And for just a minute, he allowed himself to wonder—if things had gone differently, would he and Trish have had a son? With red hair and big blue eyes?

Trish had wanted a child. Once she'd finally made the decision to get married, she'd jumped in with both feet.

When he'd had to leave, had been forced to disappear, he sweated out the first couple months, until he was sure that he hadn't left her pregnant. He still wouldn't have been able to go back, but he'd have figured out some way to ensure that his child was well taken care of. Just like he'd figured out ways to ensure that Trish was safe, protected.

He'd done a good job.

But now something had gone wrong and Trish was paying the price.

DEEP SECRETS

BY
BEVERLY LONG

Printed and bound in Spain
by CPI, Barcelona

First Published in Great Britain 2016
By Mills & Boon, an imprint of HarperCollins*Publishers*
1 London Bridge Street, London, SE1 9GF

© 2016 Beverly R. Long

ISBN: 978-0-263-91906-6

46-0616

Beverly Long enjoys the opportunity to write her own stories. She has both a bachelor's and a master's degree in business and more than twenty years of experience as a human resources director. She considers her books to be a great success if they compel the reader to stay up way past their bedtime. Beverly loves to hear from readers. Visit www.beverlylong.com, or like her at Facebook.com/beverlylong.romance.

For Kathy and Randy and their family, who have made us feel very welcome in Missouri.

Chapter One

Trish Wright-Roper stuck the fork tines through the paper napkin, ruining it. Normally, she didn't mind rolling silverware. It was a mindless activity, really. But on a day like today, when her brain was too busy remembering, it was irritating her beyond reason.

She could hear Milo finishing up in the kitchen. Earlier he'd dropped a steam table pan onto the tile floor and the clang had echoed through the empty café. She'd gone back to investigate and he'd been staring at the pan, his face flushed with anger.

Not at himself. Not at the pan. Not even at her.

For her. Because everyone who knew Trish well knew that four years ago today, Rafe Roper had died and her heart had been broken. And everybody who cared about her, which definitely included Milo, was on edge. No one would admit it, though. Instead, they'd practically turn somersaults to get her to think of something else.

Milo was no different. "What do you say you and me catch a movie in Hamerton tonight?" he asked, coming out of the kitchen. The man's hair was pulled back from his face in a tight ponytail and it hung practically to the middle of his back. He was an ex-con who'd applied for work just weeks after Rafe's death. He'd been a lifesaver because she'd been in no shape to work, to hold up her share of the responsibilities.

"You hate movies," she said. "You think it's ridiculous to pay ten dollars to see something that you'll be able to see for nothing in just a couple of months."

"Yeah, but there's this one I've really been wanting to watch."

She shook her head. "No, there isn't. You know that Summer and I usually watch some silly romantic comedy today and you also know that she's not due back from her honeymoon until tomorrow. You're *filling in*."

He drummed his thumb on the counter, a sure sign that he was frustrated. "She hated that she was going to be gone. I promised her that I had this."

When her twin sister, Summer, had married handsome Bray Hollister, the love of her life, several months earlier, they'd postponed their honeymoon until Summer's kids could take a week off school. Bray had made the honeymoon arrangements and Summer hadn't had the heart to tell him that she wanted to be back in Ravesville a day earlier.

But her twin had felt terrible about it. She and Trish had discussed it. Trish had assured her it was fine. Summer had wisely not mentioned that she intended to draft her own replacement.

"Come on. Your sister is going to be mad at me if I don't get this right," Milo said, proving that he was willing to play upon every emotion.

"Are you scared of her or her tough-guy husband?"

"Both."

She smiled at him. Milo wasn't afraid of anything. Over the years he'd been at the café, they'd had more than one disruptive customer. It was bound to happen, especially in a café that attracted one-timers, the people driving through on their way somewhere else. In those instances, with a minimum of fuss and mess, Milo would have his arm around the customer, gently pushing him out of the café, with a stern warning not to bother to come back.

He was prepared to defend them. One time when he'd been lying on the kitchen floor, fixing a temperamental fryer, she'd spied an ankle holster. She knew as an ex-con he likely wasn't supposed to have a gun. She also believed that he carried it purely for protection. For himself. For her and Summer. When he realized that she'd seen the gun, he challenged her. "You have a problem with this?" he said.

She didn't really like guns. When she'd been married to Rafe, he'd owned one and had insisted that she learn to shoot it. Had said that he wanted her to learn for safety reasons, that if there was a gun in the house, every adult needed to know how to use it safely. She'd gone along with his wishes and had got good enough that she was confident that she wouldn't shoot her own foot off. So when Milo asked, she'd shaken her head. "No problem here."

He'd smiled and gone back to fixing the fryer. As she walked past, he muttered, "Always did think she was a smart girl."

Now she stared at the man who'd become much more friend than employee. "Don't worry about me. I'll be fine."

He studied her. Kept drumming his thumb. The poor digit was going to be bruised. "I suspect Rafe would want you to keep living," he said finally.

"How do you know? You never met him," she challenged, her words clipped. She could usually count on

Milo not to offer advice. It was always a rare reprieve and it made her mad that even that had changed.

"I...I just think he would. People have to go on. Even when it's hard."

He probably knew something about that. After all, he'd survived prison. "I know you mean well," she said, her tone kinder than before. "I've actually taken that advice," she added hesitantly.

"How so?"

"I signed up for an online dating site," she said.

Thumb stopped, head jerked up. "You never said anything about that."

She hadn't. To anyone, not even Summer.

"Any matches?" he asked.

"One that looks interesting," she admitted. "We've been emailing back and forth for a couple of weeks."

"You need to be careful with sites like that," Milo said, his voice heavy with concern. "Why don't you give me this guy's name? I'll check him out for you."

She could do that or she could call Chase Hollister, Bray's brother, who'd taken over the role of Ravesville chief of police recently, and ask him to run a check. "I haven't said that I'll meet him yet," she said. "If I do that, I'll decide then whether he needs to submit his fingerprints. In triplicate, of course. Maybe give a blood sample."

He smiled, as much as Milo ever did. "I realize you're not the foolish type, Trish. But I care about you. A lot of people do."

"I know. And believe me, it helps. Now, let's finish up here. I want to go home. It's been good to have Raney and Nalana Hollister here to help in Summer's absence, but it's still been extra work. I just want to go home and take a hot shower and crawl into bed."

"You're still planning to take a few days off next week."

"I am. Payback."

"Summer will be delighted. You never take time off."

She rarely did. And on the occasional day that she did play hooky, she generally worked in her yard, which had a never-ending supply of projects. Weeds to pull. Plants to move. Trees to trim.

But this time, she was doing none of that. She felt a little guilty about not confiding in Milo, but he worried way too much about her and Summer.

"Maybe we could go fishing one day," he said. "I could teach you a few things."

She held up a hand. "I do not want to hear one more time about that bass you caught."

He tossed his head and laughed. "It's not bragging when a man has pictures."

"I suppose not. I'll let you know if I'm available to be humiliated," she added, picking up a fork.

He looked at her pile of silverware. "I've got one more load of dishes and then the garbage. Will you be ready in ten minutes?"

When it was just the two of them at the end of the night, he always insisted that they leave together. "You bet," she said and watched him walk back to the kitchen.

She glanced out the front windows of the Wright Here, Wright Now Café. All the parking spaces in front of the café were empty. The town got quiet fast, even on a pretty spring evening. Tulips had bloomed last week in the flower box in front of the law office across the street, and now they were dancing in the light wind.

Didn't matter how unbearable the winter was, those flowers always came back. And she had, too. Yes, she'd suffered a great loss. But she had much to be thankful for. A wonderful sister. Her nephew, Keagan, and her sweet little niece, Adie. Her new brother-in-law, who made sure she knew that every one of the Hollisters considered her family.

And now that she was almost thirty-eight years old, it was time to get on with her life.

A soft sob escaped and she looked around the empty café, grateful that no one was there to witness her lapse. Most of the time she was able to fool people. She could laugh and joke with the best of them. Only a precious few knew how much she mourned Rafe, who'd had the bad luck to go on a stupid float trip with his buddies. Only a precious few knew that sometimes she would go to the river and stare at the murky depths, so angry that it had taken her husband from her, not even generous enough to give her back a body to bury.

She rolled the last knife, fork and spoon and gently laid the napkin on the top of the stack. Then she carefully slid the tray of rolled silverware under the counter, where it would be easy to grab in the morning. Tables would fill up fast. She loved it when the place was really busy, when there were customers to wait on, tables to clear and money to take at the cash register. She loved the noise and the energy of people enjoying a good meal.

And while the café had a very different feel at the end of the day, when it was empty and quiet, it was satisfying to sit on a counter stool and look around at the clean floor, the shiny counters, the freshly washed pie case and know that she and Summer had built this from practically nothing.

They had purchased the café more than five years earlier. The previous owners had let the place get run-down and business had dwindled. Once she and Summer had signed on the dotted line, they'd had to close the place for a month just to get it ready to open again. Walls had been painted, floors and counters replaced, booths and tables repaired and all new dishes acquired. Then they'd tackled the kitchen. A new grill had been installed, the walk-in refrigerator scrubbed from top to bottom, and best of all, they'd purchased a new dishwasher.

Summer wanted the day shift to be home with her kids at night. That had been just fine with Trish. She'd always been a bit of a night owl. They'd hired a small staff and opened their doors to the grateful appreciation of all the other business owners on Main Street. The small downtown had been in danger of going the way that most small towns had, with empty storefronts and dilapidated buildings. There were high hopes for the Wright Here, Wright Now Café.

Summer and Trish Wright had grown up in Ravesville and people were willing to give the place a try. Word spread quickly that the service and food were top-notch and business had grown rapidly.

Four months after they'd opened, Trish had been just about to lock the doors the night that Rafe had blown into town. Literally. It had been a hot summer day and the weather forecasters had droned on about the possibility of tornadoes. At nine o'clock, like every night, she'd hung the Closed sign in the window. Had been grateful that the restaurant had cleared out by eight thirty. She had already sent Daisy, her night cook, home, because the woman was deathly afraid of storms.

She'd been walking back to the kitchen, to do one final sweep of the space, when pounding on the front door got her attention. She'd turned, locked eyes with the handsome stranger and, as crazy as it seemed, realized immediately that her life was about to experience a fundamental shift.

She'd unlocked the door just as the Ravesville tornado sirens started ringing. The stranger had smiled at her. "I think it's about to get interesting," he'd said.

She'd had no idea.

The café didn't have a basement, so she and the man had ridden out the storm sitting on the floor in the small space between the back wall and the counter, protected from the possibility of flying glass. They'd each had two pieces of banana cream pie because he'd convinced her if they were both about to die, there was no sense worrying about calories.

The café had survived the storm, and when he'd said goodbye, he'd touched her cheek. She'd thought she'd seen the last of her mysterious stranger, that he'd been a one-timer, but then two nights later, he was back, asking her to dinner. By the following weekend, they'd been lovers.

Neither one of them were kids. She'd been thirty-three and he was just a year older. She hadn't been especially interested in marriage. She was well aware of how miserable Summer was with her husband, Gary Blake, and she didn't have any interest in making a similar mistake. When Rafe asked her to move in with him after six weeks of dating, she said no. She liked her independence and didn't see a need to give it up.

But Rafe Roper knew how to wear a girl down. He was an amazing lover but it was more than that. He was different than the other men that she'd dated. Most important, he made her laugh. Every day. And he remembered all the little things. She'd get up in the morning and there would be chocolate doughnuts on her front porch. He'd have dropped them by early on his way to Hamerton, where he was part of the construction crew building the new mall. He would send her flowers. Never roses, because she'd mentioned just once that they weren't her favorites. He sent lilies. Always lilies.

He was a fabulous cook and could make all her favorites, including eggplant parmigiana and shrimp scampi. He'd teased her mercilessly about owning a café and being barely capable of boiling water.

She and Summer still had work to do on the café and he was always willing to lend a hand, to fix a door or paint a wall. She could still see Summer standing near the pie case, telling Trish that she'd be a fool to let him get away.

And Trish knew she was right. So when Rafe asked her to marry him after they'd been dating for three months, she didn't hesitate to say yes. And he didn't give her time to think about her decision. They were married just two weeks later. Then they bought a house together, too big for just the two of them, but she'd started dreaming about babies to fill the empty rooms. Babies with dark eyes and an amazing smile, just like their daddy.

And life was pretty darn near perfect.

Nine months later, he was dead. He'd gone back east to visit a friend who was sick. She'd assumed it was a dear friend because when he'd returned, she'd sensed that he was still upset. When he'd left the next day on a float trip with his buddies on the construction crew, she'd hoped it would cheer him up.

His raft had overturned and his body had never been recovered.

Then it was not just the rooms of her house that were empty.

Her heart. Her soul.

Her spirit.

She'd wished she was dead, too. But she'd lived. And somehow, someway, had managed to crawl her way back. Didn't expect to ever feel full again but had developed an odd contentment with the emptiness. Except for nights like this, when it became unbearable.

She'd expected to feel blue today. That was probably why earlier in the week she'd jumped at something Mary Ann Fikus had said. M.A., as everyone called her, worked at the bank and ate lunch almost every day at the café. She was just back from a week in the Ozarks. She'd been going on about the cottage where she'd stayed.

Trish had been to the Ozarks, the lake-filled, mountainous area in southwest Missouri, several times and had even stayed at the particular lake that M.A. had visited. It was a lovely area.

And when M.A. described the cottage, it had sounded like the perfect place to rest and read books and maybe, just maybe, fish. Thinking there was little chance it would be available at such late notice, Trish had called the owner and been pleasantly surprised that it was. She'd assumed they would want a credit card to hold it, but Bernie Wilberts had told her that she could simply leave a check on the table when she left. She'd been very careful to explain that she would arrive on Sunday, but he'd told her it didn't matter, that the cottage was empty. He'd given her the combination code for the lock on the door.

If Summer had been around, Trish would have told her about her plans. She'd thought about telling Milo, but given his propensity to worry about her, she'd thought better of it. She'd tell him just before she left town.

She turned to walk back to the kitchen and stopped abruptly when there was intense pounding on the door. Her heart leaped in her chest. It was like that night so long ago. She turned.

And through the glass, she saw Keagan, her fourteen-year-old nephew. With five-year-old Adie next to him. Summer and Bray were a little slower to get out of the SUV.

She opened the door and the four of them tumbled in. "What are you doing home?" she asked, hugging each of the kids. Then Bray. Finally, her sister. She hung on an extra minute. She knew why her sister was here. "You shouldn't have," she whispered.

Summer shook her head. "When I told Bray what today was," she said, grabbing her new husband's hand, "he changed our flight so that we could get back. He insisted."

She rolled her eyes in her brother-in-law's direction. "I guess I do understand why she loves you," she said.

Bray winked at her and focused on Adie, who had found her favorite seat at the counter and was whirling on the stool at warp speed.

"How are you feeling?" Trish asked, looking at Summer's still-flat stomach.

"Fine. But anything that went in circles at Disney World was Bray's domain. I stood on the sidelines and ate orange Popsicles."

It was unbelievable that Summer and Bray would be

adding to their family in just seven more months. More proof that life really did go on. She drew in a breath and smiled. "Well, Milo was insisting on a movie tonight. I guess you're all excited to see *Pretty Woman* one more time."

"How did you know that was my favorite movie?" Bray asked with a straight face.

Summer lightly punched her husband's biceps before turning back to Trish. "I'm sure you're glad that you're not holding down the fort alone any longer. Next week, I want you to rest up. You will take a couple of days off, right?"

"I think I will," Trish said.

"Where's Milo?" Summer asked, moving quickly to the next topic.

She could tell them both about her plans. "Taking out the garbage. I'll get him."

Trish went through the swinging door that connected the dining room to the kitchen. No Milo. The back door was open just a fraction of an inch, letting the cool spring air blow in. The light near the back door was on.

"Milo," she called, walking toward the door. "Summer and Bray are—"

She opened the back door and almost tripped. On a body.

Milo. *Oh my God.* "What happened?" she asked, dropping to her knees.

There was blood everywhere. On his body, on the pavement, running out of the side of his mouth. "Milo," she cried, reaching to lift his head off the cold, hard ground.

"Trish," he said, his breaths raspy. "Tell Rafe they know."

He closed his eyes and she started to scream.

Chapter Two

Tell Rafe they know.

Trish sat on the edge of a booth, her feet flat on the floor, her eyes closed. Hoping that the world would stop spinning. Somebody had draped a blanket over her.

Maybe it had been Summer. Or Bray. Or maybe even Chase Hollister, who hadn't even been on the job for six months. He was about to investigate his first murder.

Milo was dead. Knifed to death. Gutted like a fish. That was what she'd heard one of the volunteers from the fire and rescue squad say before Bray had grabbed his shirt collar and jerked him out of the room. The man had come back, said a quiet apology in her direction and been more respectful until Chase finally let them take Milo's body from the scene. Of course, it had seemed like hours before they'd moved him off the cold ground. At some point, more police had arrived. They were still here. Portable lighting had been set up behind the café, making it look even more surreal.

The images in her head were disjointed. Opening the door, practically stumbling over the body. Blood. So much blood. Bray whipping the door open, pulling her back.

Thank goodness for Bray. He'd taken charge. She and Summer had been hustled back inside the café, where Keagan and Adie waited, scared to death that their aunt had been screaming. He must have called the police, too, because within minutes Chase Hollister had arrived, looking very serious.

At some point, Cal Hollister and his pretty wife, Nalana, had arrived and taken Summer and the kids away from all the ugliness. Her twin hadn't wanted to leave, but she'd already thrown up three times and Bray had had enough. "I'll call you tomorrow," Summer said, as Nalana was guiding her out of the door. "We need to talk about a funeral."

Milo didn't have family. It would be up to them. He wouldn't want a funeral. And if he'd known about her trip, then he'd have been mad as hell at her if she canceled so that they could have one.

But funerals weren't for the dead. They were for the living, to make it easier to say goodbye. They would definitely have a funeral.

THEN SHE HAD watched Summer and the kids leave. She wasn't worried about them. Bray's youngest brother, Cal, had been a Navy SEAL. Nalana, his new bride, was still an FBI agent.

She'd stared at the floor after that. Until she'd finally got so tired that she needed to close her eyes.

"Trish," she heard someone say.

She wanted to ignore it, to pretend that the past several hours hadn't happened. But that wasn't an option.

She lifted her head. Chase was squatting down in front of her, his eyes full of concern.

"How are you doing?" he asked.

She licked her dry lips. "He was a good man," she said, choosing to ignore the question. She wasn't up to pretending that she was fine. She was so damn tired of always pretending that she was fine.

"Yes, he was," Chase said. "And we will find the person who did this. I promise you."

If anyone could, it was probably Chase. He'd been a cop in St. Louis before coming back to Ravesville, ostensibly to get his deceased parents' house ready for sale but really to guard a key witness in a murder case. He'd done more than just guard the witness. He'd married her. And now Raney Hollister was one of Trish's favorite people.

"Was there anyone unusual in the café tonight or maybe even within the last couple of days?"

The question wasn't unexpected. She'd been trying to think of the same thing for the past hour. "I don't think so," she said. "We had a few strangers, of course." That wasn't unusual. Travelers. Usually vacationers. People in need of a hot meal and a cup of coffee. "But nobody that I considered unusual or suspicious."

"Did Milo have any visitors or receive any unusual telephone calls that you're aware of?"

"No. I don't think he had any plans for after work because he'd asked me if I wanted to see a movie."

She saw Chase exchange a quick glance with Bray. "Did you often watch movies together?" Chase asked, probably wondering if he'd missed a romantic connection between her and Milo.

"Never," she said. "But he knew that today was a tough day for me."

Another glance between Chase and Bray. Oh, for goodness' sake, Bray didn't have to explain this. She was a big girl. "My husband, Rafe Roper, died four years ago today," she said.

"I'm sorry," Chase said.

She believed him. Chase Hollister was a good man. She'd known him since he was a kid. Which was why she was going to tell him everything, even though her mind hadn't made sense of it yet.

"Milo said something before he died."

Bray's head whipped up. This was news to him.

"What was that?" Chase said gently.

"'Tell Rafe they know.'"

Chase didn't look at Bray this time. He was staring intently at her. "You're sure that's what he said?"

"Yes."

Chase stood up, walked over to the window, looked out at the street. Finally, he turned. "Did Milo know your husband?"

"No. Rafe was already dead before he came to work here."

"Did the two of you frequently talk about Rafe?"

"No. I don't discuss Rafe with many people. But Milo and I had been talking earlier in the evening and his name came up."

"Is it possible that Milo was confused? That your conversation earlier in the evening was on his mind, and that's why he mentioned him before he died?"

"I guess," she said, her tone flat. It made as much sense as anything. But she'd never seen Milo confused or discombobulated about anything. He was always calm, always controlled. But then again, she'd never seen him bleeding to death on the dirty pavement, either.

"I don't know," she said, her voice breaking. "I just don't know and it's driving me crazy."

Chase reached out for her hand. It probably wasn't police protocol, but given that his brother was married to her twin sister, she and Chase were family. "It's going to be okay," he said. "I know hearing something like that would be very upsetting. But he was dying. Losing lots of blood quickly. He wouldn't have been thinking clearly."

She'd been telling herself the same thing. But for some strange reason, it really irritated her to hear someone else say it. "They were his last words. I think they were important to him," she snapped.

"Of course," Chase said.

Bray stood up. "I think I should take Trish back to my house," he said.

When Summer and Bray had got married, Bray had moved into the small house that Summer had rented with her two children. They were building a new home but the walls had just gone up. "You don't have extra space," she said. "I'll go to my own house."

"You can stay with Raney and me," Chase said immediately.

She did not want to stay with anyone. She was strung so tight that she was about to lose it. "Is there any reason to think that I'm in danger, that the attack on Milo had something to do with me or Summer or the café?"

"We have no way of knowing that," Chase said. "Milo was attacked from behind. As best as I can tell, he was in the process of putting the garbage into the Dumpster when he was stabbed. Based on what Bray has told me, I understand you opened the door to check on him and he was already on the ground. Whoever had done this was gone."

She nodded. "He'd been in prison. Do you think it could be someone from his past, someone who maybe held a grudge?" She was grasping at straws but she so desperately wanted to make sense of it.

"I don't know," Chase said. "I've asked for help from

the state. They have more sophisticated resources than we have to process the scene. We're going to be done here in just a little while, but I'd prefer it if you could keep the café closed tomorrow, just in case."

Saturdays were usually busy days. "I'll put a sign on the door," she said, getting up to find paper and a pen. The sign probably wasn't necessary. It was a sure bet that at least one of the volunteer fire and rescue squad would tell his or her spouse what had happened here tonight and it would spread like wildfire. By morning, everyone in the small town would know why the café wasn't open.

It was one of the reasons she hadn't said anything before this about Milo's last words. She hadn't wanted it to be overheard.

Because if one well-meaning person asked her what she thought about it, she might explode. She didn't know what she thought. *Tell Rafe* implied something that she couldn't even fathom. *They know.* Know what, for God's sake? "I want to go home," she said. "To my house. I have Duke. He won't let anyone get near me." It was true. The German shepherd was fiercely protective, had been since the day he'd wandered up to her doorstep without any tags. She'd searched for an owner for a week, even putting an ad in the paper, but no one had come forward. Duke had become her dog.

"A dog isn't much protection against a bullet," Chase said gently.

"This was a knife, not a bullet."

"You don't know that's the only available weapon," he said.

"The café emptied out at least a half hour before we closed. I was alone in the dining room, clearly visible if someone outside had bothered to look in the window. If they wanted to harm me, they had a chance. But they waited until Milo took the trash out. I think this was about Milo, not about me."

"Even with that final comment?" Bray asked.

"Like Chase said, Milo was dying. He might have been confused." She picked up her purse and kissed her brother-in-law on the cheek. "Thank you," she said. "Thank you for bringing Summer home early, thank you for being here and for having the wherewithal to respond."

Then she turned to Chase. "I trust you, Chase. With every bone in my body. I know that you'll do everything you can to find Milo's killer. He was a wonderful friend and he didn't deserve to die like this." Then she leaned in and gave him a quick hug.

Bray picked up his keys from the counter. "At least let me follow you home and make sure you get inside safely."

The Hollister men were very protective of the women they loved, and by virtue of being Summer's sister, she was automatically included in their circle. "Fine. Let's go."

HER FOUR-BEDROOM RANCH house was too big for one person, and tonight, more than ever, she felt as if she was drifting from room to room, looking for ghosts. She was grateful, though, for the silence.

Bray had been true to his word. He'd left, a worried look on his face, after he'd checked every room and the garage. She'd assured him that she'd set the alarm immediately and she had.

Now she stood in her kitchen and Duke crowded in next to her, almost as if he knew that something wasn't quite right. He was poking his nose at her knees, and when she reached down to pet him, she realized that there was blood on her dark blue pants.

Milo's blood. She hadn't seen it before, but when she'd knelt next to the body, the blood had got on her.

"Oh, Milo," she sobbed, catching hold of the kitchen counter to keep herself upright. *Tell Rafe they know.* "What did you mean?"

With jerky movements, she peeled off every stitch of her clothes. Then naked, she stuffed them into the kitchen garbage can. She roughly yanked out the plastic bag insert and tied it up tight. With heavy arms, she tossed the bag by the door that led to her garage.

Then, feeling very old and weary, she walked back to her bedroom and straight into the adjoining bath. She turned on the shower, as hot as she could stand it. And when she stepped under the spray, she let the tears that she'd held back all night run down her face.

Her chest heaved with her sobs and she braced herself against the wall.

She wasn't stupid. *Tell Rafe.* That implied that Rafe was alive. Was that even possible? His body had never been found. But what would keep him away? What would keep a husband away from his wife?

Four years. Four long years.

Over fourteen hundred days of heartache.

It just wasn't possible. Rafe would never hurt her like that.

RAFE HOPED THERE were no snakes in the damn grass. It was damp and scratchy and smelled like a herd of cattle had passed through. He'd arrived before dawn and had been on his stomach for the past several hours. He badly wanted a cup of hot coffee. But he didn't move.

Windows were open in the villa and music drifted up the hill. When the song changed, his gut tightened up.

They played that one at his wedding. And in the morning, his beautiful bride had been humming it.

She'd been so happy. And he'd thought it would last until balls started dropping out of the air. Accidents, some said. He knew better.

His trusted coworkers had been murdered. He didn't care what anybody said.

And he suspected the man inside, who was probably about to sit down to breakfast with his family, was responsible. Luciano Maladucci. Richer than several European countries put together and more evil than most could even imagine, he delighted in playing chess with people's lives.

Unfortunately, Rafe hadn't been able to prove Maladucci was behind the deaths. It had been his sole focus his first six months back, but every lead turned into a dead end. He had to stop when his boss told him in no uncertain terms to *let it go.*

He let it go. At least as far as most people knew. But he'd found another way to tighten the noose around this man's neck. One way or the other, he was going to see him behind prison bars.

With his binoculars picking up every detail, he watched a Ferrari Spider turn into the circle drive. What was the youngest Maladucci son doing here? The older son and his family lived in the east wing of the villa. It was rare for the two brothers to be together, probably because the younger brother had slept with the older brother's wife three years ago.

Real friendly, the Maladuccis.

Real deadly, too.

He felt the buzz from his cell phone. His private cell

phone. What the hell? Milo wasn't supposed to check in until Sunday. It was Saturday.

He shifted, pulled his phone out and realized it wasn't Milo, but someone else he trusted explicitly. He stared at the text message.

Milo is dead.

There were a hundred possibilities. Like a heart attack or a stroke?

But none of those would have warranted a special message. No. This message meant that there was danger. And it was headed toward Trish.

Chapter Three

She stayed in the shower until the hot water ran out. When she got out, she considered not drying her waist-length hair but knew that it would be a tangled mess in the morning if she went to bed with it wet.

She should have cut it years ago. But when she'd been married to Rafe, he'd convinced her to keep it long. *I love your hair*, he used to say. *Your beautiful red hair. The night of the storm, I saw it through the window of the café. It looked like liquid fire. I thought I'd never seen anything quite so wonderful.*

After he'd died, she couldn't bear to do any more than trim the ends. Wore it pulled back most of the time in a low ponytail.

Tell Rafe they know.

She sat down hard on the edge of the bathtub. It was crazy but she was so angry at Milo. The poor man was dead and she was furious that he'd said something like that and then died.

She was a bad person. Horrible. A man was dead and all she could think about was herself.

She jabbed the on button and held the dryer for too long in one spot, burning her scalp. Ten minutes later, she gave up. Her hair was still damp but she was so damn tired. She picked up her toothbrush, spread some toothpaste and halfheartedly brushed. When she tossed her toothbrush back onto the counter, a memory hit her so hard that she almost doubled over.

Rafe putting his toothbrush back just so, in exactly the same spot every time. His shaving cream and razor, too. *Everything in its place*, he used to say, lightheartedly poking fun at himself. Before she'd married him, she'd considered herself pretty neat and organized. But Rafe had been the king of patterns and order. She'd noticed it slowly, over time. He kept very little paper around, usually just a small pile of unpaid bills. If you asked, he could tell you, in the order it appeared, what was on his desk at any one time.

He never made a big deal out of it. And she had never taken it too seriously until one night they'd come home from a movie in Hamerton, entered the house, and he'd sensed that something was different. He'd grabbed her, pulled her behind him, and the gun that he always carried on him had been in his hand. *The hallway light wasn't on when we left*, he had whispered in her ear.

He'd inspected the whole house but had come up empty. But she could tell that he was bothered by the incident. It wasn't until she finally checked her cell phone, which she'd turned off at the movies, that she heard the message from Summer. She'd stopped over to borrow a dress.

When she'd told Rafe, he'd waved it off. She could tell he didn't want to discuss it. But she hadn't forgotten it. She had seen a side of her husband that night that was fascinating. It was not as if he'd morphed into someone new. No, it was more subtle than that.

He was still Rafe, the handsome construction worker who had stolen her heart and made her laugh every day.

But he was someone else, too. Someone very capable. Someone fearless.

Someone, she suspected, who would do whatever it took to protect her and their home. He'd handled the gun expertly. She'd been in awe, really.

And she'd started paying more attention to the things around her. Noticing when things changed. It was like playing a game where there was no score and she was competing only against herself. She got better at it every day. Nobody got new glasses, highlighted their hair or had their teeth fixed that she didn't pick up on it. It was just crazy small stuff but she had fun with it.

It was only one of the many ways that loving Rafe had changed her.

She left the bathroom. She didn't bother to dress. Simply crawled into bed naked. She could hear Duke pacing in front of her door, his nails scratching against the wood floor. "Good night, Duke," she said, knowing that he wouldn't settle down if that nighttime ritual wasn't observed.

The pacing quieted and she knew the big dog had taken his spot outside her door. He'd knock his hind end on the door at five the next morning, ready to go out. Until then, she could sleep.

Except that every time she closed her eyes, she could see poor Milo. After a half hour, she gave up and turned on her light. Duke immediately whined, letting her know that he knew that something wasn't right. She opened the bedroom door. "We're leaving early," she said.

She had to. She absolutely had to leave this house that she had bought with Rafe, where she had made plans, dreamed big. The memories of Rafe were still too strong here. She could see him at the stove, wearing his jeans

low on his hips and no shirt, waving a spatula in her direction. Could see him snoozing on the couch, a book
open on his chest. Could see him walk across the kitchen
naked for that first cup of coffee in the morning.

Could practically smell his earthy masculine scent.

Was it because it was the anniversary of his death?
Was it because she and Milo had been talking about him?
Was it because of what Milo said?

Probably some of all three. It didn't matter. It felt as
if she was losing her mind.

No better place to do it than a little cottage in the middle of nowhere. If she started to scream and crawl the
walls, nobody would be there to witness the meltdown
of the century.

Summer would understand and would proceed to plan
the funeral. They could have it at the end of the week,
when she was back.

With her head on straight.

Maybe with a fish story—in Milo's honor.

Duke cocked his head and watched her closely as she
dragged her suitcase out of the closet and started throwing
clothes in it. Swimsuit. Shorts. Water shoes. A couple of
summer dresses. Sandals. Some things to sleep in. Then
she added toiletries and a lightweight jacket in case the
evenings got cool. By this time, Duke was pacing, well
aware that his routine was upset.

She dressed in jeans and a long-sleeved green T-shirt
and slipped her feet into her favorite cowboy boots. Then
she went to the kitchen, where she pulled out a half-full bag
of dog food. Plenty for five days. She'd originally planned
to leave on Sunday since the café was closed. But now she
was free to leave a day early.

She pulled a sack out of the cupboard and haphazardly

picked items from her counters and cupboards. The half loaf of bread. A jar of peanut butter. Cereal. There had to be a small town nearby where she could buy milk. Two bottles of wine. She thought about adding another one but figured that was overkill. Boxes of macaroni and cheese. A jar of honey-roasted peanuts. And for the heck of it, she threw in the three bananas that she'd been ignoring for days.

She looked at her watch and debated whether she should call Summer now. Quickly discarded the idea. Summer had been so sick after seeing poor Milo's body. She needed her rest. Trish would call her in the morning to let her know her plans.

She made one more pass through her house, pausing outside her bedroom door to gaze at her pale gray bed skirt. Shaking her head, she walked into the room, got down on her knees, reached underneath the bed and pulled out her gun case.

Rafe had bought a gun for her several months after the last time she'd gone to the range with him. It had been a surprise. Initially she'd been inclined to tell him to take it back. But he'd been insistent. *You should have your own*, he'd said.

SHE HADN'T SHOT it for more than four years. Had kept it locked up, under her bed. Was it crazy to pull it out now? M.A., who was single, had been traveling with her ten-year-old niece and she'd said that she'd felt perfectly safe.

But Trish wasn't a fool. She was a woman, traveling alone. A little extra protection made sense. Especially after what she'd seen earlier tonight.

She took it out of its case and slipped it into her shoulder bag. "Let's go," she said to Duke.

He followed her to the kitchen, and when she opened the door to her attached garage, he hurried ahead of her, like he always did. When she opened the passenger side door of her two-door Jeep, Duke jumped in and promptly scrambled over the middle console into the backseat. She went around back and shoved her suitcase and sack into the rear space. In the corner of her garage was her fishing gear. She grabbed it and put it in the Jeep. Then she got in.

Took a breath. Then another. Wiped her damp palms on her blue jeans.

She didn't normally steal away in the middle of the night.

But then, there had been nothing normal about this night. The heavy weight of her gun in her shoulder bag was even more proof of that.

It was just after one when she pulled out of the garage and shut the door behind her. Determined to think about something else, she turned on the radio and hunted for a station that had music. She finally found one that was playing oldies from the '50s and '60s.

Great. She felt about a hundred. It would be perfect.

She would be in the right area in just over an hour. It might take her a while to wind around the country roads and find the cottage. Hopefully her GPS would behave nicely.

"Are you excited?" she asked Duke.

He barked just once.

"I'll take that as a yes," she said, settling back. She wasn't worried about falling asleep while driving. Her body was practically humming with energy. She would not have been able to sleep.

She'd lost a good friend tonight.

Had Milo simply been a convenient target? Was it possible that a vagrant had been hiding in the alley, and when Milo had opened the door, the attack had been a spur-of-the-moment decision? Or was it something much more sinister? Had someone been waiting for Milo, someone from his past?

She prayed that Chase Hollister would find the answer. She wanted Milo's attacker to pay for what he'd done. It wouldn't bring Milo back but it would help to know that a killer had not gone free.

She pressed down on the accelerator, fully aware that she couldn't outrun the image of Milo's dead body on the dirty cement. She could not forget about what had happened. No. That was asking too much.

But she could drive, and then tomorrow, when she woke up in her little cottage, she would make coffee and take it down to the lake and dangle her feet in the cool water.

And she would come to terms with another senseless death.

She would have to.

Sometimes the only thing one could do was keep going.

RAFE GOT OFF the damn hill as fast as he could and ran the mile to where he'd hidden his car. Once inside, he sent a quick text to others on his team, letting them know about the arrival of the youngest Maladucci.

He looked at his watch, mindful of the seven-hour time difference between Italy and home. It was almost nine, which meant it was almost two in the morning at home. Time for most people to be sacked out.

But Daniel, who had sent this message, would be awake. He would anticipate that a return message was on its way.

He picked up his private cell phone. Trish? he typed and pushed Send.

Within minutes he had his response. Left café around midnight, arrived home safely.

He took a deep breath. Then another. That was good news. But he was edgy. Had been for the past twenty-four hours. Nothing unusual about that. Always the same, year after year.

Maybe someone was walking over his grave.

Hell, he'd walked over his own grave. Less than a month after Trish had the service, he'd been back in Ravesville, with Duke in tow. Just weeks before he'd died, he'd purchased the dog and arranged for it to be specially trained. From the beginning had called it Duke because Trish had always said that if she ever got a dog, Duke would be his name. His plan had been to surprise Trish on their one-year anniversary. When he'd had to leave, he'd expedited the training and delivered the dog to Trish's backyard two months earlier than expected.

But Duke had been a champ and Rafe had rested better knowing that the dog would protect Trish. Not that Trish should have been in danger still. That should have ended when Rafe left. But he couldn't stop being extra careful. Trish was too special.

So she'd been home for more than an hour. She would be sleeping. There was no need to request an updated report. No need at all.

Screw it. He typed. Reverify. And waited.

Thirteen minutes later, he knew something was terribly wrong when his phone rang. "Yeah," he answered.

"She's gone," Daniel said.

He gripped his phone and swallowed hard. "Signs of violence?"

"None. Dog is gone, too."

Milo was dead and Trish and Duke were missing. He stared up at the sun that was bright in the blue sky. It was going to be a nice day.

Not that it mattered. He had things to do.

It was almost two thirty before Trish pulled up in front of the cottage. There was a narrow half-gravel, half-grass road leading to the small wood structure. She knew the details from M.A. One bedroom, one bath, a kitchen and a big screened-in porch that had a great view of the water. It had sounded perfect, and now that she was here, even though it was too dark to see much of anything, she realized that she'd been right.

Unless, of course, there were mice inside. Even with her gun, she was no match for rodents. "Duke, you're going to need to protect me."

He nudged her shoulder with his wet nose. *I've got your back*, it seemed to say.

There was a small light burning next to the cottage door, but even as she walked the short distance from the car, she became aware of how dark the Missouri wilderness could be. Based on what M.A. had told her, the nearest cottage was a half mile away. It didn't help when Duke decided that he needed a potty break and he took his time sniffing for just the right area.

Her heart started to beat a little faster in her chest and she was glad when the dog finally finished. When it came time to enter the combination on the lock that hung over the door handle, she had to enter it twice before she got it right. The door swung open. Duke pushed in front of her and she made no effort to hold him back. She reached inside, hoping to feel for a light switch.

It was six inches farther away from the door than she'd expected. But once she found it and flipped the light on, she felt much better. It really was just perfect. The main part of the cottage had a small living area with just a couch and a bookshelf. There was no television. It led into the kitchen, where there was a big braided rug under the table. There was a stove, refrigerator and sink.

There was no door on what she suspected was the bedroom. She walked over and found the light. It had a double bed, a small table with a lamp and a dresser. The only other room in the main portion of the cottage was a small bathroom that was off the kitchen. It was old but clean with a bath/shower combination, a toilet and a vanity.

It was the porch that really interested her. It ran the entire length of the cottage, with windows and a back door making up one whole side. It was the size of all three of the other rooms put together. The shades on the windows and door were down, which made sense. She knew that she wouldn't be able to see anything right now anyway, but she was confident that in the morning, it was going to be dazzlingly beautiful. M.A. had told her the back door opened to steps that led to a long dock where the owner kept a boat for the renters to use. Then there was water for as far as you could see.

On the porch was a small, round slate table, the size where four could squeeze in to have breakfast, with four wrought-iron chairs with padded seats. Also a forest green sofa, a couple of overstuffed chairs, and a big wooden coffee table, the kind with drawers underneath. It had rained a couple of days when M.A. had been here and she'd said the board games and cards that she'd found in the coffee table had been a lifesaver.

Trish unpacked her sack, putting the few groceries

away in the cupboard. She pulled out Duke's water and food dishes and filled both. He immediately started eating.

It probably wasn't a bad idea. She'd had nothing since lunch, more than twelve hours earlier. She made herself a peanut butter and banana sandwich and poured a glass of water from the faucet. There was a roll of paper towels in a holder next to the sink. She pulled one off and wrapped it around her sandwich. Then she went onto the porch, sat on the sofa and ate.

It had been the right decision to come. She could feel it. Both her body and mind needed rest. Then she could face what had happened tonight.

She'd always figured that Rafe would have liked Milo. Would have appreciated the man's cooking ability, liked his dry sense of humor and been satisfied that he'd kept a watchful eye on Trish and Summer. Not that Ravesville was dangerous.

But it had been earlier tonight. She'd thought it couldn't get worse than when Summer's little girl had been kidnapped, along with her ex-husband. But she'd been wrong.

Murder.

She wadded up the paper towel around the quarter of the sandwich she hadn't eaten. Then got up, found the garbage container under the sink and tossed it away. Then she took her suitcase into the bedroom and opened it. Pajama pants and a tank were near the top and she quickly undressed and pulled them on.

Duke plopped down in the doorway, and she realized that without a door she'd probably be awakened the next morning, not by a hind-end knock, but rather by a lick in the face. "Maybe you should go outside again. You drank a lot of water."

His ears perked up.

"Let me get your leash," she said. She hadn't taken more than three steps when she heard a noise.

She listened. It had sounded like a car door. Not right outside but not far away, either.

Just one door.

At almost three in the morning.

"Could you hold it until morning?" she asked, absently rubbing the fur on Duke's back. She knew the dog was confused. He was starting to push up against her leg.

Maybe it was somebody else who was simply arriving at their cottage very late.

There was probably a very reasonable explanation for the noise.

She moved away from the door and Duke came with her. But instead of returning to her bedroom, she went back to the porch, detouring through the kitchen to get her shoulder bag. She pulled out her gun and sat on the sofa with her legs curled up underneath her.

This was crazy. Not counting the nine months that she'd lived with Rafe, she'd lived by herself since she was eighteen. Almost twenty years. She was independent. Certainly not someone who got spooked easily.

She'd also never had someone's blood on her knees before.

She listened carefully, didn't hear anything else. Minutes went by. She was almost ready to relax when she heard a noise outside the back door. Footsteps on what had to be the back steps that M.A. had described.

The hair on Duke's back stood up and she could see his teeth.

And then the knob on the back door started to turn. She raised her gun.

Chapter Four

The locked door held. And the next sound she heard was a sharp knock.

She was surprised she heard it since her heart was beating so loudly. She didn't move. Duke continued his low growl.

"It's Bernie Wilberts. Is that you, Miss Roper?"

She almost dropped her gun. She managed to stuff it under the sofa cushion. Then she grabbed Duke's collar and hung on tight.

She recognized the voice. It was the man that she'd talked to on the telephone about renting the cottage.

She unlocked the door and opened it just inches. A man, his body lean and tall, with a few lines on his tanned face, stood on the back porch. He had a flashlight but it was pointed down toward the ground. He looked interested, but not terribly alarmed that he'd encountered someone in a cottage that was supposed to be empty.

"Hi," she said. "Yes, I'm Trish Wright-Roper. I arrived early."

"I saw the car and figured that was the case. And then I saw the light, so I figured I better check."

She opened the door a little wider. "You're out late,

Mr. Wilberts. I was going to call you but I didn't want to interrupt your sleep."

"Call me Bernie," he said. "I wasn't even Mr. Wilberts when I was in the corporate world. Anyway, best fishing is in the middle of the night."

That made her think about Milo and what had sent her scrambling to the cottage. He'd caught his last bass. She felt a pain in her chest and wondered when it would get easier. "Of course," she said.

By now, Duke had squirmed his way around her legs and poked his nose out the door.

"That's a fine-looking dog," Bernie said.

"He was just about to go out," she said. "Duke, sit." The dog, who normally obeyed really well, continued to pull forward, and she knew that she was about to lose her grip.

"Watch out," she said.

Duke flew past Bernie, almost knocking the man off the back steps. *Oh, good grief,* she thought, stepping out after him. Her bare feet hit the back step. There was just enough room for her and Bernie. "Sorry about that," she said.

She could hear Duke, thrashing around, but couldn't see him. It was very dark outside. "May I?" she said, pointing at Bernie's flashlight.

"Of course," he said.

She shone the light around and caught a glimpse of Duke. He was circling a log. "Get busy, Duke," she called out, her voice soft, aware that even though there weren't any close neighbors, sound carried at night.

"Looks as if he could hold his own against the coyotes," Bernie said.

That didn't scare her. She'd had coyotes in her backyard for years. But even so, she hoped the dog had the good sense to come back in. She didn't relish looking for him in the dark.

Duke came bounding back onto the steps and she stepped back inside. "Well, I'll be going, then," Bernie said. "I'll stop back at a more reasonable time tomorrow or the next day, and we can get acquainted."

"Great," she said. "I'll be interested in learning about the best fishing spots."

She watched the man walk down the steps and around the corner of the cottage, presumably toward a car that he'd parked somewhere nearby. She shut and locked the door.

She turned and looked at Duke. "Well, that was exciting," she said.

He barked once in response.

She turned off the light on the porch. "We made the right decision, Duke," she said. "We needed this."

BERNIE WILBERTS DIALED the number that he knew by heart. "She's there," he said. "Early."

"Why?"

"How the hell should I know?" He hated this. He really did. "I saw a car and I checked. She's by herself. She's got a dog. But I suspect a bullet will take care of him easy enough."

The voice at the other end was quiet for a moment. "Fine. I'll be in touch."

IT WAS CLOSE to nine before Trish woke up. Given that it had been after four before she'd dropped off, she knew she could probably have slept later. But Duke had other ideas when he put his nose in her face.

"Fine," she muttered, throwing back the sheet.

He ran to the door and then had to wait for her. She walked, scuffing her bare feet on the wood floor. Running was out of the question until she'd had coffee. She snapped on his leash and opened the front door. She took a few steps outside and let the leash out so the dog would have his choice of trees and shrubs to water.

She could hear birds singing in the trees and there wasn't a cloud in the blue sky. It was a perfect day.

She took a deep breath. Then another, expanding her lungs. The air was already warm and was heavy with humidity. The trees smelled damp and she knew it had rained here recently. There was mud around the log that Duke was once again circling.

If he got dirty, he could wash off in the lake. She might do the same.

However, he managed to stay clean, and once he was done, they went back inside. She checked her cell phone to see if there were calls from Summer. Thankfully there were not. She would have been worried if Trish had not answered.

She dialed her and it rang three times before Summer picked up. "Hey," her twin said. "I was just about to call you."

"How are you feeling?" Trish asked.

"Better," Summer said. "I'm sorry I couldn't stay last night."

"If you hadn't voluntarily left, I think Bray might have had a stroke."

"He worries," Summer said. "I've tried to tell him that I threw up every day for three months when I was pregnant with Keagan and Adie, but he's not buying it."

Her sister was very lucky. She and Bray had loved

each other since they were teenagers, but life had intervened and it had taken them fifteen years to find their way to one another.

"I need a favor," Trish said.

"Of course."

"Can you take care of the arrangements for Milo's service? I would help but I drove to the Ozarks last night."

"In the middle of the night?" Summer squeaked.

Trish almost laughed. "Yes, Mother. In the middle of the night. But I arrived safe and sound. No need to worry. And speaking of mothers, will you let Mom know what's going on?"

"Of course. But where are you?"

"Near Heelie Lake. I got a recommendation from M.A. She was here recently with her niece. You knew I'd been planning to take a few days off once you were back. After this thing with Milo, I thought about canceling, but I...I just had to get away."

"I totally get it. It's so awful. I'm going to miss him so much."

She could tell Summer was close to tears.

"I'll be back on Wednesday."

"Promise me that you'll keep your cell phone on and charged at all times. And no more driving in the middle of the night."

"Of course," Trish said.

There was a pause on the other end. Finally, Summer spoke. "It must be horrible for you, Trish. To have Milo die on the same day as Rafe. It's just too much."

"Two good men," Trish said, her own throat closing up.

"I'm glad you got away," Summer said. "I'm really glad. Just be safe. I love you. We all do."

The line went dead. And Trish knew her twin was either crying or vomiting. But Bray would be there to handle either.

Maybe if she'd had someone at home, someone to hold her, she wouldn't have felt the need to run in the middle of the night. She didn't begrudge her twin's happiness. Their lives were just different and she'd learned a long time ago to accept that.

She put her cell phone down and started a pot of coffee. Then she raised every shade on the porch, even the one on the door. M.A. had been right. The view was lovely. From the back steps, there was a little patch of grass that M.A. hadn't mentioned, maybe twenty feet wide, before one hit the edge of the water.

The wooden dock that extended another fifty feet over the water was faded but in good repair. Bernie Wilberts's boat, tied at the end, was white with brown panels. The aluminum fishing boat wasn't new but, like the dock, appeared sturdy. It would suit her just fine.

Now that the blinds were up, she realized that wasn't enough. She opened several of the windows, happy to see that there were screens to keep the bugs out. Duke rested his chin on one of the sills, looking about as happy as a dog could look.

She could practically hear the lake calling her name. *Trish. Trish Wright-Roper.*

"Give me ten minutes," she said to Duke.

She walked back into the kitchen, toasted two slices of bread and slathered them with peanut butter. She grabbed a couple of handfuls of dry cereal and chewed. She washed it all down with the coffee that was now ready.

She hadn't bothered to unpack the night before. But now she opened her suitcase and pulled out light blue capri pants and a blue-and-white tank. She slipped on a pair of sandals that she'd brought. She loved her cowboy boots but they weren't good for dangling feet in the water.

On her way out the back door, she grabbed a well-read romance novel off the bookshelf in the living room. Duke bounded ahead of her, racing up and down the dock three times before she made it to the end.

The sun was warm on her face and she could smell the heady scent of the water. There was very little algae and, when she sat at the very end of the dock, it was clear enough that she could see the bottom of the lake through the ten or so feet of water.

Two hours later, she was a hundred and thirty-eight pages into her book, pleasantly warm and, truth be told, a little sleepy. But there were things she needed to do. The idea of more dry cereal was not appealing. She needed to find a grocery store. It was a little early for lunch but she wasn't on anybody's schedule but her own. She'd grab a bite to eat and still have the whole afternoon to take the boat out for a little fishing. Bernie Wilberts might like to dangle a line in the middle of the night. Not her.

She stood up and Duke, who had been stretched out next to her sleeping in the sun, immediately woke up. He stayed close as she walked back to the cottage. Once inside, she tossed her book on the slate table and then closed and locked all the windows and did the same for the back door.

Then she grabbed her purse and keys and walked out the front door, making sure that it was locked behind her. She opened up the door of her Jeep and Duke jumped in.

It was fifteen minutes before she got to Heelie. She

wasn't sure which had come first. The town or the lake. But now each was an extension of the other. Every other place on the three-block stretch was a T-shirt shop or a souvenir store. There was one coffee shop, three ice cream parlors and two small restaurants. She parked in front of one. She rolled down the window for Duke. She wasn't worried about anybody stealing him. He'd bite the person's arm off who tried that.

The place had fewer tables than the Wright Here, Wright Now Café and there was no shiny pie case in the corner. The menu looked similar but the prices were higher.

Maybe it was time for her and Summer to increase theirs. She ordered a BLT with fries and, to test the young waitress, an Arnold Palmer to drink. The girl smiled and said, "My mom drinks those."

Trish managed to keep a smile on her face as the young girl trotted off to get her lemonade–iced tea combination. The girl's comment had been a stark reminder that she was an age where she could have a daughter working behind the counter.

But look at Summer, a little voice nagged at her, as she unrolled and rerolled her silverware, tighter than it had been before. Summer was exactly the same age and she'd be having a new baby in seven months.

You're not over the hill, she told herself.

But had she crested the peak and was the descent staring her in the face? Suddenly motivated, she pulled out her smartphone and scanned her emails, looking for the last one from the guy that she'd met online. The one she'd told Milo about.

Maybe it was time to fish or cut bait.

Barry North wanted to meet her for dinner. She found

his message and, before she could change her mind, sent him a quick note confirming that she'd be available to meet him the following Saturday.

When her BLT and fries arrived, she forced herself to eat. She was moving on. This was good. When she got back to Ravesville, she was tossing out those self-help books about dealing with loss. She was dealing just fine.

She'd just pushed her plate away when her phone dinged, indicating a new email. She picked it up, ignoring that her hand was shaking. So great to get your message. Glad we're finally going to do this. Where and when? I don't mind a drive.

She'd told him that she lived about ninety minutes southwest of St. Louis but hadn't been specific about Ravesville. She wasn't stupid. She might be new at the online dating game, but she knew enough not to give out her personal information. He lived in Kansas City.

Maybe Hamerton. It was a twenty-minute drive from Ravesville. There were a couple of good places there. She wanted someplace nice but not too fancy. She typed back. Mulder's in Hamerton. At seven.

Almost immediately came the response. Looking forward to it.

She closed her phone feeling suddenly very warm. She had a date. The idea of it made her BLT rumble in her stomach.

She pushed her chair back, walked to her Jeep and got Duke out to take a little stroll. They went up and down the streets, with Duke stopping frequently to drink out of the dog water bowls that many of the merchants left outside their entrances.

Then it was back to the Jeep for Duke while she went to the grocery store and bought milk and eggs and more fresh vegetables than she probably needed. But hopefully she'd catch a fish this afternoon and be able to cook the fish and the vegetables on the gas grill that was chained outside the cottage.

Back at the Jeep, she shoved the groceries inside the back door and slipped into the driver's seat. It was a very warm day, and through her capri pants, she could feel the heat of the leather. She leaned back in the seat gingerly, knowing that her tank wouldn't provide much protection. She'd pulled her hair into a low ponytail, like she usually wore it to work, but it felt heavy on her neck. Maybe it would be cooler on the water.

She checked both ways and then pulled out of her parking space. Duke had his head hanging out the window. There was a lot of traffic that didn't lighten up until she'd turned off onto the side road that would wind around until it led her to the cottage.

She remembered several of the hairpin turns from the previous night and realized that they were much scarier in the daytime. She hadn't been able to see how narrow the shoulder on the road was.

Fifteen minutes later, when she was back at the cottage, she let Duke out to do his thing and grabbed the groceries. She held both plastic bags in one hand so that she had a free hand to enter the combination.

She got it on the first try this time. The door swung open.

And by habit, her eyes swept the room. Call her crazy but it seemed different than it had when she'd left two hours earlier. It smelled different. And the handle of the faucet on the kitchen sink was turned to a slightly different angle. And the rug on the floor had one corner flipped up, as if someone had caught it with a shoe.

Trust your instincts.

She could almost hear Rafe's voice in her ear.

She dropped her groceries and ran for her car. Where the hell was Duke?

She was reaching for the Jeep door when someone caught her from behind. She turned, swinging her fist.

The stranger caught her arm. He was big and beefy and he smelled strongly of garlic. He was completely bald, maybe late fifties.

She opened her mouth to scream and he backhanded her. She fell to her knees.

"Shut up or we put a bullet in you," he said. "Get the dog."

She thought he was talking to her but realized that there was a second man. He was standing five feet away, holding a gun. He was much younger, with dark hair that touched his shoulders. But there was no doubt that the two were related, maybe father and son.

Her ears were ringing and she was pretty sure she had a bloody nose. She lifted her head, looking for Duke. He was fifty feet away, his fur raised, on full alert. He was going to charge the man with the gun.

"Oh, no, Duke," she cried.

The man pulled the trigger, catching Duke as he leaped into the air. She heard his sharp yelp of pain and saw him fall.

Duke's big body hit the hard ground and he lay there.

She pushed herself off the ground. She had to help him. "You bastard," she screamed. "You killed him."

And when the younger man laughed, Trish launched herself in his direction, kicking and screaming with everything she had.

It took both men to subdue her, and she only stopped

when they had her on the ground with the gun pressed up against her temple. She turned her head to see her poor dog.

He lay absolutely still.

Chapter Five

"You son of a bitch," she screamed at the younger man.

He laughed and yanked her arm, pulling her to a standing position. Then he pushed her toward the cottage and through the doorway. She stumbled over the spilled groceries. She was shoved toward a kitchen chair and her tailbone hit it hard.

The older man had followed them in and was now going through her purse that she'd dropped outside during the struggle. He pulled out her billfold, flipped it open and held it up, squinting at it. "Trish Wright-Roper. Jackpot."

He had to be comparing her to her driver's license. Jackpot. That could mean only one thing. This hadn't happened by chance. They'd been looking for her.

It made no sense. She didn't have enemies.

Maybe not, but a man had been murdered outside her café the previous night. Was that what this was about? Milo?

She sat in the chair and faced her attackers, attempting to control her spiking emotions. The idea that these men might have had something to do with Milo's death fueled an anger that she'd never thought herself capable of. And then there was what they'd done to poor Duke.

But she couldn't get so upset that she couldn't think.

"Anthony, go finish off that dog," the older man said.

He pulled Trish's cell phone out of her purse. He didn't bother to look at it. Just dropped it on the ground and stepped on it with the heel of his boot.

Anthony looked up from the cookies he'd grabbed from the floor. He tore at the packaging. "I'm eating."

"You can eat when this is over," the older man said. He spoke in a tone that made it clear he considered himself in charge.

Anthony evidently understood the pecking order because he tossed the now-open cookies onto the counter. "What the hell am I supposed to do with it?"

"This isn't that difficult. Just get it out of sight. Put the carcass in the woods, under something."

Duke deserved so much more. She was going to kill both of these men when she had the chance. And leave their bodies for the buzzards.

Anthony stalked to the door, leaving it open behind him. She couldn't see but Old Guy was watching.

"What?" he said loudly, his voice cross.

Anthony didn't answer, but perhaps he motioned or something because a look of exasperation crossed Old Guy's face. "Fine," he said. "Just come back in."

She could barely keep the smile off her face. It could mean only one thing. Duke had somehow had enough life in him to slink away.

Stay alive, Duke, she thought. *I'll try to do the same.* With that thought in mind, she once again tried to channel her anger, to make it into something productive. Her phone was out of commission but her gun was still on the porch, still stuffed underneath the cushion, where she'd left it last night. She needed to somehow find a way to get to it.

When Anthony came back inside, he picked up the

other groceries on the floor and seemed delighted that the eggs hadn't broken. He ignored the cookies he'd opened and poured himself a bowl of cereal. He added milk and noisily ate. Old Guy gave him a dirty look but didn't say anything else.

"Who are you?" she asked, proud that her voice didn't shake. She would not let these people know that she was terrified.

"Why, we have friends in common," said Old Guy. Then he laughed and wiped his sweaty brow with the back of his hand. "That makes us friends."

She was confident that she'd never seen either of these two men before. But she decided to let his comment play out. "You've got an odd way of showing it," she said.

He shrugged and turned his head to look at Anthony. "Tie her up."

Anthony set down his bowl and pulled out a small ball of heavy twine from his pants pocket. He squatted in front of her. He smelled of sweat and garlic and she fought back the urge to gag. When he roughly pulled her ankles together and wrapped the twine around four times and then tied it tight, she fought back the instinct to scream.

"To the chair," Old Guy said, frowning.

Anthony stood up. Instead of tying her wrists together, he tied each wrist to the back of the chair, at the spot where the seat curved down to the leg.

If she went anywhere, the chair was going with her.

"Now what?" she asked.

"Now we wait," said Old Guy, smiling at her.

"For?" Trish asked. She needed to figure out the plan if she hoped to outthink them.

His smile faded. "Stop asking questions or I'll gag you. You'll know soon enough."

He pulled a cell phone out of his shirt pocket. Held it up so that he could take a picture of her. Evidently not happy with the shot, he moved to the side. "Anthony," he said, motioning for the man. "Put your gun up to her temple."

Anthony seemed only too happy to do that. She could feel it, warm from either the sun or the man's body, pressing against the soft part of her skull.

Old Guy took several shots. Then he lowered the phone and typed something, using his thumb. "That should do it," he said.

Were they sending the picture to Summer? Trish's stomach twisted at the idea of her sister opening up a message and seeing this. It had been only six months since Adie had been kidnapped. Could Summer survive this again?

She could. She was strong. And now she had Bray and his brothers, too. They would find her. Save her. She had to hold on to that thought.

"He won't be able to resist that," Old Guy said.

He? He who?

But Old Guy was done talking. He walked out onto the porch and she lost her view of him. But she could hear him cross the length of the porch, heard a creak as he sat down. Probably on the couch. Maybe even on the same cushion that her gun was stuffed under. She guessed it was too much to hope for that it would accidentally go off and shoot him.

But Old Guy didn't worry her as much as Anthony, who was staring at her. With her arms behind her back, her breasts were more prominent, pushing against the thin material of her tank top.

If he touched her, that would be more than she could endure.

AFTER LEAVING THE MALADUCCIS', Rafe drove to his apartment and picked up the things he would need. On the way to the Milan airport, he made phone calls. One to Henri, to let him know that his services were going to be needed.

Nobody knew about Henri. Rafe had encountered the man years before he'd ever met Trish. It had set him back some to look across a crowded restaurant and see someone who very closely resembled him. It was widely believed that everybody had a double. Well, Rafe had met his.

He'd cultivated a relationship with Henri that had been profitable to both of them. Financially profitable for Henri because Rafe paid him very well. Rafe had benefited from the resemblance because whenever Rafe was supposedly off the clock on holiday, Henri filled in, coming and going from Rafe's apartment, making it appear as if Rafe was indeed home.

Truth be told, Rafe had actually been in the United States, spying on his wife. Nobody that he worked with knew about Trish. Not even his boss. And he intended to keep it that way. It was safer for her.

Once Rafe had been confident that Henri understood the plan, he'd made a second call to arrange transport back to St. Louis. He didn't intend to fly commercial. First of all, there were no direct flights from Milan to St. Louis. He would have to connect in New York or Atlanta and there would likely be delay after delay.

And he didn't intend for his name to show on any manifest. At least, not yet. That was essential.

For years, he'd prepared to have to make a last-minute flight back to the States. Just in case. That was going to pay off today.

His call was answered. He spoke in the common lan-

guage of dollars and, within five minutes, had secured
a spot on a charter flight that, according to the manifest, was delivering medical equipment. Perhaps there
would be an antiseptic wipe on board.

He was leaving at 10:00 a.m. his time, which was
3:00 a.m. Missouri time. It was a ten-hour flight. There-
fore, he would be there by 1:00 p.m. Missouri time.
He sent a text to Daniel to let him know where to pick
him up.

He parked his car, walked up the steps of the plane,
spoke to the pilot briefly and settled into his seat. He
listened to the engines rev up as the plane taxied down
the runway and tried to tell himself that there could be
a thousand reasons why Trish wasn't at her house. It did
not mean she was in trouble.

After all, she'd taken Duke with her. That was a good
sign. Right?

But somebody had killed Milo. It was possible that it
had been random. Even so, it was plenty enough to get
his attention and to get him back to the States. The timing was bad but he'd stay just long enough to ensure that
Trish was okay.

He slept on the plane, not because he was terribly
tired, but because he knew that it might be a while before he could sleep again.

Trish was missing. Once his feet hit the ground, he
would not stop until he knew she was safe.

The plane landed about twenty minutes early. At the
pilot's signal, Rafe lifted the hatch on the floor of the
plane and dropped down into the cargo hold. Then he got
into the empty crate and pulled the door shut. He had to
wait several long minutes before he heard the sound of

a door. Then he hung on while a forklift off-loaded him and his crate.

Fifteen minutes later, he heard a click and the door of the crate popped open. He pushed his head out. He was on a dock. Nobody around. He exited and calmly walked to the front of the warehouse. A blast of warm air hit his face. It took him a minute to figure out where he was and then he sent a quick text to Daniel.

It was just after 1:00 p.m. It would be 8:00 in Italy. The Maladuccis would have finished their predinner cocktails and be sitting down for the meal.

His phone pinged and he thought it was probably Daniel responding. He glanced at it and almost stepped off the curb in front of an oncoming semi. Trish. Oh, God. Tied up. With a gun to her head. Blood on her face. Her shirt. His hands shook as he studied the photo.

The message below the picture was brief. We'll trade her for you.

Chapter Six

With a few clicks, Rafe ran the text message through software on his phone. But it couldn't be traced. He was able to tell that the picture had been taken two minutes ago.

He texted back. He wanted to beg them not to hurt her, to tell them that he'd do anything. Instead, he typed, I'm willing to talk.

The reply came immediately. Come to Missouri. Further instruction will be sent.

He heard the sharp tap of a horn and looked up into the eyes of his trusted friend. He and Daniel had gone to college together and stayed good friends ever since. Daniel had joined the FBI years ago and was the most accomplished man that Rafe had ever met. He had a pilot's license and flew his own plane. He had scuba dived the great reefs of the world and he spoke five or six languages fluently.

He was also a chameleon, and when there had been a concern that the Ravesville police chief was involved in significant illegal activity, some of which had involved the transportation of minors across state lines, the FBI had sent him to Ravesville to play the role of small-town police officer.

It was years after Rafe had left Ravesville but still

fortuitous because it had given him another set of eyes besides Milo to watch over Trish.

With Chief Poole in jail and Chase Hollister now occupying that chair, there had been no need for Daniel's continued service in Ravesville. He was currently working out of the Chicago FBI office but he kept his ear to the ground for Rafe, passing along tidbits that he heard.

Rafe got into the car. Showed the man the text. Daniel let loose with several words that Rafe had wanted to say. He was holding his emotions in. Barely.

"Well, I guess now we know," Daniel said, finishing up. "I'm sorry, Rafe."

"I know." He was sorry, too, and more angry than he'd ever been in his whole life. But none of that did them any good. "Thank you for letting me know about Milo. How did you hear?"

"I monitor the Twitter and Facebook pages of several men on the volunteer fire department. One of them Tweeted that the cook at the Wright Here, Wright Now Café had been murdered. I got to the airport as quickly as I could, flew here and managed to arrive a half hour before Trish drove herself home, followed by Bray Hollister."

If Daniel hadn't alerted Rafe about Milo's death and then subsequently confirmed that Trish was missing from her apartment, he'd have been totally surprised by the picture of her. He'd probably have had a damn heart attack. Even now, with ten-plus hours to have anticipated the worst, it had still been pretty horrific to see that photo.

"Do you have any idea who is behind this?" Daniel asked.

"No, not for sure. I've always believed that Luciano Maladucci was behind the *accidents* that happened to my colleagues. If I had to guess, it would be him. Maybe they got tipped off that I'm getting close again."

"You need to know something. I didn't know this when I gave you the news about Milo."

"What?"

"Milo had some poignant last words. 'Tell Rafe they know.' I talked to Chase Hollister this morning. He told me to see if it possibly meant anything to me."

"What did you tell him?"

"Told him I had no idea."

"Who did Milo say this to?"

"Trish. She found him."

The news settled on him, almost taking his breath away. Trish should never have to see things like that. It wasn't the world she lived in. And what the hell would she have thought hearing those words? Maybe she'd been in such shock that the words hadn't really registered. Hadn't meant anything.

They meant something to him. Milo had wanted to warn him that danger was closing in. It had to be big. Nothing else would have made Milo sacrifice the truth. *Tell Rafe.* By that, he had opened the door that Rafe Roper might not really be dead. He'd protected the secret for a long time. Even dying, he wouldn't have said it if it wasn't vitally important.

As they pulled away from the curb, Rafe pulled out a second phone from his shirt pocket. He scanned the numbers. There were only just a handful in this particular phone. He pressed the one he wanted. "Go," he said when the phone was answered. Then he hung up.

He settled back in his seat. Right now, if they were tracking his accounts, and he assumed they were, they would see him online, purchasing a seat on a charter flight that in one hour would fly him from Milan, Italy, to the St. Louis airport. Next, they would see him arrange for a rental car in St. Louis.

If they had someone at the airport, and he suspected they would, they would know when his passport and boarding pass were scanned. His seat would be occupied. By Henri. Once the plane landed in St. Louis, he suspected that was when further instruction would arrive.

It was a ten-hour flight. The plane would land in St. Louis at midnight.

It was 1:00 p.m. now. That meant he had eleven hours to find Trish before they thought his feet were touching US soil.

He glanced at his phone, at the picture. Even bloody and bound, she was still so beautiful. So perfect in every way.

It had almost killed him to leave her. But he knew that it was the only way to protect her. They would have found him eventually. Discovered Trish. Known that the easiest way to make him pay for what he'd done to them was to hurt her.

So Rafe Roper had died.

He glanced at Daniel. "Is there anything else?"

He shook his head. "Summer and Bray Hollister were at the funeral home this morning, making arrangements for Milo. They did not appear to be distressed."

That wasn't good. It meant that Trish had probably made some kind of contact with Summer before she'd been apprehended. They weren't worried about her, wouldn't be looking for her.

But it also meant that they might have some idea of where she was. So, in order to find out where Trish was, he was going to have to go through Summer or her new husband. He'd done his research on Bray Hollister when the man had first come back to Ravesville. He'd been a DEA agent and had built a reputation as being tough as nails. He'd still be easier to talk to than Summer, who would want to skin him alive.

He opened his contacts on his telephone and found Bray Hollister's number. It had been in his phone for months. He started typing. When he finished, his message said, Need to meet. Come alone. 2nd floor, across from café. In 90 minutes.

Based on what he knew about Bray Hollister, he'd come. And he probably wouldn't tell his new bride—he wouldn't want to worry her needlessly. But he wasn't stupid. He'd have one or both of his brothers as backup. Fine. Might as well get it over with. They were a tight group, those Hollister brothers, based on what he'd heard.

In five minutes, he got a return text. Who is this? Who gave you this number?

I will explain. Milo gave it to me.

There were no other texts from Bray. He hoped that meant the man would be there to meet him when they rolled into Ravesville.

It was a bright, sunny afternoon, far different than the first night he'd rolled into Ravesville. The light had been fading fast when he'd heard the sounds of the tornado siren. He'd looked off to his left and he was pretty sure he could see the makings of a funnel cloud.

But still, he'd have tried to outrun it. If he hadn't looked through that damn window of the Wright Here, Wright Now Café and seen the most beautiful woman ever. She was tall and fit and had silky red hair to her waist.

And he decided it wouldn't be a bad idea to wait out the storm in her company. He figured it might be a couple of hours of fun and, if he got real lucky, maybe an hour of sweaty sex.

But somewhere in the middle of his second piece of banana cream pie, he realized that he was in trouble. This woman was different. This woman could make him want things that he couldn't have.

This woman was meant to be his.

And so he'd broken his own rules and hoped like hell that it would be okay. And it was better than okay. It was damn near perfect until he'd got the first call. Then the second. The team was dropping like flies. Somebody had flipped on them.

He didn't know whom he could trust.

So he'd done the only thing he could do.

But now Milo was dead.

Another death.

This time he would settle it and settle it for good. But first he had to find Trish, make sure she was safe.

EIGHTY-ONE MINUTES LATER they entered Ravesville. "I'll walk from here," Rafe said. "I'll need a vehicle."

"It'll be parked a block east. A black BMW."

"Thank you." Once he knew where Trish was, he'd be on the road again. "I appreciate your help."

Daniel smiled. "I hope it works out for you and Trish. I really do. I'll stick around Ravesville for a few days in the event you need me."

Rafe got out and walked the two blocks to the building across from the café. When he rounded the corner of the second floor, he saw that Bray Hollister had got there early. He was lounging against the wall, his stance casual.

"Thank you for coming," Rafe said.

Bray didn't respond.

Rafe already had the keys in his hand. He hadn't wanted to have to pull them out of his pocket—Hollister might get nervous and shoot him with the gun that he was sure to be wearing.

He kept his hands where Hollister could see them and turned to open the door. He walked into the empty apartment, turned and stood with his back against the wall. "There's nobody else here," he said.

Hollister must have believed him because he followed him in and shut the door.

"My name is Rafe Roper," he said.

Hollister considered him. Finally, he spoke. "You son of a bitch. Trish thinks you're dead."

"It's a long story," he said. "But right now, I need to know where Trish is. She could be in danger."

That got Hollister's attention. "From who?"

"From the people who killed Milo," Rafe said. He didn't intend to show Hollister the text message. Based on what he'd been told about the man, there was no way that he was going to leave law enforcement out of it.

And Rafe didn't know whom he could trust.

Hollister was either a really good actor or he really wasn't a bit surprised that Trish's trouble had something to do with Milo. He undoubtedly had heard about Milo's last words and he was piecing the information together.

Hollister walked over to the window, pulled back the curtain. "I saw you up here. It was around Thanksgiving. You were watching the café."

That had been the last time he'd been in the States. And he had been in Ravesville. But to the best of his knowledge, nobody had ever seen him watching over the café. "You're observant," Rafe said. "I was already on my way out of the country before I heard about Adie's disappearance. I was glad to hear that things worked out okay."

Hollister turned to look at him. "Milo had some last words. For Trish."

Rafe waited.

"He said, 'Tell Rafe they know.'"

He pretended to be surprised. No need for them to start looking at Daniel.

"Who's behind this?" Hollister demanded.

"I don't know." But if it was the people he thought, they'd killed before and were coming back to finish the job.

"Where's Trish?" Rafe asked.

"Who do you work for?" Hollister demanded.

"It's better that you don't know," Rafe said. "But I am no threat to you or your family."

"Of course you are. You just told me Trish was in danger."

"I'll handle this."

Hollister didn't look convinced but he gave up on the line of questioning fairly easily. He had probably figured out that no amount of asking was going to get Rafe to tell him anything else. "You do realize that when you find Trish you're going to have a whole lot of explaining to do," Hollister said. "I'm going to assume you left her for the right reasons. But even that might not make a difference."

He was prepared for that. It would hurt him badly but nothing was more important than finding Trish and keeping her safe. "Where is she?"

"I know an approximate location," Hollister said. "When she talked to Summer, she said she was at a cottage near Heelie Lake in the Ozarks."

"Address?" Rafe said, pulling out his phone.

"She didn't give Summer one. But she did say that the cottage had been recommended by a woman who eats in the café. M.A. Fikus."

The name meant nothing to Rafe. He keyed in information on his phone. Within minutes, he knew Mary Ann Fikus was single, worked at the Ravesville bank and had a peanut allergy. On her social media pages, she talked about making quilts and apple butter.

He kept flipping screens until he had her street address. That was where he was headed next. He put his phone back in his pocket and walked over to the door. "Hollister, will you come with me to M.A.'s house? She might not be willing to tell me anything but she knows you."

Steady eyes studied him. "You can call me Bray," he said. "After all, I think we're sort of family."

In his world, the luxury of family had always been beyond his reach. "Thank you," he said.

The BMW was exactly where it was supposed to be. He got in it and Bray followed him in his own vehicle. They pulled up in front of M.A. Fikus's house within four minutes. He was anxious to meet the woman, get the information and get on the road.

He could hear the music from the sidewalk. M.A. liked badass rock and roll and she liked it loud. That didn't fit the image he had of the quilter and apple butter maker.

He was still three feet away from the front door when he saw that it was open and the lock had been broken, as if somebody had taken a foot to the door. He pulled his gun and confirmed that Bray was indeed carrying when suddenly there was a gun in his hand, too.

The two men entered the living room. There was no

sign of distress. He motioned to Bray that he was going to look right. Bray went the opposite direction.

It was a small house, just two bedrooms and one bath. It didn't take him long. He'd just finished the bath when he heard Bray Hollister.

"Rafe, back porch."

M.A. was dressed in workout clothes but she wasn't going to have to ever worry about her weight again. She was on her stomach and she'd been shot in the back three times.

It was possible that she'd never even known that an intruder was in her house.

"Call it in," Rafe said. "You can tell your brother I was here but I'd appreciate it if my name wasn't in the police report."

"How are you going to find Trish now?"

"M.A.'s bank records. Credit card receipts. If she recently stayed there, I should be able to narrow the area fairly quickly."

"You have access to all that?"

"I do," he said simply. "Does she have family?" he asked, looking at the woman.

"I'm not sure. Summer will know."

"If there are…issues with money, you know, for paying for the funeral, I'll take care of it," he said, already moving for the door.

"Rafe," Bray said, stopping him. "Be careful. If you really get yourself killed out there this time, Trish will never forgive either one of us." He held up a finger. "And you better be as good as I suspect you are. Because if you fail and I have to tell Summer that something has happened to Trish, I'm going to hunt you down and rip out your heart."

Chapter Seven

It took Rafe less than twenty minutes to piece together M.A. Fikus's last vacation. She'd bought gas, groceries and a sub sandwich in Heelie. Had got a massage there, too. That had occurred the day after she'd rented a kayak at a marina at Heelie Lake.

Banking records told a story. Unfortunately, there were no transactions for lodging.

What role did M.A. play in all of this? Was she simply an acquaintance of Trish's who happened to mention a great vacation spot? Was she an unwitting accomplice and she'd been duped into leading Trish away from the safety of Ravesville? Had she been one of them? And had something gone terribly wrong that she'd had to be culled from the group?

So many questions but at least he had someplace to begin. He started his car, knowing that he'd be in the right area in a little more than an hour.

He would find Trish.

And then he was going to break the bastards who'd hurt her.

TRISH'S SHOULDERS HURT from being pulled back and her lower back ached like hell from having her spine arched.

The only good thing was that Anthony had left her alone in the kitchen. He had gone into her bedroom and, by the sounds of the creaking springs, was taking a nap on her bed. He'd turned on the radio next to the bed and she could hear sounds of a ball game.

Everyday stuff.

Except she was tied up. Waiting.

For who?

She wished she'd thought to tell Summer that she'd check in later during the day. If she had done that, and the call didn't come, Summer would send the cavalry. But now she would have no idea that Trish was in trouble.

It really was up to her.

Unless she got lucky and Bernie Wilberts decided to show up. But truthfully, she didn't really want that. He was a nice guy who would be quickly overpowered by these two and then she'd have someone else to save besides herself.

She decided it was time to see how much leverage she might have. "Hey," she said. "I have to go to the bathroom."

There was no answer.

"Hey," she said again. "I really do."

"Anthony," boomed the voice from the porch.

Anthony didn't answer. She suspected he was sound asleep because she was pretty confident that the baseball announcer wasn't the one snoring.

She heard noise on the porch and then Old Guy walked around the corner. He glanced into the bedroom and shook his head in disgust. But he didn't wake Anthony up. Instead, he pulled a pocketknife from his pants, extending the blade, and cut her arms and feet loose. "Out in two minutes or I'm coming in to get you."

She didn't waste any time getting to the bathroom and shutting the door. She used the toilet because she really did have to go. Then hurriedly washed her hands and face, scrubbing the dried blood off. Her nose hurt but she didn't think it was broken.

She glanced around the room, hoping for some kind of weapon. There was nothing. Not even a damn razor. She hadn't planned on shaving her legs while she was here. And there was no window in the bathroom.

She opened the door. Old Guy had taken her chair. He got up and motioned for her to sit down.

"Could I have some water, please," she said.

He shrugged.

She took that for a yes. She opened a cupboard door and pulled out a glass. Ran the water. Filled the glass half-full and drank it.

She needed to get to the porch. Her gun was less than twenty feet away but it might as well be on the moon if she couldn't find a reason to get out there. "I'm cold," she said. "Can I get that blanket off the sofa on the porch?" she asked, already starting to cross the kitchen.

He moved fast, grabbing her arm and swinging her around. "You ain't going nowhere," he said. He shoved her down into the chair and picked up the twine.

She automatically got into the position that Anthony had tied her in the first time. Old Guy wrapped the twine even tighter than Anthony had and it cut into her skin.

But she was still happy. Because when she'd got her glass of water, she'd seen the key to Bernie Wilberts's boat next to the toaster. And she'd come up with a plan. But to enact it, it was very important that she have some use of her feet. Tied together she did. Tied to the legs of the chair, she'd have been virtually immobile.

Her opportunity would come. She just had to be ready when it did.

RAFE PULLED INTO Heelie at exactly 4:17 p.m. The town of 973 occupants was south and west of Ravesville, but still north of Springfield, Missouri. The terrain was hillier and the roads wound through the limestone cliffs.

While he'd never been to Heelie or Heelie Lake, he suspected it was like many places in the Ozarks, in that the population swelled during the summer when people from all over the country hitched up their boats and drove to Missouri for whatever their particular water sport might be. Fishing. Boating. Waterskiing. Tubing. Canoeing or kayaking for those who wanted to work a little harder.

Based on what he'd seen driving in, Heelie Lake was substantially less commercial than Lake of the Ozarks to the north. Much smaller, too. But that still meant that there were hundreds of miles of shoreline and way too many properties to search efficiently.

He needed help. Which was why he started in town. Bray and Summer had heard from Trish this morning. That meant that she'd been okay at that point. Just maybe, she'd gone to town for one of those lattes that she loved and somebody had seen her.

He started at one end of the business district. At each store, he asked about a woman with long red hair and a German shepherd dog. Finally, in one tattoo parlor, he found a young girl who had seen them.

"I saw her walking by the store earlier," the young woman said. "I noticed her hair right away. It was beautiful. She didn't come in but her dog did stop for a drink." She pointed to the bowl by the door.

"What time?" Rafe asked. It was the first solid clue.

She shrugged. "At least a couple of hours ago," she said. "She was carrying some sacks. I think she'd been to the grocery store."

Then she'd probably been on her way home before the
groceries got warm. Which meant that she was probably
staying somewhere close. "Her friend Mary Ann Fikus,
everybody calls her M.A., was here just a few weeks ago.
I think she's staying at the same place. You didn't happen to meet M.A. while she was here?"

She shook her head.

It had been a long shot. He hadn't seen any tattoos
on M.A.

"You might want to talk to Bernie Wilberts. He owns
a stretch of property on Heelie Lake and his cottages are
real nice. She looked like the kind of woman who would
enjoy a nice place."

I'm not sleeping on the ground. That was what she'd
told him the one time he'd suggested they go camping.
He assured her that was no problem. He didn't plan on
sleeping and she could be on top.

That had got him a quick shot in the shoulder. Probably because her mother and sister were in the next room.
"Where does Bernie live?"

"Molson Road," she said, pointing west. "About a mile
from town. Turn right. First house on your left."

Easy enough. "Thank you," he said. His car was parked
close, and within seconds, he had the air-conditioning on
high and was driving. He found the house in less than
five minutes. Nice yard. Long lane with orange daylilies
on both sides. Two story, sided yellow. No cars outside.

He got out, knocked on the door and waited. When
there was no answer, he tried the front door. It was locked.
He walked around the house, looking in the windows.
Knocked on the back door. Tried the handle. When there
was no answer, he busted a windowpane, stuck his hand
in, flipped the lock and entered.

The smell of blood hit him. He pulled his gun and rounded the corner. There, in the narrow hallway between the kitchen and the living room, was a dead person.

A woman. So not Bernie Wilberts. He didn't need a body temperature to know that she'd been dead for several hours. She was already getting stiff.

Three gunshots to the back. A junior detective would be able to figure out that the person who'd killed M.A. had probably also killed this person.

He took a look at her face. Then studied the wedding picture that was on the shelf, next to the flat-screen television. The picture was twenty years old but he was pretty confident that the dead woman was Mrs. Wilberts.

Milo had been knifed to death but M.A. and this woman had both been killed the same way. They were all connected. He knew it.

And it made it seem very likely that the cabins that M.A. had recommended had indeed been owned by Bernie Wilberts.

He looked around for a desk but didn't see one. He started opening drawers and cupboards in the kitchen. In the fourth drawer, he found a stack of paid bills. He quickly went through them, stopping when he came to property tax bills for the previous years. There were eight separate addresses. He entered all of them into the GPS on his phone. Then he put the paperwork back, wiped off everything that he'd touched and left the house.

He would call it in. Just not quite yet. If the killers were close, he didn't want them to get nervous if they heard that their latest victim had been found. They might act rashly and that was the last thing he wanted. He looked at his watch. He still had at least five hours before they would worry about him being back in the States.

He was banking on the fact that they'd keep Trish alive to lure him in. He had no illusions that they'd let her go. Even once they had him. She was as good as dead if he didn't figure out a way to save her.

He studied the map on his phone. All the addresses appeared to be lakeside properties but, unfortunately, not all in the same area. Several were just miles apart but three of them were on the far side of the lake. It would take valuable minutes to drive the distance.

He considered the possibilities. He wanted to be able to approach without detection. With a car, even one that ran as smoothly as the one he was driving, that was impossible. And these were likely not well-traveled roads. A car on them would be noticed. By anybody who was in the mood to notice.

And while he wasn't expected for hours yet, he wasn't going to underestimate his enemy.

It was a sunny, warm day. There were lots of boats on the water. That would be the better way.

He used his smartphone to search for boat rentals. Found the nearest one and drove the seven miles. When he pulled up, there was a man and his little boy already there, renting a fishing boat.

The little guy had red hair.

And for just a minute, he allowed himself to wonder if, had things had gone differently, he and Trish would have had a son. With red hair and big blue eyes.

Trish had wanted a child. Once she'd finally made the decision to get married, she'd jumped in with both feet. Three months after the honeymoon, she'd stopped taking her birth control pills.

When he'd had to leave, he sweated out the first couple of months, until he was sure that he hadn't left her pregnant. He still wouldn't have been able to go back, but he'd have figured out some way to ensure that his child was well taken care of. Just like he'd figured out ways to ensure that Trish was safe, protected.

He'd done a good job.

But now something had gone wrong and Trish was paying the price.

Chapter Eight

Rafe walked inside the boat rental office.

He smiled at the kid behind the counter, who couldn't have been more than twenty. "Got any boats available to rent?"

"Storm's coming in. Not a great time to be on the lake."

"I'll be okay," Rafe said. He pulled out his billfold.

The kid pointed to a sign on the wall. "We rent them in four- or eight-hour increments. But we close at eight. You'll need to have it back by then."

"No problem."

The kid shrugged. "You won't get your full four hours in."

"I'm okay with that," Rafe said easily. He just wanted the kid to get the damn paperwork done so that he could get the hell out of there.

"It's four hundred and a deposit of half that. Bring it back in good shape and you'll get the deposit back."

"Fair enough," Rafe said, pulling out cash.

The kid slid a paper form across the counter. Rafe didn't bother to read the legalese. He filled in his name and showed the kid an ID when he asked for it.

There were coolers on the shelf behind the clerk. "I'll

take one of those, too, with a twelve-pack of water and…"
He grabbed a handful of candy bars from the stand next
to the counter. "And these." Trish was likely to be dehydrated and hungry and… He had to push the next
thoughts out of his head. He'd rescued women before.
Women who'd been kidnapped by men. Women who'd
been used. Badly.

He would kill the men painfully but that would never
be enough to make Trish whole again.

He drew in a deep breath. Focus. He needed to focus.
He handed the kid another fifty to cover the cooler and
the snacks and got seven dollars back.

He didn't pick up the change. Instead, he pointed to a
green hat with netting that covered the neck. "That, too,"
he said, fishing out a few more dollars.

The kid handed it to him. Rafe ripped the tag off and
put it on. It was perfect, with its wide brim.

"I'll meet you around back," the kid said. "*Flora* has
a full tank of gas."

Flora was Trish's mother's name. He hoped that was
a good omen.

He walked back to his car, started it and drove it around
to the rear of the parking lot. He'd flown with guns and
ammunition in his bag and he intended to take them with
him on the boat. He considered taking his second cell
phone but decided not to risk that it could be confiscated
if something went terribly wrong. It would be better left
in the trunk.

He got out of the car, grabbed his duffel and strolled
down the deck. He quickly inspected the boat. *Flora* was
a sturdy-looking twenty-six-footer. He climbed in and
saw that the kid already had loaded the cooler.

"There's your life vest," said the kid. "You're supposed to wear it."

If it wasn't Kevlar, it wasn't going to do him much good. Rafe put it on, then started the boat. Engine seemed solid enough. He waved at the kid and drove away from the dock. He scanned the shoreline, got his bearings. The lake was good sized, at least five, maybe more, miles across. The houses on the far side were barely visible. He would start with those and work his way back. He pulled out his cell phone and used it to identify his first stop.

He took off the clumsy life jacket and ran the boat at a moderate speed, not too slow, not too fast. Because it was a Saturday, there were lots of other boats on the water. When they passed, it wasn't unusual for someone to raise a hand in a friendly wave.

He waved back, making sure that his face was down, as if he was busy with his controls. Even with the hat, no sense letting anybody get too close a look.

When he got to the first property, he docked his boat and walked quietly up to the house that sat very close to the water. He'd always had superior hearing and now he was listening for anything that would tell him that his presence had been detected. But he heard nothing. He got all the way up to the cottage and looked in the window.

It was empty.

But people were living there. There was a pitcher of what appeared to be lemonade on the counter next to an open pack of store-bought cookies. Then he heard the voices. One low. A man. One higher. Probably a woman. But not Trish.

The woman was telling the man to hurry up, that she didn't have all day.

Not exactly sure what he'd see when he edged around

the corner, he almost smiled when he saw the man and woman, both looking as if seventy was a distant memory, playing a board game on the front porch.

He figured it was a safe bet to assume that Trish wasn't inside. He quickly walked back to his boat, got in and motored down to the next cottage.

It was similar to the first but not occupied. It didn't look as if it had been occupied for some time. There were cobwebs stretching across the front door.

He glanced at his watch. He'd already been in Heelie for over an hour. It was almost 5:30. Time was going too fast.

The third and fourth properties were several miles to the south but the GPS showed them very close together. When he got there, he saw that they were larger cottages located across the road from one another. He stood in the woods and surveyed both. There were young boys on bikes in front of one. The other had a teenage girl in a swimsuit sunbathing outside.

Four down, four to go. He got back in his boat and set off for the next location. He had to cross the lake.

He found it easily enough with his GPS but he didn't like the looks of it. It had a longer dock than the other cottages. There was a fifteen-foot aluminum fishing boat tied at the end.

It would be a long walk up that dock. He'd be a sitting duck if somebody in the cottage wanted him dead.

He passed by the dock and drove along the shoreline, as if he might be assessing the best possible place to drop a fishing line. He saw a place that had possibilities. Not for fishing. But for mooring the boat. He'd get his shoes and pants wet but he could live with that. He took off his hat. He didn't want anything to obscure his vision.

He dropped his anchor and waded to shore. Then he scrambled up the bank. He stayed in the tree line all the way back to his destination.

The back of the cottage was all porch, with windows and a door. In order to see in, he'd have to climb the five steps, but that wouldn't do him any good because the blinds were all down. He edged around to the front of the cottage.

Holy hell—there it was. Trish's Jeep.

But no other vehicles. That didn't make sense. Unless they'd come in the fishing boat. He supposed that was possible.

He pulled out his cell phone and studied the picture that he'd been sent. Now, no longer focused on the blood on her face and the gun pressed into her temple, he took in the details and then studied the cottage. She was sitting on a kitchen chair. There was a table and part of a window. He walked around the cottage. The ground sloped off on that side of the cottage, so the window was too high for him to easily see into. But the shape was the same.

The photo had been taken inside of this cottage. It didn't make sense that they'd move her.

Which meant that she was still here.

He considered his options. He had no way of knowing exactly who was inside or how many. But it was always better to divide and conquer.

Trish's Jeep had a car alarm. She'd bought the vehicle two years before and he'd had Milo convince her to get the additional security installed. Now it was going to come in handy.

He walked up to the Jeep and tried the door. As he'd hoped, the alarm started peeping. He was already moving fast, back toward the trees, up at a forty-five-degree angle to the front door.

A man stumbled out of the cottage, looking half-awake. He had a gun in his hand. In the other he must have had a key fob because he raised his arm in the direction of the Jeep and suddenly the alarm stopped.

It made it seem very quiet.

Rafe recognized him. Anthony Paradini. Only son of the New Jersey Paradini clan. His father was Big Tony, who had run the Jersey operation for at least twenty years.

Seeing him made it all the more likely that he'd been right all along. The Maladucci and the Paradini families had been associated for decades. They had competed and collaborated, depending on what particular vice was at play. Big Tony had done fifteen in federal prison for drug trafficking in his twenties and had come out with a bad attitude. Anthony would have been just a little kid when his dad got sent up.

If the Maladucci family needed assistance with something, they would call upon the Paradini family. It would cost them dearly. Nobody worked free of charge.

The price on his head must be pretty high. But even when you paid well, good labor was hard to find.

Anthony was generally considered to be a screwup. Maybe because his dad hadn't been around. Rafe was certain the family wouldn't have trusted him to do this alone. Big Tony was probably inside. Maybe someone else. Maybe not.

Now Anthony was stalking toward the vehicle, to figure out why in hell the alarm had suddenly started ringing. He walked all around the Jeep. Then he looked around.

Rafe picked up a rock and threw it thirty yards. It hit a tree, making noise. As he'd hoped, Anthony focused on the area where the rock had landed. The man raised his gun and started walking toward it.

Oldest trick in the book.

Rafe let him get ten yards into the trees before he took him down with a sharp knock on the back of the head.

He hit him hard. Hard enough to knock him out.

Rafe grabbed the man and dragged him a few feet farther into the woods. One down. But Anthony had been the easy one. Big Tony was a hell of a lot sharper.

Another five minutes and Big Tony would start to wonder where his son had wandered off to. But Rafe doubted that he'd simply barge outside. Big Tony hadn't stayed alive by being careless.

With that in mind, Rafe rolled Anthony onto his back and started unbuttoning his blue-and-white-striped shirt. He got it off, then used the duct tape in his pocket to bind Anthony's wrists together and his ankles, too. Then Rafe slapped a piece of tape over Anthony's mouth.

He left him in the woods, propped up against the tree.

Rafe put on Anthony's shirt. It was tight in the shoulders but would do the trick. Then he took the man's baseball cap and stuck in on his own head.

He stayed back in the trees but worked his way around to the back of the cottage and the lake. There was some yard between the back stairs and the edge of the water. The dock extended another fifty feet.

As quickly as he could, he walked down the dock, listening carefully for any sound from the cottage. A door opening. A window. Anything that would tell him that his presence had been detected.

He was six inches taller than Anthony and twenty pounds heavier, so there was little chance of fooling Big Tony if the man got a close look.

But Rafe got to the end of the dock without hearing anything. Then he sat down, dangled his legs over the edge of the dock and turned his back to the cottage.

To Big Tony's gun.

While Big Tony hadn't stayed alive by being stupid, Rafe Roper hadn't stayed alive by always playing it safe.

Chapter Nine

Old Guy was in the bathroom when the car alarm went off. From behind the closed door, he bellowed for Anthony to go take a look.

A minute later, Anthony stumbled out of the bedroom, swearing loudly. There was a stain on his pants that hadn't been there before and she caught a whiff of alcohol. She suspected Anthony had fallen asleep and spilled the wine on himself.

Her best hope was that he'd come back in, resume drinking and pass out. Then she'd have only the Old Guy to deal with.

"Maybe it's your damn dog," he snarled. He held up the gun in his hand. "I'll finish off the job this time."

Duke. She could feel her throat start to close up and she forced herself to breathe, to not give in to the panic that threatened to overwhelm her. She—

"Anthony!" Old Guy yelled from the bathroom.

Yes, go Anthony, she thought. With him outside and Old Guy indisposed, it was her chance. She had a plan. All she had to do was get to the boat key, grab it with her mouth, then hop, chair and all, to the back door. She thought there was a good possibility that she could turn the knob with her fingers. Once she was outside, all she had to do was hop down the steps, then the length of the dock, throw herself over the edge of the boat, figure out a way to insert the key to start the engine and gun it.

Nothing to it.

Maybe not a foolproof plan but infinitely better than sitting here, waiting for Anthony to snap or Old Guy to get bored and shoot her.

Anthony grabbed her keys off the bookshelf where he'd thrown them earlier. The minute the door shut behind him, she was moving. It wasn't possible to do it quietly, so she simply needed to do it quickly.

Three hops and she was at the counter. She bent forward, snatched the key with her teeth and straightened up. The car alarm had stopped.

Four more hops and she was in the doorway between the main cottage and the porch. Four more and she was at the back door. She turned her body, grabbed the doorknob with the fingers on her left hand and twisted.

She heard it catch at exactly the same minute Old Guy, his pants still unzipped, roared through the archway. His big hand came down on her shoulder and he spun her around so hard that the legs of her chair knocked into the wall, sending her flying.

She and her chair landed sideways on the floor, her right shoulder taking the brunt of the fall. He stood over her. Panting.

"You little bitch," he said. "You'll pay for this." He kicked her hard in the right calf.

She pressed her lips together, determined not to cry out, not to give him the pleasure of knowing that he'd hurt her.

"Anthony," he yelled. He stalked to the front door, leaving her on the floor. She was no threat to him in this position. She couldn't get herself and the chair upright without help. It was like being a crab trying to climb out of a bucket.

It was so frustrating. The only consolation was that he was back within a minute, looking pretty darn frustrated himself.

He yanked her and the chair up and pushed her back into the kitchen. Once all four legs of the chair were back on the ground, he leaned close. He cut the twine that bound her ankles together. Then he quickly tied each ankle to a chair leg.

"I swear to all that's holy," he muttered, "between you and that kid, a man can't even have a moment of peace to do his business in the bathroom."

She didn't intend to give these two any peace. This was a momentary setback but she wasn't giving up.

"What do you want from me?" she asked.

He stared at her. "I don't want anything from you," he said finally. "You're simply a means to an end."

"What end?"

He smiled and pinched her bruised cheek hard. "Justice, sweetheart. Long overdue, from what I understand."

Then he walked over to the front door one more time and looked out. Shaking his head, he went out to the porch.

She could hear the blind being raised. Then the sound of a door opening. "Anthony, get your ass back inside this cottage," Old Guy yelled.

"ANTHONY, GET YOUR ass back inside this cottage."

He'd been right. It was Big Tony.

Rafe kept sitting.

He heard footsteps on the stairs. Then nothing. He assumed Big Tony was crossing the yard.

So far, so good.

Then heavy footsteps on the dock, making it shake just a little. "This ain't a damn fishing trip," Big Tony said, agitation clear.

Rafe didn't move.

Now the footsteps came faster. "I'm talking to you, boy."

Rafe judged him to be about five feet away. He pulled his legs up, got them under him and sprang up and around, all in one motion.

Big Tony was close enough that Rafe's first punch landed squarely on the man's haggard cheek.

To Big Tony's credit, he responded faster than Anthony ever would have, getting in one good punch, knocking Rafe's head back. But Rafe was faster, more agile, and in less than thirty seconds, the fight was over.

Big Tony was flat on his stomach, his arm twisted behind him, breathing heavily. Rafe, with one knee in the middle of Tony's back, leaned close to the older man's ear.

"I'm going to let you live. For the moment. But if we get inside and I see that you've harmed one hair on her head, I'm going to kill you. And it will be an extremely painful death."

Big Tony didn't answer.

And Rafe found himself hesitating. He had been full steam ahead when it had been about getting here and making sure that Trish was safe. But now? Now that he was about to give the woman that he'd loved the surprise of her lifetime, he was scared.

He'd never wanted to hurt her. Had never wanted to cause her pain. And he'd done exactly that.

But he'd kept her alive.

That was what was important.

All the while keeping an eye on the cottage, he slapped a piece of duct tape over Big Tony's mouth, then secured his wrists and ankles. He left him lying facedown on the dock. If the idiot was stupid enough to roll around and fall into the water and drown, that wasn't his concern.

He took off Anthony's striped shirt and baseball hat. Then he drew in a breath, steadied his nerves and continued up to the house.

He was fairly confident that it was only Anthony and Big Tony in the cottage but he wasn't going to be stupid about it. He opened the back door and edged his head around the frame. The porch was empty. He listened, didn't hear anything.

But he knew Trish was close. Could feel her presence.

He crossed the porch and stepped into the main room of the cottage. There, tied to a chair, was his one true love.

She stared at him, her pretty green eyes registering shock. She opened her mouth, as if to speak, then closed it.

"Trish," he said.

Her eyes rolled back in her head and she fainted.

He took one extra second to clear the bedroom and bath, making sure that there was nobody else in the small cottage. Then he took his knife and sliced through the twine that bound her wrists and her ankles. The coarse material had worn against her delicate skin, and his hands, his always-steady hands, shook as he balled up the twine and tossed it aside.

Just as she was coming to, he saw the bruise on her

cheek. He reached out to touch it but dropped his hand. He didn't want to see her go lights-out again.

If he'd expected her to throw her arms around him and swear to love him forever, he would have been sadly mistaken. Instead, she pushed her chair back, away from him. When there was space, she got up, on unsteady legs, and backed away from him until she came up against the wall that separated the bath from the kitchen.

She still hadn't said a word. It rattled him.

"Did they touch you?" he asked. He knew immediately it was the wrong thing to say first but he couldn't help it. She looked so vulnerable and he couldn't stand that she'd been terrorized by Big Tony and his idiot son.

She did not respond for a long moment. Then finally, she shook her head. "I thought…you were dead," she said, her voice barely a whisper.

And a dozen lies popped into his head. He could pretend that he'd been badly injured and just recovered his memory. He could say that he'd been taken prisoner. He could…

He was tired of the lies. So tired. "I know," he said.

"You bastard," she said, her voice rising sharply.

Mindful of the two men that he had tied up outside, he didn't defend himself. "Where's Duke?" he asked, looking around.

Now her eyes were big. "How do you know my dog's name?"

He wasn't doing well here. But he knew something was wrong if Duke wasn't close. She hadn't left him in Ravesville. "I'll explain. Where is he?"

"Anthony shot him," she said.

Rafe clamped down on the rage that arched through

him. He was well aware of how much Trish loved that dog. "I'm sorry," he said.

"I think he's dead," she said. "He managed to get away into the woods."

He couldn't worry about it right now but he would find the dog. He was a fine animal and he certainly deserved better. "Just give me a few minutes to get things right here."

She was shaking. That just about killed him. But there really were things to do.

"Please," he said, before going out the front door. Anthony was still where he'd left him. The man was conscious but definitely not firing on all cylinders. Rafe put his gun in the man's face and waited until it registered. Then he pulled the man to his feet. And punched him in the mouth. Hard. The man went to his knees. Rafe yanked him up again. "That was for the dog," he said.

Then he shoved him in the direction of the cottage. Once inside, he tied him to the same kitchen chair where Trish had been restrained.

"Let's see how you like it," Rafe said, wrapping his wrists tight to the back of the chair. Then he went out the porch door to get Big Tony. He brought him inside.

Trish had moved from the wall to the sofa on the porch. "I'll just be a minute," he said to her. He was finishing tying Big Tony to another chair when he heard the back door open and close. He moved fast.

Trish was outside. Halfway down the dock, bent from the waist. He didn't think she was throwing up but maybe she felt faint.

He understood. His own knees were damn weak.

He understood why he'd given almost no thought to what he might say to her when he saw her. There were really no words that were adequate. And what he'd said could certainly have been better. But he would explain. Maybe not everything. But enough that she would understand he'd done the only thing he could do.

He went back to make sure that he'd done a good job with securing both of the Paradinis. He had questions for them but it could wait until he made sure that Trish was okay.

He was putting his knife back in his boot when he heard the sound of an engine turn over, sputter for a minute, then smooth out. He was out the door and down the steps in one leap. Then it was full steam ahead as he saw Trish yank on the tie rope of the fishing boat.

She was leaving.

Over his dead body.

She was behind the wheel. Giving it gas. It had better pickup than he would have anticipated.

He realized he wasn't going to be in time to stop her. Damn it. He ran through the trees and waded out to *Flora*. He pulled up his anchor and took off. Unless her boat ran way faster than it looked, it would be no contest.

Sure enough, in just minutes, he caught up with Trish. Her hair was blowing in the wind and she had both hands on the steering wheel, white-knuckled. She was not wearing a life vest. He recalled that she was not a terribly strong swimmer.

He did not want her to do something stupid and end up in the water. He slowed his own boat down, hoping that she'd do the same. But she didn't let up.

"Slow down," he yelled.

She didn't respond.

He looked around. It was after seven and there would normally be more than an hour of daylight, but the storm was rolling in and it was getting dark. Most of the boats were off the lake. But there could still be people onshore who might get interested if they heard too many shouts coming off the lake.

He gave her some space. He followed, but not so close that anyone would get the impression that he was chasing her. He didn't intend to let her get away, and if she got in any trouble, he wanted to be close enough to quickly help.

"Just don't do anything stupid," he murmured, then realized he wasn't sure if he was talking to her or to himself. Probably to himself, he realized.

Because right now he was feeling pretty damn dumb. How had he thought he could ever really leave this woman? How had he thought he could be content with just observing her life from afar?

He wanted to be a part of her life. To be with her.

But despite all his efforts, all the sacrifices, he'd put her in danger. And if he didn't end it now, it was going to hang over their heads like a guillotine. Just waiting. A sharp blade at the ready.

Chapter Ten

Trish felt as if her head was going to explode. Rafe. Alive.

The events of the past half hour were more than any one person could be expected to take in, to process. It was asking too much. All she could do, it seemed, was drive the boat.

She had no destination in mind. Had already lost track of where she'd started. Not that she had any intention of going back to the cottage. She would make arrangements for her Jeep to be returned to Ravesville. Bray would do it for her. She could ask him to look for Duke, too. It was a long shot to even hope that he'd somehow survived but he certainly deserved to have a decent burial.

Her hands started to shake and she gripped the steering wheel tighter. She'd lost a dog and gained a husband.

Who was following her in his boat.

She'd heard him yell at her to slow down but there had been no way in hell she was doing that. Her emotions were too raw.

She had mourned him for four years. And he'd been living the whole time. It made her feel stupid, as if someone smarter would have figured it out.

She had never, not even once, considered that he might still be alive. Even when his body had never been recovered.

Because what kind of person did something like that? What kind of person would put another human being through the trauma of having a loved one die?

Certainly not the man that she'd married. Or that she thought she'd married.

But maybe she hadn't really known Rafe Roper at all.

If that was even his real name. If everything else was bogus, then maybe his name was, too.

For years now, she'd politely corrected people when they'd called her Trish Wright. *Trish Wright-Roper*, she would say. Well, ha-ha, maybe the joke was on her.

She'd seen him a hundred times in her dreams. And she'd talked to him. On her good days, she'd told him over and over again how much she loved him. On her bad days, she'd railed at him for being careless in the river.

But he'd never answered her, never said anything.

Today, when he'd said her name, his voice sounded rusty. But yet so familiar.

It had been too much.

When he'd been tying up Anthony and Old Guy, she'd felt as if she was about to crawl out of her skin. She'd had to get outside, get some fresh air. As she neared the back door, she saw the boat key that she'd dropped on the floor when Old Guy had stopped her escape attempt. She picked it up, with still no plan in mind.

But she'd had the presence of mind to get her gun from underneath the sofa cushion. She walked outside, hoping to catch her breath. She stood and looked across the lake. Saw the black clouds rolling in. She felt as if they were going to roll right over her and she would be smothered.

And just that quick she decided that she had to leave. She ran for the small fishing boat. And he almost caught her. In fact, she'd been afraid that he was going to leap from the dock into her boat.

She hadn't realized that he had a boat just down the shoreline. But he must have known it would easily catch up to hers, even with her head start.

And now the lake was really getting dark and the wind was picking up. Even with the headlights on, it was getting difficult to see the shore. She looked at her gas tank. It was nearing empty. She did not want to be stranded on the water all night in the middle of a raging storm. That was just stupid.

Would Rafe just keep circling her? Waiting for some indication that she was ready to talk?

It was ironic. A day ago, she'd have said that she'd give anything to have just one more conversation with him, to tell him how much she loved him. But now she didn't know how she was going to do it. But putting it off wasn't going to make it easier.

She throttled down the boat and headed for shore. When she saw an empty boat slip, she cut her speed even further and managed to slide into place, bumping the side of the boat just once against the wooden dock. She grabbed the tie rope and tossed the looped end around one of the wood posts.

She reached for her gun that she'd had on the seat next to her. Then she got out and was standing on the dock, her arms wrapped around herself, when Rafe smoothly docked his own boat on the other side. When he killed his lights, the area was very dark.

There were a few lights still on the water, boaters who were probably hurrying to shore. Bits of light from nearby cottages split the dark woods.

"Hi," he said softly, coming to stand next to her. He

had a flashlight in his hand. He didn't try to touch her. "Are you okay?"

"Not really," she said. She unwrapped her arms and he must have seen her gun because he held up his hands.

"Planning on using that on me?" he asked, his tone casual.

"I had it stuffed under the sofa cushion on the porch," she explained, choosing not to answer his question.

"I'm glad you've got it," he said. "And I'm sorry," he added. "I'm sorry I surprised you and that I did a horrible job of explaining what was going on."

"What is going on, Rafe?" she asked. "If that is your name."

"My name is Rafe Roper," he said, his voice tight.

She'd offended him. Well, tough. "Well, then, maybe you want to explain why everything I've believed for the last four years has been a lie? A deliberate lie."

"I—"

"And how the hell did you know I was here?" she asked, interrupting him.

He waited, maybe to see if another question was coming. Maybe because he was thinking of a good lie. She had no idea. She didn't know him.

"Well?" she said, her tone impatient.

"I learned of Milo's death and I anticipated that you might be vulnerable."

"Milo," she repeated. "You…" Her voice trailed off. "You didn't even know Milo. What difference would his death have made to you?"

"I knew Milo," he said.

"You were already…dead," she said, her voice breaking.

"I was gone," he said. "Not dead. Milo and I had

worked together for years. He was in Ravesville because I arranged for him to be there."

"He had been in prison," she said.

"No. Never. That was a story that was invented for him."

He was dismantling everything she'd believed to be true. Her chest felt tight. The air heavy. It was hard to breathe. "You arranged for Milo to be there. To do what? To spy on me?"

"To look after you. I was attempting to manage a difficult situation."

"Manage a difficult situation," she again repeated his words, her tone flat. "That's great. Just great," she emphasized, more agitated. "I was mourning a dead husband and you were *managing me.*"

He didn't answer. She was so angry that it was taking everything she had not to push him off the dock into the water.

"I'll tell you everything," he said. "But I need to deal with those two back at the cottage first. We can't risk them getting loose or someone coming to assist them."

The idea of having to deal with Old Guy and Anthony again was chilling.

"Will you come with me in my boat?" he asked.

He was stiff and formal, acting as if one wrong word on his part would send her running off into the woods. It almost made her feel bad.

If she didn't go with him, she would have to stay here, by herself, in the dark. Plus, her Jeep was back at the cottage. She could get it and drive herself home. She would find Duke's body and she would drive both of them home. "Yes," she said. She would pay someone to come get Bernie Wilberts's boat and return it to the cottage.

He held out his hand to help her into the boat but she ignored it. She wasn't ready yet to touch him. He didn't force the issue. He waited until she was in, then stepped over the edge, untied the line and started the engine.

She had no idea where they needed to go but he didn't seem worried. He aimed the front of the boat toward the far-off shore. He sat behind the wheel. She sat in the back, as far away from him as she could get.

BERNIE WILBERTS HAD a buzz going that wasn't helping him as he navigated the winding roads. He'd left his house more than fourteen hours ago, shortly after having a silent breakfast with his wife. There had been a time when he and Amy had talked, laughed, loved. But lately, because of the situation, conversation between the two of them was forced.

She didn't understand that this was the only way to protect the family. He hadn't worked his whole life to provide for his three daughters and his wife only to have it go up in smoke because of a few mistakes. His youngest was still in college. And his middle daughter was getting married in the fall. All of that cost money.

He'd found a way to atone for his screwup at work that had cost him his job. He'd replaced his income. His wife should be congratulating him, not busting his chops. She was still able to stay home and do enough online shopping to keep the UPS driver busy. She wasn't complaining about that. Nope.

Everybody in this part of the country made a living off drugs—in some form or fashion. It wasn't that big of a deal. Who cared if a few idiots overdosed and died? They were losers.

Not like his girls. All three of them had been on home-coming court. Beautiful, they were.

Like that woman, Trish. She was something with all that red hair, down to her waist. And really sweet, too.

The idea that something bad was going to happen to her in the next day or two had settled on his chest and he hadn't slept well. Which was why, after breakfast, he'd packed up his fishing gear and gone out onto the lake. He'd stayed out past dinnertime and it was dark by the time he'd got back to shore, grabbed a bite at the Hoot and Shoot Diner. The storm was about to break.

He felt sick. The twelve-pack on the boat and then the two whiskeys straight up at the diner probably contributed to that.

Indecision and alcohol didn't mix.

He'd weighed his options. Do nothing. That was the easiest, probably the best for everyone. Well, not for pretty Trish. Or he could stop at the cottage and tell her to go home. Not tell her why but simply tell her to get the hell home and not tell anybody that he'd warned her.

Could he trust her to keep her mouth shut? Even if she did, would DT take it out on him that she'd disappeared? If she told the truth, it was a foregone conclusion that DT would enact his revenge.

Getting mixed up with that man had been his big mistake. But what choice had he had? He'd had some bad luck with cards. And then hadn't been able to pay back the loans. That was when DT had come into the picture. DT had told him that he could either treat the offer to join his operation and regain financial stability as the gift it was or if he refused, DT would make him regret his lack of manners. And then DT had laughed and asked if he'd got his mail yet that day.

He had. It had been a picture of Amy and his daughters having lunch at a local restaurant.

So, he'd gone along. And the money had been good. The local kids were hungry for their heroin and Amy was happy because he told her their investments were doing well. Then one day, he hadn't been careful enough and Amy had found his inventory. It had been right about the same time that a couple of his customers overdosed and died.

Amy was a teacher and she'd had the kids in her fourth-grade class just six years earlier. She acted as if he was some kind of monster. He hadn't been able to tell her the truth. If she'd known that their girls were at risk, she'd have never forgiven him. He told her he had it under control. She said he'd crossed a line that he could never step back over.

Now what would she think of what he was doing with Trish? He hadn't even understood the plan at first. All he'd been told was to keep the cottage available. Then he'd been told that M.A. Fikus would be renting it. She'd stayed a few days, but when he'd stopped in to see her, she'd been cold to the point of rudeness. He'd dismissed it until DT had mentioned that M.A. Fikus would be referring the cottage to Trish Wright-Roper and that he should cut the rate by half.

He'd been irritated about the reduced rent, but since DT was paying him well for other things, he'd kept his mouth shut. But he had said he was surprised that M.A. Fikus was referring anyone, since she hadn't seemed happy while she was here.

DT had laughed and said that if she wanted to keep her employer from learning that she had a nasty little heroin habit, she'd do what she was supposed to do.

He hadn't asked DT why it was so important to get Trish Wright-Roper to the cottage. He didn't want to know.

But once he'd seen her, he suspected the worst. Stories about young women captured and hidden away for years to be used by the men holding them had kept him up most of the night. Was that her future? He'd always suspected DT was a little bent.

She probably wasn't all that much older than his oldest daughter, whom he'd taken, along with her sons—his only grandchildren—out onto the lake just two weeks ago.

He didn't think Trish had any children but still.

His decision made, he cranked the wheel sharply and headed for the cottage. He'd warn her. What she chose to do with that warning was her business. He parked his car next to Trish's Jeep. There were no lights on in the cottage, which meant that she might be sleeping. But better to lose a few hours of sleep than...

He didn't even want to think it.

He rested his forehead against the steering wheel. He'd made a damn mess out of his life. Got himself in a hole that he couldn't climb out of.

Disappointed Amy. That was for sure. And she'd been a good wife. Most of the time.

He didn't think they could go back to where they'd been, but maybe this was one step in the right direction. Maybe saving Trish would make the difference. He pulled out his cell phone and sent a text to his wife. I'll be home soon. Stopping at one of the rental cottages.

He got out of the car. She hadn't turned on the outside lights and it was very dark. If he hadn't known the area so well, he might have fallen.

He knocked.

No one answered.

Not knowing what else to do, he entered the combination and opened the door. The room smelled bad.

His stomach rolling with whiskey and grease, he hit the light. Two men were tied to chairs. He did not know them.

They both had duct tape on their mouths. He ripped the tape off the younger one's mouth.

"Thank God," he said.

Bernie stared at him. "Who are you?" he asked.

"Anthony," the man said.

That meant nothing to Bernie. "Who's that?" he asked, pointing to the older man.

"My father. Untie us."

Bernie shook his head. Where was Trish? What had happened here? He walked over to the older man and ripped the tape off his mouth.

"What the hell are you doing here?" the man asked.

Bernie recognized the voice. It was him. DT. That was what Bernie had dubbed him because he was always telling him what to do. Do this. Do that. DT.

"Don't just stand there like a dumbass," DT said, in the same demanding tone that Bernie had grown to hate more each day.

"Where's the woman?" Bernie asked.

"Not far enough," DT said. "And when I find her and her husband, they will both be very sorry."

So she was married. "Maybe you should just cut your losses and call it a day," Bernie said.

DT stared at him, his eyes hostile. It reminded him of how angry the man had been when Bernie had told him that Amy had discovered what was going on. DT had become so angry on the telephone, had said he wouldn't tolerate any more careless mistakes.

He was probably outliving his usefulness to DT. Maybe this was the way it was all supposed to end. His ultimate penance for crimes committed. Odd, but that gave him the sense of the peace he'd been searching for the whole damn day on the lake.

But what about Amy?

He opened the kitchen drawer to find a knife.

Chapter Eleven

Trish sat as still as a statue for most of the ride. But once they had got across the lake and close to shore, she made her way up to the front of the boat. "What are you going to do with them?" she asked.

"Trust me on this," he said, then winced when he realized how inappropriate the words were. "They'll pay for what they did to you, to Milo, to Duke, to the others," he finished.

"The others?" she said, her eyes wide.

There was really no good way to tell her. "M.A. Fikus is dead."

"What?" She paused. "I don't understand," she added.

Her voice sounded weaker and he was afraid that she was going to faint again. He reached for her, but when she flinched and drew back, he dropped his hand. "Please, sit," he said. He relaxed when she did, lowering herself awkwardly into the passenger seat.

"You found out about the cottage from M.A., right?"

"Yes."

"I don't think that was an accident. She told you about the cottage for a reason."

"M.A. was my friend," she said, shaking her head.

He understood. She was questioning whether it was

another betrayal. "Maybe she didn't have bad intent. Unfortunately, we may never know. Or perhaps one of the two inside will fill in the missing blanks if they think it will help them in some way."

"With the police?" she asked.

He ratcheted back the throttle as they got closer to shore. Big Tony and Anthony wouldn't be as concerned about the police as they would be their boss, once it became known that they had failed. But he didn't have time to explain all that right now. He wanted a chance to question them and then he would call his team, call his boss. "Yes, the authorities will be notified."

She closed her eyes. "And then what happens."

Then he was going to finish this. Once and for all. "I stash you somewhere safe, under twenty-four-hour guard."

"I'm going home," she said. "Back to Ravesville."

"We can discuss that," he said carefully.

She held up a hand. "Do. Not. Try. To. *Manage*. Me." She spit out each word. "I think you've done enough of that." She turned, so that her back was facing him. Her spine was straight. Brittle.

It dawned on him that maybe she hated him. That thought made him want to vomit over the side of the boat.

This was not going to be easy.

He focused intently upon the shore. He needed to deal with one thing at a time.

The sky was heavy with swirling clouds. When he cut his lights three hundred yards out, it was as if they were moving in a sea of blackness. He slowed way down and used his flashlight to find his way to the dock. He killed the engine. "I want you to stay in the boat," he said quietly. "Please," he added, realizing she wasn't inclined to do anything he suggested. "If you have any reason to think anything is wrong, then get the hell out of here. Don't worry about me."

"Don't you think you're taking a big risk that I'll simply leave you here?" she asked.

She'd left him once already tonight. But she'd had a chance to calm down. Had learned some things that might give her pause before she ran off in the dark night. "I guess I'll have to take my chances."

He tied up and turned to her. He kept his hand over his flashlight, mostly obscuring the light. But he could see her shape. "Get down," he said, "on the floor. There's less chance of anyone seeing you. Keep your gun in your hand. If anybody besides me approaches the boat, shoot them. Don't make small talk first. Just shoot them."

He waited until she got down on the floor of the boat. Only then did he turn and step up on the dock. He listened carefully for any sound that told him his presence had been detected.

He didn't hear anything.

Then he did. And saw a familiar arc in the night sky.

But it still caught him off guard when he was knocked back by a fiery blast.

THE BLAST SHOOK the dock and the boat. And then a heavy splash sent the water rippling.

And the stench of burning wood filled the air.

Trish felt as if she couldn't catch her breath. The cottage had blown up and was now burning. And Rafe— *oh my God*—Rafe had been blown off the dock, into the lake.

She had to find him. The fire lit up the space and she saw his body. Facedown, five feet from the dock.

She threw herself over the edge of the boat and slogged through the chest-high water. When she reached him, she yanked hard on his right shoulder, to flip him over.

He wasn't breathing.

Cognizant that there must be danger nearby, she didn't yell or scream. But she shook him.

No response.

She grabbed him under his arms and towed him back to the dock. Even with the buoyancy of water, he was very heavy. Panting hard, she braced herself against the ladder at the end of the dock. She had his back against her front. With her knee bent and under his lower back, it gave her enough leverage to keep his head out of the water.

"Damn you," she cried, her mouth close to his ear. "Don't you die on me now." She wrapped her arms around him and squeezed, the heels of her hands digging into his chest. She did it three times in a row. Hard.

And when he sputtered and spit water, it was the best sound she'd ever heard. Then he was twisting in her arms.

He was running his hands over her arms, holding her face. "Are you injured?" he demanded.

"No. You are. You almost drowned," she said.

He ignored her. "We have to get back in the boat. We have to get out of here."

And with more strength than she would have anticipated, he was pushing her up and over the side of the boat. Then crawling in himself. Before pulling away, he leaned over the side and grabbed his flashlight off the dock, dropping it in her lap.

She turned it on and pointed it at him.

There was blood running down the side of his face from a substantial gash in his forehead, near the hairline.

She suspected he'd hit his head on the dock before he'd gone into the water.

"You're bleeding," she said. "You need a doctor."

He reached up to feel his head. "It's fine," he said. "Hang on." He started the boat.

"What happened here?" she demanded.

"Rocket launcher," he said as if that was all she needed to know. He took the flashlight from her hand and focused it forward.

As they drove away, she turned her head to look at the remains of the cottage. She had never seen anything like it. It was all just too much. The men holding her prisoner. Rafe. Learning that everything she'd believed to be true for four years had been a lie. Now this.

Rafe had not yet turned on the lights, and as they edged away from shore, the light from the fire diminished. She forced herself to stand and move to the front of the boat. "Hold this," he said, handing her the flashlight.

He reached into his wet jeans and pulled out a cell phone. She expected him to try to turn it on, to see if it had survived the lake. But, instead, he removed the battery.

"What are you doing?" she asked.

"We're going off the grid," he said.

She waited for something more, but when it didn't seem to be coming, she grabbed his arm. "What the hell are you talking about?" she said. "We have to call someone. Get help."

He shook his head. "Ain't no helping anybody who was inside. They're dead."

He was undoubtedly right and that sat heavy in her stomach. A chill spread through her. Some of that, she realized, was that she was in wet clothes, speeding along in a boat. But mostly she was cold to the bone because had the explosion happened an hour earlier, she'd have been inside. She'd be dead now, too.

"I don't understand any of this," she said.

He turned his head. It was too dark to see his eyes but she knew what she would see. Grim determination. She could hear it in his voice. "I don't, either. And until I do, we're staying away from the cottage."

"But—"

He held up a hand. "Listen, Trish. This wasn't an accident. We have to figure out what's going on."

If it hadn't been an accident, then there were really only two choices. "Was it someone going after me or after those men?"

"I don't know. Listen, there are things you don't know."

The part of her that was fed up with surprises wanted to stop him. She couldn't handle anything else. But she said nothing. This was a dangerous situation that didn't appear to be getting any better. She needed to know everything if she had any hope of getting out of this alive.

Alive. Summer. The two thoughts collided in her head at the same moment. She pulled again on Rafe's arm.

"I have to be able to call Summer. My Jeep was at that cottage. It's a simple matter for them to trace it back to me, then to Ravesville. If they contact the local police, that's going to be Chase Hollister. He's going to tell Summer."

"We may not be able to help that."

She grabbed him, hard enough to swing him her direction. "I am not going to have Summer believe that I'm dead. Not for one minute. I know what that does to a person."

She could feel the emotion in his big body. And she felt bad that she'd blurted it out just that way, given that earlier she'd noticed that his voice was filled with pain.

She suspected that he probably had a concussion in addition to the laceration that needed attention. But he needed to understand that this was nonnegotiable.

"We'll find a phone," he said. "As quickly as possible. I promise."

After everything that had happened, it was crazy to think that she could ever trust him. But oddly enough, she believed him.

"But first," he said, "we're going back to where we landed earlier. I saw a cottage set back from the lake about two hundred yards. There were no lights."

"Maybe they were in bed."

"Maybe. But we should at least check it out. It's going to rain, maybe even storm, and I'm not crazy about spending the night on the lake in a boat in those conditions."

"Why are we looking for shelter? We should be going to the police," she said, again trying to make him see reason.

"No," he said.

She knew there was no use arguing. They moved quickly across the lake. As they got closer to shore, he cut the engine back. Now she could hear the very distant noise of sirens. The explosion would likely have been heard for miles. Firefighters were responding. She was very grateful for the recent rain and that the ground and surrounding foliage was wet. Perhaps the fire would not spread too far.

He held a finger up to his lips. She understood. They were near shore and wouldn't want their voices overheard. She would not have been able to identify the right spot were it not for Bernie Wilberts's boat that was still tied on one side of the U-shaped dock.

He docked the boat and tied it up. "Bring your gun," he said. Before he stepped out, he pulled on a fishing hat that had been in the boat. Then he got out and turned to offer her a hand. Instinctively, she took it but knew immediately it was a mistake when her skin, her traitorous flesh, heated up fast.

She had always loved his touch.

Had missed it so.

The minute her feet were on the dock, she dropped her arm, breaking contact. This man had let her think he was dead for four years.

And now he was back, with trouble everywhere.

"This way," he said softly. He also had his gun in his hand. The flashlight in the other.

He led her away from the lake. The grass was long, up to her knees in places. The wind whipped it around them. It did not bode well if the cottage was still burning.

She turned around to look and realized the angle was wrong. She could no longer see the other shore, see the cottage where she'd been so happy and relaxed this morning, only to be held prisoner there later.

The long, wild grass turned into a short, mowed lawn. The cottage was just in front of them. If the grass had been mowed recently, how likely was it that the cottage was empty? But Rafe kept going.

They walked around to the front. There was no garage and no car in the driveway. So far, so good.

"Stay right here," Rafe whispered, pulling her off to the side.

"What are you doing?" she rasped.

"I'm going to knock on the door," he said. "If somebody answers, I'll give them some excuse about trouble with my boat. Just stay out of sight, no matter what."

"I should knock. You'll scare them. You've got blood all over your face."

He pulled his hat lower onto his forehead. "Your hair is…memorable. We can't take the chance."

She watched him walk away. *Memorable.* He used to call her hair sexy. When they would make love, he would run his hands through it. When she would wake up in the mornings, he would often have thick strands of it wrapped around his hand, and she would know that at some point in the middle of the night, he had reached out for her.

It was so dark that even though she was probably less than ten feet away from him, she could not see him. But she heard him knock loudly on the door. Then a second time.

"This way," he said, his voice soft and close to her ear.

She couldn't quite keep her squeal inside. She hadn't heard a thing as he'd walked back to her. How the hell did he do that?

"Sorry," he said, his voice sounding amused for the first time. "I'm going in through the window around back. Then I'll open the back door for you. I'll need you to hold the light for me."

When she shone the flashlight, she realized he had a knife in his hand. In less than a minute, he'd scored a neat square in the glass. He pushed it through with his palm and reached his hand and arm inside, up to the elbow. She heard the sound of a latch flipping.

She moved the light, enough that she could see his face. Sweat was running off it, yet he was shaking. "Rafe," she said. "You need to—"

"Stay here," he interrupted her. Then he raised the window, threw a leg over the side and was out of sight.

It dawned on her that there was a great deal that she didn't know about this man that she'd married.

He opened the back door. "Come in. The place is empty."

Empty, yes, but definitely recently inhabited. With the help of Rafe's flashlight, she could see that there were clean dishes in the rack next to the sink and newspapers on the table. When she got closer, she could see they had last Sunday's date. When she lifted up the paper, she saw an electric bill for Edith and Harry Norton.

She opened the refrigerator. It contained the basics: ketchup, mustard, mayonnaise, jelly. And in the produce compartments, sweet potatoes and onions. Things that wouldn't spoil quickly. There were no milk or eggs. She closed the door.

There wasn't much to see in the rest of the space. Next to the kitchen was a small living room, then a bedroom and a bath. It was very similar to Bernie Wilberts's cottage except that it was smaller, with no back porch.

That didn't matter, she realized. She didn't intend to stay long. Just long enough for the storm to pass and for Rafe to provide her with some explanation of what was going on.

"I think it's likely that the Nortons use this cottage on the weekends," Rafe said.

"This is the weekend," she said. "It's Saturday."

"I know. So I think that's good news. If the people who come here aren't here by Saturday night, they aren't coming this weekend. I think we just got lucky."

He might be right or maybe the people were coming on Sunday this week. There could be a thousand reasons for that. But she didn't deny that it felt good to be off the lake, away from the potential of the upcoming storm. And she was pretty confident that Rafe couldn't go much longer. He was trying to hide it, but she didn't miss that he was leaning against the counter, as if his legs were not quite up to carrying his body weight.

"You need to get that cut cleaned up. Sit down," she said, as she gently pulled him toward one of the kitchen chairs.

She set the flashlight on the counter to give off some light. Then she grabbed paper towels off the roll that hung next to the sink. She ran the kitchen faucet until the water got warm. "Can we turn on the lights?" she asked.

"I'd rather we didn't," he said. "But we can light this," he added, nodding at the large candle that was in the middle of the kitchen table. He picked up the book of matches next to the candle and struck one.

"There's no phone," she said, unable to keep the disappointment from her voice. "We can't call Summer."

"We wouldn't take the chance of doing it from here anyway. It's possible that they've thought ahead far enough that they've got some kind of tracking device on your sister's phone and they'd be able to locate us here."

Who were these people? "Would you have thought to do that?"

He nodded. "Yes. I'd have identified anybody who might be in your support network and made sure that I was monitoring their activity."

And she'd thought she couldn't feel any more helpless. Guess that was another thing she was wrong about.

She pushed the candle closer to him. It wasn't much light but certainly better than nothing.

Using the damp paper towel that she'd had clutched in her hand, she gently wiped away the blood on his face. The cut was several inches long but not too deep. He did have a hell of a knot about an inch above his right eyebrow. "I think you hit the deck before you went into the

water. Hard enough that it knocked you out. You probably have a concussion."

"It'll be fine." He dismissed her concern. He gently
caught her wrist. "Thank you," he said softly. "I'd have
drowned if you hadn't helped me."

She stepped back, suddenly chilled in the overly warm
room. "This time for real," she said.

The words hung in the air.

"I'm going to see if there are any first aid supplies in
the bathroom," she said, desperately needing to put a few
feet between them. He didn't try to stop her.

She shut the door behind her and turned on the light.
Her legs were shaking and she lowered herself to the floor
in the small bathroom. *This time for real.* It had been a
mean thing to say. And that wasn't generally her style.
But while she hadn't hit her head, she still felt pretty
damn off-balance.

M.A. was dead. The two men in the house as well.
And, of course, Milo. Was that where the trail started?

It had somehow led them to this cottage. She knew
pure determination had fueled Rafe for the past fifteen
minutes. The blast, the knock on the head, the time in
the water… It had all taken a toll. But if she hadn't seen
it all, she'd have never known.

Rafe Roper was a hell of an actor.

And that was why she was sitting on the floor, pretending to be studying the contents of a bathroom cupboard.

She was afraid. Afraid that she was going to learn that
it had all been an act. Maybe that was why she'd snapped
first. To get the first swing in so that when the knock-
out punch came, she'd at least have one small victory to
hang on to.

This time for real. Take that, Rafe Roper.

She heard the scrape of a chair and knew that he was just seconds from coming to check on her. She grabbed what she needed and stood so fast that her reflection in the mirror almost seemed blurred.

She looked horrible. Her hair was wet and snarled from her time in the water, her face pale, her eyes dark. But, she realized, if Rafe hadn't freed her from that cottage, she'd look a whole lot worse because she'd be dead.

She turned off the light before she opened the door. Then she walked back to the kitchen and placed the tube of antibiotic ointment on the table. Then the adhesive strips. "I think the butterfly kind would be better to close the cut, but this is all they have."

"It'll be fine," he said.

She placed the last thing on the table, a big bottle of ibuprofen. "I thought this might come in handy," she said.

He smiled. "I think it's good that I've got a hard head."

She stood close to him and liberally spread the ointment on the cut. Then she opened three of the strips and covered it.

"Can I get you anything else?" she asked, rather formally, perhaps, for the circumstances.

"I'm good," he said.

He wasn't but there might not be time to waste. "I want to know something," she said. "Before he died, Milo said to me, 'Tell Rafe they know.' I thought he was delirious. But he wasn't, was he? They? Who is that? Who is doing this? And what is it that they know?"

Chapter Twelve

She wanted answers. Well, she deserved some. But it would likely have been easier going if his head wasn't pounding and he wasn't seeing double.

Although two of Trish was not necessarily a bad thing. She'd saved his life. He was confident of that. All he basically remembered was the heat from the explosion, the force of it knocking him back, falling, pain and then nothing.

Except for that his very last thought had been of her. And a prayer that somehow she had escaped injury and would follow his orders to get the hell out of there.

Instead, she'd gone overboard and dragged his sorry hide out of the water. He'd been unconscious, yet he'd heard her. Had heard the panic in her voice. The need. And that was what had pulled him back from the edge, had allowed him the strength to dispel the water in his lungs.

He would answer her question, but first, she needed to know a few things. "Earlier today, I received a text. It was a picture of you, with blood on your face, tied up, with a gun to your head."

She nodded slowly. "I didn't know who they were sending it to."

"They wanted a trade. Me for you."

"And you said yes?"

"Of course."

"But you didn't contact the police? Why?"

This was where it got complicated. He must have hesitated for too long because she slapped her hand down flat on the table. "Do not lie to me. Please."

He nodded. "First of all, they didn't give me an exact location. They told me to return to Missouri and that I would get further instruction. So I didn't know where to send the police. Even if I had, I wouldn't have taken the chance that they'd screw it up. Not when your life was at stake."

"Where were you?"

"They thought I was in Italy. I had been but I'd left as soon as I was informed of Milo's death. I was in the States hours before they expected me. The element of surprise was in my corner."

"How did you find me?"

This was going to be hard on her. But she'd asked him not to lie. "I contacted your brother-in-law, Bray Hollister. I wanted to know what he knew about your absence. I figured you'd told Summer and that she'd probably told him. I didn't want to go directly to Summer if I didn't have to."

"She's pregnant."

"I know," he said. He smiled. "I'm happy for her."

She gripped her head in her hands as if holding her brains in. "This is surreal. You know all about my life and I know nothing about you."

There was nothing much he could say about that. "Bray said that you were at Heelie Lake and that you'd rented a cottage based on a recommendation from M.A. Fikus.

I went to see her and… Well, you know that part. I still didn't know exactly where you were but I headed for Heelie. I got a lead that Bernie Wilberts owned a lot of cottages in the area and I wanted to identify his properties. I went to his house. His wife…" He stopped, not wanting to tell her. Too much death.

"What?" she demanded.

"Trish, his wife was dead. Shot three times at close range in the back. Just like M.A."

She sucked in a deep breath. "By the men who had me?"

"I don't know. But I'm guessing they had some involvement. What time did they grab you?"

"Just after lunch. A little before one."

"If I had to guess, Mrs. Wilberts was killed several hours before that. Big Tony and Anthony were likely responsible."

"Big Tony?" she repeated. "I heard him call the young one Anthony, so I knew that. I thought they were probably father and son."

"Anthony Sr. and Anthony Jr. Paradini."

"In my head, I called the father Old Guy."

He smiled. "Big Tony probably wouldn't have been happy about that. He dates women who are barely old enough to vote. Spends a lot of money on them. That's usually enough to convince them to stick around for a few months."

"You seem to know a lot about him."

"About seven years ago, I infiltrated the organization he works for."

"*Infiltrated?* Like a spy?" She practically spit the last word.

"Intelligence," he corrected. "For a small agency connected with the United States Department of the Treasury. We protect the financial system."

"You're an accountant?" she asked, doubt in her tone.

She was probably remembering that he didn't even balance his own checkbook. "While we protect the financial system, very few of us actually have accounting or finance backgrounds. I have a master's in biochemical engineering."

"You're a federal agent."

Her tone was bemused. Or maybe that was just his ears ringing.

"I thought you were a construction worker. Every day you packed a lunch and went to work, to build the mall in Hamerton. Or was that a lie, too?"

Her words stung. But it was important to keep going. "I was always good with my hands. When I wanted to stay in Ravesville, that seemed like the best job for me." He paused, closed his eyes. Centered himself. "The night of the storm, I was passing through, with no intent to stay. But something happened between us that night, as we sat on the floor eating pie. And I couldn't go. Because of you, Trish."

He pushed his chair back from the table, the legs scraping on the wood floor. He stood up fast, which was a mistake. It made his head roll. He sank back down. "But you have to know," he said, "that if I thought I was bringing any danger to you, I would never have done it. I thought it was safe. That I was safe."

"I don't understand."

"The people who have the power to *upset* the entire monetary structure that sustains this country are the same people who facilitate terrorist plots, bankroll drugs and deal in weapons of mass destruction," he said. "Seven years ago I successfully infiltrated an organization in the Middle East that we believed was attempting to engineer a biochemical weapon that had the potential to kill millions if released in an urban area under exactly the right conditions."

"They were terrorists," she said.

"Yes. And over a period of three years, I managed to become one of them. My cover was that of a well-educated, financially advantaged, disenfranchised American. Ryan Weber. That was my name. Ivy League college education. High school track star. Born in Connecticut. Parents deceased. Access to substantial trust fund. A whole persona was built, one that would have stood the scrutiny of the best background investigations."

"Ryan Weber." She repeated the name as if she was trying to reconcile everything that he was telling her.

"Ryan Weber worked side by side with them on developing exactly the right formula as well as the right components."

"Components?"

"Something that could be transported easily and not detected. It could be perfect, but if they couldn't get it into the country, it did them no good."

"It wasn't Ryan Weber doing this. It was you helping them." She said it without inflection, her voice sounding dull.

"Every day," he admitted. "And every night, I was transmitting information back to my team, who were supporting me. I was attempting to foil and delay the group's progress in multiple ways, all without them having a clue that I was playing both sides. But I did it. Ultimately, the group decided to make a trial run at an event in England, targeting the London Tube system. We couldn't let it go forward, of course."

"What happened?"

"I continued to play my role. Up until the final moment. Ideally, the principals of the operation needed to be apprehended with the goods on them, so to speak, so that arrests could be made without compromising my involvement."

"And that happened?"

"Yes."

"You say it as if it was no big deal," she said.

It had been a freakin' huge deal and fraught with multiple opportunities for failure. But that was not important now. "Suffice it to say that the necessary arrests were made before the chemical was released. The operation was shut down. People were going to prison with no hope of parole. And I needed to disappear."

"That's when you came to Ravesville?"

"Yes. I returned to the States. I was going to continue my work with the agency but in a domestic position, located on the West Coast. I stopped in Ravesville on my way there. But…well, you know the next part. You weren't going to leave your twin sister and your business. And I…I couldn't leave you. So I made a decision. I contacted my boss, told him I was out."

"All without telling me?"

He'd wanted to. Had wanted her to know that he'd been playing the part of someone else for so long, that he felt like a stranger in his own skin. Had wanted her to know that it was only with her that he felt like Rafe Roper again. "I couldn't. And then nine months after we were married, things started to fall apart. I got word that one of the people on my team had jumped in front of a subway train and been killed. Ruled a suicide but I wasn't convinced. Especially when three months later, a second one was killed when an elevator malfunctioned in his building and fell multiple stories. I knew it couldn't be a coincidence. My old boss said I was imagining things. But I knew our identities had been compromised. I knew that they would come for me. And I wasn't going to take the chance that you'd get caught in the cross fire."

"So you faked your own death."

"I did. And while I desperately wanted to tell you the truth, I knew that I couldn't. You're a genuine person, Trish. You would have struggled to hide the truth from people you loved. Not being able to tell Summer the truth would have eaten at you. And I couldn't do that to you."

"You thought dying would be easier on me?" she asked, as if trying to make sense of the logic.

"Nothing was going to be easy. But if you and everyone else believed I was dead, then you were safer. That was what was important."

"And what was Milo's role? Was he part of your team?"

"Not on this particular project but I'd known him for years. Respected his abilities. He had lots of family money and had retired early. He was happy to watch over you and Summer so that I could do what I needed to do."

"He worked so hard," she said, shaking her head. "I could never have guessed."

"That's why he was perfect. By the way, he loved working with you and Summer. Said that you two were the daughters that he never had."

He could see her swallow hard and realized that of everything he'd told her, that might have been the most difficult for her to hear.

"I had to find out who was behind the attacks on the

team," he continued. "Find out who had compromised all of us. I told my boss I wanted back in. He was reluctant. Said I was coming back for the wrong reasons. Ultimately, I told him I'd go to his boss if necessary, all the way up to the president if necessary."

"The president of the United States?"

"Yes. My fabricated background wasn't all that different from my real background. I did my graduate work at Harvard. The president's son was my roommate when his dad was vice president. I'd been to the West Wing of the White House often enough over the years that I knew how to get a late-night pizza delivered there without it getting hung up in security."

"Amazing," she said, shaking her head.

He understood. Not amazing that he'd been in the West Wing ordering pizza. Amazing that she'd never known any of these things.

"It took me some time but I finally figured out that I wasn't the only one who was a pretty good liar. The entire time that I was working in the Middle East, I had no idea that the organization was financed by a man living in Italy, posing as a winemaker. Luciano Maladucci."

"Someone in Italy, a winemaker, is supporting terrorists?"

She clearly didn't believe him. "There are people all over the world supporting terrorism. People in the United States. People in countries that we consider allies in the fight against terrorism. Everywhere. For all different reasons. Sometimes it's as simple as a screwed-up ideology. This time it was much more basic. Financial. Luciano Maladucci has a significant financial interest in a pharmaceutical company that is developing an antidote to just the kind of chemical weapon we stopped. He stood to make billions."

She said nothing.

His stomach was roiling and he was pretty sure he was about thirty seconds away from losing its contents. He probably did have a concussion. "Listen," he said. "We'll stay here through the night and in the morning make the necessary decisions."

"You still haven't answered my question," she said. "Why did Milo say, 'Tell Rafe they know'?"

"I suspect he meant that the Maladucci family knows that I'm alive."

"Because they still want to kill you?"

"Even more now," he said.

"I don't understand," she said.

He needed to get horizontal. "We can talk tomorrow. I'll take the love seat."

"You're two feet too tall for that," she said.

"It'll be fine," he said.

"For God's sake," she said, her voice shaking. "Just please take the damn bed."

Fine. He couldn't fight about it. He got up more slowly this time and congratulated himself on not falling over.

"But—"

"Can it wait, Trish?" he asked, interrupting her.

She stared at him so intently that he wondered just what she was seeing. Finally, she nodded. "Yes, it can."

TRISH SAT AT the worn kitchen table, staring at the nicks and grooves that the candlelight danced over. She was worried about Rafe. He was putting on a good show but she wasn't fooled. He'd gone into the bathroom and vomited. He'd tried to hide it from her by turning on the water in the sink and the shower, too, but she'd heard the un-mistakable sounds of someone retching. Then he'd gone into the bedroom and she'd heard the sounds of the bed creaking as he lowered himself down.

He needed a doctor. Head injuries were tricky. Everybody knew that. She waited another five minutes but couldn't stand it.

She picked up the candle and went to the bedroom door. His eyes were closed. But even ill, he'd heard her. "Yes," he said.

"Why can't we go to the police or to the hospital?" she asked, her words clipped with frustration.

He sighed. "Because right now, I don't know who I can trust. I trust myself and you. Until I figure out who else can be invited into the circle, we stay low."

"We can trust Summer. I think we can trust the Hollisters. They would help us."

"We might be putting them in danger," he said.

She thought of her twin and her unborn baby, of Adie and Keagan. "There has to be someone else," she said.

He didn't answer. After a long minute, she turned around and walked back to the table. She could hear the wind now. It was really blowing. And just then, a crack of lightning broke the sky, visible through the cotton curtains on the windows.

She knew she should be grateful to have shelter. A night on the water in a bad storm would be terrible. And she was suddenly very tired. She'd been tense every single minute of the hours that she'd been tied up and it had taken a toll on her. And she was hungry, too. It had been a long time since her early lunch.

Knowing what was in the refrigerator and that it wasn't much, she opened the freezer. There were a few packages of frozen meat and a loaf of bread. She pulled out a package of bacon and the bread and tossed both of them on the counter.

She felt bad about consuming the Norton's food but she would send them money once she got home.

That thought settled around her like a heavy, wet blanket. She'd left Ravesville less than twenty-four hours ago but it seemed like a lifetime. So much had happened. So many truths revealed.

How could she go back and pretend that Rafe was dead?

It dawned on her that he'd been right about one thing. It would have been very difficult for her to pretend that he was dead when he wasn't. To lie every single day to Summer. That was just not something that she would have been able to do.

But now she would have to do that? Right? She and Rafe hadn't actually talked about that piece of it. Was he going to slip away again to go fight bad guys?

She wanted to know what he was thinking but knew that it would have to wait. The man was injured. She was worried about that. What the hell would she do if he suddenly lapsed into a coma or worse? But he did not intend to seek medical attention. The only thing she could do was wait.

Wait for him to wake up. Wait for him to tell her his plans. Wait for him to leave again.

Wait to be alone again.

She walked back to the doorway of the bedroom. He was stretched out, his breaths deep and even. Just listening to it stirred memories of all the nights she had lain in bed next to him. Listening to him sleep. Her own body humming from making love to him.

She had thought she was the luckiest woman in the world. And then her world had stopped turning on its axis and the ride she was on had come to a jarring stop.

She'd become a widow.

Now, as she walked back out to the small living room and sat on the love seat, she leaned her head back and stared into the darkness. It would not be the first time she'd slept sitting up. For months after Rafe's death, she'd slept in a chair, unable to return to the bed that she'd shared with him.

And as if it had been lurking in the back of her mind, just waiting for the opportunity to pop up, the memory of a joke she'd seen somewhere online came to her. She couldn't remember the joke but the graphic was in her head. An old lady, a cat in her lap, sleeping in her chair, the black hairs on her sagging chin blowing back and forth with the force of her snores.

She thought about the text that she'd sent earlier that day when she'd been eating lunch. She'd done it because she'd finally turned a corner and realized that she didn't have to be alone, pining away for Rafe Roper.

Of course, she hadn't known at the time that Rafe was alive. That she was still married.

Even if it was in name only. And she wasn't the type that could turn her back on that. She had a date next Saturday night. Wasn't that a kick in the pants? First date in four years and she'd made it on the day her dead husband rose from the grave.

She closed her eyes. No time to worry about that right now. She needed to focus on surviving. In the dark cottage, safe from the raging storm, it was peaceful. But in her heart, she knew this was simply a temporary interlude. Danger lurked.

Chapter Thirteen

"Rafe."

It was a whisper of a breath across his cheek. He smiled. This was going to be one of his good dreams.

Over the years, he'd quickly learned to tell the difference. In the good dreams, Trish had been smiling, maybe standing at the counter of the café, coffeepot in hand, pushing a piece of pie in his direction. Or in her blue jeans, planting flowers in their garden, dirt on her cheeks. Or even better, lying naked in their bed, her face flushed with desire.

The bad ones had been Trish at his funeral, her body bent with grief, or Trish lying faceup on some sidewalk, her body lifeless, a bullet hole in her forehead, blood seeping out of her.

When the good dreams came, he would fight to stay asleep, fight to hold the joy. When the bad dreams came, he'd jerk himself awake, no matter how tired, and that would be it for sleep that night. He wouldn't take the chance of sinking back into hell.

"Rafe."

He felt her warm hand on his forehead. Her skin was always so soft, smelled so damn good. Tasted better.

In his really good dreams, he would taste her. Everywhere. And when she came apart, convulsing in his arms, he would lick the sweetness of her body.

"Rafe."

More insistent. Needy. Wonderful.

He reached out, wrapped his hand around her wrist, brought it to his mouth. Touched her with his tongue.

"Hey?" she cried and jerked away.

He opened his eyes and quickly shut them when he was temporarily blinded by the flashlight.

"What the hell was that about?" she asked.

Embarrassment flooded his system. Rafe Roper didn't get caught short. "If you'll get the damn light out of my eyes, it would help," he said, attempting to buy a couple of seconds.

He heard the soft click of it being turned off. Took in two more deep breaths and then opened his eyes. He didn't need any light to know that Trish sat on the edge of his bed. How was it possible that she still smelled of sunshine after the day she'd had?

"I'm sorry," he said. Hell, he should just get it stamped on his forehead.

"Why did you do that?" she asked.

Could he tell her about the dreams? Would it make her feel any better to know that she hadn't been the only one hurting? Was he looking for some sympathy? Like, *Hey, look, I suffered, too*.

That was pretty damn pathetic. "I don't know," he lied.

She snorted, as if to say that she didn't buy it but quite frankly wasn't expecting more out of him. "I was worried about your head injury," she said. "I remembered reading somewhere that the injured person should be awakened every couple of hours."

"I'm going to be fine." He thought that was true. A

few days of rest and he would be good to go. Unfortunately, they didn't have a few days. Much less than that before it would start to fall apart.

His internal clock told him that he'd been sleeping for a couple of hours. The fire at the cottage would have been extinguished but it was likely that they'd still be sifting through the rubble, attempting to identify bodies. He had no idea whether Big Tony or Anthony carried identification on them. He assumed they did.

So it was just a matter of time before word got out that the men were dead. He had to assume that whoever had launched that rocket would be expecting other bodies inside. Trish, for sure. Even in the unlikely event that the attacker hadn't known she was inside, her Jeep was there.

He didn't want to bring it up but he thought that it was entirely possible that Summer had already been notified that her sister was suspected dead. They, of course, wouldn't be able to confirm it without a body.

He wished he'd thrown in his second cell. He wouldn't worry about using it. He was confident that it had never been compromised. He'd considered returning to his rental car to get it but ultimately decided not to in the event that the BMW had been traced to him.

It was a risk to go look for a telephone, but when he'd been driving around this afternoon, he'd passed several marinas and he thought he recalled seeing telephone booths at a couple of them. Throwbacks to a different time. They needed gas for the boat anyway, so perhaps it was a good way to kill two birds with one stone.

It was a bad analogy because right now, he felt as if he and Trish were the birds. Dumb birds, because somebody was just waiting for them to show themselves and then they were going to get blasted.

"Did you sleep?" he asked.

"Some."

He was pretty sure she was lying. "You take the bed," he said, attempting to sit up.

She put her hand flat on his chest and pushed him back. "Oh, please," she said. "I found some bacon and bread."

It was his favorite sandwich. Toasted bread piled high with bacon and a little ketchup. Was she remembering? Or was it just coincidence and he was trying to convince his sorry self that she still cared?

"There wasn't much choice," she said.

That answered that. He closed his eyes. "I'll get something when I wake up the next time. Then we'll take off, look for a phone. Get the lay of the land."

"Are we in trouble here, Rafe? Big trouble?"

He opened his eyes. "It's trouble," he said simply. "But nothing that we can't handle." He sincerely hoped that was true.

"I hope you're not lying to me again," she said. Then got up and left the room.

And he was alone. Again. Still.

TRISH, WHO WOULD have sworn on a stack of Bibles that she couldn't sleep a wink, woke up when a gentle hand shook her shoulder.

"It's morning."

When she and Rafe had been married… Wait—they were still married… Well, when they had been living together, he used to wake her up with *It's morning, darling*. She wondered if he still remembered that.

She opened her eyes and stretched. Her neck hurt from the awkward angle caused by the arm of the love seat.

She pushed herself to a sitting position. Rafe stood in front of her.

It was daylight and he'd opened one of the curtains partway, letting in natural light. It was the best conditions she'd seen him in and he, quite frankly, looked like hell.

His eyes were shadowed with pain, his face was spotted with dried blood that she'd missed with the damp paper towel and he needed a shave. But he seemed steady enough on his feet.

She sniffed and realized it was bacon that she smelled. Somehow he'd managed to cook without her hearing anything. Her stomach growled and she put a hand on it.

He smiled. "Let's eat," he said.

"What time is it?"

"Just after six," he said. "The marina should be open."

"Marina?"

"Yeah. We need gas for the boat and I'm hoping we can find a phone there."

"What can I tell Summer?"

He looked surprised, as if he hadn't expected the question. "Last night, you said that it might be possible that Summer's phone is bugged. I want to make sure I don't say anything stupid to get us into more trouble."

"I appreciate that," he said. He walked over to the counter and pushed four pieces of bread into the toaster. "I think our best bet is to call Chase Hollister."

"Bray is her husband, not Chase."

"I know. But Chase is the police chief. I don't think anybody would have thought to put surveillance on his phone. He can get word to Summer and Bray. Do you know his number?"

She really, really wanted to talk to Summer, wanted to tell her how crazy mixed-up this whole thing was and that she wasn't sure of anything at this point. Summer would understand. But she would do nothing that might put Summer in danger. "I don't know his cell but I know the police station number. I learned it years ago in case there was an emergency at the café. What can I tell him?"

"Reassure him that you're alive and well. Give him permission to tell Summer but make sure he understands that them telling anyone that they've heard from you could further endanger us. And I'd appreciate it if you didn't tell him where you are. I don't want to have to deal with the Hollisters coming here en masse to try to save the day. Then I'll have more people to worry about getting hurt or killed."

He put two sandwiches together, dribbled ketchup on his and nothing on hers, and brought them over, along with a paper towel for each. "The people who own this place must not be coffee drinkers. I couldn't find a pot or any of the fixings."

"Barbarians," she said.

He smiled. He loved coffee as much as she did. "Maybe we can catch a cup at the marina."

"I thought you were worried about me being so recognizable. My hair," she added.

He pointed toward the shelf near the door. "Ball cap. You're going to need to put it up as best you can. And those and some duct tape will add some bulk." He moved his index finger to point at the stack of pillows he'd placed on one of the kitchen chairs.

She pointed to her tank, which maybe wasn't skintight but she sure as hell wasn't getting a pillow under it. "I don't think so."

"There are men's and women's clothing in the bedroom closet. We're going to borrow."

What hadn't he thought of? "You've been busy. How long have you been up?"

"Long enough that I'm fairly confident that I'm not going to fall down." He picked up two of the pillows. "I'll change in the bathroom."

She finished her sandwich and went to examine the closet. She pulled out a large navy blue shirt that buttoned up the front and some gray pants. She felt dumpy just looking at them.

She left her own clothes on but pulled the pants on over them. She zipped and buttoned and gathered the waist. She used her own belt to secure the pants. She was struggling to get the pillows taped into place when the bathroom door opened. Rafe wore a green shirt and pants and the fishing hat that he'd worn in from the boat the previous night. It did a good job of obscuring his cut. He looked twenty pounds heavier.

"Need some help?" he asked.

She didn't want to delay them. "Okay."

He came into the bedroom and stood close. She could smell the soap that he'd used to wash his face and hands. "Just hold them," he said, motioning to the two pillows that she awkwardly clutched above each hip.

She did and he wrapped the duct tape around her body, slipping it under her right arm, around her back, under her left arm, across her breast.

The two pillows didn't quite meet and the tips of his fingers swept across the valley of her breasts. Her thin cotton shirt was barely a barrier. He jerked his head up. "Sorry," he mumbled. He cut the tape and started wrapping again, this time lower, securing the pillows around her stomach.

Higher. She almost begged. Her traitorous breasts remembered his touch and she could feel her nipples tighten in response.

As soon as the tape was secured, she jerked away, turning so that he couldn't see her face. The curse of being a redhead was that she blushed easily—when she was scared or mad or aroused.

With shaking hands, she buttoned up the ugly 1X shirt. Still with her back toward him, she reached both arms up, separated her long hair into three different sections and efficiently braided it. When she was done, she secured the braid with a rubber band that she'd found in the kitchen drawer.

Finally, she turned to him. His mouth was slightly open, his gaze fixed. He was standing perfectly still except that the thumb on his right hand was rubbing against his index and middle fingers.

And she felt heat in her core, knowing that she wasn't the only one in the room experiencing ill-timed lust.

"Trish," he said, sounding needy.

It would be so easy to slip back, to forget the pain that she'd battled through these past four years. "I have a date on Saturday," she blurted out. "I've moved on."

Someone not familiar with Rafe would have thought the news had no impact upon him. But she saw the subtle shift in his dark eyes.

"Who's the lucky guy?" he asked casually, as if he was asking about the weather.

"No one that you would know."

"From Ravesville?" he asked.

"No."

"How did you meet him?"

He'd given up his right to ask questions four years ago. "None of your business," she said.

He shrugged, turned and walked out of the bedroom. He picked up the baseball hat on the shelf and, without looking at her, tossed it in her direction.

She put on the hat, hoping that it would keep her brain stuffed into place because clearly it had to be rattling around right now, muddying up the clear connection between thought and emotion.

She didn't like people who were deliberately hurtful. Tried to avoid them. But lashing out had been infinitely better than asking him to touch her, to kiss her, to make love to her.

Still, she had a very sour taste in her mouth.

It would take more than coffee to wash it away.

"Do you have your gun?" Rafe asked.

She walked over and pulled it out from beneath the love seat cushion. "I'm not sure how to carry it. Especially now. These pants are too loose. If I stick it in the waistband, it might fall through and I'll end up shooting off my foot."

He pointed to the pockets. "Use those. If you need to shoot, don't worry about pulling your gun out. Just stick your hand in your pocket, flip off the safety and aim in the general direction of the bad guy."

"How will I know who the bad guy is?"

"He'll be the person trying to kill us."

There wasn't a hint of humor in his tone. "I should be able to figure that out, then," she said. She put the gun in her pocket. It weighed down her pants on one side, and if someone looked really closely at her, they might put two and two together and come up with locked and loaded. "I'm ready."

He pointed at the two pairs of sunglasses that were on

the shelf next to the door. "Take whichever pair fits the best. I'll take the other."

He waited while she tried both and selected one. When he put his glasses on, he really didn't look much like Rafe anymore.

His hand was on the door, but for some reason, he wasn't turning the knob. Finally, he turned toward her. "I don't want to take you," he said. "But I can't leave you here by yourself, either. There's no damn safe place."

She didn't want to stay at the cottage. As mad as she was at Rafe, she felt safer with him. "Let's go," she said. "It'll be fine. As long as the marina has coffee, that is."

He HADN'T BEEN kidding when he'd said that he didn't want to take her. But leaving her was not an option. He couldn't protect her if he was halfway across the lake. They would stick together.

For now, he realized. *I've moved on.*

Those words had been like a knife to the gut. Which was ridiculous. Wasn't that what he'd wanted? Wasn't that what he'd told Milo time and time again? Insisted. *Find someone for her*, he'd said. *I don't want her to be alone.*

Hadn't he given up every damn thing so that she could be safe?

He supposed that might be the fundamental problem. They both saw themselves as the aggrieved party. There wasn't much to be gained by playing the I-hurt-more-than-you game.

The lake was quieter than his tumultuous thoughts, yet still not empty. With the naked eye, he could see five other boats. Probably fishermen wanting to get an early start. Hopefully not anyone looking for them.

When Trish headed for the back of the boat, he pointed

to the passenger seat up front. He wanted her close in case something happened.

Once she was seated, he started the engine and pulled away from the dock. He was satisfied that she was disguised as well as he could have hoped. The pillows and the big clothing made her look overweight and sort of sloppy. She'd stuffed her braided hair up inside the ball cap. As long as it stayed there, they might just pull this off.

If it had been only Trish's need to communicate with Summer, he might have held the line and told her that it was simply going to have to wait. But he needed to get out, to start gathering intelligence, to figure out what the heck had happened last night.

He drove the boat to the middle of the lake, far enough away from shore that from there it would be hard to distinguish their features without good binoculars. He kept his speed steady, not too slow, not too fast. Ten minutes later, he saw the marina. Now there was no choice but to return to shore.

There were three people visible on the dock. One, a young man, maybe twenty-five, wearing a white T-shirt and gray shorts, holding a clipboard. He was waving his arms toward a row of boats, as if to tell the young couple he was facing that they could have their choice of craft.

The woman pointed at what appeared to be a sweet twenty-six-foot Rendezvous and the couple climbed in. While Clipboard Guy was busy giving them last-minute instructions, Rafe docked the boat and tied up. With his index finger, he discreetly pointed at her, then at the pay phone that was ten feet away from the marina office. Trish did not acknowledge the instruction. He wasn't sure she was breathing.

"Relax," he said under his breath. "We're just a couple out for an early morning fishing trip. No reason for anybody to think anything different." He waited until she gave him a jerky nod before stepping out of the boat. He held out a hand for Trish.

She took it and he realized her fingers were ice-cold. He wanted to assure her that everything was going to be fine, but since she'd asked him not to lie to her anymore, he wasn't going to offer up any assurances that might not be true.

"I don't have any money," she said when she was standing close to him.

He'd thought of that. He had cash but he thought there might be another way that would ensure the call got answered. "Make it a collect call. Tell the operator that you're Raney Hollister."

"That's Chase's wife. How do you know that?" she asked, her eyes wide.

"That's probably not the most important thing right now. Chase will accept the call." He added, "I'll get the gas and then go inside for the coffee."

He was surprised when he didn't have to prepay for the gas. Showed how much people in this area still trusted.

And speaking of trust, it was a risk letting her talk to Chase without him listening in. She might unconsciously give away their location. Might do it on purpose, he realized. He wasn't confident that she trusted him.

Or would ever trust him again.

But the only hope of getting them back on the right path was to show that he trusted her. With an eye still on her, he dragged the gas hose away from the pump and stuck it into the boat's tank. She had the phone up to her ear with her back to him.

She was still talking when the automatic shutoff clicked off. The young couple were in their boat now, putting on their life jackets. Clipboard Guy was about to untie them.

He put the gas cap back on and walked toward the marina shop. When he opened the door of the shop, he could smell freshly brewed coffee and knew that the trip wasn't going to be a total bust. There was no one else inside, not even a clerk. Clipboard Guy must handle the whole show during the early mornings.

Rafe wondered around the small space. There were only three aisles. He found some bug spray and sunscreen, which he figured could come in handy. He remembered how easily Trish burned. He picked up a gallon of milk and was studying the candy bars in the small freezer at the front of the store when the young man entered.

"Morning," Rafe said. "Going to be another hot one." The weather was always a safe topic.

"Ninety-two," said the kid. He walked behind the cash register and leaned his butt against the back counter.

Rafe walked away from the freezer and set what he had in his arms on the counter before moving on to the coffeemaker in the middle of the room. "Smells good," Rafe said, nodding his head at the pot. "Outside, it smells like somebody had a big bonfire."

"Did you see it?" the kid asked, his eyes wide.

Rafe shook his head. "Just rolled into town this morning."

"Well, then you missed the most excitement this place has had in years. A cottage blew up, just exploded. And then, just like in the movies, two cars caught on fire and they blew up, too. One of them was a sweet black BMW. That had to be fifty thousand just up in smoke."

When they'd left the cottage the first time, there had

been only Trish's Jeep in the driveway. Somebody driving a BMW had arrived in that twenty minutes that they'd been gone. "Anybody get hurt?" Rafe asked, picking up a package of powdered doughnuts.

"I'll say. Three people are dead. I heard that they can't even tell if they are men or women."

He knew two of them were men. Big Tony and Anthony. He wasn't sure about the mystery guest. "That can't be good for tourism."

"I know. My mom works for the county dispatch center. She talks to the cops all the time," he said proudly. "They think they know one of the people. His license plate survived the blast. They went…" The kid hesitated, as if he knew that he shouldn't be repeating something that his mom had discussed at home.

Rafe turned, just far enough that he could see Trish getting back into the boat. He listened for the engine, thinking it was possible that she might try to leave him there. But it was quiet.

He added a bag of popcorn to the stuff already on the counter. He pulled out a hundred-dollar bill. "This plus $68.20 at the pump. They went?" he prompted.

"The police. When they went to his house to tell his wife, she was already dead. Shot in the back."

Was it possible that more than one woman had been shot in the back in this small community? He didn't think so. The third person in the cottage had to be Bernie Wilberts.

"The cops found the woman's phone and there was a text on it from her husband saying that he was going to be home soon, that he was stopping at their rental cottage first. They said it came in around eight o'clock but that she never would have gotten it. She was already stiff."

He said it as though it was no big deal. It made him think of how Trish hated it when her nephew, Keagan, played violent video games. She said it was ruining young people, making them desensitized to violence.

"I imagine the police will figure it out."

"My mom said they're getting some help from the state. Forensics. Maybe somebody like Abby from *NCIS*."

He'd seen the show. Over the years, he'd worked with a dozen Abbys but none that ever wore roller skates. "That would be cool."

The kid handed him his change and then put the two large coffees in a cardboard carrier. The rest of the items went into a white plastic sack.

Rafe opened the door of the shop. But before he could step outside, he saw the boat, idling at low speed. A hundred yards out from the far edge of the dock. Two men, both midforties, both with dark hair. One had twenty pounds on the other, but besides that, they were eerie replicas of each other. He did not recognize either one of them. And while they were dressed as fishermen, there was something not quite right about their appearance. Their clothes looked brand-new.

They were studying Trish, who had her back to them.

Chapter Fourteen

Rafe forced himself to stay put. He got ready to lose the coffee that he was carrying in his right hand. The milk and other purchases were in a sack, looped over his left wrist. He mentally adjusted for the slight difference in his center of gravity.

He was an excellent shot. But two against one were never good odds in a gunfight. Four years ago, Trish had been a decent shot. He'd made sure of that. But by the time she figured out what was going on and got to her gun, it would be over.

The two men looked at one another and one shook his head. They revved up their engine and moved toward the open water.

Rafe let out his breath. The kid at the marina wouldn't have been able to stop talking for weeks if there had been a gunfight on his dock.

"You okay, man?" asked the kid, from behind him.

"Yes," Rafe said without turning around. He watched the men. They were picking up speed, moving quickly away.

He moved out of the doorway and walked the length of the dock. He stepped into the boat and handed Trish the coffee carrier. She removed both cups and handed him back one.

"I spoke to Chase," she said.

He wanted to demand to know what she'd said but he didn't ask. Just untied the boat, started the engine and pulled away from the dock. When they were fifty yards out, he opened the sack, pulled out the bag of powdered doughnuts and gently tossed them in Trish's lap.

"I found out something," she said.

"Me, too. You first."

ME, TOO. YOU FIRST. It was their game. It would usually start within minutes of both of them getting home from work in the evening. They would be in the kitchen, working on dinner. One of them would start by saying *I saw something interesting today* or *I heard something funny today* or *I did something for the first time today.* The other one would automatically have to say *Me, too. You first.*

And it would begin. Laughing and talking about their day. Most nights they would end up in bed before dinner could be cooked.

Sharing everything.

Well, not everything. That was obvious now. She pushed those ugly thoughts away. "You were right. The local police tracked my license plate back to Ravesville and contacted Chase."

"I imagine he was surprised to hear from you."

He had been grateful but not that surprised. "The officer he spoke with confirmed that my body had not been identified. That, along with whatever it was you said to Bray, must have been enough for them to keep positive."

"Had he told Summer?"

"No. He and Bray made the decision not to. But they're going to tell her now that they know I'm okay."

"Did he want to know where you are?"

"Yes. But I told him that I'd promised you that I wouldn't say."

He turned to stare at her. "Thank you," he said.

"He wasn't very happy about that, so I did tell him that I'd check in tomorrow, too."

"Okay, we'll make that happen."

She opened the bag of doughnuts. "The cop told Chase that there were *three* people in the cottage."

"I know. The kid at the marina told me the same thing. They tentatively identified one as Bernie Wilberts, based on his license plate. Same as they did for you."

The doughnut tasted chalky in her mouth and she washed it down with a big swig of too-hot coffee. It was crazy, really. She'd met the man only once, had one additional telephone conversation, but she felt as if she'd lost someone that she knew well.

Maybe it was because of what Rafe had told her about Mrs. Wilberts. A whole family had been wiped out in one day. "So it was bad timing on his part?" she asked.

Rafe didn't answer. That made her nervous. "What are you thinking?" she demanded.

"The kid at the marina told me that Bernie Wilberts drove a black BMW. I was also driving that same kind of car. I think it's very possible that when Bernie got there, somebody mistook him for me, and the cottage was attacked."

Rafe and Bernie Wilberts didn't look anything alike. Did they? Both had dark hair. Same height. Approximately the same weight. Rafe was all hard muscle, and Bernie… Well, not so much. But from a distance…

The morning wind was picking up and their boat was stirring the water. She watched the trail of wake. It was how her brain felt. Insubstantial. Frothy. But one thing was clear. "Then what you're saying is that you were the target. Not Big Tony or Anthony or me." It was a warm sunny day and a chill ran down her spine.

She had preferred it when she thought she might be the target. Rafe had just come back from the dead. Sort of. And she was very, very angry with him about his deception.

But she couldn't bear to lose him again.

They were nearing the cottage. "Now what?" she asked.

"Let's get out of sight until I figure out what to do next."

He had his hand splayed across his forehead, as if protecting his eyes from the bright sun. He was wearing the clunky sunglasses that he'd found at the cottage but she suspected the quality was poor. He'd probably started the day out with a headache and this couldn't be helping it. But maybe there were details that needed attention before they returned to the cottage. "You said you were driving a car. Where is it?"

"In town, in the public lot near one of the boat rental places."

"Can it be traced to you?"

He shook his head. "This boat either. I rented it under the name Bill Wood."

"They didn't make you show an ID?"

"I have one."

Of course he did. He probably had four or five different IDs in his pocket. This husband of hers that she really truly didn't know. "Pretty soon nothing you say will surprise—"

She heard the noise a millisecond before she hit the floor of the boat with Rafe's big body covering her. She managed to raise her head.

Rafe already had a gun in his hand, his own head raised, scanning the horizon. His body was taut with barely contained energy.

She heard the sound again and was able to track the origin. A boat on the near shore, its engine backfiring. She realized Rafe had come to the same conclusion when he moved off her and extended a hand to help her up.

"Sorry," he mumbled.

Maybe he was full of surprises. Maybe there were a thousand sides that she had yet to see. But this man would protect her. He would give up his own life to save hers.

That spiked an emotion that she wasn't ready yet to deal with and she turned away from him.

SECONDS AGO, WHEN the damn boat had backfired, his first thought had been that the two men in the boat had somehow circled back without him noticing and had decided that they'd missed something the first time. He needed Trish to be aware that danger might be very close. "There's something you should know."

She had turned away from him and for a second he thought that maybe she was giving him a message that she was done listening, that she'd heard about all she could handle. But slowly she swiveled in her seat.

"I saw two men in a boat this morning. They cruised past the marina. I thought they were giving you a close look."

She motioned to herself. "In these clothes with an extra forty pounds, there's not much to look at."

"You could dress in a gunnysack and you'd be beautiful," he said.

Her fair complexion colored fast. She wasn't used to receiving compliments. That was his fault. That and so much more.

"Did you recognize them?" she asked.

"No. But they weren't fishermen," he said. "I suspect they're hired help. They'd been given a description of a slender, red-haired woman and they couldn't see past a big blue shirt. That tells me they aren't very smart. Or motivated. Or maybe either."

They could be as dumb as rocks, but still, seeing them that close to Trish, with her unaware, had been almost too much.

What if they'd been just a little smarter? What if they'd been told to shoot first and ask questions later?

He swallowed. The morning sun felt too hot on his face, even though his hat provided shade. The water seemed very blue. Maybe it was the cheap glasses. But then he saw a slim piece of red hair that had escaped from Trish's tight braid. It swung in the breeze, caressing her neck, like a single spike of fire.

Everything was exaggerated. Especially the need that raced through his body. He turned away from Trish, not wanting her to be able to look too close. She had always been able to see too much.

He tied up, scanning the area while he did so. He didn't see anything that concerned him. But then again, a rifle with a scope didn't necessarily require close proximity. He needed Trish inside, with at least the benefit of solid walls.

Not that that had helped Bernie Wilberts all that much.

He just needed to make sure that nobody discovered that they were holed up at the Norton cottage.

He slowed the boat and expertly pulled in next to the dock. After he tied up, he turned to Trish.

"Do you mind carrying these?" he asked, very formally, nodding his head toward the sack of groceries and the still-full coffee cups. "I'd like to keep my hands free."

"Of course," she said, just as formally, as if they were two strangers. Certainly not as if they had been close once, as close as people could be.

He led the way, his gun in hand. When they got to the short grass, he held up his free hand, stopping her. Turning, he whispered, "Let me check it. Run like hell if you hear anything odd."

He crossed the space from the tree line to the back door, a flashback from the night before at the edge of his thoughts. He was confident that he'd not been followed either last night or this morning...but still.

But he got to the door without incident. Then he was inside. The cottage had not been touched. Within seconds, literally, he was back at Trish's side. "All clear," he said.

She didn't answer.

"Are you okay?" he asked.

She made a deliberate look to the right, then the left. "Another day in paradise. What's to complain about?" she snapped.

A small smile escaped before he shut it down. Trish had always hid her nerves with sarcasm. It was silly but just seeing that that one thing hadn't changed made him feel good.

He opened the door to the cottage and let her go inside first. She set the milk down on the counter with a thud. The bug spray rolled out of the sack and onto the tile floor. "Maybe I'd be better," she said, "if I understood what the hell was going on."

He sat down at the table and took off his hat and sunglasses. He desperately wanted to lie down and close his eyes. But she'd given him a pass last night. "There are some things that haven't exactly made sense over the years. And now I think I might know why. I told you last night that we were successful in stopping the London Tube incident and that arrests were made. There were two brothers that were both charged with terrorism-related offenses, all punishable by many years in prison."

"What doesn't make sense about that?" she asked.

"I knew they were brothers. But the whole time that I was working alongside of them, I thought that they did not have other family. No one else was ever mentioned, nor did my team ever identify any other family. And believe me, we're pretty damn thorough. For us to miss that was a big miss."

"How did you find out that it was missed?"

"After my two teammates were killed and I went back to the agency, I started investigating. There's an old rule. Follow the money. And that's what I did. That's when I was finally able to connect the two that we'd arrested with the person who had to have been bankrolling the operation."

"The winemaker in Italy," she said.

"Yes. But I was shocked to learn that the winemaker wasn't just the money guy—he was their father. He'd never been married to the mother. She'd ultimately married someone else. The two sons had been raised by their mother and stepfather."

"But somehow got reunited again with their biological father."

"Shortly after finishing college, we think."

"Last night, you said something about the fact that the Maladucci family had more reason now than ever to come after you."

"Mr. Maladucci had two more sons with a second wife. What we've been able to discover is that one of them has picked up where his older half brothers left off."

"A real family business," she said.

"We're pretty confident that the youngest brother, Demí, is not involved. He's a well-known European philanthropist. But Mario, the older brother, is his father's right hand. I was successfully able to convince one of the secretaries in his office to help me—"

"Did you sleep with her?" she asked, her voice hard.

It knocked him back. "What?"

"In your little cloak-and-dagger world, isn't that how things are done? People trade sex for favors."

She was right. Sometimes. He held up a finger. "I did not sleep with her." But the secretary had slept with Mario. She claimed it was a small price to pay for justice.

Trish braced her elbow on the table and rested her forehead in the palm of her hand. "I'm sorry," she said. "I don't know where that came from."

He understood. Her nerves had to be brittle. In the span of two days, she'd seen Milo killed, Duke shot, been kidnapped, had a husband come back from the dead, heard about multiple people with gunshots to their backs, and was now being told that it was likely worse than what she'd imagined. She was probably hanging on by a thread. And when that happened, people lashed out. And her accusation wasn't unreasonable.

But it still hurt that she could so easily conjure up the accusation. What other things was she thinking but hadn't yet voiced?

He probably didn't want to know. "I convinced her to help me after I uncovered that her brother was killed in a café bombing in France. I thought she might be sympathetic to my efforts and I was right. Luciano and his older son have picked up where the two older half brothers left off. They don't have the technical knowledge but they've hired that expertise. It's more of the same. Another biochemical attack."

"Do you know where?" she whispered.

"At the Kentucky Derby. Opening ceremonies."

She gasped. "That's just a few weeks away."

"I know. And we were moving swiftly. Arrests of Luciano and Mario Maladucci would have been made by the end of next week. That's why I don't think the timing of this is coincidental. Somehow, I think they found out."

"How?"

"That's the big question. Maybe the secretary decided that it was too big of a risk and she confessed her involvement. I don't know. There are always loose ends in operations like this. Of course, this is not the only case I've worked on during the last four years. There have been many others. There is no lack of people doing bad things in this world and I have made some enemies. But from the very beginning, this felt personal. The attack on Milo. Taking you hostage. Somebody wants me to know that they can get to the people that I hold dear. My family, so to speak. I believe it's revenge for what I've brought down on their family. Maybe a counterattack. Maladucci may know that the agency is close to dismantling his operation once again and he's striking first."

"Would the secretary have known that? Would she have been privy to that information?"

"Not from me. And maybe it wasn't her. Maybe it was someone else."

SHE COULD HEAR it in his voice. He was angry. Hurt. She understood. Being deceived by someone you trusted was like a knife in the gut. She thought better, however, of pointing out her observation.

They would deal with their personal situation. One way or another. But in order to have that opportunity, they both needed to stay alive. And based on what Rafe was telling her, there was somebody determined to make sure that didn't happen.

"Do you know who?"

"No. But somewhere along the way, I've trusted the wrong person. Made a mistake."

She sipped her coffee. "You said before that Big Tony and Anthony were owned by the Maladuccis."

"They are little fish," he said. "Anthony probably accepted that. He had much smaller ambitions than his father, much to his father's disappointment. They were muscle supporting a strong revenue stream derived from the sale of illegal drugs and gambling. Maybe a little human trafficking thrown in. You'd be surprised at how diversified these organizations are. Makes Wall Street look like a bunch of amateurs."

Muscle. "I think you might be right. When they took that awful cell phone picture of me, they said something about you not being able to stay away. I didn't know who they were talking about, of course. But Big Tony said something along the lines that it wasn't about me, that it was about making things right."

"Big Tony always had a way with words. Or at the very least, a big mouth."

"So here's what I don't understand. If Big Tony and Anthony were following somebody's orders to kidnap me and kill you, then why blow up the cottage with them in it. That doesn't make sense."

"Agreed."

"So what are the possibilities?" she asked.

"I've settled on these three," he said. "It was somebody who had it out for Big Tony and Anthony, and anybody else who happened to be in the cottage was collateral damage. You, me, Bernie Wilberts. They probably didn't care."

She waited. If he really thought that, they wouldn't be puffing themselves up with pillows and pretending to be Ma and Pa Fisherman.

"Or," he said, "it was somebody in Big Tony and Anthony's infrastructure who wasn't confident that they could get the job done and decided to take matters into his or her own hands."

"In that case," she said, "they were collateral damage. And when it becomes known that we weren't killed, the bad guys are going to keep at it."

"Yes. I imagine so." He rocked his chair back and reached to snag the popcorn off the counter. He opened it and extended it in her direction. She shook her head. Maybe his stomach wasn't a wreck. He lived in this world but her world was eggs over easy and a stack of pancakes. Simple.

"What's the third possibility?" she said.

"A slight variation from door number two, but in this version, the bad guy isn't part of the Maladucci organization. He's a part of my organization." He pushed back his chair and started pacing around the small room. "I've been wondering why now. I've been back with the agency for four years. I didn't think anybody knew about you. But I could have been wrong. You've been in Ravesville the whole time. Why now is there a need to lure you here so that I'll follow? It could have happened anytime in the past four years. Why now?" He tossed back the handful of popcorn and chewed.

It indeed was something to chew on. "Who knew you were close to bringing down the Maladucci family again? This time probably for good."

"Only a handful of people. Hell, not even that. Two trusted coworkers, Daltry and Miara. My boss, Kevin. His boss, Michelle. I suppose even her boss, but since that's the president of the United States, I'm taking that off the table. Four people. Two men, two women."

"Tell me more about them," she said. "These four."

"I've worked with Daltry and Miara since rejoining the agency four years ago. I like both of them, trust both of them."

"As much as the two partners who were killed?" she asked.

He shook his head. "I didn't let myself get that close."

She had figured as much.

"Both Daltry and Miara were part of the surveillance team on the Maladucci house. So they were aware that I abruptly left the property. I told them I wasn't feeling well. They might have wondered about that, but I'm not known for skipping out of work, so they probably would have cut me some slack."

"What about your boss?"

"Kevin Leonard has been my supervisor for a long time. Before I came to Ravesville and then after. He's just a little older than me. We have a good partnership. He doesn't like fieldwork, hates to get his hands dirty. But he's really good at reporting and relationship-building, all the things that I find tedious. He likes wearing suits and his shoes are always polished."

She smiled at the last part. "That's very helpful to know." She considered what he'd told her. "Does he also think you're ill?"

"Yes. Once I'd made the decision to leave Italy, I called him and told him that I wasn't feeling well and would likely be out for several days."

"Was he okay with that?"

"I think he was concerned. Putting the Maladucci family on ice is sort of a big deal. It will get some attention from people higher up in the agency, maybe from even outside the agency. He's ambitious. Smart. I'm sure he wants it to go smoothly and end well. He wants all hands on deck. I could tell that he was a little upset or maybe nervous. He stutters a little when that happens."

"And his boss, Michelle?"

"I rarely interact with her."

"What about support personnel. Surely these people have administrative assistants and things like that. Maybe it's more than four?"

"It's possible, but there is certain work that gets done that is so confidential that it is not shared with support personnel. All correspondence is directed on secure lines only to the intended recipient. Messages can't be copy and pasted, can't be forwarded."

"That doesn't prevent somebody from inviting another person into their office and letting them read over their shoulder."

"You're right about that."

"And what about the computer people? Everybody knows that the people who are responsible for the computer system can see anything they really want to see."

"It's possible, but quite frankly, lots of the messaging was done on secure phone lines and never put in writing."

She sighed. "This is complicated. I don't have a concussion and even I have a headache."

"I'll figure it out," he said. "I have to."

Chapter Fifteen

He needed to check his phone. If somebody had been trying to reach him it might give him one more clue as to who was interested in knowing whether he'd survived the explosion. But he could not check it from here.

Heelie Lake was a big lake. He could take the boat several miles south and put his cell phone battery back in there. If they caught the signal, he'd be long gone before they could get someone in the area. Unless the two guys he'd seen at the marina just got lucky and were close by.

He needed to take the chance. But he did not want to leave Trish, who, even now, probably didn't understand the gravity of their situation.

"I'm guessing that the two we saw on the lake are not the only two looking for us," he said. "It's possible that there are people in multiple places, both on the water and land."

She seemed to consider this as she studied her hands. "You need to use me," she said finally. "To flush them out. We need to find them, demand to know who they're working for. We need to hunt them down, rather than the other way around. I'll show myself," she added, as if she was discussing a walk in the park.

"No," he said. "Absolutely not."

"You said it yourself. They're looking for me. But I'm the small fish. According to your own theories, this probably isn't about me. It's you they want. They aren't going to hurt me. They'll want to use me, to lead them to you."

"They'll still kill you," he said. "Once you've done what they needed."

"We'll have to figure out a way to stop that," she said.

He was always the one with nerves of steel. And now she was the one showing the guts. He hated this but it made sense. Still. "I can't let you do it," he said. He would not, could not, take a chance with her life. But neither could he send her back to Ravesville. The Hollisters would protect her, likely with their lives, but their attacker had already shown that he or she was ruthless and didn't care about others getting hurt.

It was a damn mess. "I can't let you," he said.

"That's ridiculous," she said.

"It's not," he said, barely keeping control of his patience.

"You're not listening to reason. Why can't I do this?" she pushed.

Because he loved her. *I'm moving on.* "Just because, damn it."

The words hung in the air.

"We have to figure out if those two men were indeed looking for me and if so, how many more might be scattered around the area."

"They aren't going to just volunteer the information, Trish," he said.

"We have to figure out a way to convince them to talk to us," she said. "I don't think we should lead them back here. So far, this seems like a pretty safe place for us."

"Agreed."

"I might know a place. I've stayed at the other end of the lake several times. On the west side, it's developed. On the east side, there are a series of small coves. There aren't any cottages because it's federal ground in that area. So it can be pretty isolated."

"What are you proposing?" he asked.

"We take Bernie Wilberts's boat there. It's slower but I think it's in our best interests to keep our boat under wraps as much as possible so that when we're disguised, we feel comfortable driving it."

He tilted his chin down to look at her. "Are you sure you haven't done undercover work?"

She ignored the question. "I'll drop you off and then I make myself visible. Maybe I can do a little shopping on-shore. Hopefully the two men you saw this morning are still in the area. Once I've done that, I'll head back your direction. When they follow me, you can deal with them."

SHE MADE IT sound so simple. But there were a thousand things that could go wrong. The Maladucci family had a lot to lose. Desperate people did stupid things. But hiding out and doing nothing was not his style. And it wasn't making her any safer. "If we do this, I don't want you out of your boat," he said.

"Will you trust me to do what I need to do?" she asked.

Well, hell. "I have always trusted you," he said. He had trusted that she would have the spirit to go on. That alone had kept him sane more than a few nights.

He trusted her enough that he was going to tell her about Henri. Not another living soul knew about him.

"We may have one ace up our sleeve," he said. He told her the story of Henri and how he'd met him. And that he'd stepped in and impersonated him before. He was not specific about the times or the reasons.

When he was finished, she looked a little amused. "So it freaked you out to see your double?" she asked.

"A little. But he's been extraordinarily helpful. There is one pretty significant limitation, however. He's German and doesn't speak English well. He understands it better than he speaks it. So he would never pass for me if it required him to interact with someone. But I think there's a way we can go with your idea to use you as bait." He stopped and shook his head. He hated even saying the word. "And use my relationship with Henri, who is right now cooling his heels somewhere outside St. Louis until he gets word from me."

"I'm ready," she said.

"First, we need to get Henri here. I need to make contact with him. Let's go back to that pay phone at the marina."

Twenty minutes later, Rafe finished his call to Henri. He'd been a little afraid the man wouldn't answer the call because it hadn't come from Rafe's second phone. But he had and the conversation had been relatively easy.

Carrying out the plan would be significantly harder.

Before he got back into the boat, he went inside and purchased two large coffees. A different young man was working and barely spoke to him.

When he got back to the boat, Trish smiled at the coffee. "Thank you," she said.

"I knew that one cup earlier wasn't going to cut it," he said, starting the boat.

"Well, what did he say?" Trish asked, her tone impatient.

"He can be here in two hours. I asked him to trailer a boat so that he doesn't have to rent one once he gets here. Less chance of someone seeing him. He'll meet us on the west end of the lake. He'll be wearing a red baseball hat and a white T-shirt."

"I hope there aren't a lot of Cardinals fans on the lake," she muttered.

"Let's hope he's got a strong bat and we knock it out of the park," Rafe answered.

She stared at him, her green eyes intense. He realized that she'd forgotten her sunglasses. "That was fun when you played softball," she said.

His first and only summer in Ravesville, he joined the men's softball team that played at the local park. They'd needed a third baseman. After being undercover for many years and continuously living on the edge, he'd enjoyed the easy camaraderie that existed between the players. Had loved looking up in the stands and seeing Trish cheering for him.

Had looked forward to going home with her those nights and making love to her. And she would tease him in bed. *Make it a good throw, Roper.* And when she would come apart in his arms and he would follow her over the edge, he would whisper in her ear, *Home run for Roper.*

"Trish," he said, his voice sounding rusty.

"Yes," she murmured.

"We have two hours until we have to meet Henri. I...I want you."

She'd asked him to be honest. He couldn't get much more brutally frank than that. He braced himself for her refusal. *I've moved on.*

She made him wait. Then she gave him a half smile. "I've got an idea for the seventh-inning stretch."

His damn heart flipped over in his chest. Just flipped over.

He pushed the speed up another five miles per hour and hummed "Take Me Out to the Ball Game" all the way back to the cottage.

ONCE THEY WERE safely inside the cottage, he caught her in his strong arms and pulled her tight to his body. He smelled like the lake and the coffee that he'd just drunk. His skin was warm and she ran her hands up his arms, over his biceps, across his chest.

And then he bent his head and he kissed her. Consumed her, his mouth greedy, his tongue stabbing into her mouth. With a hand on each side of her face, he held her tight.

Not that she had any intention of pulling away. They were in danger. Someone wanted to kill Rafe, maybe her, too. If they didn't both survive this, she would not have wasted this day, this time.

Still kissing him, she tried to unbutton her ugly blue shirt. She wanted it and the pillows and everything else gone. She wanted to touch him, skin to skin.

He lifted his head. His eyes were dark. "Need some help?" he asked, his tone guttural.

She nodded.

He put a hand on each side of the shirt and ripped. Buttons flew everywhere. "I'll leave them enough money for three shirts," he said, his mouth close to her ear. Then he was licking her collarbone.

And she felt as if the pillows and duct tape were strangling her. There was such need in her body.

"Get a knife," she moaned.

"Kinky, huh?" he teased. He put his hands on her butt and pulled her against him. He was rock hard.

"Rafe Roper," she said, "if you don't get these awful pillows off me in the next ten seconds, I...I don't know what I'm going to do," she finished weakly when he stuck his hand down the front of her baggy pants and touched her.

Even though her cotton capris and her thin panties still separated them, her body responded, as it always had, to his touch.

He knew what she liked.

All was fair in love and war. She unbuckled his belt, unbuttoned his jeans, pulled at the zipper. Started to drop to her knees.

He groaned and held her up. "You win, darling," he said, his mouth against her neck. He put his hands under her bottom and boosted her up. She wrapped her legs around his waist.

And on the way to the bedroom, he snagged the scissors off the table.

Chapter Sixteen

She must have slept. Because when she woke up, she was on her side, with Rafe spooned around her. He had one arm draped over her stomach, her hair curled around his hand.

It had been fast. Electric. Nerve endings that maybe weren't dead but certainly asleep had jumped and saluted. She came minutes after he'd entered her and he'd pounded into her, his wonderful body slick with sweat.

They had not used protection. Hadn't discussed it. But even now, the knowledge that a child could have been created was almost overwhelming. When she'd believed Rafe dead, the thing she had mourned the most was that she hadn't been pregnant. She would never hold one of Rafe's children in her arms.

But now. Maybe.

"Are you awake?" he asked softly, his mouth close to her ear.

"Yes."

"Everything okay?"

She turned to face him. She studied him. "Your cut looks better but the bruise on your forehead is worse."

"I'm fine," he said. He stroked her shoulder. "Are you avoiding the question?"

She stared at his sexy brown eyes and ran the pad of her thumb over his right eyebrow. "I'm not sure everything is okay but I have no regrets," she said.

He sighed but didn't push her for a better explanation, and for that she was grateful. Her emotions were all over the place. Making love to Rafe again had been amazing but there was so much unresolved between the two of them. While he might have had his reasons, and they might even have been good reasons, to have left her and let her believe him dead for four years was not something that someone got over easily.

And then, of course, there was the small matter that someone was trying to kill one or both of them. "Can we talk about next steps?" she asked.

He rolled onto his back and put one arm under his head. The other he kept securely around her. "Sure."

Which was nice and agreeable but his actions weren't matching his words. He was gently rubbing his fingers up and down her naked stomach. His tanned skin was a stark contrast to her very pale skin.

"Stop—that tickles," she said, stilling his hand. It did but it also was distracting—making her think of all the places that she wanted those fingers to go, all the ways he had made her come in the past without ever taking his pants off.

He smiled. She sensed he knew exactly why she'd made the request.

She sat up in bed. She was done letting him run the show. "I'll be back. I need to use the restroom."

When she returned, she got in on the other side of the bed, so that his back was facing her. He started to roll over but she stopped him.

She ran her finger down the middle of his back. Let it dip below the base of his spine.

"Trish," he growled.

"Yes?" she said sweetly.

"What are you—"

"Doing? Why, I'm taking charge."

She pulled on his shoulder so that he lay flat on the bed. Then she straddled him and she was pretty sure his eyes rolled back in his head.

"Go for the grand slam," he said weakly.

AN HOUR LATER, they left the cottage. Trish had her hair up inside the ball cap and wore another ugly shirt, this time a green-and-white stripe, but without the padding. She wore just her own capri pants and they were tight enough that she could stick her gun in the back of her waistband and not have to worry about it falling through. It was damn uncomfortable, however.

Rafe had changed his clothes, too, picking out a tan shirt and pants. He wore the same green fishing hat. He had his gun in his holster and the knife in his boot. He'd grabbed the flashlight at the last minute and she figured that was a good call. If nothing else, knock the hell out of the bad guy.

They both wore sunglasses and took two fishing rods and a tackle box from the Norton shed. As they walked from the cottage to the boat, she was confident that they shouldn't attract undue attention. They looked like any other fashion-challenged couple on the lake. She got in first and Rafe handed her the equipment. As she'd suggested, they took the smaller boat. She knew there was some risk with that. After all, the bad guys might know about Bernie Wilberts's boat and be on the lookout for it. But fortunately, there was nothing too distinctive about it.

They set off at a moderate speed in the middle of the lake. Her nerves were strung tight. She knew this was really their only option. It was hard to fight an enemy when you didn't know who it was. They needed information. Their only lead was the two men that Rafe thought looked suspicious.

Fifteen minutes later she tapped Rafe on the shoulder. "It's just up there a little ways, around the bend in the lake."

"Okay," he said. They were across from a marina larger than the one they'd stopped at earlier. It had multiple places to gas up and there was a row of shops across the street. It looked like a souvenir store, a bar and maybe a small grocery store.

"This is as good a place as any," he added, as he removed his cell phone and battery from his pocket. He snapped the battery in and powered up his phone. He scrolled through the recent calls.

"Anybody?" she asked.

"At least one from everybody on my team. A couple from my boss. Two from blocked numbers."

"What time did they start and stop?"

"First one came in just minutes after I removed the battery. They've continued sporadically since then."

It was just now two o'clock. That meant that Rafe's phone had been dead for about eighteen hours. Not such a long time, really.

But so much had happened. It felt as if it had to be much longer. She watched him scan his contacts and select one. "Who are you dialing?"

"My dentist."

She narrowed her eyes at him, which was a wasted effort because she had on sunglasses. "Suddenly remembered you're due for a cleaning?"

He held up a hand, asking for silence. She heard someone answer on the other line. It was a voice recording. Of course. It was Sunday. The dentist office would not be open. He listened to the whole recording.

Then he disconnected the call and immediately removed the battery. "That will be enough for them to pick up activity," he said.

"What are they going to think if there's activity and you haven't checked in?"

"The worst. Our rule is that if we can, we check in. No exceptions."

She could tell that it bothered him that he'd disregarded a rule that he'd probably helped set. "Maybe you could at least call your boss?"

He shook his head. "I can't. Maybe his phone has been hacked. I just can't take the chance."

The boat was moving fast, the aluminum bottom hitting the water hard. She understood. If they would be able to trace the call back to this area, he would want to get the hell out of there fast.

It was ten minutes later that they saw a boat similar to the one that Rafe had rented slowly cruising the lake. The driver wore a red baseball cap and a white T-shirt. "Is that our relief pitcher?" she asked.

"Relief pitcher, designated hitter, utility guy. Pick your position." Rafe raised his arm and waved.

The boat came closer. And Trish had to remember to shut her mouth. The resemblance was amazing. Of course, there were differences. The man's eyes were just a little rounder, his lower lip just a little less full. But the skin tone was spot-on, he was the same height and weight, and the hair color and cut were perfect.

She could see how if he was coming and going from Rafe's apartment that anyone watching and expecting to see Rafe would think that they had.

The two men nodded to one another. Rafe motioned to her. "Henri, my wife, Trish. Trish, my good friend Henri."

Trish smiled at him. "Thank you for coming."

"What is our plan?" he asked, his German accent quite noticeable.

"Follow us," Rafe said. "We're headed that direction." He motioned toward the far west side of the lake.

When they reached the area that Trish remembered, it was not terribly impressive. There was a relatively narrow channel away from the main body of the lake that quickly broadened into a large circle. Unlike the rest of the lake that was smattered with cottages, docks and boats, this was still undeveloped land. Boaters who ventured into the area probably lost interest relatively quickly—there wasn't much to see except long grass and trees.

Years ago when she and Summer had brought Adie and Keagan to the Ozarks for a few days, they'd gone on a hot air balloon ride. She'd had the chance to see this area from that angle. It had been amazing. The two coves were almost perfect semicircles, a palette of greens contrasting beautifully with the blue water.

In the first cove, there was a boat with two fishermen. Rafe glanced at Trish and she pointed toward the second cove. Ideally, it would be better to have no one else around. That might prove to be impossible but they should try.

The second cove was empty. Trish knew that might be only a temporary reprieve. By the time she dropped Rafe off and returned, hopefully with the men on her tail, one or more boats might have ventured into the area. It wasn't known to be a great fishing spot but the isolation would appeal to some.

She hoped it appealed to the two men, that they didn't smell a trap. If they did, would they just shoot her and be done with it, figuring getting her out of the way was one less body to deal with later?

She voiced none of these concerns. She knew that Rafe was a thread away from shutting down the whole effort, that he was scared for her. She wasn't going to add to that.

She needed to be confident.

Rafe pointed the nose of the boat toward an area at the far side of the cove. There was no sandy shore. The water simply got shallower until it washed up against solid land. He slowed down and motioned for her to get ready to drop the mushroom anchor over the front of the boat. She grasped the nylon rope in her hands, grateful that this wasn't the first time she'd ever done this. Rafe cut the engine and she carefully let out the rope in the waist-high water. The heavy base of the anchor settled into the muddy bottom.

Then Rafe got out of the driver's seat and motioned for her to take his place. She knew what to do. She turned on the engine and slowly backed the boat toward shore. At Rafe's hand signal, she stopped and he was over the rear of the boat, barely making a splash in the water. He waded to shore, pulling the boat after him.

Then he helped her from the boat. It was very quiet, with just a gentle lapping of the water against the land and the occasional squawk of a bird. They did not talk while they waited for Henri to join them.

Once he was there, Rafe led them from the lake, deeper into the tree line. She was grateful for the knee-high fishing boots that she'd borrowed from Mrs. Norton. The grass was long and she worried about snakes. Five minutes later, he stopped.

"This might work." They were the first words he'd said and his voice practically made her jump.

This was a small area that had clearly been someone's campsite at one time. There was a ring of rocks where they'd had a small fire. There was enough space that someone could have pitched a small tent.

He was rubbing his forehead and she wondered if he had a headache. She understood. She had one herself. "I think you're right," she said, hoping she sounded more confident than she felt.

He walked around the perimeter of the cleared space. Every few feet, he would stop and pick up a sturdy-looking stick. When he had an armful, he turned to her. "Remember what I said earlier, that you couldn't get out of the boat? I'm changing my mind. We need to set this up to be believable." He walked over and dumped his load in the fire pit. "If I was right and they were tracking my phone, they will undoubtedly still be in the area of that marina. Once you leave here, go to the grocery store that was across the street. Buy some lighter fluid and matches and maybe some hot dogs and buns. Hell, buy some marshmallows if you want. When you return, come directly to this spot."

He pointed to Henri. "You'll be here. Feeding the fire. Looking unconcerned."

"It's a beautiful day. Why would I be concerned?" Henri asked, his tone light.

Trish knew he understood the risks. Rafe had told her exactly what he'd told Henri before he'd asked the man to participate in their ruse.

"Exactly," Rafe said. He smiled but it didn't reach his eyes.

He still hated this. "Where will you be?" Trish asked.

"Somewhere near, where I can see what's happening."

Where he could manage the situation as best he could. He would protect both her and Henri with his own life.

She really hated this, too.

He turned to her. "You'll need to be vigilant and watch when you pick up a tail. Once that happens, it's straight back here, no more stops, no more delay. I don't think they'll try anything on the open part of the lake. Too many eyes. But once you turn into this cove, they might try to stop you, thinking that they won't run the risk of losing you in the woods."

"What do I do?"

"Do whatever you can to reach land. If they try to apprehend you on the water, you need to use your gun. Once you get on land, I'll be able to protect you, but on the water, I can't be a lot of help to you."

She pressed on her chest because it hurt. "I should go," she said.

"Yeah."

She swallowed hard and started walking. She got five steps before she felt a strong hand on her shoulder. She turned and she was in his arms, as if it was the most natural thing in the world.

"Oh, Trish," he said, his mouth close to her ear. And then he was cupping her face, kissing her. Gently at first. Then more insistent. It reminded her of their last night before he'd disappeared, when they'd made love gently, and then toward morning, he'd taken her again with an urgency that had surprised her.

He kissed her as if he was never going to stop. His

tongue in her mouth, his hands sure and confident as they gripped her. But finally he pulled away and rested his chin against her forehead.

"You won't see me when you get back," he said.

"But you'll be here," she said.

"Yes. Whatever happens, know that I'm here."

"I trust you," she said.

Three little words. Not the three little words that usually made a heart go soft. But in this case, maybe trust was better than love.

"Be safe," he said, his breath coming hard. "Please be safe."

RAFE FOLLOWED TRISH back to the boat and made sure that she got the anchor raised. At the last minute, she took off her striped shirt and her baseball cap and threw them to him.

Then he gave the boat a final push out into deeper water, heard the motor turn over and resisted the overwhelming urge to throw himself into the vessel and wrestle the wheel away from her.

His head hurt. When he moved too quickly the world swam for just a brief second.

Not a good thing if he had to get a shot off quickly.

He wanted to avoid that if at all possible. Truth be told, he, who never ran from any battle, wanted to avoid any altercation. The possibilities of Trish getting hurt were simply too high. He let himself imagine staying on the island with Trish, living off the land, making love a couple of times a day. Of course, that might work in a poorly done movie but in real life it wasn't an option. She had Summer and Adie and Keagan. She had her café.

At one time, she'd had him.

I've moved on.

When he'd made love to her it sure as hell hadn't felt like it. Afterward, for the first time since he'd rescued her from the kitchen chair and she'd backed away from him like a scared animal, he'd felt a little hope.

They couldn't change their history but they could forge a new future. The new guy could get lost. He'd tell him so in no uncertain terms.

But he was jumping the gun. He knew that. Trish was a loving, giving woman but he had perhaps underestimated the pain that she'd endured.

Maybe because that was the only way he could deal with it. Maybe he'd told himself that she'd be sad but that her heart would heal. Maybe he'd been afraid to consider the alternative. That he had dealt her a blow that had knocked her to her knees. Maybe he was doing more of the same right now.

One thing at a time, he told himself. *Concentrate on the most important things. Keeping Trish and Henri safe. Catching the people responsible for all the killing.*

He walked back to the cleared area and found Henri gathering sticks for the fire. "She is very beautiful," Henri said. "She is the one you've been coming to see all these years."

Coming to watch. But there was no need for specifics. "Yes."

"I did not realize that you were married. You surprised me when you said she was your wife."

It had rolled off his tongue pretty easily. It felt right. "We've been estranged," he said.

Henri shook his head. "She does not look at you in that way. She looks with wanting."

Henri might be English-challenged but he had a way with words. Did she want him?

Like for forever?

They hadn't talked about it. There hadn't been much time, really. They'd been together for less than a day after a four-year absence. No wonder things felt strange.

In bed there'd been no strangeness, no awkwardness. He had slid into her body and felt as if he'd finally come home. Peace. There was no other word for it.

But peace rarely lasted and he'd just sent her out as bait. What the hell had he been thinking?

"I don't want her to get hurt," he blurted out.

Henri shrugged. "Then we'll have to work very hard to make sure she isn't."

Chapter Seventeen

As she drove the boat across the lake, Trish was overly conscious of her hair flying in the wind. After all, it was her blue-light special signal. *Red-haired woman here. Come and get me!*

She tied up at the marina and wiped her sweaty hands on the edge of her shirt. When she crossed the street, she made it a point to look both ways twice. Not because she was worried about the traffic, but because it gave her a chance to look around. She did not see two middle-aged men like Rafe had described.

She knew that did not mean they weren't there.

She opened the door of the small grocery store and almost sighed when the cool air hit her. It was another hot afternoon in Missouri. It dawned on her that just a day ago when she'd bought groceries, her biggest concern had been getting them home before they got hot. Now it was getting them back to Rafe before she got shot.

Hot, shot or worse. Taken. Funny how that could be worse than getting shot and dying. But the hours she'd spent yesterday with Big Tony and Anthony had been horrible. She'd felt so vulnerable. She didn't ever want to feel that way again.

And if she was taken, she knew Rafe would do whatever it took to get her back safely. Even if he died in the process.

Better to just get it over with with a bullet to the brain.

Not that she was hoping for either alternative. What she really wanted was to buy her few groceries, get in her boat, have the men follow her back to the island and then let Rafe deal with them on his terms.

And she'd just stand off to the side and watch.

She wasn't cut out for this kind of stuff. And up until yesterday, she'd never imagined that Rafe was, either. But she was learning about this man that she'd married.

He'd figured out a way to fool everyone who was tracking his movements from Italy to the United States. Then he'd found her at the cottage and disabled both Big Tony and Anthony to free her. And that was basically nothing compared to what he'd done after the cottage had exploded. After nearly drowning, he'd managed to get both of them back in the boat, across the lake and into the Norton cottage. With a head injury.

He was amazing, really.

Now, likely with a concussion, he was getting ready to confront the enemy. All she had to do was lead them there.

She wandered up and down the aisles of the small store. There were only four with a small freezer section across the back wall. As Rafe had suggested, she picked up a package of hot dogs and buns. She skipped the marshmallows, thinking something that sweet would make her sick for sure. She bought two bottles of water. No telling how long this might last and she didn't want either of them getting dehydrated.

And because the potato chips that she'd bought the day before had been scattered from here to wherever by the blast, she added a bag of those. Comfort food in an uncomfortable situation.

She took her merchandise up to the cash register and waited behind two women both dressed in swimsuits with cover-ups thrown over them. They had on cute sandals that made her very conscious of the tall rubber boots that she wore. She felt clumsy and out of place.

All the better to attract attention, she told herself. Which, she realized, was exactly what she'd done when she shifted to pull money out of her pocket and saw a dark-haired man in the corner of the store. Watching her.

Her twenty-dollar bill fluttered down onto the check-out lane. "Sorry," she mumbled.

The clerk smiled and picked up the money. Then she bagged Trish's groceries and gave her the change. Trish stuffed it back in her pocket, telling herself to breathe, just breathe.

She looped the plastic sack over her wrist, keeping her hands free. Then she walked out of the store, looking twice each direction before she crossed the road again.

She forced herself to walk, not run, down the long dock. Then she was in the boat, untying the ropes, tossing them on the floor of the boat. She started the motor and pulled away. Slowly. A careful boater.

Certainly not a woman whose heart was about to jump out of her chest. She did not look behind her. But she listened for the sound of another engine.

And she was pretty sure she heard one.

RAFE HAD CHOSEN his spot carefully. He was uphill from the clearing. He could see both the lake and Henri. When he heard Trish's boat, he took in three very deep breaths to settle his nerves.

She dropped her anchor close to shore, got out of the boat with plastic bags on her arm and sloshed through the water to the shore.

She waved to Henri and he waved back. Then she showed him what she'd bought. When she pulled a magazine out of her sack and tossed it in his lap, he realized that she was brilliant.

She needed to give them an excuse for not talking. That excuse was this week's *People* magazine.

Henri caught on and started flipping pages. Trish sat next to him and got busy putting hot dogs on the ends of sharp sticks that Henri had placed near the fire.

Nice day for a picnic.

They were playing it perfectly.

And he thought it might be for naught when he didn't see another boat follow her into the cove. And after about ten minutes, he was just about to call it a good effort, when out of the corner of his eye, he saw movement on-shore.

The two men that he'd seen that morning were furtively walking along the shore. They each had a gun in hand.

They must have thought it was too dangerous to bring their boat into the cove. They had probably left it just around the edge, in the main part of the lake.

He saw the exact moment that they saw Henri and Trish. They stopped in their tracks, looked at one another and nodded. He got ready. If they raised their guns, he was going to have to take them out.

But they didn't. He wasn't that surprised. He thought they might attempt to take him alive. All the better so that he could be tortured later.

He waited for them to split up, so that one could approach from behind.

But they did nothing. Except the man in the lead pulled out a cell phone and appeared to be sending a text. Did they really need instructions? Or permission? Who the hell was pulling the strings in this operation?

Meanwhile, Trish had cooked two hot dogs, put each one inside a bun and handed one to Henri. They were eating and Henri was looking through his magazine, his head bent down.

Rafe wanted to rush the men and demand answers. But he waited.

Twenty-seven minutes and forty-two seconds later, his patience was rewarded.

And then sorely tested because something was happening but he wasn't exactly sure what. The man with the phone had quickly pulled it out of his pocket, looked at the screen and then nodded, as if satisfied. Then he pointed to his partner to circle around behind the clearing.

Rafe followed the man who was moving. As he did so, he heard the engine of a boat. He looked over his shoulder. He still had a clear view of the lake but the boat was out too far for him to clearly see the person at the wheel.

But he didn't doubt for one minute that it had something to do with the information that had come across the man's phone.

The boat was drawing closer. Henri and Trish had to hear it but they were continuing to act unconcerned. Trish had relaxed back on the sand, as if her primary goal in life was to catch some rays on her face.

It humbled him that she trusted him to figure out a way to save them all.

He hoped to hell it wasn't misplaced.

TRISH STRETCHED BACK, her upper body propped up by digging her elbows in the sand. She kept swallowing because otherwise she thought she might vomit her recently eaten hot dog. What the hell was happening? It was taking forever. She wanted to know what Rafe was thinking, what he was doing.

I'll be there. It had been his promise. She would not doubt him.

But when she heard the engine of the boat, she wanted to leap up from the sand and call out to him, to warn him. But instead, she closed her eyes and lifted her face to the sun.

She knew something was wrong when Henri, who had been humming softly under his breath, stopped. She opened her eyes just as two men emerged from the trees with guns in their hands.

Chapter Eighteen

One was the man that Rafe had described. Midforties, brown hair, dressed in brand-new clothes. The other was much older, balding, with more gray than brown in his hair. He wore a linen shirt and what looked to be silk trousers. They were wet up to the knees where he'd waded to shore.

Henri tossed his magazine aside and had stood up. He stepped in front of Trish, as if protecting her.

"Search them," the older man snarled.

Forties Guy did. All he found was a pack of gum in Henri's pocket.

"I prefer to meet in my home, in civilized conditions," the older man said, his tone condescending. "But your actions, Mr. Roper, rendered that impossible. Or should I call you Ryan Weber? That is, after all, what my sons knew you as."

Luciano Maladucci. It had to be. He had a soft Italian accent.

Henri said nothing. She knew that he was going to avoid talking as long as possible.

Maladucci stepped closer, close enough now that Trish could smell the expensive cologne that he'd evidently bathed in. With his free hand, he batted away a bug from his neck.

Then he clamped that same hand on her biceps and roughly yanked her toward him. Henri made a move to pull her back but Forties Guy stepped forward with his gun pointed at Henri's heart.

"I'm dreadfully sorry to interrupt your picnic," Maladucci said, "but your husband has caused me a great deal of trouble and I simply can't allow it. He needs to understand the consequences of his continued interest in my family. It means I will have an interest in *his* family."

Rafe had been right.

Where the hell was Rafe?

Waving his gun in the direction of the lake, Maladucci said, "In my country, little boys are taught to fish before they can walk."

Huh?

"Knowing how to scale a fish is a useful skill," he added. With his thumb, he lifted up the edge of his expensive shirt and put his gun back into the small leather holster that he wore on his hip. Then he pulled a knife.

Long, shiny, maybe a ten-inch blade, slightly curved.

And he put it up to her throat.

But he looked at Henri. "You're going to watch her die. And know how I feel every day when I think about my sons rotting in that prison. I have waited a long time for this," he said. "Too long. Demí said that it wasn't worth it. The risk was too great. But he's wrong. It is absolutely worth it."

He grabbed a big swath of her hair, knotting it up in his fist. "This is very pretty," he said, his voice almost purring. "I'll bet you like it," he said, again looking at Henri.

No response from Henri. That seemed to agitate Mala-

ducci even more. "You are not much of a man if you will
not defend those that you love," he said. Then he swung
his knife toward her and the sharp blade connected, just
above his clenched fist, and a foot of hair floated to the
ground.

Her heart was thudding in her chest. Not over the
loss of some hair. But that knife was very sharp and he
seemed to know how to use it.

It had stunned Henri. He was white-faced and was
looking from side to side.

Maladucci noticed. "There's no one coming," he said.
He pointed toward Forties Guy. "I sent his partner up onto
the hill where he'd have a clear view of the lake so that
he could make sure that we're not interrupted."

Maladucci tilted his head back. "Monty," he called
out. "Are we still alone?"

There was silence. Maladucci looked at Forties Guy,
who shrugged.

"Monty?" Maladucci called out.

When there was no answer, he pointed to Forties Guy.
"Go find him," he said.

She turned her head to watch Forties Guy climb the
hill but soon lost him in the trees. She heard him crashing through the brush.

Then there was nothing.

"Jacques?" Maladucci yelled.

Jacques didn't answer.

Maladucci moved faster than she would have anticipated. He wrapped his arm around her throat and the
knife came frighteningly close to cutting her carotid ar-
tery. She did not move.

"What the hell is going on?" he demanded.

Henri shrugged.

"Why the hell don't you say something, you bastard," Maladucci yelled, sounding insane. He tightened his grip on her neck, cutting off her air. She started grabbing at his arm and quickly realized that he was too strong.

It was now or never. She clenched her fist and jammed her elbow back. She heard a pop and he sagged behind her, almost taking her down with him.

She scrambled away. Oh, God. Had she pushed a rib into his lung? Had she seriously injured him? It wasn't until she looked at him that she realized he had a bullet hole in his forehead. And Rafe was running down the hill like a high school track star.

"Get away," he yelled.

She couldn't. Her legs had given out on her. She sagged into the sand. "He's dead," she said.

Rafe didn't even break stride. He got close, checked for a pulse and, only then, turned to her. "Oh my God, Trish. Are you okay?" he asked.

Before she could answer, he bent to the ground and picked up the pile of hair. "Your hair. Your beautiful hair."

"I needed a trim," she said and grimaced when her own voice trembled. She needed to be strong. He certainly had been. "The other men. Monty and Jacques?" she asked, her voice stronger.

"Incapacitated. Not dead."

"That was close, man," Henri said, regaining some of his aplomb.

"Now what?" she asked.

Rafe was already pulling out his phone. "We call the police. You'll both need to give statements. I'll call my boss, let him know what's going on. We'll have to move on arresting his older son for his involvement in the biological warfare."

"It's really over," she said. "I can go home."

"Yes."

She didn't want to have this conversation with Henri listening in. But she needed to know. "Are you coming back to Ravesville, Rafe?" she asked, as casually as she could when her heart was racing in her chest.

"Do you want me to?" he asked.

"I think we have things to talk about," she said.

He drew in a deep breath. "We'll talk," he said.

Chapter Nineteen

Summer cried when she walked in the door. Just like she had every time she'd seen Trish for the past week. She hugged her so hard that Trish was confident she'd bruised a rib.

"You know, with your hair shorter, we look more alike than ever," Summer said.

True. Summer had worn her hair shoulder-length for years. After Trish's stylist had evened out her hair, it was just a few inches longer.

Plenty left for Rafe to wrap his hands in.

Except that Rafe was MIA. Well, not really missing. She knew where he was. He'd had to return to DC to meet with his boss shortly after he'd taken care of pesky little details like getting people arrested and transported to the appropriate place.

It had been a little hard to piece the puzzle together with Luciano Maladucci dead. But there was a ballistics match to Jacques' gun for M.A. and for Mrs. Wilberts. The hits had been ordered by Maladucci, or so Jacques said, and there was little reason to disbelieve him.

Both Jacques and Monty had denied any involvement in Milo's death and Trish had been inclined to believe them. She would always believe that it had been Maladucci. He was good with a knife and he seemed the type to gloat over a dying man, which had probably prompted Milo's deathbed warning.

The part that didn't make sense was the rocket launcher to the cottage, killing the Paradinis and Bernie Wilberts. Again, Jacques and Monty denied involvement, said that they'd arrived at the lake the following morning after being summoned by Luciano Maladucci in the middle of the night.

Maybe it had been Maladucci and he'd got Bernie Wilberts confused with Rafe. If so, he'd no doubt been very angry when the police identified Bernie as the victim based on his license plate. But that didn't really make sense because Maladucci wouldn't have expected Rafe to even be in the States at the time of the explosion. He was supposedly still in the air, on his way from Italy. In the end, she supposed it didn't matter. Knowing the truth wouldn't bring them back. The cops had found some text messages on Bernie Wilberts's phone that showed he was a bad guy. They'd told her that he sold a bunch of drugs, the kind that were killing teens.

And it was hard to be sympathetic about the Paradinis. They had planned to kill her. They had killed Duke.

She was grateful to the Hollister brothers, who had helped her look for Duke's remains. They'd been unsuccessful in finding them, and because hope really did spring eternal, she'd stapled his picture on every fence post and fishing pier in the area, just in case.

But there'd been no word and it had been a week.

"When's Rafe coming home?" Summer asked.

"I'm not sure. We had almost no time to talk before he had to return to DC."

Summer lowered her voice, obviously cognizant that

her handsome husband was in the kitchen, getting them tea. "Are you going to be okay, Trish?"

"I don't know," she said. "Things are no more settled then they were when he walked into the kitchen and I fainted dead away."

"Don't say the word *dead*," Summer said. She wasn't teasing.

She was right. Too many dead people. And Milo's funeral was tomorrow. Rafe had sent an email, promising that he'd be back. She'd tried his phone and got his voice mail.

They'd sort of connected. Kind of like they were sort of married.

"Rafe will make it," Summer said, as if she'd been reading her mind. Having a twin was really scary sometimes.

"I'm sure he'll do his best," Trish said. Her voice sounded tight and pinched and she knew that Summer heard it.

"Give him a chance," Summer said. "I saw the way he looked at you before he left. He loves you."

And she loved him. Always had. Always would.

But was it enough? He'd deceived her. For what he'd thought were good reasons, but the four years of pain she'd endured could not be so easily forgotten.

"We're planning to talk," Trish said. It was all she was willing to commit to. "Now, let's make sure we've got things covered tomorrow."

An hour later, she left Summer's house and went by the café. They'd stayed closed the entire week. They would re-open on Monday, the day after tomorrow. Food and paper products had been delivered yesterday. She'd shoved the refrigerated items into the cooler but had left the boxes of canned goods in their boxes. She needed to get those unpacked and on the shelves. It wouldn't hurt to cut up some vegetables for soup, either.

An hour later, things were looking pretty good when her cell phone buzzed. She pulled it out and her pulse kicked up. Rafe was twenty minutes out.

WHEN SHE MET him at the door of the café, she leaned forward for a chaste kiss on the cheek. So, that was the way it was, huh?

No way. He'd had some time to think this week. He was coming back to Ravesville and they were going to have the life that they'd started four years ago.

"How are you?" he asked.

"Fine. Come in," she said, stepping aside.

It felt weird, her treating him like a guest. He wanted to grab her and kiss the hell out of her but knew that wasn't what she had in mind when he took a stool at the counter and she walked behind it.

She looked tired. But good. "I like the hair," he said.

"Thanks," she said as she took a seat beside him. "I may keep it this length. I mean, I know you liked it long, liked to…" Her hands fluttered at her sides.

She was nervous. He'd been gone too long and they hadn't had time to talk before he'd left.

But there had been a lot to handle. The first thing he'd done while he, Trish and Henri were still in the cove was call his boss. When he'd given him a rundown of everything that had happened since he'd abruptly left Italy, there'd been long periods of silence on the phone. Rafe knew the man was surprised and probably trying to figure how best to proceed.

It had taken a week but now he had good news to share

with Trish, news that should quiet her nerves. "Mario Maladucci and a host of others have been arrested. There are a myriad of charges, the most serious dealing with conspiracy and intent to commit a terrorist act on American soil."

"It's over? Really over."

"It is," he said.

The silence stretched. He ran his index finger along the edge of the counter. Back and forth.

She watched him. "We had that custom-made," she said. It was easier to talk about counters than the things that really mattered.

He nodded. "I know. I remember the day they delivered it. You were so excited."

She stood up, very straight. "You'd been gone for over a year when the counter was delivered."

He stilled his hand. There could be no more lies. "I told you that Henri would take my place when I needed to get away."

"Yes."

"I would come here. I rented the apartment on the second floor of the building across the street."

"What?" She was blinking her eyes fast.

He swallowed hard. "Sometimes I just needed to be close," he said.

The color drained from her face as she sat again. "Are you telling me, Rafe Roper, that you *watched* me?"

He would tell her all of it. "Yes. More than once. I was in your house, too, when you weren't home."

She stood up, her motions awkward. "My heart was breaking and you had the capacity to make it better. All you had to do was walk across the street. Or wait for me to come home one night. My God, Rafe. Why didn't you do that?"

"I couldn't."

"Yes. You could have," she said. "You could have told me the truth and let me make the decision. Instead, you made it for me."

He was losing her. He could tell. "But you, you were always talking, laughing. You seemed happy. How the hell was I supposed to know?"

She opened her mouth, then shut it. She turned and started to walk away.

"Trish," he said. They had come through so much. How could he lose her now? "Where are you going?"

She turned, just halfway. "I...I can't be with—"

She stopped. Her cell phone was buzzing. She fished it out of her purse and read the screen.

"Trish," he said. He was not above begging.

"I have a date tonight," she said, sounding almost dazed. "That's where I'm going. On. My. Date."

"No," he said.

She stared at him. "You lost the right to tell me what to do a long time ago."

She took three more steps, turned the door handle and walked out the back door of the café to where her new Jeep was parked.

TRISH WALKED THROUGH the empty rooms of her house, touching nothing. The space felt huge.

She would sell the place. Should have done it years ago. What would Rafe have thought when he sneaked into town and saw the big For Sale sign?

You were always talking, laughing. Had she been so convincing that he was fooled? Surely Milo would have told him? But to be fair, she never let Milo see more than a little of her despair. She'd always figured the poor man had his own problems—he didn't need to shoulder hers, too.

Maybe if Milo had gone to Rafe and said, *Hey, buddy, she's falling apart.* Maybe that would have made the difference?

She'd been so angry with Rafe. When her cell phone had buzzed, she'd almost ignored it. But then had realized it might be about Duke. Maybe someone had found him. When she'd seen the text, it had jolted her back into the reality of her life.

She'd intended to cancel the stupid date but had forgotten to do so. But just that quick, she'd been grateful that she hadn't. She needed to think of something else besides Rafe's duplicity. She'd be poor company tonight but she would meet Barry North and they would have dinner. She would pay for her own. Heck, she'd buy his, too, just for the principle of it.

Then she'd tell him that she wasn't interested in a second date. Because even if she couldn't ever forgive Rafe, she also couldn't imagine ever loving anyone else.

She stopped walking when she got to her bedroom. After dressing in a black skirt and a sleeveless white silky blouse, she caught a glimpse of herself in the mirror. Her skin had actually tanned while she was in the Ozarks.

A visible change.

So many more beneath the surface.

She pulled her long hair into a ponytail and then wrapped it tight into a bun at the nape of her neck. She slipped her feet into black sandals with delicate gold buckles.

She drove to Hamerton and found the restaurant. She checked her watch. She was twenty minutes early.

It gave her too much time to think. What was Rafe doing right now? What was he thinking? Was he tying up the loose ends of his investigation so that he could leave after Milo's funeral?

She pressed a hand against her stomach, knowing that the sudden pain was not from hunger but something much more elemental. Love. Loss.

Indecision.

She pulled out her cell phone, thought about calling him. Couldn't. She wasn't ready to talk to him yet. Instead, she sent a quick text to Summer. At Mulder's in Hamerton. Date with Barry North from Kansas City. Ever since her lake experience, she'd felt the need to check in more frequently, to make sure that somebody else had key information.

She turned her phone to Silent. That was enough for now. Summer would have a thousand questions and she didn't want to answer them just yet.

At ten minutes before seven, she opened the heavy front door of Mulder's. The foyer was dimly lit with sconces on the wall. There was a woman, dressed all in black, her arms wrapped around several menus. Before Trish could give her name, a man approached from the dining room.

"Trish?" he asked, his voice tentative.

"Yes," she said, her voice higher than usual. She was nervous.

"I recognized you from your picture," he said, smiling.

She extended her hand. His online picture had been of him skiing down some mountain. Up close, he was a good-looking guy. He was probably midforties with an athletic build and a full head of hair.

If she'd been looking, he would have warranted a second glance. She was going to have to make sure that he understood that it was her, not him, that precluded a second date.

"I was just about to walk out to my car," he said.

She glanced at her watch. "Was I late?" she asked.

"I just realized that I forgot my billfold out there."

She started to tell him that he wouldn't need it, that she intended to cover dinner. But she didn't want to have that conversation now, before they'd even ordered drinks.

"You can wait here or you're welcome to walk with me," he said. "It's a beautiful night."

It was. It was still light outside and they were on the main street of Hamerton. It was safe. Trish smiled at the hostess. "We'll be right back."

He held the door for her. "That way," he said, pointing a finger.

They passed her new Jeep and got to the end of the block. He turned right. "Just got my car painted," he said. "Didn't want to park too close to anyone else."

The side street was much quieter than the main street and she felt suddenly uncomfortable. Maybe her experience at the lake had made her hypersensitive but she wasn't ignoring her gut. "You know, I just forgot that I need to make a phone call," Trish said. She started to turn. "I think I'll head back to the restaurant and do that—"

He yanked on her arm, pulling her into a dark doorway. His hand was over her mouth before she could scream.

"Sh-sh-shut up," he said, his mouth very close to her ear. "Shut up or I'll k-k-kill you here."

RAFE HAD LEFT the café and had gone to the only other place that he felt comfortable—the empty apartment across the street. He prowled around the space. The idea of Trish going on a date with another man ate at him, making him want to lash out at someone.

He needed to do something productive.

Hell, maybe he'd mow Trish's grass. It had rained several times this past week and the grass had to be growing like crazy.

He drove to Trish's house and let himself in with the key that he'd always had. He supposed that she'd want it back.

He wandered around the empty house, knowing that he was stalling. If he didn't start the yard soon, it would get dark before he got it finished.

He made one more pass through the house. He could smell her perfume in her bedroom and he clenched his fist thinking of another man sniffing at her damn neck. And at all the other places where he knew she liked to dabble a little scent.

He saw Trish's computer on the desk. She'd never said how she'd met her date. Had it been online? The guy could be a major creep.

Or he might be a really nice guy that she liked.

Which one was he more afraid of?

He ran his finger along the edge of the computer as he sat down at the desk. Would she think he was out of line? He hesitated for just one more second.

He'd rather be out of line than lose her to some other guy. He flipped open the lid. Fortunately, there was no password. He opened the internet browser and went right for the tab that appeared to be for the online dating website. A click, a simple click, and he would have information on Trish's date.

He stopped. She was already so angry with him. Would this push her over the edge?

He closed the computer, pushed his chair back. Rubbed the back of his neck. Christ, he was tired.

He stood, pulling his keys out of his pocket. He'd mow the grass tomorrow, before Milo's funeral. He hadn't given Trish the privacy she deserved before. He sure as hell could now.

He had his hand on the doorknob.

Aw, hell.

In six steps he was back at the desk and within seconds he had the computer open. He clicked on the right tab.

And his damn head about exploded.

He'd recognize that profile anywhere. The ski jacket added a little bulk and the stocking cap hid the high forehead.

But it was his boss.

Kevin Leonard.

There was no good reason for him to be dating Trish.

But a slew of bad reasons. And each one of them had something to do with what had happened at the lake.

He picked up Trish's landline phone and quickly dialed. Summer answered on the second ring. "What is going on, sis?" she asked. "I just got your text and—"

"It's Rafe," he said. "I'm at Trish's house. She sent you a text? Where is she?" he asked.

"Why?" she said, her tone more guarded.

"Listen, Summer. I don't have time to explain. But I think she's in trouble."

"In Hamerton. At Mulder's. Oh, Rafe—"

"Don't worry," he said, interrupting her. "I'll find her. And when I do, I'm never letting her out of my sight again."

BARRY NORTH HAD hit her hard in the stomach, then stuffed her in the trunk of his car while she was trying to catch her breath. It was dark and hot and she felt as if she was going to throw up. She'd found the emergency trunk release and realized that it was somehow disconnected.

This hadn't been a spur-of-the-moment decision.

He'd planned this. He'd led her down the side street on purpose. He'd lied about his car being just painted. When he'd put her in the trunk, she'd seen the heavy white dust on the black car.

Think. Think, she told herself. What else had he said? *Shut up or I'll kill you here.*

Horrible, horrible words. He'd stuttered when he'd said them.

Hadn't she just heard about someone who stuttered when they were nervous? *Oh my God.* It had been Rafe's boss, Kevin Leonard. What else had Rafe said about him? All she could remember was that his shoes were always shined.

She breathed in hot air and told herself to think. Why would Rafe's boss have struck up an online relationship with her? Why would he stuff her in the trunk of a car?

There could be only one explanation. Rafe had been right all along. He'd been concerned that it was someone on his own team that might be trying to kill them. It was the person leading the team.

The only reasonable explanation was that Kevin Leonard was working with the Maladuccis. But they'd been arrested. Why keep going?

But not all of them had been arrested. Not the younger son. What was his name?

Demí. That was right. When Luciano Maladucci had held the knife up to her throat and talked about getting revenge against Rafe, he'd said that Demí had said it wasn't worth it, that the risk was too much.

In everything that had happened, she'd forgotten to

tell Rafe that and he hadn't heard it himself because he'd been too far away.

But the younger son had to be a part of this. Was Kevin Leonard somehow in cahoots with Demí?

It was more than she could fathom. But she needed to wrap her head around it. She also needed to pay attention to everything else. She needed to keep track of how long they drove so that she could estimate the miles once they stopped. Were there other sounds? Trains? Car horns? Anything that would give her an idea.

They were going fast, which told her that they'd left the city limits of Hamerton. She let out a small scream when he turned hard and she slid to the side, knocking her shoulder into the side of the trunk.

She'd been such a fool. But she'd been so intent on teaching Rafe some kind of lesson.

Rafe. Oh, God. She loved him so much and she was never going to get the chance to tell him.

The car stopped suddenly and she prepared herself to come out swinging, scratching, screaming. Whatever it took. She wasn't going to make it easy for this guy.

She heard his door open then shut. Then nothing.

Seconds turned into a full minute.

Was he simply going to leave her here? To die a slow death in a hot trunk.

It was crazy.

And as much as she didn't want to face the man, she didn't want to die alone.

She started to scream.

RAFE MADE THE twenty-minute drive to Hamerton in twelve minutes. He pulled into an empty parking spot and was out of the car and opening the restaurant door in seconds.

He stepped across the small foyer and into the dining room. He scanned the tables.

Damn. She wasn't there. Had Summer been wrong?

Trish would not have lied to her about it. There would be no reason to. He turned to see a young woman, walking at a leisurely pace. "Sir?" she asked. "Table for one?"

"I'm looking for a woman, long red hair, with a man, midforties, brown hair."

She glanced around the room. He resisted the urge to get in her face in an attempt to hurry her.

"She would have arrived about fifteen minutes ago," he said.

The woman's blue eyes opened a little wider. "There was a woman, really pretty, who had red hair. I'm not sure how long it was. It was in a really cute bun."

"Where is she?"

"The gentleman that she was with forgot his wallet in his car. They went to get it. She said she'd be right back but that didn't happen. I just gave their table away."

"What direction?" he asked. "What direction did they turn when they left?"

She shrugged. "I think to the right."

He started running. Saw her car and searched it quickly. It was empty. When he got to the end of the block, he debated whether he should turn left and cross the street or turn right.

He thought about his boss. Conservative Kevin. Suit always pressed. Silk tie. Hair always trimmed.

He turned right.

And ran, stopping just long enough to look in every parked car. He got all the way to the end of the block. In Washington, DC, Kevin drove a Toyota Camry. But he'd have rented a car here. It was like looking for a needle in a haystack.

He ran his hand through his hair. Tilted his head back. And saw the man.

Second-floor window. Sitting in his chair. Watching the street.

Rafe crossed the street, stood underneath the window. He waved his arm. "Hey, sir," he yelled. "I'm looking for a woman, red hair, in a bun. Have you seen her?"

The old man stood. He was wearing pajamas. "I already called the police," he said, his Southern drawl heavy.

"What? Why?"

"Because where I come from, young man, you don't hit your woman and lock her in the trunk."

TRISH STOPPED SCREAMING when she started choking on her dry throat. No one was coming. No one was going to help her.

The man hadn't told her to be quiet, hadn't threatened her. That told her one thing. She was in the middle of nowhere.

How long did it take to die of thirst in a hot car?

A day? Two at the most. It wouldn't be an easy death.

But she couldn't simply give up. Summer knew that she'd gone on the date. She'd be expecting to hear from her in a couple of hours. When that didn't happen, she'd summon help.

Rafe would look, too. He'd been full-time busy saving her life this past week.

He would not stop until he found her. *Please, please, let him be in time.*

RAFE PACED THE SIDEWALK, waiting for the police. The man in the pajamas had come downstairs and was standing on his porch. But he wasn't talking. *I'll tell my story to law enforcement.* That was what he'd said when Rafe had demanded to know more about the man, the car, the direction they'd gone. Rafe had pulled his badge. "I'm a federal agent," he'd said.

The man just shook his head. He wasn't impressed.

Right now Rafe wasn't all that impressed with being a federal agent. Not when his boss could do something like this.

He'd thought about pulling his gun and forcing the old guy to talk but knew that was only going to ultimately delay him. He might need the local police.

He used his time to call Chase Hollister. When the man answered, Rafe quickly filled him in. "It's Rafe Roper. I think Trish has been kidnapped by my boss, Kevin Leonard, outside Mulder's restaurant in Hamerton."

"Got it," Chase said, knowing better than to waste time with stupid questions. "We're on our way. Stay in touch."

Next he called Daniel, who had hung around Ravesville all week. He was intending to go back to Chicago after Milo's funeral. Rafe wanted all the help he could get.

He'd just finished his conversation with Daniel when he heard the sounds of approaching sirens. Two squad cars pulled up. A male officer in one, a female officer in the other. Probably everybody on duty on a quiet night in Hamerton, Missouri.

He kept his identification in his hand. Maybe they'd be more impressed.

"I'm Officer Wagner and this is Officer Billet," said the male officer when they got close. "Which one of you made the call?"

Wagner and Billet were both in their thirties and he
suspected they had several years of experience, based on
the quiet confidence of their approach. But he doubted
they'd ever come up against anyone like Kevin Leonard before. The man was exceptionally smart. That was
something Rafe had always admired about him.

Rafe stepped forward. "I'm Rafe Roper and I'm a federal agent." He held out his badge for them to examine.
"This man saw a woman get assaulted and pushed into
the trunk of a car. My…" He stopped. It might do more
harm than good to identify Trish as his wife. They would
doubt that he could be impartial.

They would be right.

"The woman is Trish Wright, a witness in my protection. The driver of the car is Kevin Leonard, also a
federal agent."

The two officers looked at each other. Officer Billet
recovered first. She stepped forward and addressed the
old man. "What's your name and what did you see?"

"My name is Walter Wilson and I saw these two
people—a couple, I thought. Not walking hand in hand
but chatting, like they knew each other. Then, all of a
sudden—" his voice lowered, as if he was enjoying the
storytelling "—the man yanked her into that doorway,
right there, and then he hit her. Like he was going for
middleweight champion of the world."

Rafe was going to rip Leonard apart.

"Then when she was bent double, trying to catch her
breath, he popped his trunk open and pushed her inside.
Then he took off."

She was injured. No doubt scared to death. He'd been
so damn stupid to be satisfied with catching Luciano

and Mario Maladucci. His gut had told him that it went deeper.

A few things made sense now.

The reluctance that Kevin Leonard had had about Rafe coming back on his team four years ago. The feeling that the Maladuccis were sometimes a step ahead of them. And most recently, that first phone call to his boss. Kevin had seemed shocked at the news he was telling him. He hadn't been shocked by that. He'd been shocked to hear from Rafe because he knew that Maladucci intended to kill him.

"What kind of car?" Rafe demanded.

Both of the cops gave him a dirty look.

"We're wasting time," he said.

The old man held up his hand. "He was driving one of them new Cadillacs. A nice black one. Shame to let a car like that get so dirty. Lots of white dust. If I had to guess, it's spent some time parked near the quarry."

Rafe knew the quarry. He'd spent a year working in Hamerton, building the new mall. They had got cement from the quarry. It was almost straight east, just a few miles outside of Ravesville.

It would help considerably to have an area to start. But dust could blow some distance and that meant there would still be multiple country roads, with multiple houses and outbuildings to search. It would take time. Time that Trish might not have. "Listen to me," he said. "He'll be armed and dangerous. I have backup coming. Chief Hollister from Ravesville."

"We know Chase Hollister," Officer Wagner said.

"Good," Rafe said, already running for his car. "Communicate with me through him," he said, over his shoulder. "He's got my number."

Rafe got into his car and headed east, driving ninety on roads meant for fifty-five.

He was going to be too late. He could feel it in his gut.

RAFE WAS GOING to be too late. That was her first thought when the trunk lid suddenly popped open and she saw *her date* standing there, now holding a hacksaw.

He motioned for her to get out of the trunk and she saw that he also had a gun.

She didn't want to get any closer to the saw or the gun but there was absolutely no chance of running away if she didn't get out. She summoned every bit of courage that she had and threw a leg over the side. Soon she was standing next to the vehicle. Her legs were not steady and she tried to calm herself by taking a few quick deep breaths.

She glanced down and knew she was right about the identity of her captor. The car might be filthy but her date was neatly dressed and his shoes were super shiny. "So, Barry," she said, "or should I just call you Kevin?"

He reared back in surprise. "W-w-well," he said. He drew in a deep breath as if he, too, needed to settle his nerves. "I guess the need for introductions is over."

"Why are you doing this?"

He didn't answer. Just looked at her.

It didn't matter why. What mattered was getting away. She'd been right. The area was deserted. It felt a bit like the end of the earth. The gravel road dwindled away into patches of dirt and grass just twenty yards past the one-story white bungalow that had probably been new in the '40s and got its last coat of paint in 1970. There were no screens on the windows and several of the panes were cracked. There was no yard, just an accumulation of crabgrass and weeds.

She was not going in that house. He'd have to kill her outside.

"That's going to be messy," she said, looking at the saw, buying time. "Based on what you told me in your emails, I thought you were the orderly sort. You know, clean kitchen counters and such."

"It's not for me," he said.

She looked around. "I'm not sure that squirrel in the tree has the strength to use it."

He smiled, showing even, white teeth. "You're quite funny. I noticed that in your emails. It's no wonder Rafe Wonder likes you."

Rafe *Wonder*. Was that another one of his aliases?

Kevin Leonard laughed. "That's what I call him. Rafe Wonder. Because he's a damn Wonder Boy. Always getting it right. Tenacious. Patriotic to a fault. Guess that's good when you're in a position to be having Sunday dinners at the White House with your old college roommate and his father."

He was jealous of Rafe. Was that what this was about? It had to be more.

He looked at his watch and scowled. This had to be about the person he was expecting. The person the saw was for.

"I would think you'd be happy," she said. "After all, isn't Rafe catching Luciano Maladucci a feather in your cap? After all, you lead the team."

"The agency pays me a pittance," he said. "If you want to get rich, don't work for the government."

"So instead, you work for the Maladuccis," she said.

He looked at the saw with distaste. "This wouldn't be necessary if you and Rafe had died at the cottage the way you were supposed to."

"You launched that rocket," she said. It was the only thing that made sense.

"Yes. When Rafe called to tell me that he'd left the surveillance site because he was ill, I knew he was lying. Rafe would have stuck it out, you know, country before self. There was a reason he left and it had to be a good one. I thought it was possible that he'd gotten word about Milo and his unfortunate demise."

"You did that," she accused. She had not thought it was possible to hate the man more.

He shook his head. "That was Luciano's handiwork. It was humorous, really. Rafe was watching Maladucci's house and the man was already in the United States, had already killed Milo. Anyway, it gnawed at me that Rafe had left a trail that we could so easily follow. Buying the charter flight ticket, renting the car. He was usually much sharper in the field. And I just knew that, somehow, Rafe had managed to leave Italy earlier than we thought. I followed that hunch to Heelie Lake and some lovely young woman with way too many tattoos confirmed that hours earlier a handsome guy driving a BMW had been inquiring about a woman with long red hair. I drove to the cottage, saw the black BMW and thought it was my chance to end it all. The Paradinis, you, Rafe. Everyone dead. Maladucci would have thought I was brilliant to tie things up so neatly."

"You must have been really upset when that plan didn't come together," she said.

"Sh-sh-shut up," he said. He looked down the gravel road.

"Don't you hate it when people aren't on time?" she said, turning slightly, trying to get a better angle to see if he'd left the keys in the ignition.

He had. Fool. Her heart started to race in her chest.

He was a foot too far away for her to land a good kick, but when he came closer, she was going to be ready.

She needed to disable him and get the hell away. Wherever the road led, it had to be better than being here, waiting for some maniac who did his best work with a hacksaw.

Fueled by determination, she got ready.

But then realized that her chances of escape had got significantly less likely when she saw a white SUV crest a hill, still more than a mile away.

"Finally," Leonard said, relief in his voice.

RAFE FOUND THE quarry easily. The front gate was locked up tight for the night. Over the top of the four-foot gate, he could see several buildings but he decided not to search them. One, because he didn't see a black Cadillac. Two, there were no fresh tracks in the heavy dust. And three, most important, she wasn't here; he could feel it.

He knew that a hunch was about the poorest investigative tool a man could employ, but with Trish, he always had a sense when she was nearby.

He kept driving and turned down the first gravel road. He drove fast, with gravel spraying up behind him. They would lose the light within the hour and that would make the search much more difficult.

He drove with one hand, working the edge of his shirt with the other. He had to find her. He could not lose her now.

His phone rang. It was Chase. "Yeah," Rafe answered.

"You've got me and Bray in my car. My other brother, Cal, is in his own car. Daniel Stone is five minutes behind us."

The cavalry had arrived.

"I've called in air support to assist the Hamerton police in looking for the vehicle," Chase said.

"Thank you." It was a good call but somehow Rafe knew that it wouldn't come in time. "I checked the quarry and am—" he waited a couple of seconds until the sign at the crossroads came into view "—just now crossing Tedrow on Rigger."

Chase said something but it didn't register.

Because at just that moment, when he'd crossed the intersection of the two gravel roads, he'd caught a glimpse of another car crossing Tedrow as well, more than half a mile south.

If the crossroads hadn't been perfectly aligned, he'd never have seen it. He hadn't caught the exact make or model of the vehicle but he knew it was a white SUV going way too fast.

That was enough to make him interested. He interrupted whatever it was that Chase was saying. "I just saw a white SUV going east on the first road south of Rigger. I'm going to try to intercept it."

"We'll be on your six," Chase said, promising backup. "ETA of seven minutes."

Rafe hung up and pushed the speedometer up over a hundred. The next crossroad was farther than he'd anticipated and he cursed the idiots who'd plotted the roads. Finally, he got to it. He slowed to forty-five and made a wide turn. Then he picked up speed from there.

Go. Go. Go. For once his heart and his head were saying the same thing.

DEMÍ MALADUCCI WAS a handsome guy. Didn't look much like a killer, she thought. But when she saw his eyes as he approached, she knew, beyond a shadow of a doubt, that was his intent.

He did not greet Kevin Leonard. He simply extended his arm and Leonard handed him the hacksaw. Demí weighed it in his hand.

"Your husband has caused my family a great deal of trouble," he said.

She licked her lips. "I think he'll be even more focused after this."

Demí laughed. "I have an excellent alibi for tonight. Multiple witnesses who will support that I was nowhere near here. He'll know but he'll never be able to prove it. It will eat him alive."

It would. Rafe loved her. Had always been willing to make great sacrifices to ensure her safety. To know that he failed in the end would be horrible for him.

"Of course, I'll have my own trophy," Demí said.

He reached for her and grabbed her arm. Then he dragged her along, across the scraggly lawn, until he stopped and pushed her down on the ground.

She realized she was next to an open well pit. They were going to put her down there.

"Now I'm going to cut off your hand. And it will give me peace when I look at it later knowing that he knows that you died a slow and painful death, bleeding out, with the rats and the snakes sucking at your blood."

He raised the hacksaw and—

Fell face forward, his body pitching into the well.

Trish rolled away from the pit.

When she looked up, she saw Rafe running across the yard, gun in hand. She realized that he'd shot Demí in the back of the head.

"Hands in the air, Leonard," Rafe yelled.

But he didn't have to shoot him because Kevin Leonard took one look at the man charging toward him, took his own gun, put it in his mouth and pulled the trigger.

Chapter Twenty

Reverend Clara Brown, who had married Trish and Rafe four years ago and most recently performed the marriage services for all three of the Hollister brothers, did the funeral service for Milo. As always, she did a beautiful job. She spoke eloquently about the last years of Milo's life and the relationship he'd had with Summer and Trish.

It was a private service. There was Chase and Raney Hollister, Cal and Nalana Hollister, Bray and Summer Hollister, and Rafe and Trish Wright-Roper, along with just a few of the other employees from the Wright Here, Wright Now Café.

Trish held Summer's hand during the service with Rafe at her other side. He kept an arm around her. He pretty much hadn't stopped touching her since he brought her home last night and made love to her in their bed. It seemed as if he needed the assurance that she was alive and well and truly safe.

They were singing the last song when the back door of the small church opened. A woman, maybe fifty-five, with short, crisp, gray hair, came in.

With a dog.

Duke. With a big, clean bandage wrapped around his middle.

The singing stopped and Trish was running down the aisle.

"I'm sorry," the woman apologized. "I didn't realize there was a service going on."

Trish was on her knees, hugging her sweet dog.

"He wandered up to our house about a week ago. He'd been shot. I've been a nurse for thirty years," she said, "and I thought I could fix him up. I didn't realize he was your dog until I went into town this morning. I drove straight here and the people at the gas station on the main street told me I could find you here."

Trish looked up at her husband, who had tears in his eyes. And then she sat on the dusty floor of the old church and let her big dog climb into her lap.

* * * * *

"So we agree to work as a team. For Tommy's sake."

"For Tommy's sake." Lucy took a step closer, and Niall inhaled the scents of baby powder and something slightly more exotic that didn't have anything to do with the infant she was pushing into his arms.

"Since I've convinced you that we're on the same side now, would you feel comfortable watching him for about ten minutes? That's all the time I'll need to freshen up and change so we're ready to go."

Her fingers caught for a moment between Tommy and the placket of Niall's shirt, and even through the pressed cotton, his stomach muscles clenched at the imprint of her knuckles brushing against his skin. But she pulled away to drape a burp rag over his shoulder, apparently unaware of his physiological reactions to her touch and scent.

APB: BABY

BY
JULIE MILLER

MILLS & BOON

First Published in Great Britain 2016
By Mills & Boon, an imprint of HarperCollins*Publishers*
1 London Bridge Street, London, SE1 9GF

© 2016 Julie Miller

ISBN: 978-0-263-91906-6

46-0616

Our policy is to use papers that are natural, renewable and recyclable products and made from wood grown in sustainable forests. The logging and manufacturing processes conform to the legal environmental regulations of the country of origin.

Printed and bound in Spain
by CPI, Barcelona

Julie Miller is an award-winning *USA TODAY* best-selling author of breathtaking romantic suspense—with a National Readers' Choice Award and a Daphne du Maurier Award, among other prizes. She has also earned an *RT Book Reviews* Career Achievement Award. For a complete list of her books, monthly newsletter and more, go to www.juliemiller.org.

For my husband, Scott E. Miller.

I'm so proud of you for writing your stories
and getting them published.

(Welcome to the joys and headaches of being an author.)

Prologue

Dr. Niall Watson would rather be at the crime lab conducting an autopsy instead of standing at the altar, babysitting his brothers.

But saying no to his baby sister on the day of her wedding wasn't an option. Putting on the groomsman's suit and facing the crowd of smiles and tears that filled the church was as much a gift to Olivia and her fiancé as the sterling silver tableware he'd bought at the online department store where they'd registered. If Olivia, the youngest of the four Watson siblings, and the only sister, asked him to keep older brother Duff and younger brother Keir in line today, then Niall would do it. It was a brilliant strategy on her part, he silently admitted. Not only would their rowdier brothers be kept in check, but asking the favor of him was sure to keep Niall engaged in the ceremony. It was smart to give him a specific task to focus on so his mind didn't wander back to the dead body he'd analyzed yesterday morning at the lab in southeast Kansas City, and the follow-up notes he wanted to log in, or to the facts on a drowning victim he wanted to double-check before turning his findings over to the detectives supervising those particular cases.

As a third-generation cop in a close-knit family of law enforcement professionals, it was practically impossible not to be filled with investigative curiosity, or to have dedication and responsibility running through his veins. When it came to work and family, at any rate. And for Niall, there was nothing else. Work filled his life, and the Watson family filled his heart.

Except when they were screwing around—like Duff beside him, running his finger beneath the starched collar of his white shirt and grumbling something about Valentine's Day curses while he fiddled with the knot on his cherry-red tie. Or Keir, chattering up the aisle behind Niall, saying something outrageous enough to the bridesmaid he was escorting to make her giggle. Then Keir patted her hand on his arm and turned to wink at Millie, the family housekeeper-cook they'd all grown up with, as he passed the silver-haired woman in the second pew. The older woman blushed, and Keir blew her a kiss.

Niall adjusted the dark frames of his glasses and nailed Keir with a look warning him to let go of the bridesmaid, stop working the room and assume his place beside him as one of Gabe's groomsmen, already.

"Natalie is married to Liv's partner, you know." The tallest of the three brothers, Niall dropped his chin to whisper under his breath.

"Relax, charm-school dropout." Keir clapped Niall on the shoulder of the black tuxedo he wore, grinning as he stepped up beside him. "Young or old, married or not—it never hurts to be friendly."

Olivia might be the youngest of the four siblings, all third-generation law enforcement who served their city proudly. And she might be the only woman in the tight-knit Watson family since their mother's murder when Niall had barely been a teen. But there was no question that Liv ran the show. Despite Duff's tough-guy grousing or Keir's clever charm or Niall's own reserved, logical prowess, Olivia Mary Watson—soon to be Olivia Knight—had each of them, including their widowed father and grandfather, wrapped around her pretty little finger. If she asked Niall to keep their headstrong Irish family in line today, then he would do exactly that.

With Keir set for the moment, Niall angled his position toward the groom and best man Duff. He didn't need to adjust his glasses to see the bulge at the small of Duff's back beneath the tailored black jacket. Niall's nostrils flared with a patience-inducing breath before he whispered, "Seriously? Are you packing today?"

Duff's overbuilt shoulders shifted as he turned to whisper a response. "Hey. You wear your glasses every day, Poindexter. I wear my gun."

"I wasn't aware that you knew what the term *Poindexter* meant."

"I'm smarter than I look" was Duff's terse response.

Keir chuckled. "He'd have to be."

Duff's muscular shoulders shifted. "So help me, baby brother, if you give me any grief today, I will lay you out flat."

"Zip it. Both of you." Niall knew that he was quickly losing control of his two charges. He scowled at Keir. "You, mind your manners." When Duff went after the collar hugging his muscular neck again, Niall leaned in. "And you stop fidgeting like a little kid."

A curious look from the minister waiting behind

them quieted all three brothers for the moment. With everything ready for their sister's walk down the aisle, the processional music started. Niall scanned the rest of the crowd as they rose to their feet. Their grandfather Seamus Watson hooked his cane over the railing as he stood in the front row. He winked one blue eye at Niall before pulling out his handkerchief and turning toward the aisle to dab at the tears he didn't want anybody to see.

And then Olivia and their father, Thomas Watson, appeared in the archway at the end of the aisle. A fist of rare sentimentality squeezed around Niall's heart.

His father was a relatively tall, stocky man. His black tuxedo and red vest and tie—an homage to the date, February 14—matched Niall's own attire. Niall knew a familiar moment of pride and respect as his father limped down the aisle, his shoulders erect despite the injury that had ended his career at KCPD at far too young an age. Other than the peppering of gray in Thomas's dark brown hair, Niall saw the same face when he looked into the mirror every morning.

But that wasn't what had him nodding his head in admiration.

His sister, that tough tomboy turned top-notch detective, the girl who'd never let three older brothers get the best of her, had grown up. Draped in ivory and sparkles, her face framed by the Irish lace veil handed down through their mother's side of the family, Olivia Watson was a beauty. Dark hair, blue eyes like his. But feminine, radiant. Her gaze locked on to Gabe at the altar, and she smiled. Niall hadn't seen a glimpse of his mother like that in twenty years.

"Dude," Duff muttered. He nudged the groom beside him. "Gabe, you are one lucky son of a—"

"Duff." Niall remembered his charge at the last moment and stopped his older brother from swearing in church.

Gabe sounded a bit awestruck himself as Olivia walked down the aisle. "I know."

"You'd better treat her right," Duff growled on a whisper.

Niall watched his brother's shoulders puff up. "We've already had this conversation, Duff. I'm convinced he loves her."

Gabe never took his eyes off Olivia as he inclined his head to whisper, "He does."

Keir, of course, wasn't about to be left out of the hushed conversation. "Anyway, Liv's made her choice. You think any one of us could change her mind? I'd be scared to try."

The minister hushed the lot of them as father and bride approached.

"Ah, hell," Duff muttered, looking up at the ceiling. He blinked rapidly, pinching his nose. The big guy was tearing up. "This is not happening to me."

"She looks the way I remember Mom," Keir said in a curiously soft voice.

Finally, the gravity of the day was sinking in and their focus was where it should be. Niall tapped Duff's elbow. "Do you have a handkerchief?"

"The rings are tied up in it."

"Here." Niall slipped his own white handkerchief to Duff, who quickly dabbed at his face. He nodded what passed for a thank-you and stuffed the cotton square into his pocket, steeling his jaw against the flare of emotion.

When Olivia arrived at the altar, she kissed their father, catching him in a tight hug before smiling at all three brothers. Duff sniffled again. Keir gave her a thumbs-up. Niall nodded approvingly. Olivia handed her bouquet off to her matron of honor, Ginny Rafferty-Taylor, and took Gabe's hand to face the minister.

The rest of the ceremony continued with everyone on their best behavior until the minister pronounced Gabe and Olivia husband and wife and announced, "You may now kiss the bride."

"Love you," Olivia whispered.

Gabe kissed her again. "Love you more."

"I now present Mr. and Mrs. Gabriel Knight."

Niall pondered the pomp and circumstance of this particular Valentine's Day as the guests applauded and the recessional music started. Logically, he knew the words Liv and Gabe had spoken and what they meant. But a part of him struggled to comprehend exactly how this sappy sort of pageantry equated to happiness and lifelong devotion. It was all a bit wearing, really. But if this was what Olivia wanted, he'd support her whole-heartedly and do whatever was necessary to make it happen.

Following Duff to the center of the aisle, Niall extended his arm to escort bridesmaid Katie Rinaldi down the marble steps. Despite his red-rimmed eyes, Thomas Watson smiled at each of his children. Niall smiled back.

Until he caught the glimpse of movement in the balcony at the back of the church. A figure in black emerged from the shadows beside a carved limestone buttress framing a row of organ pipes.

In a nanosecond frozen in time, a dozen observations blipped through Niall's mind. The organist played away upstairs, unaware of the intruder only a few yards from his position. The figure wore a ski mask and a long black coat. Clearly not a guest. Not church staff. The pews were filled with almost two hundred potential targets, many of them off-duty and retired police officers. His new brother-in-law had made more enemies than friends with his cutting-edge editorials. What did he want? Why was he here? Didn't have to be a cop hater with some kind of vendetta. Could be some crazy with nothing more in mind than making a deadly statement about a lost love or perceived injustice or mental illness.

The gleam of polished wood reflected the colored light streaming in through the balcony's stained-glass windows as the shooter pulled a rifle from his long cloak. Mauser hunting rifle. Five eight-millimeter rounds. He carried a second weapon, a semiautomatic pistol, strapped to his belt. That was enough firepower to do plenty of damage. Enough to kill far too many people.

Time righted itself as the analytical part of Niall's brain shut down and the years of training as a cop and medical officer kicked in. *Move!* Niall shoved Katie to one side and reached for his father as the shooter took aim.

"Gun!" he shouted, pointing to the balcony as his fingers closed around the sleeve of Thomas Watson's jacket. "Get down!"

The *slap, slap, slap* of gunshots exploded through

the church. The organ music clashed on a toxic chord and went silent. Wood splintered and flew like shrapnel. A vase at the altar shattered. Flower petals and explosions of marble dust rained in the air.

"Everybody down!" Duff ordered, drawing the pistol from the small of his back. He dropped to one knee on the opposite side of the aisle and raised his weapon. "Drop it!"

"I'm calling SWAT." Keir ducked between two pews, pulling his phone from his jacket as he hugged his arms around Natalie Fensom and Millie Leighter.

Niall saw Gabe Knight slam his arms around Liv and pull her to the marble floor beneath his body. Guests shouted names of loved ones. A child cried out in fear, and a mother hastened to comfort him. Warnings not to panic, not to run, blended together with the screams and tromping footfalls of people doing just that.

"I've got no shot," Duff yelled, pushing to a crouching position as the shooter dropped his spent rifle and pulled his pistol. Niall heard Keir's succinct voice reporting to dispatch. With a nod from Katie that she was all right and assurance that her husband was circling around the outside aisle to get to her, Niall climbed to his knees to assess the casualties. He caught a glimpse of Duff and a couple of other officers zigzagging down the aisle through the next hail of bullets and charging out the back of the sanctuary. "Get down and stay put!"

Niall squeezed his father's arm. He was okay. He glanced back at the minister crouched behind the pulpit. He hadn't been hit, either. The man in the balcony shouted no manifesto, made no threat. He emptied his gun into the sanctuary, grabbed his rifle and scrambled up the stairs toward the balcony exit. He was making a lot of noise and doing a lot of damage and generating a lot of terror. But despite the chaos, he wasn't hitting anyone. What kind of maniac set off this degree of panic without having a specific—

"Niall!" His grandfather's cane clattered against the marble tiles. Niall was already peeling off his jacket and wadding it up to use as a compress as Thomas Watson cradled the eighty-year-old man in his arms and gently lowered him to the floor. "Help me, son. Dad's been shot."

Chapter One

Niall stepped off the elevator in his condominium building to the sound of a baby crying.

His dragging feet halted as the doors closed behind him, his nostrils flaring as he inhaled a deep, weary breath, pulled the phone from his ear and checked his watch. Two in the morning.

Great. Just great. He had nothing against babies—he knew many of them grew into very fine adults. But he'd been awake going on twenty hours now, had been debriefed six ways to Sunday by cops and family and medical staff alike, hadn't even had a chance to change his ruined fancy clothes, and was already feeling sleep deprived by switching off his typical nocturnal work schedule to be there for Liv's wedding. No way was he going to catch a couple hours of much-needed shut-eye before he headed back to the hospital later this morning.

He put the phone back to his ear and finished the conversation with Duff. "You know we can't investigate this shooting personally. There's a huge conflict of interest since the victim is family."

"Then I'm going to find out which detectives caught the case and make sure they keep us in the loop."

"You do that. And I'll keep track of any evidence that comes through the lab."

"We'll find this guy." Duff's pronouncement was certain. "Get some sleep, Niall."

"You, too." Niall disconnected the call, knowing he couldn't comply with his older brother's directive.

But it wasn't the pitiful noise of the infant's wails, nor the decibel level of distress that solid walls could only mute, that would keep him awake.

His brain's refusal to let a question go unanswered was going to prevent his thoughts from quieting until he could solve the mystery of where that crying baby had come from and to whom the child belonged. As if the events of the day—with his grandfather lying in intensive care and an unidentified shooter on the loose in Kansas City—weren't enough to keep him from sleeping, now a desperately unhappy infant and Niall's own curiosity over the unexpected sound were probably going to eat up whatever downtime he had left tonight. Cursing that intellectual compulsion, Niall rolled his kinked-up neck muscles and started down the hallway.

Considering three of the six condos on this floor were empty, a retired couple in their seventies lived in one at the far end of the hall and Lucy McKane, who lived across the hall from his place, was a single like himself, the crying baby posed a definite mystery. Perhaps the Logans were babysitting one of the many grandchildren they liked to talk about. Either that or Lucy McKane had company tonight. Could she be watching a friend's child? Dating a single dad who'd brought along a young chaperone? Letting a well-kept secret finally reveal itself?

Although they'd shared several early-morning and late-night chats, he and Lucy had never gotten much beyond introductions and polite conversations about the weather and brands of detergent. Just because he hadn't seen a ring on her finger didn't mean she wasn't attached to someone. And even though he struggled with interpersonal relationships, he wasn't so clueless as to think she had to be married or seeing someone in order to get pregnant.

So the crying baby was most likely hers.

Good. Mystery solved. Niall pulled his keys from his pocket as he approached his door. Sleep might just happen.

Or not.

The flash of something red and shiny in the carpet stopped Niall in the hallway between their two doors. He stooped down to retrieve a minuscule shard of what looked like red glass. Another mystery? Didn't building maintenance vacuum out here five days a week? This was a recent deposit and too small to identify the source. A broken bottle? Stained glass? The baby wailed through the door off to his right, and Niall turned his head. He hadn't solved anything at all.

Forget the broken glass. Where and when did Lucy McKane get a baby?

He'd never seen her coming home from a date before, much less in the company of a man with a child. And he was certain he hadn't noticed a baby bump on her. Although she could have been hiding a pregnancy, either intentionally or not. He generally ran into her in the elevator when she was wearing bulky hand-knit sweaters or her winter coat, or in the gym downstairs, where she sported oversize T-shirts with one silly or motivational message or another. And then there were those late-night visits in the basement laundry room, where there'd been clothes baskets and tables between them to mask her belly. Now that he thought about it, Lucy McKane wore a lot of loose-fitting clothes. Her fashion choices tended to emphasize her generous breasts and camouflage the rest of her figure. He supposed she could have been carrying a baby one of those late nights when they'd discussed fabric softener versus dryer sheets, and he simply hadn't realized it.

If that was the case, though, why hadn't he seen the child or heard it crying before tonight? The woman liked to talk. Wouldn't she have announced the arrival of her child?

Maybe he'd rethink other options. It was the wee hours after Valentine's Day. She could be watching the child for a friend out on an overnight date. But why hadn't Lucy gone out for Valentine's Day? The woman was pretty in an unconventional kind of way, if one liked a cascade of dark curls that were rarely tamed, green eyes that were slightly almond shaped and the apple cheeks and a pert little nose that would make her look eternally young. She made friends easily enough, judging by her ability to draw even someone like him into random conversations. And she was certainly well-spoken—at least when it came to washing clothes and inclement weather, gossip about the building's residents and the news of the day. So why wasn't a woman like that taken? Where was *her* date?

And why was he kneeling here in a stained, wrinkled tuxedo and eyes that burned with fatigue, analyzing the situation at all? He needed sleep, desperately. Otherwise, his mind wouldn't be wandering like this.

"Let it go, Watson," he chided himself, pushing to his feet.

Niall turned to the door marked 8C and inserted his key into the lock. At least he could clearly pinpoint the source of the sound now. The noise of the unhappy baby from behind Lucy McKane's door was jarring to his weary senses. He was used to coming home in shrouded silence when his swing shift at the medical examiner's office ended. Most of the residents in the building were asleep by then. He respected their need for quiet as much as he craved it himself. He never even turned on the radio or TV. He'd brew a pot of decaf and sit down with a book or his reading device until he could shut down his thoughts from the evening and turn in for a few hours of sleep. Sending a telepathic brain wave to the woman across the hall to calm her child and allow them all some peace, he went inside and closed the door behind him.

After hanging up his coat in the front closet, Niall switched on lamps and headed straight to the wet bar, where he tossed the sliver of glass onto the counter, unhooked the top button of his shirt and poured himself a shot of whiskey. Sparing a glance for the crimson smears that stained his jacket sleeve and shirt cuffs, he raised his glass to the man he'd left sleeping in the ICU at Saint Luke's Hospital. Only when his younger brother had come in to spell him for a few hours after Keir and Duff had hauled Liv and her new husband, Gabe, off to a fancy hotel where they could spend their wedding night—in lieu of the honeymoon they'd postponed—

had Niall left Seamus Watson's side. "This one's for you, Grandpa."

Niall swallowed the pungent liquor in one gulp, savoring the fire burning down his gullet and chasing away the chill of a wintry night and air-conditioned hospital rooms that clung to every cell of his body. It had been beyond a rough day. His grandfather was a tough old bird, and Niall had been able to stanch the bleeding and stabilize him at the church well enough to keep shock from setting in. He'd ridden with the paramedics to the hospital, and they had done their job well, as had the ER staff. But the eighty-year-old man had needed surgery to repair the bleeders from the bullet that had fractured his skull and remove the tiny bone fragments that had come dangerously close to entering his brainpan and killing him.

Although the attending surgeon and neurologist insisted Seamus was now guardedly stable and needed to sleep, the traumatic brain injury had done significant damage. Either due to the wound itself, or a resulting stroke, he'd lost the use of his left arm and leg, had difficulty speaking and limited vision in his left eye. Seamus was comfortable for now, but age and trauma had taken a toll on his body and he had a long road to recovery ahead of him. And as Niall had asked questions of the doctors and hovered around the nurses and orderlies while they worked, he couldn't help but replay those minutes at the end of the wedding over and over in his head.

Had Seamus Watson been the shooter's intended target? And since the old man seemed determined to live, would the shooter be coming back to finish the job?

Was Grandpa safe? Or was his dear, funny, smarter-than-the-rest-of-them-put-together grandfather a tragic victim of collateral damage?

If so, who had the man with all those bullets really been after? Why plan the attack at the church? Was the Valentine's Day date significant? Was his goal to disrupt the wedding, make a statement against KCPD, or simply to create chaos and validate his own sense of power? Even though others had been hurt by minor shrapnel wounds, and one man had suffered a mild heart attack triggered by the stress of the situation, the number of professionally trained guests had kept the panic to a minimum. So who was the shooter? Duff said he'd chased the perp up onto the roof, but then the man had disappeared before Duff or any of the other officers in pursuit could reach him. What kind of man planned his escape so thoroughly, yet failed to hit anyone besides the Watson patriarch? And if Seamus was the intended target, what was the point of all the extra damage and drama?

And could Niall have stopped the tragedy completely if he'd spotted the man in the shadows a few seconds sooner? He scratched his fingers through the short hair that already stood up in spikes atop his head after a day of repeating the same unconscious habit. Niall prided himself on noting details. But today he'd missed the most important clue of his life until it was too late.

His brothers would be looking into Seamus's old case files and tracking down any enemies that their grandfather might have made in his career on the force, despite his retirement fifteen years earlier. Duff and Keir would be following up any clues found by the officers investigating the case that could lead to the shooter's identity and capture. Frustratingly, Niall's involvement with finding answers was done—unless one of his brothers came up with some forensic evidence he could process at the lab. And even then, Niall's expertise was autopsy work. He'd be doing little more than calling in favors to speed the process and following up with his coworkers at the crime lab. Although it galled him to take a backseat in the investigation, logic indicated he'd better serve the family by taking point on his grandfather's care and recovery so his brothers could focus on tracking down the would-be assassin.

Niall picked up the Bushmills to pour himself a second glass, but the muted cries of the baby across the hall reminded him that he wasn't the only one dealing with hardship tonight, and he returned the bottle to the cabinet. He wanted to have a clear head in the morning when he returned to the hospital for a follow-up report on his grandfather. He could already feel his body surrendering to the tide of fatigue, and despite his unsettling thoughts, he loathed the idea of dulling his intellect before he found the answers he needed. So he set the glass in the sink and moved into the kitchen to start a small pot of decaf.

While the machine hissed and bubbled, he shrugged out of the soiled black tuxedo jacket and draped it over the back of a chair. After pulling out the rented tie he'd folded up into a pocket and laying it over the coat, he went to work unbuttoning the cherry-red vest he wore. Typically, he didn't wear his gun unless he was out in the field at a crime scene. But with his family threatened and too many questions left unanswered, he'd had

Duff unlock it from the glove compartment of Niall's SUV and bring it to the hospital, where he'd strapped it on. Niall halted in the middle of unhooking his belt to remove it, opting instead to roll up his sleeves and leave himself armed. Until he understood exactly what was going on, it would be smart to keep that protection close at hand.

Whether it was the gun's protection, the resumption of his nightly routine or the discordant noise from across the hall receding, Niall braced his hands against the edge of the sink to stretch his back and drop his chin, letting his eyes close as the tension in him gave way to weariness.

The distant baby's cries shortened like staccato notes, as if the child was running out of the breath or energy to maintain the loud wails. Maybe Miss McKane was finally having some success in quieting the infant. Despite how much she liked to talk, she seemed like a capable sort of woman. Sensible, too. She carried her keys on a ring with a small pepper spray canister in her hand each time he saw her walking to or from her car in the parking lot. She wore a red stocking hat on her dark curly hair when the weather was cold and wet to conserve body heat. She sorted her jeans and towels from her whites and colors. Okay, so maybe she wasn't completely practical. Why did a woman need so many different types of underwear, anyway? Cotton briefs, silky long johns, lacy bras in white and tan and assorted pastels, animal prints...

Niall's eyes popped open when he realized he was thinking about Lucy McKane's underwear. And not folded up in her laundry basket or tucked away in a dresser drawer, either.

Good grief. Imagining his neighbor's pale skin outlined in that tan-and-black leopard-print duo he'd found so curiously distracting tossed on top of her folding pile was hardly appropriate. Exhaustion must be playing tricks on him. Pushing away from the sink, Niall clasped his glasses at either temple and adjusted the frames on his face, as if the action could refocus the wayward detour of his thoughts. It was irritating that he could be so easily distracted by curves and cotton or shards of glass or mystery babies who were none of his business when he wanted to concentrate on studying the events before, during and after the shooting at the wedding. Perhaps he should have skipped the shot of whiskey and gone straight for the steaming decaf he poured into a mug.

He added a glug of half-and-half from the fridge and carried the fragrant brew to the bookshelf in the living room, where he pulled out a medical volume to look up some of the details relating to his grandfather's condition. He savored the reviving smell of the coffee before taking a drink and settling into the recliner beside the floor lamp.

Niall had barely turned the first page when the infant across the hall found his second wind and bellowed with a high-pitched shriek that nearly startled him into spilling his drink.

Enough. Was the child sick? Had he completely misjudged Lucy McKane's competence? Niall set his book and mug on the table beside him and pushed to his feet. Maybe the muted noise of a baby crying didn't bother anybody else. Maybe no one else could hear the child's distress. He was so used to the building being quiet at this hour that maybe he was particularly sensitive to the muffled sounds. And maybe he'd come so close to losing someone he loved today that he just didn't have the patience to deal with a neighbor who couldn't respect his need for a little peace and quiet and time to regroup.

In just a few strides he was out the door and across the hall, knocking on Lucy McKane's front door. When there was no immediate response, he knocked harder. "Miss McKane? Do you know how late it is? Some of us are trying to sleep." Well, he hadn't been. But it wasn't as though he could if he even wanted to with that plaintive racket filtering through the walls. "Miss McKane?"

Niall propped his hands at his waist, waiting several seconds before knocking again. "Miss McKane?" Why didn't the woman answer her door? She couldn't be asleep with the baby crying like that, could she? In a heartbeat, Niall's irritation morphed into concern at the lack of any response. That could explain the infant's distress. Maybe Lucy McKane *couldn't* help the child. He flattened his palm against the painted steel and pounded again. "Miss McKane? It's Niall Watson from across the hall. Are you in there? Is everything all right?"

He reached down to jiggle the knob, but the cold metal twisted easily in his hand and the door creaked open a couple of inches.

Niall's suspicion radar went on instant alert. What woman who lived alone in the city didn't keep her door locked?

"Miss McKane?" he called out. But his only response

was the even louder decibel level of the crying baby. He squinted the scratches on the knob into focus and quickly pulled his phone from his pocket to snap a picture. A familiar glint of red glass wedged between the frame and catch for the dead bolt higher up caught his eye. The tiny shattered orb looked like the source of the shard he'd found in the carpet.

Finally. Answers. But he didn't like them.

There were deeper gouges in the wood trim around it, indicating that both locks had been forced. His brain must have been half-asleep not to have suspected earlier that something was seriously wrong. Niall snapped a second picture. "Miss McKane? Are you all right?"

For a few seconds, the concerns of his Hippocratic oath warred with the procedure drilled into him by his police training. His brother Duff would muscle his way in without hesitation, while Keir would have a judge on speed dial, arranging an entry warrant. Niall weighed his options. The baby was crying and Lucy wasn't answering. His concern for the occupants' safety was reason enough to enter a potentially dangerous situation despite risking any kind of legalities. Tonight he'd forgo caution and follow his older brother's example.

"Hold tight, little one," he whispered, unstrapping his holster and pulling the service weapon from his belt. Although he was more used to handling a scalpel than a Glock, as a member of the KCPD crime lab, he'd been trained and certified to use the gun.

He held it surely as he nudged open the broken door. "Miss McKane? It's Niall Watson with the KCPD crime lab. I'm concerned for your safety. I'm coming in."

The mournful wails of a baby crying itself into exhaustion instantly grew louder on this side of the walls separating their living spaces. He backed against the door, closing it behind him as he cradled the gun between both hands. A dim light in the kitchen provided the only illumination in the condo that mirrored the layout of his own place. Allowing his vision to adjust to the dim outlines of furniture and doorways, Niall waited before advancing into the main room. He checked the closet and powder room near the entryway before moving through the living and dining rooms. Empty. No sign of Lucy McKane anywhere. No blood or signs of an accident or struggle of any sort, either. In fact, the only things that seemed out of place were the bundles of yarn, patterns and knitting needles that had been dumped out of their basket onto the coffee table and strewn across the sofa cushions and area rug.

He found the baby in the kitchen, fastened into a carrier that sat on the peninsula countertop, with nothing more than the glow of an automatic night-light beside the stove to keep him company. A half-formed panel of gray knitted wool hung from the baby's toes, as if he'd once been covered with it but had thrashed it aside.

Niall flipped on the light switch and circled around the peninsula, plucking the makeshift blanket off and laying it on the counter. "You're a tiny thing to be making all that noise. You all alone in here? Do you know where your mama is?"

The kid's red face lolled toward Niall's hushed voice. It shook and batted its little fists before cranking up to wail again. Niall didn't need to take a second whiff to ascertain at least one reason why the baby was so unhappy. But a quick visual sweep didn't reveal any sign of a diaper bag or anything to change it into besides the yellow outfit it wore. Had Lucy McKane left the child alone to go make a supply run?

Niall moved the gun down to his side and touched the baby's face. Feverish. Was the kid sick? Or was that what this ceaseless crying did to someone who was maybe only a week or so old?

The infant's cries sputtered into silent gasps as Niall splayed his fingers over its heaving chest. Not unlike his grandfather's earlier that day, the baby's heart was racing. A quick check farther down answered another question for him. "You okay, little man?"

How long had he been left unattended like this?

And where was Lucy? There was no sign of her in the kitchen, either, despite the dirty dishes in the sink and what looked like a congealed glob of cookie dough in the stand mixer beside it. It seemed as though she'd left in the middle of baking a dessert. Why hadn't she completed the task? Where had she gone? What had called her away? And, he thought, with a distinct note of irritation filtering into his thought process, why hadn't she taken the baby with her?

"Hold on." Niall's gaze was drawn to a screwdriver on the counter that didn't look like any piece of cooking equipment he'd ever seen his late mother or Millie Leighter use.

After a couple of silent sobs vibrated through the infant's delicate chest, Niall pulled his hand away. Tuning out the recommencing wail, he opened two drawers before he found a plastic bag and used it to pick up the tool. The handle was an absurd shade of pink with shiny baubles glued around each end of the grip. He rolled it in his hand until he found what he suspected he might—an empty space in the circle of fake stones. Niall glanced back through the darkened apartment. The bead stuck in the frame of her door suddenly made sense. But even if his neighbor had lost her key and had to break into her own place, she'd turn on the lights once she got in. There'd be signs of her being here. And she'd damn well take care of the baby.

Unless she wasn't the one who'd broken in.

"Don't go anywhere," he ordered needlessly. Wrapping the screwdriver securely in the bag, Niall slipped it into his pocket and clasped the gun between his hands again. "I'll be right back."

A quick inspection through the bedroom and en suite showed no sign of Lucy McKane there, either. He didn't see her purse anywhere, and her winter coat and accoutrements were missing from the front closet. There was no baby paraphernalia in any of the rooms.

Had she been kidnapped? What kind of kidnapper would leave evidence like the screwdriver behind? Had she been robbed? Nothing here seemed disturbed beyond the topsy-turvy knitting basket, and anything of typical value to a thief—her flat-screen TV, a laptop computer—was still here.

More unanswered questions. Niall's concern reverted to irritation.

This child had been abandoned. Lucy McKane was gone, and the woman had a lot of explaining to do.

Niall was surprisingly disappointed to learn that she was the type of woman to leave an infant alone to run errands or enjoy a date. She was a free spirit, certainly, with her friendly smile and ease at striking up conversations with neighbors she barely knew and ownership of far too many pairs of panties. But she'd told him she was a social worker, for pity's sake. He wouldn't have pegged her to be so self-absorbed and reckless as to leave a child in an unlocked apartment—to leave the child, period. *If* she'd left by choice.

With the mandate of both his badge and his medical degree, and three generations of protecting those who couldn't protect themselves bred into him, Niall could not walk out that door and abandon this baby himself. So, understanding as much about children as his medical books could teach, he tucked his gun into its holster, pulled his phone from his pocket and picked up the baby in its carrier. He spared a glance at the soft wood around the deadbolt catch, debating whether or not he should retrieve the decorative bead jammed there or report Lucy as a missing person. Making the crying infant his first priority, Niall closed the door behind him and carried the baby into his apartment before dialing the most knowledgeable parent he knew.

The phone picked up on the third ring. "Niall?"

"Dad." He set the carrier on the island in his own kitchen and opened a drawer to pull out two clean dish towels. A quick glance at his watch indicated that perhaps he should have thought this through better. "Did I wake you?"

"It's three in the morning, son. Of course you did." Thomas Watson pushed the grogginess from his voice. "Are you still at the hospital? Has there been a change in Dad's condition?"

"No. The doctors are keeping Grandpa lightly sedated. Keir will stay with him until one of us relieves him in the morning."

"Thank God one of my boys is a doctor and that you were there to give him the treatment he needed immediately. We should be giving thanks that he survived and no one else was seriously injured. But knowing that the bastard who shot him is still…" Thomas Watson's tone changed from dark frustration to curious surprise. "Do I hear a baby crying?"

Niall strode through his apartment, retrieving a towel and washcloth along with the first-aid kit and a clean white T-shirt from his dresser. "Yes. Keir will contact me if there is any change in Grandpa's condition. I told Grandpa one or all of us would be by to see him in the morning, that the family would be there for him 24/7. I'm not sure he heard me, though."

"Dad heard you, I'm sure." Niall could hear his father moving now, a sure sign that the former cop turned investigative consultant was on his feet and ready for Niall to continue. "Now go back to the other thing. Why do you have a baby?"

Niall had returned to the kitchen to run warm water in the sink. "Can I ask you a favor?"

"Of course, son."

"Dad, I need newborn diapers, bottles and formula. A clean set of clothes and some kind of coat or blanket or whatever babies need when it's cold. A car seat, too, if you can get your hands on one at this time of night. I'll reimburse you for everything, of course." Niall put the phone on speaker and spread a thick towel out on the counter, pausing for a moment to assess the locking mechanism before unhooking the baby and lifting him from the carrier. "Good Lord, you don't weigh a thing."

"The baby, Niall." That tone in his father's voice had always commanded an answer. "Is there something you need to tell me?"

"It's the neighbor's kid," Niall explained. "I'd get the items myself, but I don't have a car seat and can't leave him alone. Oh, get something for diaper rash, too. He needs a bath. I can use a clean dish towel to cover him up until you get here, although I don't have any safety pins. Do you think medical tape would work to hold a makeshift diaper on him until you arrive?"

"You're babysitting? I never thought I'd see the day—"

"Just bring me the stuff, Dad."

Another hour passed before Thomas Watson arrived with several bags of supplies. His father groused about bottles looking different from the time Olivia had been the last infant in the house and how there were far too many choices for a feeding regimen. But between the two of them, they got the baby diapered, fed and dressed in a footed sleeper that fit him much better than Niall's long T-shirt. At first, Niall was concerned about the infant falling asleep before finishing his first bottle. But he roused enough for Thomas to coax a healthy burp out of him before drinking a little more and crashing again. Niall was relieved to feel the baby's temperature return to normal and suspected the feverish state had been pure stress manifesting itself.

The infant boy was sleeping in Thomas Watson's lap as the older man dozed in the recliner, and Niall was reviewing a chapter on pediatric medicine when he heard the ding of the elevator at the end of the hallway. He closed the book and set it on the coffee table, urging his waking father to stay put while he went to the door.

He heard Lucy McKane's hushed voice mumbling something as she approached and then a much louder, "Oh, my God. I've had a break-in."

Niall swung open his door and approached the back of the dark-haired woman standing motionless before her apartment door. She had turned silent, but he knew exactly what to say. "Miss McKane? You and I need to talk."

Chapter Two

"The man wasn't following me," Lucy chanted under her breath for the umpteenth time since parking her car downstairs. She stepped off the elevator into the shadowed hallway, trying to convince herself that the drunken ape who'd offered to rock her world down on Carmody Street wasn't the driver of the silver sports car she'd spotted in her rearview mirror less than a block from her condominium building a few minutes earlier. "He wasn't following me."

Maybe if she hadn't spotted a similar car veering in and out of the lane behind her on Highway 71, she wouldn't be so paranoid. Maybe if her voice mail at work didn't have a message from her ex-boyfriend Roger that was equal parts slime and threat and booze.

"Guess what, sweet thing. I'm out. And I'm coming to see you."

Maybe if it wasn't so late, maybe if she'd felt safe in that run-down part of Kansas City, maybe if she wasn't so certain that something terrible had happened to Diana Kozlow, her former foster daughter, who'd called her out of the blue yesterday after more than a year of no contact—maybe if the twenty-year-old would

answer her stupid phone any one of the dozen times
Lucy had tried to call her back—she wouldn't feel so
helpless or alone or afraid.

Fortunately, the silver car had driven past when she'd
turned in to the gated parking garage. But the paranoia
and a serious need to wash the man's grimy hands off
her clothes and skin remained. "He was *not* following me."

She glanced down at the blurred picture she'd
snapped through her rear window the second time the
silver roadster had passed a car and slipped into the lane
behind her on 71. Her pulse pounded furiously in her
ears as she slipped the finger of her glove between her
teeth and pulled it off her right hand to try and enlarge
the picture and get a better look at the driver or read a
possible license plate. Useless. No way could she prove
the Neanderthal or Roger or anyone else had followed
her after leaving the rattrap apartment building on Carmody, which was the last address she had for Diana. Not
that it had been a productive visit. The super had refused
to speak to her, and the only resident who would answer
her questions about Diana was an elderly woman who
couldn't remember a young brunette woman living in
the building, and didn't recognize her from the old high
school photo Lucy had shown her. Ape man had been
willing to tell her anything—in exchange for stepping
into the alley with him for a free grope.

None of which boded well for the life Diana had
forged for herself after aging out of the foster system
and leaving Lucy's home. Lucy swiped her finger across
the cell screen to pull up the high school photo of the
dark-haired beauty she'd thought would be family—or

at least a close friend—forever. "Oh, sweetie, what have you gotten yourself into?" she muttered around the red wool clasped between her teeth.

She glanced back at the elevator door, remembered the key card required to get into the building lobby.

"Okay. The creeper didn't follow me," she stated with as much conviction as she could muster. "And I will find you, Diana."

She was simply going to have to get a few hours' sleep and think this through and start her search again tomorrow. Except...

Lucy pulled up short when she reached the door to 8D. The late-night chill that had iced her skin seeped quickly through the layers of clothing she wore.

"Oh, my God. I've had a break-in."

So much for feeling secure.

The wood around the locks on her apartment door was scratched and broken. The steel door itself drifted open with barely a touch of her hand. Lucy retreated half a step and pulled up the keypad on her phone to call the police. After two previous calls about Diana's failure to show up for lunch or return her calls, they were probably going to think she was a nutcase to call a third time in fewer than twenty-four hours.

"Miss McKane? You and I need to talk."

Lucy's fear erupted in a startled yelp at the succinct announcement. She swung around with her elbow at the man's deep voice behind her, instinctively protecting herself.

Instead of her elbow connecting with the man's solar plexus, five long fingers clamped like a vise around her wrist and she was pushed up against the wall by a tall, lanky body. Her phone popped loose from her slippery grip and bounced across the carpet at her feet. Her heart thumped in her chest at the wall of heat trapping her there, and the loose glove she'd held between her teeth was caught between her heaving breasts and the broad expanse of a white tuxedo shirt. What the devil? Diana was missing, and she had no idea why her tall, lanky neighbor was glowering down at her through those Clark Kent glasses he wore.

"Wow," she gasped, as the frissons of fear evaporated once she recognized him. No one else roamed the hallways this time of night except for him. She should have known better. "Sorry I took a swing at you, Dr. Watson." She couldn't even summon the giggly response she usually had when she said his name and conjured up thoughts of medical sidekicks and brainy British detectives. Not when she was embarrassingly aware of his hard runner's body pressed against hers. Nothing to giggle about there. The full-body contact lasted another awkward moment. "I didn't hurt you, did I?"

"Of course not." Once he seemed certain she recognized him as a friend and didn't have to defend himself, Niall Watson released his grip on her arm and stepped away, leaving a distinct chill in place of that surprising male heat that had pinned her to the wall. "I shouldn't have startled you."

"I thought you…were someone else."

"Who? Were you expecting someone?"

"I, um…" She wasn't about to explain her paranoid suspicions about ape man or Roger and the silver car, so she covered her rattled state by stooping down to retrieve her glove and phone. "Sorry if I woke you. I've

had a break-in. I thought this was supposed to be a secure building in a safe neighborhood, but I guess there's
no place that's truly safe if someone is determined to get
to you. That's probably why I swung first. A girl has to
take care of herself, you know. I'd better call the police."

Niall Watson's long fingers reached her phone first.
He scooped it up and tapped the screen clear. "A 911
call won't be necessary."

Frowning at his high-handedness, Lucy tilted her
face up. "Why not?" She was halfway to making eye
contact when she saw the crimson spots staining his
rolled-up sleeve. She stuffed her loose glove into her
pocket, along with her phone, and touched her fingertip
to the red stains on the wrinkled white cotton clinging
to his long, muscular forearm. There were more drop-
lets of blood on the other sleeve, too. Irritation vanished,
and she piled concern for him onto the fears that had
already worn her ragged today.

"Are you hurt? Did you stop the intruder?" She
grasped his wrist in her hand, much the same way he'd
manhandled her, and twisted it to find the wound. Despite the tempting awareness at his toasty-warm skin
beneath her chilled fingers, she was more interested in
learning what had happened. She knew he was affiliated
with the police. Had he stepped in to prevent a burglar
from ransacking her place? Had Roger followed his release from prison with a road trip to Kansas City? Had
Diana shown up while she was searching the city for
her? Now she looked up and met those narrowed cobalt
eyes. "Have you already called for help? Do I need to
take you to the hospital?"

A dark eyebrow arched above the rim of his glasses

before he glanced down to see the source of her concern. Blinking away his apparent confusion, he pulled out of her grip to splay his fingers at his waist. "This isn't my blood."

"Then whose…?" His stance drew her attention to the holster strapped to his belt. Had she ever seen Niall Watson wearing a gun before? His badge, yes. But she'd never seen the erudite professional looking armed and dangerous the way he did tonight. Had he just come from a crime scene? "You wore a tuxedo to work?" Wait. Not his blood. That meant… A stone of dread plummeted into Lucy's stomach. Was that Diana's blood? "Oh, God." Before he could say anything, she spun around and shoved open the door to her apartment. "Diana?" Niall Watson was a doctor. But he wasn't hurt. That meant someone else was. "Diana? Are you here?"

She called out again for some sign that the young woman she'd been searching the city for all day and night had somehow shown up here.

The vise clamped over her wrist again and pulled her back to the door. "Miss McKane."

"Let go of me." She yanked her arm free and charged toward the mess on the couch. "Diana?" She paused a moment to sift through the pile of unraveling yarn and interrupted projects before snatching up the overturned basket and inspecting the insides. Lucy always kept a twenty or two hidden beneath her work. The only other person who knew where she stockpiled for a rainy day was Diana. "She was here. She took the cash," she whispered, her sense of dread growing exponentially.

"So it *was* a robbery?"

She startled at the deep voice beside her. "What? No. I would gladly give her the money."

"Give who the money?"

"Diana?" Lucy tossed the basket onto the couch and took off for the light in the kitchen.

But she hadn't taken two steps before Niall Watson's arm cinched around her waist and pulled her back against his chest. "Miss McKane. There's nothing for you to see here. I need you to come with me."

She gasped at the unexpected contact with a muscled torso and the surprising warmth that seemed to surround her instantly and seep through the layers of coat and clothing she wore. "Nothing? I have to..." For a split second, her fingers tightened their grip around the arm at her waist, needing his strength. She'd had a bad feeling all day. Diana Kozlow hadn't shown up for a long-overdue lunch and gab session. And then that phone call...

If the answer was here—even one she didn't want to be true—Lucy had to see for herself. With a renewed sense of urgency, she pushed the doctor's arm and body heat away and turned. "You need to stop grabbing me, Doctor. I appreciate your concern, but I have to—"

She shoved at his chest, but he released her waist only to seize her by the shoulders. He squeezed enough to give her a little shake and hunched his face down to hers. "Lucy. If you would please listen."

Lucy? Her struggles stilled as she assessed the stern expression stamped on his chiseled features. When had her taciturn neighbor ever addressed her as anything but a polite *Miss McKane*? That couldn't be good. The tight grip on her upper arms and the piercing intensity of those blue eyes looking straight at her weren't any kind of reassurance, either. She curled her fingers into the wrinkled cotton of his shirt and nodded, preparing herself for the news she didn't want to hear. "What's wrong? What's happened? Did you see a young woman here? Is she…" Lucy swallowed hard. "Is she okay?"

He eased his grip and straightened, raking one hand through his short muss of espresso-colored hair as he inhaled a deep breath. But he kept the other hand on her arm as if he suspected she might bolt again. "If you would come with me." He pulled her back into the hallway and closed the door to her condo behind them. "I need to ask you some questions."

Now he wanted to talk? After all those friendly overtures she'd made to her seriously hunky and completely-oblivious-to-a-lady-dropping-a-hint neighbor, tonight of all nights was when he wanted to have a private conversation with her? Somehow she doubted that he'd finally clued in on the crush she had on him. Preparing herself for a worst-case scenario, Lucy planted her feet before blithely following him into his condo. "Just tell me. Did you find a dead body in there? You told me you were a medical examiner during one of our elevator rides together when I first moved in. That's when I told you I was a social worker—that I've seen some pretty awful things, too. But my bodies weren't dead like yours. Just damaged in one way or another." Her mouth was rambling ahead of her brain. "I'm sorry. But you can tell me. Is this a crime scene? Is that why I can't go in there?" She touched the blood on his sleeve again. Although it was dry, its presence was disturbing. "Is this Diana's? Don't feel you have to spare my feel-

ings. I've been sick out of my mind with worry all day.
I just need a straight answer about what's happened. I
can deal with anything—I'm good at that—as long as
I know what I'm facing."

"You can deal with anything?" He angled his head
to the side and his eyes narrowed, as if her plaintive assertion baffled him. Then he shook his head. "There is
no dead body," he answered starkly. "I don't know who
Diana is. This blood is my grandfather's. He was shot
yesterday afternoon at my sister's wedding."

"Shot? Oh, my God." Lucy's fingers danced over the
ticklish hair of his forearm, wanting to act on her instinct to touch, to comfort, to fix the hurts of the world.
"Is he okay? I mean, clearly he isn't. Getting shot is
really bad. I'm sorry. Is he going to be all right?" His
brusque answers explained the remnants of the James
Bond getup, as well as the stains on what had once been
a neatly ironed shirt. But what any of that had to do with
the break-in or her or possibly Diana, she hadn't a clue.
Lucy curled her fingers around the strap of her shoulder bag and retreated a step. "You don't need to worry
about my problems. You should be with your family."

"Miss McKane." They were back to that now, hmm?
"I'm sorry if the blood upset you—I haven't had time
to change since coming home from the hospital." He
scraped his palm over the dark stubble dotting his chin
and jaw before sliding his fingers over his hair and literally scratching his head. "I can see I haven't explained
myself very well. Your sympathy is appreciated but
misplaced. My grandfather's condition is serious, but
please, before you go off on another tangent, would
you come inside? I do have a problem that concerns

you specifically." He glanced toward the end of the hallway. "And I don't think we should have that conversation here."

She remembered the retired couple down the hall and nodded. "The Logans. I suppose it would be rude to wake them at this hour."

A man with a wounded grandfather, a gun and a badge, and an inexplicable sense of urgency could take precedence for a few minutes over her suspicions and the futile desperation that might even be unfounded. Lucy hadn't seen Diana Kozlow in months. Perhaps she'd read too much into the telephone message at the office this morning. She was probably chasing ghosts, thinking that Diana had really needed her. Roger Campbell hadn't needed her for anything more than sex and a punching board. The only reason her own mother had needed her was to ensure her own meal ticket. How many times did she have to repeat that codependent mistake?

Inhaling a deep breath, Lucy pulled off her left glove and cap and stuffed them into her pockets, too, as Niall opened the door for her to precede him. "So what concerns me specifically besides a busted front door…" She tried to smooth her staticky curls behind her ears. "Oh, hello."

At this late hour, she was surprised to see another man—a stockier version of Niall Watson, with a peppering of silver in his short dark hair—rising stiffly from a recliner as she stepped into the living room.

She extended her hand because she was that kind of friendly. "I'm Lucy McKane from across the hall. Sorry to visit so late, but Dr. Watson invited me…" The older man angled his body to face her, and she saw the blanket with tiny green and yellow animals draped over his arm. "You have a baby."

"Can't put anything past you," the tall man teased in a hushed voice, in deference to the tiny infant sleeping contentedly against his chest. "Thomas Watson." He easily cradled the child in one arm to shake her hand. "I raised three boys and a girl of my own, so I've had some practice. I'm Niall's father."

"I could tell by the family resemblance. Nice to meet you. You seem to be a natural." Lucy stepped closer to tuck the loose blanket back around the tiny child's head. The newborn's scent was a heady mix of gentle soap and something slightly more medicinal. A tightly guarded longing stirred inside her, and she wanted to brush aside the wisp of dark brown hair that fell across the infant's forehead. She wisely curled her fingers into her palm and smiled instead. "And this is…?"

Niall's crisp voice sounded behind her. "I was hoping you could tell us."

Lucy swiveled her head up to his as he moved in beside her. "I don't understand. Isn't the baby yours?" She glanced at Niall's father. He was older, yes, but by her quick assessment, still a virile man. "My apologies. The baby is yours."

"No, ma'am."

The older man grinned, but Niall looked anything but amused when he reached across her to adjust the blanket she'd tidied a moment earlier. "*I* broke into your apartment, Miss McKane."

"You? To steal twenty dollars? Why on earth would you do that?"

"I wasn't the first intruder. I found a screwdriver that had apparently been used to break into your place." He pulled a tiny gem from his pocket and held it up between his thumb and forefinger, twisting it until she could see the fracture in the clear red glass. "I believe this came off it."

"A screwdriver?" Lucy clutched at her purse strap, the bittersweet joy of seeing the baby momentarily forgotten. Diana *was* in trouble. "A pink one with glitter on the handle?"

He picked up a bag marked with numbers and the scratch of his signature from the coffee table and folded the excess plastic out of the way so she could see the contents inside. "This one."

"Oh, my God." Lucy plucked the screwdriver from his open palm and turned it over in her hand. The room swayed at the instant recognition. Diana hadn't wanted jewelry or dolls for birthdays and Christmas. She'd been a tomboy and tough-kid wannabe from their first meeting. Diana had wanted a basketball and running shoes and a toolbox, although she'd seemed pleased with the bling on this particular set. Lucy blinked away the tears that scratched at her eyes and tilted her face to Niall's. "Where did you get this?"

"Is it yours?"

"Answer my question."

"Answer mine."

"Niall," Thomas gently chided.

A deep, resolute sigh expanded Niall Watson's chest before he propped his hands at his waist again in that vaguely superior stance that emphasized both his height and the width of his shoulders. If it wasn't for his glasses and the spiky muss of his hair that desperately needed a comb, she might have suspected he had an ego to go with all that intellect. "Apparently, someone jimmied the locks on your door several hours before I got home, and I suspect they used that tool to do it. I let myself in when I heard this child crying in distress. I thought, perhaps, you weren't being responsible—"

"With a child?" He thought…that she… Lucy didn't know whether to cry or smack him. "I would never. My job is to protect children."

"I know that." Her burst of defensive anger eased as he continued his account.

"But then I suspected that you might be in some kind of distress yourself. I entered the premises to make sure you were all right." He plucked the screwdriver from her fingers and returned it to the table along with the shattered bead and another bag that appeared to be holding the beginnings of the gray scarf she'd been knitting for a coworker. She could see now that the markings meant he'd labeled them all as evidence. "I found it on your kitchen counter beside the baby. I brought him here since there didn't seem to be anyone else watching him. We've given him food, clean clothes and a bath. Other than a nasty case of diaper rash, he seems to be healthy."

That explained the medicinal smell. "It's a boy?" She turned back to the older man cradling the sleeping infant. "He was in my apartment? All alone?"

"I believe that's what I've been saying." Niall Watson could sound as irritated with her as he wanted. He'd saved this child, and for that, she would be forever grateful.

Lucy pressed her fingers to her mouth to hold back

the tears that wanted to fall. Tears that wouldn't do anyone any good. Diana's cryptic phone message that had sent Lucy on a wild hunt all over Kansas City finally made sense. "That's what she wanted to show me. I had no idea. The baby is what she wanted me to take care of. But why wouldn't she stay, too?"

"What are you talking about, Miss McKane?"

"I have a favor to ask, Lucy. I don't know who else to call. I need to show you something, and I need you to keep it safe."

"Why didn't she tell me?" Lucy whispered. She couldn't help but reach out to stroke her finger across the infant's cheek. His skin was as velvety soft as it looked, and she was instantly in love. "You precious little boy."

"Do you know who is responsible for this child?" Niall asked.

"Possibly." Lifting her gaze to Niall's father, Lucy held out her hands. "May I?"

"Of course."

Lucy sighed with a mixture of longing and regret as the baby's sweet weight filled her arms and settled against her. "He's so tiny. How old do you think he is?"

"I'd say a week. Two, tops," Niall answered from behind her. "Obviously, pediatrics isn't my area of expertise, but I know enough to handle the basics. I still think he needs to see a pediatric specialist to ensure a clean bill of health. Now what can you tell us about his parents?" Niall stepped aside as she circled the coffee table and sat on the edge of his sofa to hold the baby more securely. She heard a huff of what could be resignation a second before the cushion beside her sank with his weight. When she tumbled toward her tall neighbor at her shifting perch, his hands shot out to balance her shoulder and cradle her forearm that held the baby. "Easy. Don't let go of him."

"I couldn't."

Niall's hand remained beneath her arm, making sure of her hold on the infant. His chest pressed against Lucy's shoulder, and for a split second she was overcome by the normalcy of the family she'd never known and would never have. A mother, a father, a child they shared together. The yearning inside her was almost painful.

Blinking rapidly to dispel the impossible image of the brainy doctor cop and her creating a perfect little baby together, Lucy scooted away to break the contact between her and Niall Watson, although she could still feel that crazily addictive warmth he radiated. "What's his name?" she asked, craving the information as much as she needed to put space between her and her errant fantasies.

"He didn't come with an ID," Niall answered. "He didn't come with anything. Not even a fresh diaper. If you could answer at least some of my questions—"

"Son." The older Watson chided the tone in Niall's voice and offered her a smile. "I nicknamed him Tommy. But that's just a family name I was using so we could call him something besides 'little munchkin.' We were hoping you'd be able to fill in the blanks for us. But I take it you're not the mother."

His green eyes were kind, but Lucy still felt the sting of truth. "No. I... I can't have children of my own."

"I'm sorry. You seem like a natural with Tommy, too."

His kind words enabled her to smile back. "Thank you." But a glance up to the man seated beside her indicated that answers were the only thing that was going to soften that empirical focus zeroed in on her. He was this baby's champion, and nothing short of the entire truth was going to satisfy him. "I think... Tommy..." She stroked her fingertip over his tiny lips, and they instinctively moved to latch on, even though he was asleep. "I have no idea who the father is. But I think he belongs to my foster daughter, Diana Kozlow."

Niall's posture relaxed a fraction, although that stern focus remained. "The woman whose name you kept calling out."

Lucy nodded. "Technically, she's my former foster daughter. Diana was with me for six years until she aged out of the system. She's twenty now. We kept in touch for a year or so. But I lost contact with her after that. She changed her number, changed her job. I had no idea she'd gotten pregnant." She nodded toward the screwdriver on the coffee table. "I gave that to her in a tool set one Christmas. I guess she broke into my apartment to leave the baby with me. Probably took the twenty I had stashed in my knitting basket. She called me out of the blue yesterday—said she had some*thing* she wanted to show me. I invited her for lunch today, but she never came. I tried calling the number she used, but the phone went straight to voice mail."

She rocked back and forth, ever so subtly, soothing the infant as he began to stir. "I went to my office to look up her most recent address and phone number to make sure I had it right—and discovered she'd left me a pretty disturbing message on my answering machine there. I've been out looking for her ever since. One of the neighbors at the last address where I knew her to live said Diana had a boyfriend move in with her about six months ago. She never knew his name, so that was a dead end. Shortly after that they moved to Carmody Street, she thought—"

"Carmody?" The elder Watson muttered a curse under his breath. "That's not a good part of town. You didn't go there to look for her by yourself, did you? At the police department, we call that part of town no-man's-land."

"I can believe it." The two men exchanged a grim look. "No one there recognized Diana, and they couldn't tell me the boyfriend's name, either. I wasn't sure where to look after that. How does a young woman just…disappear?" Lucy's thoughts drifted to all the morbid possibilities that had driven her to search for Diana. "Why wouldn't she keep Tommy with her? Why wouldn't she stay at my place with him if she was in trouble?"

"*If* she's the mother," Niall cautioned. "We'd have to blood-type him and run DNA on both mother and son to be certain."

A DNA test couldn't tell Lucy what she already knew in her heart. "He looks like her—the shape of his face, the thick dark hair. What color are his eyes?"

Thomas shrugged. "You know, I don't remem—"

"Brown," Niall answered.

Lucy glanced up when he reached around her to tuck in the tiny fist that had pushed free of the blanket. She didn't mind Niall's unvarnished tone quite so much this time. He'd put his clinical eye for detail to work on doing whatever was best for this baby. "Diana has brown eyes."

Niall's startling blue gaze shifted to hers for a moment before he blinked and rose from the couch. He paced to the kitchen archway before turning to ask, "Did you save that message?"

Lucy nodded.

The two men exchanged a suspicious sort of glance before Thomas picked up a notepad and pen from the table beside the recliner. Niall adjusted his glasses on the bridge of his nose before splaying his fingers at his waist and facing her. "Maybe you'd better tell me more about your friend Diana. And why you thought she might be dead."

Chapter Three

Lucy added another round of quarters to the clothes dryer. "Oops. Sorry, munchkin."

She quickly apologized for the loud mechanical noise and leaned over the infant fastened into the carrier sitting on top of the dryer. But she needn't have worried. Tommy was still asleep, his tiny body swaying slightly with the jiggle of the dryer. She smiled, resisting the urge to kiss one of those round apple cheeks, lest she wake him again. He'd fussed and bellowed for nearly an hour upstairs before she remembered the advice she'd once heard from a coworker about tricks to help stubborn babies fall asleep and got the idea to bring Tommy and all his new clothes and supplies down to the basement laundry room to wash them.

Instead of disturbing him again, she opted to pull a blanket dotted with red, blue and yellow trucks from the basket of baby clothes she'd just unloaded and drape the cotton knit over him, securing him in a warm cocoon. Then she picked up the basket and set it on the neighboring dryer to start folding the rest of the light-colored sleepers and towels and undershirts. She was handling more than one problem here. She'd removed the noisy

baby from Niall Watson's apartment so the enigmatic
doctor could get some much-needed sleep. Since she
had no chair to rock the baby in, she'd found the next
best thing down here in the laundry room. And at this
time of the morning, before the residents stirred to get
ready for church or work, she'd found a quiet place
for herself to think without being distracted by hunky
neighbors with grabby hands and hard bodies, or caring
for the needs of a newborn with too little sleep herself,
or worrying about the unanswered calls and cryptic
clues surrounding her foster daughter's disappearance.

When the second load of darker clothes was done
in twenty minutes or so, she'd take Tommy back up to
Niall Watson's apartment and sneak back in without
waking him. Then she'd have another hour or two to
curl up on his stiff leather couch and try not to notice
how much the smell of it reminded her of the man himself. Crushes were terrible things when they were one-
sided like this. Niall Watson, ME, was a good catch,
according to her mother's standards—not that she cred-
ited Alberta McKane for giving her any useful set of
values to judge a man by. But he was as dependable as
he was curiously aloof, and that was a quality Lucy val-
ued more than several framed degrees or the amount of
money a man made. She vowed to be a good friend to
her socially awkward neighbor, but she didn't have to
torture her dreams with the vivid memory of his body
flattened against hers as he pinned her to the wall. If
he was a different man he'd have kissed her then. And
chances are, she would have responded to that kiss with
a purely female instinct.

But Niall Watson wasn't that man. He had a set of

rules he lived by, an order of right and wrong he believed in. He wasn't a smooth talker. He wasn't much of a talker, period. But, awkward body contact aside, he treated her with respect. He put Tommy's and his family's needs above anything he and his hormones might feel. And that made him so much more attractive to her than anything her mother could have envisioned.

Stress, fatigue, the rhythmic sound of the dryer and the warmth of the insulated laundry area were beginning to have the same hypnotic effect on Lucy as they did on Tommy. After several big blinks, her thoughts drifted and her hands came to rest in the pile of warm cotton garments. Her chin was dropping toward her chest when hushed voices entered her dreams. "Down here."

"Are you sure?"

"If her car's outside, but she's not at her place, then yes."

"This is a mistake."

"I just have to know—"

"Get out of here."

Lucy snapped her head up at the slam of a heavy door from somewhere above her. The muffle of words weren't inside her head. They were as real as the terse, angry exchange of voices bouncing off the concrete-block walls outside the laundry room. She touched the gentle rise and fall of Tommy's small chest, reassuring herself that he was safe, while she blinked the grogginess from her eyes and reoriented herself to the waking world. "Hello? Is someone there?"

"I know you're here," came a heavily accented voice. "You can't take what is mine."

Lucy thought she heard a bell. Someone getting off the elevator?

Or on it. "Move. Don't let him see you. Go!"

"Where is she?" the louder voice shouted. "You know what I want."

Lucy whirled around to the vicious argument, wondering if she was still half-asleep since she couldn't make out all the words.

"You stay away from her."

"You mind your own business."

Then she heard a grunt and a gasp plainly enough, before running feet stomped up the stairs.

"Diana?" Had she heard a woman's voice in the middle of all that? Or only dreamed it? Lucy fingered the phone in her jeans pocket. But the sounds of the argument were fading and she didn't want to panic the good doctor upstairs unnecessarily by waking him from a sound sleep.

"You stay away from her."

Oh, no. "Stay away from *me*?" Maybe Niall was already awake and dealing with some kind of trouble that she'd missed. What if someone *had* followed her to their apartment building and her neighbor had come downstairs to confront him? "Niall?"

If he got hurt, it would be her fault for getting him into this mess.

After ensuring that Tommy was still sleeping, Lucy ventured out into the hallway. It was empty now. Nothing but concrete walls and utility lights. Had the two parties she'd overheard arguing split up? The elevator was moving on the higher floors of the building, and whomever she'd heard run up the stairs had exited either out the side entrance to the parking lot or into the building's lobby. "Niall? Is that you? Who was—"

Lucy jumped at the loud thump against the steel door at the top of the stairs. Outside. They'd taken what could only be a fight, judging by the low-voiced curses and rattling door, out to the parking lot. "Niall!"

Lucy charged up the stairs, pulling her key card from her jeans and hurrying out the door to the harsh sounds of a revving engine and tires squealing to find traction along the pavement. She saw the silhouette of a man racing between the cars. "Niall? Hey! Don't hurt him!"

She glanced toward the front entrance as one of the glass doors swung open. Was help coming? Or more trouble? She should call 911. She reached for her phone.

But when she saw the running figure lurch as if some invisible force had jerked him back a step, she sprinted forward to help. "Stop!"

There were two men trading blows out there. One had ambushed the other.

"Lucy!" The warning barely registered as her feet hit the pavement. She glimpsed the man hitting the ground a split second before a pair of headlights flashed on their high beams and blinded her.

Forced to turn away, she stumbled back a step. She thought she heard another car door open. She knew she heard the terrible sound of a transmission grinding too quickly through its gears. The headlights grew bigger, like a nocturnal predator bearing down on her. The lights filled up her vision. The roar of the engine deafened her. The heat of the powerful car distorted the chill of the early February morning.

"Lucy!"

Two arms slammed around her body and lifted her out of harm's way. She hit the hard earth with a jolt and tumbled, rolling two or three times until she wound up flat on her back with Niall Watson's long body pinning her to the ground.

She noted the flash of a silver sports car speeding past, bouncing over the curb into the street and disappearing into the night before the strong thigh pressed between her legs and the muscled chest crushing her breasts and the hot gasps of Niall's deep breaths against her neck even registered. "I knew that car was following me..." Lucy's triumphant words trailed away in a painful gurgle as the pain of that tackle bloomed through her chest. "Oh, man. That hurts."

"Not as much as getting mowed down by that Camaro would have." She flattened her palms against his shoulders and tried to push, but he only rose up onto his elbows on either side of her, leaving their hips locked together. He glared down at her through those dark frames. "What were you thinking? Didn't you see him driving right at you?"

"I thought you were hurt." She sucked in a deeper breath and found more voice as the ache in her lungs eased. "There was a fight outside the laundry room. He knocked the other man down. I thought it was you."

"It wasn't."

"Duh." Her breath returned in shallow gasps. "What are you doing here, anyway?"

"Saving you, apparently."

"You're supposed to be asleep."

"You're supposed to be in my apartment."

Lucy was blatantly aware of cold ground and damp

clothes and the black KCPD T-shirt that left little of that sleekly muscled torso to her imagination now. But Niall flattened himself right back on top of her when another vehicle engine roared to life in the parking lot. She found herself flat on her back a second time, pinned beneath Niall's body as the second car raced past.

Only after it turned into the street and sped away after the silver Camaro did Niall raise his head again. "Do you recognize that vehicle, too?"

Lucy shook her head. She hadn't even gotten a look at it. A fat lot of help she was. As her body warmed in places it shouldn't, Lucy gave him another push. "You can get off me now."

Without even so much as a *sorry for invading your personal space and making your brain short-circuit again*, Niall rolled to his feet and extended a hand to help her stand up beside him. While she brushed at the mud on her knees and bottom, he bent down to pick up her key card and phone and pressed them into her hands. "Are you hurt?"

"No."

Despite her answer, he turned her hands over and inspected the muddy smear on her elbow. "What are you doing out here at this time of the blessed a.m.?"

Lucy plucked away the dead bits of grass that clung to the scruff of his beard and hair. "Are *you* hurt?"

"Lucy," he prompted, dismissing her concern. "Give me an answer."

She pulled away and shrugged, wondering how long she was going to feel that stiff catch in her chest, and how much of it had to do with hitting the ground so hard and how much had to do with learning Niall's shape in a far-too-intimate way. "I heard voices. Someone was fighting on the basement stairs, and they ran out. One of them got on the elevator, maybe. I was half-asleep."

"Where's the baby?"

"Tommy." Her blood chilling at what a doofus she was turning out to be at this whole instant-motherhood thing, Lucy ran back to the side exit. She slid her key card into the lock and pulled the door open.

Niall was right behind her. "I woke up, and you and Tommy were gone." That explained the bare feet and pseudo pajamas he was wearing. "I saw the sacks with all his clothes had disappeared, too. When you weren't in your apartment, either, I came down to look for you. Then I heard the engine outside. For a second I thought—"

"What? That I'd run off and taken the baby?" She hurried down the steps. Niall followed right behind her. "I would never do that. You're just as important to him as I am." The door to the laundry room had closed, and she quickly accessed it with her key card while Niall glanced up at the numbers lighting up on the elevator behind them. But he caught the door and followed her in as she hurried to the baby carrier still rocking on top of the clothes dryer. Her breath rushed out with relief when she saw those sweet brown eyes tracking their movement across the room. "Thank goodness. He's fine. He was being so fussy. I fed him and changed him and still couldn't get him to stop crying, and you said you hadn't slept in forty-eight hours. So I remembered a trick that one of the older women in my office said worked for her kids when they wouldn't sleep. Besides, all these new things need to be washed before he can wear them."

"You left him here alone?"

"I must have dozed off myself until I heard the argument out in the hallway." Lucy unhooked the straps on the carrier and reached for Tommy. "There you are, sweetie. See? He's fine. Wide-awake again, hmm—"

"Wait." Niall's hand on her arm startled her. "Don't touch him."

She glanced up to the narrow-eyed scrutiny behind his glasses. "What's wrong?"

"How long were you gone?"

"I don't know. A few minutes, maybe…" And then she zeroed in on what had put Niall on alert. There was a lipstick mark on Tommy's forehead. Without asking, the scientist beside her captured Lucy's chin and tilted it up to run his thumb over her mouth with a friction that tingled across her lips and made her tremble from head to toe.

Despite her body's traitorous response to his firm touch, it wasn't meant to be a caress. Niall released her and held the tip of his thumb beside the mark on Tommy's forehead. The gloss she wore was rosy pink. The color on Tommy's skin was a tannish coral.

"Oh, my God." She *had* heard a woman's voice earlier. Another woman had been in here when Tommy was alone. That whole fight must have been a distraction—a way to get Lucy to leave while another woman sneaked into the laundry room. She'd kissed the baby while Lucy had been chasing shadows and dodging cars.

"Someone was here," Niall pronounced.

Not someone.

"Diana." Lucy quickly glanced around, realizing what she should have seen when she'd unhooked

Tommy from his carrier. The clean, warm blanket she'd covered him with was missing. "She took the blanket I put over him. She was right here."

And now the young woman was gone.

Again.

Chapter Four

Niall clipped his badge onto the belt of his jeans, debated about leaving his gun locked inside its metal box, then decided to strap it on. If Diana Kozlow was in serious trouble, as Lucy claimed—and the twenty-year-old hadn't simply punked out on the responsibility and expense of caring for a baby—then he'd do well to be prepared for any contingency that could come back to harm Tommy or Lucy.

It wasn't just his civic-minded sense of duty that prompted him to take a proactive role in guarding the security of his building and neighbors—too many unanswered questions surrounding the baby still nagged at him. Before he'd left, Thomas Watson had suggested Niall keep an eye open for further suspicious activity around the building. Certainly, alleged fights and a silver Camaro nearly running down Lucy—either intentionally or as collateral damage in a speedy getaway from the second driver—qualified as suspicious.

He couldn't tell yet if that woman was simply a magnet for trouble or if she was truly embroiled in a legitimate missing-person case. Niall trusted his dad's gut warning him that something felt seriously wrong here as

much as he trusted his own assessment of the clues surrounding Tommy, the violation of Lucy's apartment and
those two near misses in the parking lot last night. The
break-in had been an act of desperation, not planning.
The mark of lipstick on Tommy's forehead that didn't
match Lucy's dark pink color indicated a kiss. From a
guilt-ridden mother reluctant to say goodbye to a baby
she couldn't take care of on her own? Or a frightened
young woman who saw no other option to keep her son
safe than to abandon him to her most trusted friend?

But safe from what? Or whom?

If he hadn't been reliving the nightmare of the shooting at his sister's wedding and woken himself up to
clear his head, he wouldn't have discovered Lucy and
Tommy missing from his living room. He wouldn't have
gone looking for them and seen his pretty neighbor
blinded by the car barreling toward her. He wouldn't
have known that gut-wrenching sense of helpless in-
adequacy knowing that someone out there was a step
ahead of him, luckier—if not smarter—than he was
when it came to taking care of an impulsive woman
and an innocent child.

And Niall needed to be able to take care of Lucy and
Tommy. He hadn't spotted the shooter soon enough.
He hadn't prevented his grandfather from stroking out.
And unless a dead body showed up on his autopsy table,
there wasn't a damn thing he could do to help his family
figure out who had targeted Seamus in the first place.
But watching over Lucy and Tommy was something
he could do. Helping them find Diana Kozlow and the
other answers they needed was the challenge that would

keep him busy and his mind occupied. Helping them was the worthwhile difference he *could* make.

Besides, there was something about a tiny baby who quieted at the sound of his voice or the touch of his hand that awakened something so alien inside Niall that he'd almost forgotten the words his mother had once spoken to him as a child. He'd been bewailing going to a new school after moving across Kansas City. Athletic Duff and outgoing Keir had made new friends easily enough. But gangly, bookish Niall, who'd inherited his mother's shy genes, had spent the first few weeks of fourth grade feeling utterly alone. She'd climbed up into the tree house where he'd been hiding out to share a hug and some loving wisdom. *"There are certain people in this world, Niall, that we are destined to have a special connection to. You don't need a lot of friends. Just one or two who understand you. Who'll have your back. Who need you to be their friend, too."*

Perhaps she'd been referring to his brothers and sister sharing that kind of closeness with him. But the very next day, he'd met another new student on the playground, and the two of them had become good friends who'd gone through middle school and high school together. Although they'd taken separate college and career paths, he and Jack Riggins still kept in touch.

The moment he'd picked up Tommy, Niall had felt a similar, irrational connection being made. Tommy liked him. Tommy needed him to be his friend. Whether as a doctor or rescuer or simply as an authoritative presence to quiet his tears, Niall Watson intended to be there for Tommy Kozlow—or whatever the little boy's name turned out to be.

Tommy's real identity was only one of several questions Niall intended to find answers to today. As soon as he checked in with his grandfather at the hospital and reported any medical updates to his family, he wanted to assess Diana Kozlow's fitness as a parent, determine whether the danger Lucy suspected was genuine and track down the missing mother. And, if Diana wouldn't share the father's name, or a birth certificate couldn't be found, Niall planned to work out the legalities between guardianship and what was in the child's best interest and obtain permission to draw some of Tommy's blood to run his DNA to locate the boy's father. Lucy had already put the paperwork into motion to secure temporary foster placement of the baby with her. Her permission would be enough to run Tommy's DNA and give him his real name, so there was that conversation on his agenda today, as well.

That should be plenty to keep him busy until he reported back to work at the lab tonight.

Prepared with a plan for the next several hours, Niall ran a comb through his damp hair and picked up his mug of cold decaf off the dresser before heading out into the living room, where he'd left Lucy and Tommy sleeping a couple hours earlier.

His structured day quickly hit its first glitch when he saw that the lamp beside the sofa was on and his guests were both wide-awake. Niall stopped, his eyes narrowing on the crown of Lucy McKane's dark curls as she leaned over the baby in her lap. Nerve endings in his chest and thighs awakened with a mysterious sense memory, recalling the impression of soft curves pressing against his harder angles during that tussle in the hallway and that tumble across the grass last night. He was equally fascinated by her hands. Royal blue yarn dangled from her fingers as she deftly twisted knots onto the slender pair of knitting needles she worked. The glossy kinks of her hair bobbed against her shoulders and over the curves of the mud-stained sweater she still wore as she played peekaboo with Tommy.

She knit several stitches, then clutched her work to her chest and teased Tommy with an "I see you" that made his little fists pump with delight. The baby gurgled and cooed when she brushed his nose and shook her hair against his fingers. Then he calmed when she went back to knitting and obscured her face again.

Niall studied the interchange twice before Lucy looked up and smiled. "You know, you can stare at the details for so long that you miss the bigger picture."

He hadn't missed a thing. Abandoned baby. A woman who was proving more intriguing to study than she should be, making herself at home on his couch. Apparently, despite his insistence that her apartment wouldn't be safe for her and Tommy until maintenance could come and replace her locks, she'd sneaked inside a second time. "Excuse me?"

Lucy cupped the half-formed cap she'd been knitting over Tommy's head before tying it off and pointing to the wet bar. "Diaper. You don't smell that? Our little friend here has been very busy since I gave him his last bottle. I left the changing pad over there and didn't want to risk moving him in case he made a mess on your nice leather sofa. Your place isn't exactly babyproofed."

Niall glanced at the stockpile of supplies his father had brought over and crossed the room to get the things she needed. "The sofa has no sentimental value. It can be cleaned. You should have called me if you needed help with the baby."

"You were in the shower."

He returned to the couch, nodding toward the basket of knitting supplies she'd retrieved from her apartment. "Longer than I thought, apparently. You went back to your place. After that incident in the laundry room last night, I thought we'd agreed that you'd stay put."

"No. You suggested it. I promised to be careful," she clarified. "Tommy was sound asleep on the pallet we made for him, so I figured it'd be fine to go across the hall to gather up my knitting. I like to keep my hands busy. Especially when there's a lot on my mind." She thanked him for the supplies and set up a changing station beside her before moving Tommy onto the pad and dropping down to her knees in front of the couch. "I didn't want to wake you because, well, I already woke you once, and I could tell you needed to sleep." She turned her face up to his and winked. "You still look tired, if you ask me."

"I didn't." Niall picked up the soiled diaper and carried it to the kitchen trash. "I'm used to keeping odd hours. I'm fine."

"No, you're not," she insisted, strapping a fresh diaper into place. "How can it be with everything you've had to deal with in the past forty-eight hours or so? I imagine your job is pretty stressful, but I'm guessing your weekends don't always include a wedding, your grandfather going into the hospital, and the wacky neighbor lady and a baby taking refuge in your living room."

Wacky? His analysis of Lucy McKane had included terms like *caring, vibrant, sensual.* Although *garrulous, stubborn* and *unpredictable* were certainly apt descriptors, too.

Niall shook his head, puzzled by how easily his thoughts seemed to derail around this woman. Perhaps the shower and shave hadn't revived him as much as he'd hoped and he needed to switch to caffeinated coffee to unfog his brain. The important point here was that she'd taken another unnecessary risk, negating the whole purpose of him insisting she and Tommy take refuge in his apartment. He picked up a new outfit from the laundry she'd folded and carried it to the couch. "What if the intruders had come back?"

"You mean Diana? Then I would have brought her here and helped her, too."

She was making assumptions that couldn't yet be proved. "What if Diana had nothing to do with breaking into your apartment? What if hers wasn't the woman's voice you heard last night?"

"Who else would kiss—"

"What if someone took advantage of her connection to you, borrowed her toolbox and broke in to surrender a baby without any legal hassles?"

"And knew where I hid some extra cash?"

Fine. If Lucy was so certain Tommy was Diana's son, he had a reasonable argument for that, too. "What if the threat that prompted Diana to abandon Tommy in the first place followed her to your apartment? What if those men you heard last night had come back for you? To finish something they'd started? You could have been seriously hurt."

Her fingers stopped. Everything about her seemed to pause for a split second before Lucy shook her head, spilling her hair over the neckline of her sweater. As quickly as she'd frozen, she went right back to changing the baby, lifting Tommy to position the new sleeper beneath his back. "I appreciate your concern. But I was only gone a few minutes—long enough to clean up the cookie dough spoiling in the kitchen and gather up my knitting. If I'd sensed anything was wrong, I would have come straight back. Nothing happened."

"This time." Niall adjusted his glasses, averting both his gaze and the unexpected flare of curiosity about her reaction to the suggestion that she, and not Tommy or Diana, was the one in danger. Was it wrong of him to want to push her to reveal just what had caused her to hesitate like that? And he wondered if she knew she had a long tendril of hair caught in the nubby tweed of her sweater. He could easily reach down and free the strand for her. When he'd knocked her out of the way of that speeding car last night, he'd inadvertently discovered that her hair was as silky as it looked. That the ends were cool to the touch and the length of it was as strongly resilient as the woman herself. His fingers itched to tangle in those curly locks again, to re-create the chance touch and confirm his observations. Niall blinked away the thought. *That* wasn't on the agenda for today. She was changing Tommy's diaper, for pity's sake, not seducing him. "Lucy, I need to know that you're taking this seriously. I believe Tommy was in grave danger yesterday. That means you could be, too. I need you to be able to take care of him so that I can conduct my investigation."

"So that we can conduct *our* investigation," she corrected, as if he had misspoken. Lifting Tommy into her arms, she stood, cradling the infant against her chest and gazing down into his attentive brown eyes. "I appreciate more than you know that you and your father promised to help me find Diana and reunite her with her son. I'm grateful that you offered to let us stay with you until maintenance can replace the locks on my door. I wouldn't have felt safe there."

"You weren't. You still aren't."

She looked up at him then. "I'm grateful that you probably saved me from my own impulsiveness last night. But don't think for one moment that I don't know how serious this situation is. If Tommy and I are in danger, then Diana must be facing something worse. If she has anything to do with those men I heard arguing last night, then I know she is. I know her better than anyone. At least, I used to. You need my help."

"And if I don't accept it, you'll go off searching the city for her on your own again, won't you."

Lucy's expression brightened with a wry smile. "Now *that* is an accurate conclusion, Dr. Watson."

Not understanding the giggle that followed, Niall simply nodded, conceding the wisdom of having someone with inside information on Diana Kozlow to guide his investigation so he could either confirm or rule out Lucy's belief that Tommy was her foster daughter's baby. It pleased him, too, to know that Lucy would have temporary custody of Tommy as a foster parent, keeping the little boy close by so that Niall could keep watch over him, too. "So we agree to work as a team. For Tommy's sake."

"For Tommy's sake." She took a step closer, and Niall inhaled the scents of baby powder and something slightly more exotic that didn't have anything to do with the infant she was pushing into his arms. "Since I've convinced you that we're on the same side now, would you feel comfortable watching him for about ten minutes? That's all the time I'll need to freshen up and change so we're ready to go." Her fingers caught for a moment between Tommy and the placket of his shirt, and even through the pressed cotton, Niall's stomach muscles clenched at the imprint of her knuckles brushing against his skin. But she pulled away to drape a burp rag over his shoulder, apparently unaware of his physiological reactions to her touch and scent. "You still want to drive us to my office to pick up a bassinet and some other supplies?" she asked, gathering up her boots and purse and sweater coat.

"*I'm* the one with a car seat, so yes, I'm driving." Niall shook off his weary brain's inability to focus and shifted Tommy to one arm, catching the door as she stepped into the hallway. "I want to listen to that message from your foster daughter, too, before I bring you back here." He entered her living room right behind her, frowning at how easy it had been for her to push open the damaged door. He plowed into her before realizing she had stopped. "What are you doing?"

Her hands went straight to Tommy, even as she stumbled back a step. "What are *you* doing?" she asked. She released her grip once she seemed assured that there was no chance of him dropping the baby.

Niall looked over the top of her head to scan the empty, seemingly undisturbed living room. "I want to check your apartment before allowing you to remain here for any length of time on your own."

She nodded her understanding of his intention and crossed to a lamp to flip it on and fill the room with light. She opened the powder-room door so he could see it was clear, as well. "Your dad said we have to wait twenty-four hours to file an official missing-person case on Diana with KCPD. I'm glad you both agreed that we could start looking for answers sooner."

He followed her to the kitchen and saw that, other than the dishes she'd washed, it, too, showed no signs of the intruder returning. "Tommy needs his mother. If we can locate her and reunite them—"

"And make sure she's okay—"

"—and ensure she's competent enough and able to care for him—"

"Competent?" Lucy planted her feet, and Niall nearly knocked her flying again. But she put up a hand with a huff of exasperation, and it was Niall who retreated a step this time. "Diana would never abandon Tommy unless something was terribly wrong and she thought it was for the best. People like her and me, we have issues about family. When you've never had one, once you get one…you protect it with everything you have in you. I have to believe that, whatever's wrong, she left Tommy here in order to protect him."

"Then why come back for him? If that was her in the laundry room last night."

"Her instinct may be to protect him, but giving up the family you love, especially your brand-new child… I can't imagine how hard that would be. I don't know if I could be strong enough to say goodbye to this little one." Lucy reached out to stroke Tommy's hair as if she'd already convinced herself that Tommy was her family now. A conclusion founded purely on emotions, no doubt.

Niall—and the law in the state of Missouri—required more incontrovertible proof. "You told Dad your mother was still alive when he was taking down your personal history, asking about other people Diana might have contacted. You have family."

"Trust me, I don't. Family are people who love you unconditionally. People you can trust and rely on. The man who sired me left before I was ever born, and my mother and I have been estranged since I emancipated myself at seventeen. She's not a part of my life anymore. She never will be again."

"What happened?"

Lucy curled her fingers into her hand and turned down the hallway. "Any number of things from not always having a place to live to the revolving door of men she *did* try to make a home with. But my breaking point was when we had a difference of opinion about my boyfriend." Although she laughed, Niall was certain there was no humor in that wry sound. "It's not what you think. I wasn't some kind of teenage rebel wanting to date a bad boy. In fact, she did everything she could to encourage me to keep the guy I was trying to get away from."

"Get away from?" Niall wondered at the fist of suspicion that hit him as squarely as discovering a clue on his autopsy table. "Why? What did he do to you?"

When she faced him this time, her eyes had dulled to a mossy shade of green. "Funny. My mother was more upset about what I'd done to him." Niall waited for her to elaborate. Lucy didn't disappoint. "Roger was Falls City's golden boy—you know how it is in a small town—the high school's star quarterback, Daddy runs the manufacturing plant that employs most of the town. But Roger and I weren't a good fit."

"How so?"

"No question is too personal for you, is it?" Her typically direct gaze dropped to the middle button of his shirt. Instead of giving an immediate answer, Lucy pulled a towel from the linen closet and hugged it to her chest before turning and tilting her gaze back up to his. "All that mattered to my mother was that Roger was rich. He was going to take over the family business one day. And if he was interested in me, then no matter how awful that relationship was I needed to suck it up and…" She paused midsentence to lean in and press a kiss to Tommy's temple as the baby dozed in his arms. Niall felt that wistful caress as though her mouth had made the connection against his own skin. Before he could question his empathetic response, Lucy shook her head and headed into the bathroom to set the towel on the edge of the sink. "I realized I was just a tool for her. It was easier than I expected to leave her and move to Kansas City. I've been on my own ever since. With the exception of Diana, of course. There's no blood between us, but she's family more than my mother ever was."

Niall considered the vehemence of her statement, detecting not one trace of melancholy or regret as he followed her into the small room. "And Roger?"

Her slender shoulders sagged briefly before she

straightened. "Testified against him. Sent him to prison instead of college."

"For what?"

Her eyes met his in the mirror. "No more questions right now, okay?"

Niall needed a last name. He intended to follow up on this Roger lowlife and decide if he had anything to do with Tommy's abandonment—or even if he could be the child's father. But he'd follow up on a different tack until Lucy opened up again. "I'd give anything to see my mother again."

"I have a feeling you were raised very differently than I was. Your father is funny and kind, and I believe he truly cares about Tommy and Diana, and maybe even me. The way he told me all about your brothers and sister and his dad?" She turned, sitting her hip back on the counter of the sink. She was smiling again, and for some reason, seeing the soft curve of her lips seemed to take some of the edge off the concern that wasn't entirely professional. "I could tell that Thomas is really proud of each of you. And clearly, he loves you and supports you. It's not every son or daughter who has a parent who drops everything in the middle of the night to do some emergency shopping for them. Even when you're a grown-up. You're lucky."

Niall concurred. "I know."

A genuine laugh echoed off the tile walls. "You are one of a kind, Doctor. You see everything in black-and-white, don't you? Sometimes I envy your ability to ignore your emotions."

Funny, he'd been thinking he'd better understand his reactions to her and that mysterious Roger devil he'd never met if he could turn off the emotional responses she seemed to evoke in him and take the time to analyze whether it was fatigue, the sense of duty he was raised with—or the fact he hadn't interacted this closely with a woman on a personal basis since some time back in med school—that was clouding his perceptions.

Lucy curled her finger into Tommy's tiny hand and tucked it in beside Niall's arm. "I'm sorry about your mother. If a man like your dad loved her, I'm sure she was someone special."

"She was."

"Diana never met my mother. I wouldn't let Alberta McKane get close to anyone I cared about. The woman is toxic." A chilly palm print marked Niall's shoulder as she pushed him out the door into the hallway. "Now go. I still need ten minutes."

Lucy was dressed in jeans and a Kansas City Royals sweatshirt and was ready to go in nine. Since she was motivated to work and Tommy was content to watch them do so, it made sense to set aside his curiosity about Lucy McKane's past and focus on the very present problem of locating Diana Kozlow and identifying Tommy's birth parents and possibly the man who had nearly run down Lucy with his fancy car.

Niall loaded a bassinet and stroller into the back of his SUV while Lucy packed a new diaper bag with items they'd picked up en route to her office at Family Services. They stopped to feed Tommy four more ounces of formula before he fell asleep on Lucy's shoulder. Only then did the dark-haired woman with the riot of silky curls tumbling over her shoulders sit down at the pod of four desks surrounding a power pole and play the messages on her answering machine.

After the first beep, a man's voice, possibly slurred by alcohol, came on the line. *"Hey, Luce, it's me. I know I screwed up. I need to see you, sweet thing. I just want to apologize. Make things right between us. Please don't—"*

Lucy's cheeks reddened and she punched the button, cutting off the rest of the drawling message. "Ignore him."

"Is that a client?"

He wondered if she would ever tell him a lie to escape answering one of his questions. "Roger Campbell. High school ex. Somehow he's gotten my work number. I guess it's not tricky. We're a state institution listed in the phone book. He must have asked the main desk to transfer his call to my extension."

"Could he have your personal information, too? Does he know where you live? If you testified against him—"

She shook off his questions and pulled up the next message on the machine. Not a lie. But not an answer, either. "Here's the recording I want you to listen to."

"Lucy? It's Diana. I won't be able to make it for lunch. I know that doesn't makes sense after calling you yesterday when I hadn't called you at all for a while and I changed my number and... I'm sorry. I have so much to tell you, but...there's really no time right now." The younger woman's voice was already hurried and breathless, but now it dropped to such a soft whisper that Niall sat on the edge of the desk and leaned in to hear it over the muted mechanical noises grinding in the background. *"Something's come up and I have to*

*take care of it. I thought I could handle it myself, but...
I have a favor to ask, and I don't know who else to call.
I need to give you something, and I need you to keep it
safe while I..."* There was a sniffle and a hushed gasp.
Diana was crying. Niall looked across the desk to discover Lucy's eyes tearing up, as well. *"We're family,
right? I need you to have my back even though I don't
deserve it. I really made a mess this time. But I can fix
it... I have to fix it..."*

There was another sob, and Lucy's fingers began
a slow massage up and down Tommy's back. A quick
gasp ended the weeping on the answering machine.
The muffled shout of someone calling through a door
or wall triggered the sound of quick footsteps. *"I have
to go. I'll get there as soon as I can, but I can't stay.
I'll explain everything when there's more time. You're
the only one I can count on. Please."* Then, in a louder
voice, Diana added, *"I'm here. Yes, I'm alone. Who
would I be talking to? Just hold your—"*

He heard a muffled commotion at the end of the message, as if Diana had been hiding the phone in her purse
or pocket before she finished disconnecting the call.
Even with Niall's limited imagination, it was impossible to miss the distinct sounds of the young woman's
distress.

Niall had never seen the stoic expression lining Lucy's
face before as she pressed a button to save the message.
"I waited at my apartment for her to bring me this mysterious *thing*, and when she didn't show up, I went looking for her. Of course, I didn't know where to go. I went
to the hair salon where she used to work, but they said
she hadn't been there in ages. I tried her old apartment.

The boyfriend I knew said she'd moved out months earlier. Then I went to the place on Carmody Street. I hit a dead end. How does a twenty-year-old drop out of sight like that?"

"And you tried the cell phone number she called you from? You said her voice mail was completely full?"

Lucy nodded. "I'm right to be worried, aren't I? Tommy is the *something* she wanted me to keep safe. And it sounded to me as if she didn't want anyone on her end of the conversation to listen in." When Lucy rolled the chair away from her desk and stood, Niall did the same. "I didn't recognize the other voice, but it sounded like a man, don't you think? I couldn't make out what he was saying, though. Just like that argument last night."

"Because the man wasn't speaking English." Niall had been listening to more than just the recorded words. "Does she know a foreign language? Would she have understood the man?"

"She took Spanish in high school. That wasn't Spanish. I know enough of that to at least identify it."

It would require a bit of research, but Niall was thinking the words had been something more Russian or Germanic. They'd been angry words. And Diana Kozlow had definitely been afraid. Even though he expected it to be archived, he wanted to read through Diana's Family Services file to see if there was any friend or reference or job connection that might link her to a man with a foreign accent.

After staring at him expectantly for a few moments, Lucy swiped away her tears and made efficient work of strapping Tommy into his carrier and covering him with a blanket. She replaced the cap on his bottle and folded the burp rag to tuck into the diaper bag. "What are you thinking, Niall?"

Although Diana had been vague in her request and had never mentioned a baby or Tommy's real name, he could see that Lucy believed the younger woman and this child had been in terrible danger. For the moment, Niall agreed. Certainly, Carmody Street was no place for a young woman with a baby to take refuge. He reached out and stopped Lucy's hand from zipping the bag shut. "You can't go back to the apartment by yourself until we know more." And he damn sure didn't want her there by herself until he'd run a background check on Roger Campbell. "I need to analyze that recording at the crime lab. I have a friend who's a sound engineer there who owes me a favor. I'll call him, and we'll go there after the hospital."

Her gaze darted up to meet his, and he felt her skin warming beneath his touch before she turned her hand to squeeze his fingers then pull away to finish packing. "But we've already been too much of an imposition. You need to go by Saint Luke's to visit your grandfather and spend time with your family. I've already kept you from them longer than you planned this morning. I can grab the car seat and call a cab so you don't even have to drive us. Tommy and I will be fine—as long as you don't mind us staying in your apartment. Maintenance said there was a chance they could get someone to see to my locks today."

"And they also said it could be Monday morning." No. Tommy needed Dr. Niall Watson of the KCPD crime lab to be his friend right now. And no matter how independent she claimed to be, Lucy needed a friend, too. Right now that friend was going to be him. Niall shrugged into his black KCPD jacket and picked up the sweater coat she'd draped over the back of her chair. "I work quickly and methodically, Lucy. I will find the answers you and Tommy need. But I can't do that when I'm not able to focus. And having half the city between you and me when we don't know what all this means or if you and Tommy are in any kind of danger—"

"Are you saying I'm a distraction?"

Nothing but. Confused about whether that was some type of flirtatious remark or whether she was simply seeking clarification, Niall chose not to answer. Instead, he handed her the sweater and picked up Tommy in his carrier. "Get his things and let's go."

Chapter Five

"I'm so sorry to hear about your foster daughter. If Niall says he'll find her, he will. I've never known that boy not to solve a puzzle. Don't give up hope."

"I won't." Lucy tried to imagine how different her life might have been if she'd had Millie Leighter for a grandmother or a sweet spinster aunt or even just a friend growing up in Falls City. With Tommy charmingly blowing bubbles and taking an instant liking to the plump silver-haired woman, too, Lucy had spent the last hour in the fifth-floor lobby waiting area at Saint Luke's Hospital getting to know the fellow knitter along with a little Watson family history.

Millie had been hired by Thomas Watson when Niall had barely been a teenager, after the murder of Mary Watson. Seamus had come to live with the family then, too, to help give the stunned, grieving children and their father a sense of normalcy and security. By turns touched and then genuinely amused, Lucy listened to Millie's stories about Duff's penchant for making trips to the emergency room, Niall's awkward shyness, Keir's vivid imagination and Olivia's ability to keep the brothers who were twice her size in line. But all the while

Lucy kept remembering flashes of her own childhood and teen years, when her mother had sent her out to beg for coins so they could buy dinner. Or later, when her mother would send her to the park to play to keep her away from the trailer they sometimes lived in while Alberta slept with the crooked local sheriff to stave off getting arrested for shoplifting. Millie's humorous rendition of the New Year's celebration when Seamus had reheated a bunch of leftover pizza and she'd had to come home from her vacation to take care of an entire family stuck in the bathroom with food poisoning made Lucy laugh at the miserable story. But she couldn't help but feel the sting of useless jealousy.

She had no such loving anecdotes to share about growing up, no dear friend she'd been able to call when she really needed someone. She'd gotten herself to the hospital that night Roger Campbell had beaten her so badly. And the only reason her mother had come to visit her after the emergency surgery that had nearly gutted her was to advise her to accept Roger's apology and take him back.

It was almost impossible for her to imagine being part of a family as close and supportive as Niall's, despite the tragedies the Watsons had faced. But she could very well imagine her being a friend to a generous woman like Millie Leighter.

"Oh, my. Little Tommy's dropped off again." Millie glanced up as the elevator dinged across from the carpeted waiting area. An orderly rolled a noisy cart of lunch trays into the hallway, trading a greeting with the clerk at the floor's main desk. "I'm surprised all this hustle and bustle hasn't kept him awake."

Lucy smiled at the tiny bundle of baby nestled against Millie's chest. "Are you getting tired of holding him?"

"Not on your life."

"He's content. I'm sure he enjoyed your stories as much as I did."

Millie's cheeks warmed with a blush. "Pish-posh. You're a dear for letting me rattle on so."

"It fills the time while we're waiting to hear about Seamus. I know I can talk ninety miles a minute when I'm nervous or worried about something."

"I don't believe that." The older woman smiled. "You're trapped here with me because Niall didn't leave you a way to get home. But I thank you for listening." Millie's smile faded. "I live in a house with police officers, and I know their work is dangerous. I've been through a lot with them—kept the ship running through good times and tough ones, so to speak. But I've never been in the middle of a shooting myself, and I'm not handling this very well. I'll never forget the awful sound of all those guns firing, and the screams, and…watching Seamus crumple to the floor like that. There was so much blood. I thought… I was certain…"

Lucy reached across the gap between their chairs to comfort the other woman. "I can't imagine what it must have been like to be there."

Millie sniffled away the tears that threatened to spill over. She patted Lucy's hand before pulling up the cotton blanket Tommy was swaddled in to shield his face from the hospital's bright lights. "New life like this is always the best antidote for a horrific experience like that. And so is friendly conversation. Now why don't you tell me something about you. What were you like as a little girl?"

Not Lucy's favorite topic of conversation. She sat back in the cushioned chair, running through the short list of memories she was willing to share. "Well… I had a next-door neighbor who taught me how to knit when I was in the fourth grade. I made everybody I knew a pot holder for Christmas that year. They got scarves the year after that."

"And now you're creating intricate patterns like those beautiful socks you're wearing. The curved needles give me fits. I invariably drop a stitch. If you have any hints—" A door opened down the hallway and Lucy turned as the older woman straightened in her seat to look across the carpeted waiting area. "There are Thomas and the boys. I wonder if they have any news."

Duff came out of the room first. "That guy disappeared like a freakin' magician. One minute I'm running after him on the roof, and then poof—he jumps onto the next building and he's gone."

Keir Watson followed. "He probably had help to make his getaway."

Lucy sat up straighter when Niall appeared. The three brothers gathered in the hallway, close enough for her to eavesdrop on their conversation. "Then I'm guessing he's not a crazy. Most shooters like that work solo. They're expecting notoriety after the fact and don't care if they get caught or not. I've got a couple of guys at the lab combing social media to see if there's any kind of suicide note or manifesto posted. This guy had a purpose for being there."

"To take down Grandpa?" Keir asked.

Duff swore under his breath. "To take down some-one. Either he's a lousy shot and Grandpa is collateral damage—"

"Or he hit exactly who he was aiming for," Niall concluded.

Thomas Watson entered the hallway after his sons. "And the man with the best shot at telling us why he was targeted can't talk."

The raised male voices were instantly shushed by a middle-aged woman sporting green scrubs and a honey-brown ponytail. She shut the door behind her and moved past them, speaking as if she expected the four men to follow her. "I thought the doctor made it very clear, Mr. Watson. No more than two visitors in the room at the same time. And only for a few minutes. And I find you all in there grilling him for information? You'll tire your father out."

Thomas lengthened his rolling stride to catch up to the nurse's quick steps. "But he wants to see us. We have decisions to make about his care, and I want his input."

"Input?" The nurse stopped in the waiting area, un-fazed by the circle of Watson men towering around her. "You asked him one question about hiring me, then went right back to your investigation. Seamus can't speak, and having him squeeze your hand so often to indicate yes and no is taxing on his fine-motor muscles and the neural transmitters he needs to slowly learn how to master all over again. You saw how agitated he was."

"We were reassuring him that we're staying on top of KCPD's investigation into his getting shot," Thomas explained. "He's a retired cop. He needs to hear that."

The nurse seemed unimpressed by his argument. "He needs to rest."

Millie stood with the baby. "Is Seamus all right?"

Thomas propped his hands at his waist, echoing the stance Lucy had seen Niall use so many times. "I think *frustrated* is the word for it, Millie. Clearly, his ideas and stubbornness are intact, but he's struggling to communicate what he means."

The nurse, whose name badge read Jane Boyle, RN, tilted her face up to admonish Thomas. "Small steps, Mr. Watson. Your father needs to take small steps if he's going to recover fully. And if you intend to hire me, then we'll follow the doctor's orders and do exactly as I say with my patient. And that means no interrogations."

Niall's older brother, Duff, crossed his massive arms beside their father. "We haven't signed on the dotted line yet, lady."

Millie's voice sounded much older than it had just a few moments earlier. "You're hiring someone to take care of Seamus when he comes home?"

Thomas nodded. "Dr. Koelus said Dad needs round-the-clock care for a couple of weeks and physical therapy for some time beyond that. He recommended Ms. Boyle here. She's a private nurse with PT experience. But we're trying to decide if she and Seamus are compatible. Hell, we're trying to decide if she and I are compatible. If she's staying at the house…"

Millie's blue gaze darted over to Lucy, and she turned her head to whisper, "I think Tommy needs to be changed. Do you mind if I take him to the ladies' room?"

"Of course not. Do you want me to take him?"

"Don't be silly, dear. I can manage."

"Thank…you?" Although her nose hadn't detected any telltale odor, Lucy deferred to the older woman's experience. But when she handed her the diaper bag, Lucy read something else in Millie's eyes before she scurried away down the corridor. Of all the family meetings she'd imagined being a part of, they'd never included taking any member for granted. Perhaps worry and fatigue had clouded Niall's keen powers of observation. Or maybe it was a guy thing that all four men were oblivious to what was so painfully clear to Lucy.

Before Lucy could mention Millie's distress, Jane Boyle dismissed herself from the conversation. "I select my assignments very carefully, Mr. Watson. If I don't feel good about the patient's home environment, then I don't take the job."

"Home environment?" Thomas pointed a finger at the nurse. "Are you questioning my—"

"I'll be in Dr. Koelus's office for another ten minutes if you want to continue the interview. Then I'll be looking for my next potential assignment."

The younger brother, Keir, was a shorter, twenty-twenty version of Niall. He eased a low whistle between his teeth as the nurse brushed past him to turn the corner into the crossing hallway leading to the doctor's office. "You get a load of that lady? She's full of herself, isn't she?"

Duff needed a shave and something to take the edge off the wary tension surrounding him. "The fact that she didn't succumb to your questionable charm is the only thing she's got going for her."

"Hey, I get along great with older women. Isn't that

right, Millie? Millie?" Keir turned to discover Lucy's new friend had disappeared. "Where did she go?"

"Is Tommy all right?" Niall asked, noting the baby's absence.

Lucy tilted her chin to see concerned looks on the faces of all four men. But it was Niall's probing gaze she answered. "The baby is fine. None of you have any clue to what just happened, do you? Millie cares about Seamus—she thinks of your family as her own."

Keir's blue eyes narrowed. "She *is* part of the family."

Lucy shrugged. "She might even have extra feelings for your grandfather."

"Extra?" Niall adjusted his glasses on the bridge of his nose, demanding clarification.

"I think she's sweet on him. Or whatever it is that a woman in her seventies feels for an eighty-year-old man."

Duff scrubbed his fingers over the stubble of his beard. "She's got the hots for Grandpa?"

Thomas silenced him with a look and urged Lucy to continue.

"She certainly cares about him." Lucy gestured down the main hall to the room where Seamus Watson lay just a few doors away. "She hasn't even been allowed in to see him yet because, strictly speaking, she's not a relative."

"Of course she's family." Thomas shook his head as if her statement didn't make sense. "The two of them have lived in the same house for twenty years. I've been so preoccupied with Dad, convincing Olivia and Gabe to take some sort of honeymoon, and trying to make sense of the whole damn shooting—"

"You're not in this alone, Dad. We all dropped the ball." Niall reached over to squeeze his father's shoulder. But he was looking to Lucy for an answer. "How do we make it right?"

Lucy wasn't sure it was her place to interfere, but she was starting to get used to explaining people and emotions to her intellectual neighbor. "She's always taken care of all of you, right? I think she's hurt because you're hiring someone else to do her job."

Thomas muttered a rueful apology under his breath. "Ms. Boyle is a registered nurse. She'll be Dad's caretaker and physical therapist. I don't expect her to do anything else. And I'm certainly not kicking Millie out of the house."

"Don't tell me. Tell her. Let her know she's welcome, that she's important to each of you, that you still need her…even if it is just to cook and clean, or to spell the nurse when she needs a break. And she probably wants to be close to Seamus. She's feeling like there's nothing she can do to help right now."

Duff swore under his breath. "I can relate to that."

Thomas agreed. "We all can."

Lucy startled when Keir leaned over to kiss her cheek before thumping Niall's arm and leaving the carpeted waiting area. "Thank you. You know, I like that Niall's finally got a real live girlfriend."

"Oh, I'm not—"

"Excuse me?" Niall frowned at his brother's teasing assertion.

Keir ignored both protests and headed down the hallway. "I was beginning to think Dr. Frankenstein was going to have to build one in that lab of his."

"Where are you going?" Thomas asked.

"To find Millie. I'll take her to lunch and make amends, while you and Duff and that battle-ax Boyle make arrangements to take Grandpa home and get him set up." He turned, backing down the hallway without missing a step. "You *are* hiring her, right? I mean, who else is going to put up with his guff? She stood up to all of us, didn't she? Not an easy task, is it, Luce? You said what we needed to hear."

"I was just pointing out—" Keir winked at Lucy and then turned, including her in that sideways compliment before planting himself outside the ladies' restroom.

"You need to learn to keep your mouth shut, Lucy Claire McKane. No man on this planet likes a woman who doesn't know when to zip it. Now you go right back to the Campbells' house and apologize to Roger."

"But Mama, he slapped me."

"Well, he wouldn't if you ever learned to stop talkin' when it's not your business. How he treats his own dog isn't your affair. And put on them tight jeans I got you before you go back to see him. Those curves will help him see how sorry he is for mistreatin' ya. He's a Campbell—the best ticket out of this two-bit town we're ever gonna get."

Lucy squeezed her eyes shut against the bile rising in her gullet at the remembered incident. She'd never learned to keep her opinions to herself. And while, idealistically, she never regretted standing up for someone in need, she had learned to regret speaking those opinions without thinking through the consequences first.

Dropping her head, Lucy crossed back to the chair where she'd sat to go through her purse, ostensibly looking for something to busy her hands with until she could bury the painful flashback in her memories and concentrate on the present again—and how best to apologize to the Watsons for butting into their family business when they already had plenty on their plate to worry about.

With some sort of tacit agreement reached, Duff and Thomas followed Nurse Boyle around the corner to Dr. Koelus's office while Keir called someone on his cell phone and paced back and forth at the far end of the hall. Lucy pulled a tube of lip balm from her cosmetic bag and ran it around her mouth before she realized Niall was still standing behind her shoulder, staring down at her. She recognized that look, as though she was a specimen under a microscope he wanted to understand.

She dropped the lip balm back into her purse and turned, chin tipped up to meet his studious gaze. "What?" she asked, hearing a defensive edge to her tone she instantly wished she could take back. That only made him curious to ask more questions.

"You're avoiding me. Did Keir embarrass you with the girlfriend comment? He's a relentless teaser."

Those blue eyes were perfectly serious. Bless his stoic heart. The man could earn a medical degree and help solve crimes for the police department, but he still had no clue about the crush she'd had on him since their first meeting in the laundry room. Keir might have tuned in to her interest in his older brother, but she wasn't about to explain that attraction to Niall and risk the alliance they'd made for Tommy's and Diana's sakes. She also wasn't about to embarrass herself with any more details about her past than she'd shared with him earlier, either. "Don't worry. I know you and I are just friends. I hope I didn't overstep the boundaries of our agreement by butting in to your personal family business. Perhaps I didn't choose the best time to mention my suspicions about Millie."

He nodded, although what Niall was agreeing to, she couldn't be sure. "Keir was right about one thing. You have a real talent for reading people. You understand the subtleties of emotion in a way I never will."

"That's not true. I know you rely on that brain of yours, but you have good instincts, too." Lucy tucked a stray curl behind her ear and smiled up at him. "You knew where to find me last night when I needed you. And look at the bond between you and Tommy. You know when he needs you, too. I think he's already forming an emotional attachment to you. He senses you care about him."

Niall's gaze followed the movement of her hand. And then he surprised her by capturing one of the strands of hair that had curled beneath the neckline of her sweatshirt between two fingers and freeing it. She tried to dismiss the way he held on to the curl, arranging it just so behind her shoulder. It was probably just a scientist's impulse to have everything in a neat and tidy order, but her pulse was having other ideas. "I'm a calm presence, that's all. I'm guessing he's had a lot of upheaval in his young life."

Upheaval, yes. She could relate. With Lucy's pulse leaping at his curiously intimate touch, her words held double meaning. "Some people find security in that sort of quiet confidence."

"I hope he knows one day what a champion you are for him." As he pulled away, Niall paused, brushing away the imaginary mark his brother's lips had left on her cheek.

If the tangle of his fingers in her hair hadn't been unsettling enough, the warm stroke of his thumb across her cool skin made her remember that pragmatic touch in front of the clothes dryer last night, and she shivered. Her words came out in an embarrassingly breathy stumble. "You are, too. A champion, I mean."

Niall's fingers splayed along the line of her jaw, his thumb lingering against the apple of her cheek. When his eyes narrowed behind his glasses and the distance between their heights disappeared, Lucy caught her breath in a gasp that was pure anticipation.

Lucy's awareness of the world around her—the bustle of hospital workers, the constant beeps and whirrs of medical equipment, and the medicinal smells wafting through the chilly air—shrank to the subtle pressure of Niall's warm mouth curving over hers. Her palm found a button at the middle of his shirt and settled there, balancing her as she tipped her head back to move her lips beneath his. They shared a quiet, deep kiss that heated Lucy's blood all the way down to her toes.

She wasn't sure when her heels left the floor or when her fingers curled into the crisp cotton of his shirt, or even when her tongue boldly reached out to touch his. But Lucy was blatantly aware of her world shifting on its axis, of a two-year-old fantasy coming to life—of something stirring inside her that felt as dangerous as it was desirable. Niall Watson was kissing her. It was sweet and patient and thorough and perfect, made all the more sexy by how clueless he was of his masculine appeal. His mouth was an irresistible combination of tender purpose and firm demand. And that crazy heat he exuded that drew her like a moth to a flame—

An abrupt chill filled the air around her when Niall pulled his mouth from hers. His chest expanded against her hand as he drew in a deep breath and slowly exhaled. But his blue eyes remained locked on hers. "Was that all right? Your pupils dilated. Did I misread the signal you were sending? Or did I just interpret it the way I wanted to?"

"The signal? No. You read me just fine." Lucy pulled away from the tempting warmth radiating through the Oxford cloth she'd crinkled beneath her hand. She wished she wasn't blocked by the chair behind her or she'd put some serious distance between them while she gathered her wits. *Did I misread the signal?* "Was that an experiment to test your people-reading skills?"

"An experiment?" He shook his head. "I wanted to thank you. Millie means a lot to me—to all of us."

"Oh. Of course. Glad I could help." Lucy managed a smile, salvaging some pride at the knowledge that her first, and most likely only, kiss with Niall Watson hadn't been in the name of science. Still, that tender exploration wasn't any admission of a mutual attraction. He'd intended to express his gratitude while she'd taken another step toward falling in love with the man. He probably thought her traitorous pupils and the goose bumps that prickled beneath the warm fingers still resting against her neck were some sort of involuntary response to the cold, filtered air inside the hospital. "I kind of specialize in creating healthy family relationships. It's the least I could do after all you're doing to help Tommy and Diana."

"Lucy—"

He opened his handsome mouth to say something more, but Thomas Watson appeared around the corner and called for his son to join them. "Niall. I'd like your two cents on this, too. Sorry. Am I interrupting?"

Lucy sidled away the moment Niall turned to his father's bemused smile. "What do you need, Dad?"

"I thought you'd have a better idea of where we can fit all of Dad's medical equipment. There's more room in the guest suite, but if we have to accommodate Ms. Boyle for a few weeks, then she'll want a private bathroom—"

"You'd better go." Lucy gave Niall a nudge toward his father. "It's important."

He glanced over the jut of his shoulder at her. "So is this. I think there's been some kind of misunderstanding between us."

"Not at all. You said thank you, and I said you're welcome." They were friends, allies—and she was grateful for that. But a few minutes apart would allow her to clear her head of any of the misguided fantasies that were still firing through her imagination. "Looks like we might be at the hospital a little longer. Could I borrow your keys and get my knitting bag out of your car? It'll help me pass the time. Tommy will be fine with Millie until I get back."

After a momentary pause, he reached into the pocket of his jeans and handed them over. "Straight there and back, all right? If you overhear any arguments, call me before you go investigate on your own."

"I won't be gone more than ten minutes. Then I'll come back and spell Millie with the baby."

"Ten minutes," he clarified.

"Okay." She uttered the promise in as conversational a tone as she could muster, not wanting him to suspect just how eager she was to put some thought-clearing distance between them.

He didn't release the keys once she'd wrapped her fingers around them, holding on without actually touching her. "I haven't forgotten about Tommy and Diana. We'll go to the lab right after this."

"I know." She could never question his commitment to finding answers.

Lucy pocketed his keys and hurried to the elevator, knowing Niall continued to study her retreat, probably trying to make sense of her passionate response to a simple thank-you kiss. But she refused to look back and let him see the confusion and embarrassment that was no doubt evident on her face. Last night he'd touched her, more than once. They'd traded some full-body contact that had ignited more than a distant fantasy. And now he'd kissed her. With any other man—like that drunk in the disreputable neighborhood the police had dubbed no-man's-land—she'd think he was into her. But Niall Watson didn't quite understand the intricacies of attraction—and these increasingly intimate interactions that were wreaking havoc on her heart and hormones were nothing more than gratitude and practical necessities to Niall.

When the elevator opened, Lucy dashed inside and pushed the button for the lobby. When she did dare to look back across the hallway, she saw that she was still the object of Niall's piercing scrutiny. It wasn't until she held up ten fingers right before the doors shut that he finally turned away to Dr. Koelus's office. And it wasn't until she broke contact with those blue eyes that she was finally able to release a deep sigh of relief.

The elevator descended, and with each floor, a little more common sense returned. She was foolish for letting her feelings for Niall simmer into anything more than a stupid crush. Maybe these weren't real feelings, anyway. It made sense for a woman with her background to idolize a man who was the complete opposite of a volatile glory seeker like Roger Campbell, to be drawn to a man to whom family was so obviously important. But that didn't mean she was falling in love with the quiet mystery man across the hall. She had far more important things to worry about than her love life, anyway. Like finding Diana. Making sure Tommy felt safe and nurtured. Even just finishing the blue cap she was knitting for him.

When Lucy stepped outside the hospital's sliding glass doors, she was hit by a sharp blast of damp wind that cut through her sweatshirt and camisole, reminding her that she'd been in such a hurry to escape before Niall started grilling her with questions she didn't want to answer, that she'd left without her sweater coat. Spring was trying to come to Kansas City, but it wasn't here yet. Although the temperature was well above freezing, the drab day did little to perk up her spirits. She crossed her arms in front of her and surveyed the dingy landscape of sooty snow melting against the curb and the muddy mess of brown grass surrounding a few denuded trees. Even the evergreen shrubs had a grayish cast that reflected the low, overcast sky.

Maybe the promised rain would wash away the last dregs of winter and she wouldn't worry quite so much about Diana being out in this. Was money the reason she'd left Tommy with her? There'd been nothing with the infant but the clothes on his back. She and Niall and Thomas Watson had bought or borrowed everything Tommy could need. But did Diana have a warm coat to wear? A safe place to stay out of the weather? Food to eat? Did she know how much Lucy ached to see her foster daughter's beautiful smile and hug her in her arms again?

Warmth of a different kind trickled down Lucy's cheek and she quickly wiped the tear away. Crying wouldn't do Diana or Tommy any good. And she certainly didn't need to embarrass herself any further by standing here in front of a big city hospital crying her eyes out, especially after that humiliating lapse in judgment with Niall upstairs.

Shaking off both the cold and the negativity of her fatigue-fueled thoughts, Lucy crossed the driveway and followed the sidewalk around to Saint Luke's visitors' parking lot. She found Niall's SUV easily enough and slung the long strap of her knitting bag over her shoulder and across her chest before locking it again.

Glimpsing a distorted movement reflecting off the side window, she shut the back door and swung around. She slowly released the breath that had locked up in her chest and nodded to the older couple walking past the rear bumper. Of course. It was probably them that she'd seen, reflecting at a weird angle as they approached and then passed Niall's SUV. After that close call outside their condominium building last night, she was probably being extra paranoid about silver cars and parking lots. Still, it was hard to shake the sense that there was something unseen just beyond the corner of her eye, something that she was missing.

A shiver skittered down her spine that had nothing to do with the penetrating breeze. Had she imagined the car following her? Or simply confused another resident's new vehicle with something similar she'd seen down in no-man's-land? Holding the strap of her knitting bag in both fists, she walked to the rear of the SUV and looked up and down the lane of parked cars. Was someone watching her? She seemed to have a sixth sense for when Niall was studying her, and she lifted her gaze to the hospital's fifth floor. Was he spying on her from the waiting-area windows, making sure she didn't disappear before all the mysteries swirling through that brilliant head of his could be solved? Lucy frowned. All the glass on the front of the building reflected the sea of clouds, making it impossible to tell if anyone inside was overly curious about her. Best to get moving and go back inside.

Although she felt fairly certain that neither Roger nor the drunk from the aptly named no-man's-land Thomas Watson had described would have any clue how to track her to this part of the city, she still found herself looking at all the cars she passed as she hurried across the parking lot. She was specifically looking for a silver sports car, but it was daunting to see exactly how many gray and silver vehicles there were in the parking lot, and impossible to know whether any of the people walk-

ing in and out of Saint Luke's main doors belonged
to one of those cars or if anyone, seen or unseen, was
watching her.

The uneasy suspicion remained when she reentered
the hospital's lobby and moved through the main visitors' area to the bank of elevators. Maybe it was just
the chill of the dreary February air staying with her.
Maybe that's why she'd felt someone's eyes on her—
they'd thought she was a fool for venturing outside without mittens or a cap or even so much as an umbrella to
ward off the coming rain.

The elevator doors opened, and Lucy watched with
an envious tug on her heart as a nurse pushed out a
wheelchair with a new mom holding her baby while the
dad and a big brother and sister followed them with bal-
loons and flowers and a basket of gifts. And though she
managed a smile and "Congratulations" to the expanding family, Lucy's arms tightened around her middle.
That was never going to happen for her. Roger Campbell and her mother had seen to that. Despite her good
fight to remain optimistic, a gloom as chilly and blah
as the weather outside settled around her shoulders.

Once the elevator was clear, Lucy stepped inside.
She had five floors to push the past out of her head and
fix a legitimate smile on her face for Niall and Tommy
and Millie and the Watsons and the rest of the world
she intended to take on until she located Diana and reunited her with Tommy. She retreated to the back rail
as two men converged on the waiting elevator, giving
them space to come in. But the younger man darted past
the gentleman carrying a bouquet of flowers, pushing
a button as he slipped inside.

"Hey, I think that guy wanted—" The young man pushed the close button with rapid-fire repetition, nearly catching the other man's outstretched hand between the sliding doors before he wisely pulled back to wait for the next car. "Okay."

Guess you're in a hurry.

Lucy arched an eyebrow at his rudeness and kept her distance from the preoccupied man. With his back to her and the collar of his leather jacket turned up, masking all but the top of his coal-black hair, she could only speculate whether fear for a loved one's health or excitement over a new birth or simply being self-centered were what drove him to get to where he needed to go so quickly. She couldn't even see around him to find out what floor number he'd pushed. But he certainly smelled good—if one liked the scents of Italian cooking that filled the elevator. He must be a chef or come from a family who—

"You were downtown yesterday, asking about Diana Kozlow?"

Lucy's wandering thoughts smashed into the steel door of reality. Her gaze shot to his upturned collar and her heart raced with a wary excitement. "You know Diana? Can you help me?" She took a step forward but quickly retreated to the far corner of the car when he shifted his back to her, not only to keep his face hidden, but to expose the sheath of a long knife, strapped to the waist of his dark jeans. "Where can I find her?"

"You need to stop asking questions." His accent, a mix of guttural consonants and rolling *r*'s, reminded her of the argument outside her laundry room and the answering machine message at her office.

"Were you at my building last night? Was Diana with you?" Was he the man Diana had sounded so afraid of on the answering machine? Had he hurt her? Had he threatened her with that knife? Hell, he wasn't that much taller than Lucy, but he was muscular enough to do damage with his bare hands.

His only answer was a terse "Shut up. You're only making it worse."

"Making what worse?" She desperately wanted him to answer. "Who are you? Is Diana okay? Where is she?" One answer. Any answer. She was beginning to understand Niall's obsession with resolving loose ends. "Please. She's like a daughter to me. I just need to see her and know she's okay. Can you help me? I need to talk to her."

His shoulders hunched inside his jacket, and he exhaled an audible groan of what—impatience? Frustration? "What about the baby?"

He knew about the baby? "Tommy is hers, isn't he?"

"Tommy?" The man angled his face partway toward hers, although she still couldn't make out much more than olive skin with beads of sweat making the black strands of hair stick to his forehead.

"Tell me the baby's real name. What does Diana call him?"

"Is he safe? He is well?" Was that a wistful note in his cryptic words?

He cared about Tommy. He *knew* Tommy. "Yes. Didn't you see him last night? I think Diana did. He needs his mother. Can you take me to her?"

"Tommy is a good name. Whatever you do, don't let

that baby out of your sight. And don't let him anywhere near Diana again."

Again? Diana *was* the woman who'd left the lipstick kiss on Tommy's forehead. "How can I? I don't know where she is. What's going on? Did you break into my apartment? Wait. What kind of car do you drive?" The elevator slowed its ascent and stopped with a soft bounce. She glanced up. Fourth floor. He was getting off without telling her anything except veiled threats that made her even more afraid for Diana. "Please. Is she okay?" He slipped between the sliding doors before they were fully open. Forgetting the knife and the muscles, she lunged forward and grabbed his arm to stop him. "I just want to talk—"

He winced and muttered a foreign curse before he jerked free of her grip and shoved her back into the elevator. Lucy barely caught a glimpse of dark eyes and sharp cheekbones before he reached back in to push the door-close button.

"Hey. Hey!" She clipped her elbow on the steel railing, sending a tingle of momentary numbness down to her fingertips, before landing on her bottom. But she ignored the bruising pain and scrambled to the control panel to reverse the command. She caught the door as it stopped, then opened again, narrowing her gaze on the bloody palm print sliding out of sight between the elevator and outside wall.

Confused shock stopped her for a moment. That was *her* palm print. The blood was on *her* hand.

But she wasn't bleeding.

The mysterious man was injured.

And he was getting away.

"Hey, stop!" The staff and visitors walking the hall paused and turned as she rushed out. "Come back!"

"Miss?" A black man wearing a white lab coat over his tie and dress slacks put a hand on her arm. "Are you all right?"

She twisted away, taking a step one direction, then the opposite, looking for a leather coat. "Did you see a man get off the elevator? A dark-haired man?"

The woman beside him also wore a lab coat and carried a tablet computer. "Are you hurt?"

"I'm fine. There was a man in the elevator. He must have been running."

"This is Dr. McBride," the woman introduced her companion. "Do you need him to look at that hand?"

"No." Lucy flashed a smile and dismissed their concern. "This is his blood. I have to find him."

"Him?"

"Did you see—" An elevator beeped beside the one she'd exited. "Do you know if that's going up or down?"

The woman shrugged an apology as Dr. McBride asked, "What's the man's name?"

"I have no idea. I've never met him before."

The doctor crossed to the nurses' station and ordered them to notify security about the injured man.

"Do you need to wash up?" his assistant offered.

"No. I need to find…" Lucy's gaze zeroed in on the door marked Stairway gently closing and took off at a run. "Excuse me."

She pushed open the door and stopped on the concrete landing, glancing up and down, adjusting her hearing to the sudden quiet compared to the noises and voices out on the hospital floor. There. Footsteps running down the stairs.

"Wait!" she shouted, hurrying down the steel and concrete stairs. "I need your help."

Lucy wasn't an athlete by any stretch of the imagination, but she'd walked miles on the treadmill in the gym back in her building, so she pushed herself to move faster and catch the man before he exited the hospital. She slung her bag behind her back and balanced her hand against the railing, leaving her bloody mark as she spun around one landing and the next. She was nearly breathless, as much from desperation as from her sprint down four flights, when she burst through the stairwell exit onto the sidewalk outside.

"Where..." So many cars. Too many people. Too many bushes and trees.

Lucy almost headed over to the main entrance to see if the man who'd given her the cryptic warning had taken a turn somewhere and come out into the main lobby. But then she saw the small red blob seeping into the sidewalk a few feet away. She jogged out to the edge of the driveway, spotted another blood droplet on the opposite curb and hurried across into the main parking lot. There. A spot on the fender of someone's car. Another one on the white arrow marking the turn lane to the exit. She wasn't aware of the gray sky anymore, was barely aware of the damp chill in the air as she hurried behind the bloody trail. She was nearly to the road at the far end of the parking lot when the path she was following ended.

"No." Her nostrils flared as she took a deep breath to slow her panic. "You're my best lead." She scanned the grassy brown berm for one more clue to finding the man, praying she hadn't reached a dead end. "Help me. Help…"

Lucy looked up and saw an orangey-red pickup truck, its noisy engine idling and sending out plumes of stinky exhaust as it waited to turn onto the hilly road that ran in front of Saint Luke's. She saw the driver, staring at her through the window.

Dark hair. Brown eyes. Sad brown eyes.

Lucy's heart leaped in her chest. "Diana!"

The how and the why didn't matter. Overwhelming relief gave her a second wind. Lucy charged up the hill.

"Diana!" The young woman splayed her fingers against the glass, turning away and shaking her head. Was that a wave goodbye? "No. Wait!"

She saw the blur of movement between two parked cars a second too late.

"I said to leave us alone!"

She caught a glimpse of shiny gray steel before something hard struck her in the temple, spinning the world around her. Lucy crumpled to her hands and knees as the man in the leather jacket charged past her.

Her jeans and sweatshirt were soaking up the moisture from the grass by the time she heard the squeal of tires against the pavement and her world faded from gray to black.

Chapter Six

Niall would allow Lucy ten minutes to come back from her errand.

At eleven minutes, he excused himself from the meeting with his father and Jane Boyle, which had somehow devolved into a discussion about overstepping personal boundaries and who'd be in charge of what once she moved in to care for Seamus. Leaving the two of them to butt heads, Niall went back to the waiting area, looking for dark curls and a knitting bag but finding neither. Adjusting his glasses on the bridge of his nose, he scanned up and down the hallway. No Lucy. Something was wrong.

Although he still hadn't figured out why she'd pulled away from that kiss—and hadn't even had time to fully process the impulse that had prompted him to put his fingers in her hair and taste every inch of her rosy lips in the first place when a verbal thank-you would have sufficed perfectly well—there were two things he knew for certain about Lucy McKane: she was a woman of her many words, and she didn't want to be away from Tommy any longer than was necessary. If she'd prom-

ised to be right back, she should be here by now. She
would be with the baby.

While assessing his options and formulating a plan,
Niall rubbed his palm on the thigh of his jeans, trying to erase the memory of Lucy's silky curls twisting around his fingers as if they'd grabbed hold of him
with the same enthusiasm her grip against his chest had.
He needed to concentrate on the clues around him and
figure out his best plan of action. Realizing her purse
and cell phone were still sitting there in the chair where
she'd left them, and that calling her wasn't an option,
he quickly moved on to plan B.

Spying Keir and Millie conversing outside the ladies'
room, Niall strode down the hallway to join them. "Is
Lucy in there?"

Millie shifted back and forth on her feet, rocking
the cooing infant on her shoulder. "No. Tommy and I
were the only ones in there. I haven't seen Lucy since
we left."

"Keir, have you seen her?" Niall wondered at the
little gut punch of satisfaction when Tommy shifted
his alert brown eyes to him at the sound of his voice.

"No, bro." Keir gave him a playful punch on the
arm. "Aw, come on. I liked her. You haven't scared her
off already, have you?" His teasing grin quickly faded
when he didn't get a rise out of Niall. "Hey, just kidding. Is something wrong?"

Niall couldn't wait here and play negotiator while
his father and Ms. Boyle tried to reach a compromise.
And he sure as hell didn't have time to be responsible for keeping Duff's mouth shut in there to prevent
a serious rift between the family and the woman they

needed to see to their grandfather's recovery. Instead, he took Millie's arm and walked her toward Seamus's room. "Are you okay watching Tommy a little longer?"

"Of course. What's happened, Niall?"

"Lucy went out to the car. She should have been back by now."

"She said she thought someone had been following her the past couple of days. Do you think he found her?"

"What?" Niall stopped and looked down into Millie's crinkled blue eyes. "Who's following her?"

"She didn't know. Someone in a silver car."

"Ah, hell. There was a car like that at our building last night. Silver Camaro. Nearly ran her over."

Millie wrapped her hand around the back of Tommy's head, as if she didn't want him to hear this surprising tidbit of news. "She said she spotted it downtown when she was looking for her foster daughter and then again about a block from your building. She didn't mention anything about last night."

"Probably because she didn't want to upset you," Keir suggested. "But if this guy has located where she lives and saw you two leaving this morning—"

"He could have tracked us to her office and then the hospital." Niall raked his fingers through his hair, berating himself for making such a rookie mistake. "I wasn't even looking for something like that."

"When you work a crime, you're used to the people being dead, not chasing after you," Keir pointed out. "It's been a long time since your academy training."

"That's no excuse."

"Maybe it's her foster daughter, trying to make contact again," Millie suggested.

Niall doubted it. "Or the creep trying to hurt Diana and Tommy."

Keir was the detective here. He pulled out his phone. "I can do a search for silver Camaros in Kansas City. If you're thinking about tracking one down without a license plate or even make and model, though, it'll be a long shot. Maybe we can narrow down the search grid to certain neighborhoods."

Niall nodded and resumed walking. He wondered why Lucy hadn't mentioned seeing the Camaro more than once when she'd seemed so open about everything else, including some disturbing hints regarding her past. If someone had been following her, that could explain her instinct to punch first and ask questions later, or run outside to confront whoever was tailing her.

When they reached room number 5017, he pushed open the door and ushered them inside. He dropped the diaper bag on a chair and crossed to the bed where Seamus Watson lay. The old man's bright blue eyes tracking Niall's movements were the only color in his wan face. "Grandpa, I brought someone to keep you company." He leaned over and kissed Seamus's forehead beside the layers of gauze that covered the bullet hole and surgical incision there. "I have to go to work. Millie's going to introduce you to little Tommy. He belongs to a friend. He's…" He palmed the small, warm head resting on Millie's shoulder. Tommy's eyes looked up at him, too. "…a baby."

Seamus's eyes opened as wide as the stroke would let him, and his lips fluttered with a remembered task. Clearly, there was a question there.

But Niall didn't have time to answer. He headed for

the door before he lost his focus again. With Lucy's penchant for being led by her instincts and emotions and not thinking things through, she could be in real trouble. "Millie will explain."

Keir stopped him at the door. "You want backup?"

"No." They still had no leads on their grandfather's shooting—whether it was an accidental hit, or if somebody would be coming back to finish the job. And he couldn't focus on two mysteries that hit so close to home at the same time. "I need to know these people are safe."

Keir pulled back the front of his jacket, tapping his belt beside the badge and sidearm holstered there. "They will be. I'll find out what I can about the car."

With a nod, Niall strode from the room. When he got on the elevator, he was more certain than ever that something was terribly wrong. A crimson palm print, half the size of his own, stared at him from the closed steel door. He inhaled a deep breath to counteract the rush of unaccustomed anger that heated his blood. It wasn't necessarily Lucy's. The blood didn't mean she was hurt. His gaze dropped to the number-four button and the smudge of a bloody fingerprint marking it. It was too big to come from the hand that marked the door.

There'd been two people on this elevator. A man and a woman. And at least one of them was seriously injured.

Ah, hell. Niall pushed the button, stopping the elevator at the next floor. When the doors opened, he stepped out. "Lucy?"

A quick visual sweep of the people moving on the fourth floor revealed no curly-haired brunette. But two security guards were converging on the nurses' station.

Niall held up his badge as he approached the doctor standing there. "Have you seen a dark-haired woman? Thirtyish? Wearing a Royals sweatshirt?"

The other man turned from the guards he was giving a report to. "She was here a few minutes ago. She said there was an injured man on the elevator. Last I saw she was heading—"

Niall didn't need to hear the rest. A second scan picked up the elongated blood drops on the tiles leading to the stairwell exit. Directional spatter. Whoever had been injured on the elevator was running—away from someone or after someone, he couldn't tell. Logic indicated that one of them had to be Lucy.

The blood left a clear trail down the stairs. Too much of a trail. Niall took the stairs at a jog, skipping two steps at a time, burning inside at the idea any drop of it could be Lucy's.

He found another bloody print on the door handle leading outside and pushed it open. "Lucy?"

A half dozen people on the front sidewalk turned at his shout. Not her. None of them were her.

A sprinkling of rain spotted his glasses. He looked through the drops to zero in on the next bloodstain on the opposite curb. Even with the growing intensity of the rain, thinning the spot into rivulets that washed away in the gutter, he could tell that the blood marks were getting bigger, more circular. Whoever was injured was slowing down, succumbing to his or her wound. The instinct to run to his truck and grab his kit to preserve some of the blood so he could ID its owner blipped into his brain and out just as quickly when he saw four or five people converging at the far edge of the parking lot.

Good Samaritans running to help.

Help whom?

"Lucy? Lucy!" Niall stretched his long legs into a run, zigzagging between parked cars until he saw the woman on her hands and knees wearing muddy clothes and the people helping her to her feet. When she turned to thank one, he got a clear glimpse of the sticky red substance matting the hair beside that warm, velvety cheek. Niall had his badge in his hand by the time he reached the group and moved them aside. "KCPD crime lab. I'm a doctor."

"Niall." Lucy reached out her hands and tumbled into him as the others stepped back. He caught her in his arms and sat her down on the curb. Why was she smiling? Was she delirious? How bad was that head wound? "I saw her. I saw Diana. She was right here. She's alive."

"I'm tired of seeing you muddy and beat up. Where are you hurt? What happened?"

She was urging him to retreat as much as clinging to his arm for support. "We're getting wet. Where's your car? If we don't hurry we'll lose her again—"

"Stop talking." He quickly assessed her injuries, pushing her back onto her bottom and kneeling beside her when she tried to use him to stand again. The blood on her hand was washing away as the skies opened up and the rain began to fall in sheets around them. No cut or scrape there. But she winced as he pushed the damp curls away from her temple and saw the ugly gash in her hairline where the skin had split open. He pulled a white handkerchief from his back pocket and pressed it against the wound.

"Ow. Damn it, Niall, you need to listen to me."

"Can you see this?" He held up a finger in front of her face and moved it from side to side, watching her green eyes track the movement.

"Of course I can. There's nothing wrong with my eyesight. I *saw* Diana. She was right there." Since there was no obvious indication of a concussion, Niall shifted his attention, running his hand along her shoulders, elbows, hands, knees, ensuring there were no other injuries needing immediate attention. "Let me up. I'm soaked to the skin. We have to do something. Have you heard a word I've said?"

Niall was obliquely aware of a break in the rain hitting the top of his head as Duff ran up beside him. "Oh, hell. Is she all right?" A quick glance up to his big brother asked for an explanation and thanked him at the same time. Duff understood. "Keir called me. Said there might be a problem. What do you need?"

"Have you got a handkerchief on you?" Duff pulled a blue bandanna from his pocket. Niall wrapped it around the cuff of Lucy's sweatshirt and tied it off, trying to preserve some of the blood that had soaked in there. Since she had no injury to her hand or wrist, he suspected it would match the bloody fingerprint in the elevator and possibly give him a name for the culprit who had cracked her head open. "Look for a silver Camaro. Someone's been following her."

Lucy shook her head, dislodging the compress that stuck to the wound at her temple and moaning at the sudden movement. "No, Diana drove away in a red pickup truck. I mean, yes, there was a car yesterday. And last night. But just now...they turned north. Diana and the man from the elevator. They left together."

"What man?" Duff asked, pulling out his notepad and pen.

"He warned me not to try to find Diana. But I did. They were here together."

"Can you describe him?"

"He was bleeding." That made sense. Lucy's blood was redder, fresher, than the mess he'd found inside. Niall plucked up the soiled handkerchief from the shelf of her breasts. It was already getting too wet to do much good as a compress, so he used it to dab at the bruising and swelling so he could get a clearer look at the wound there. "He warned me not to try to find her. But she was here. She saw me...and then he..." She pushed Niall's hands away. "It's hard to think when you're doing that."

"I need to see how badly you're hurt."

"It's not my blood."

He held up the blood-soaked handkerchief. "The hell it isn't!"

"Easy, Niall." Duff rested his big hand on Niall's shoulder and knelt down beside him to talk to Lucy. "Can you give me a description of the truck?"

Lucy's wide eyes had locked on to Niall's at his irrational outburst. But she blinked away the raindrops glistening on her dark lashes and turned to Duff. "Faded red. Rusted around the wheel wells. Small. But I never saw a license plate. I didn't think to read it at the time, but it had words and a logo on the side of the door— like a business name."

Duff jotted down the information while Niall tried

to ignore the irony of Lucy's calm recitation of facts when he'd been the one distracted by his emotional reactions. "And the guy?" Duff asked.

"Black hair. Black leather jacket and jeans. Mediterranean looking. He smelled like a restaurant, if that helps."

Duff pushed to his feet and turned to the people who'd gathered around to make sure Lucy was all right. "Did anybody else see the truck or the man who hit her?"

He took statements from a couple of bystanders who'd stayed to make sure she was all right. But Niall had collected his thoughts enough to understand they had little to add beyond confirming the details Lucy had shared. "Your perp has lost a lot of blood, too. He couldn't risk coming to this hospital, but he'll have to go somewhere for treatment soon or you'll be looking for a dead body."

"I'll put a call out to notify area hospitals and clinics. I'll check in when I know something." Duff pulled out his phone and punched in a number as Niall pulled Lucy to her feet. "You'll get her to the ER?" Niall nodded. "Sorry this happened, Luce. Stay strong. We'll find him. And don't let this guy scare ya too much."

Duff jogged away while Niall wrapped an arm around Lucy's waist and pulled her to his side, shielding her from the rain while keeping her close enough to hold the compress to her temple. "Let's get you inside."

Although the man in him was certainly aware of her sweetly rounded curves pressed against his body, the doctor in him was concerned about the chill he felt through the wet clothing where denim and cotton rubbed together. He tried to quicken her pace, but he had to shorten his stride when he felt her fingers dancing at the right side of his waist looking for a place to hold on to for balance. Finally, she slipped her cold thumb beneath the waistband of his jeans and latched on to a belt loop. "You know, sometimes I forget you're a cop as well as an ME. With your gun there, I'm not sure where to put my hand."

"You hang on anywhere you can. I've got you."

Three more steps, then a hesitation to blink the rain from her eyes, then another step. "Why would your brother think I'm scared of you? I'm not, you know. I mean, I get frustrated..." She tried to laugh, but the sound ended up more like a groan and she stopped, laying her hand over his on her forehead. "Okay, I guess I am hurt."

"Could we keep moving?" he suggested.

They made it past the next row of cars before she stopped again. "Wait a minute. Where's Tommy? Is he okay? That man knew about him. He said not to let Tommy out of my sight. And I don't even know where he is."

"Tommy's fine. He's with Keir and Millie. He's meeting Grandpa. He'll be safe with them." She smiled, and he took a little more of her weight and pulled her into step beside him again.

"That's sweet. And Millie got to see Seamus. A visit like that will make all three of them feel better. Thank you for listening. And taking the time to come help me. Again. I know I said I'd be right back, but I couldn't pass up the chance to learn something about Diana. Oh, wow. You don't even have your jacket. You're getting so wet."

Chatty woman. Sometimes, he enjoyed the melodic sound of her voice filling up the silences he was far too accustomed to. But was there anyone she wasn't going to mention before she started taking care of herself? Or was the rambling an indication of some undetected head trauma?

Barely missing a step, he reached down behind her knees and swung her up into his arms, knitting bag and all. "Too much talking and not enough walking."

"Put me down."

He ignored the protest of her hands pressing against his chest and quickened his pace, carrying her straight to the hospital's main entrance. They could reach the ER through the lobby. "Put your arm around my neck and keep pressure on that wound."

Instead of obeying his instructions, she squiggled against him, trying to free herself from his grasp. "I can't afford to be an invalid, Niall. You do realize that I'm the only family Diana has. I mean, we can't exactly count Tommy when it comes to helping out. We're not like your family where your dad and your brothers and Millie and all your lab and cop friends jump in and help out. It's just me. I *have* to be there for her."

So what was he in all this? Who was ignoring the breast squeezed against his chest and the rain smearing his glasses to keep her from bleeding until she fell unconscious? Who'd rescued Tommy from hours alone without food or attention, or torn a hole in his UCM sweatpants saving her from that speeding car last night? Who'd agreed to team up with her for the baby's sake? How was she alone? "I swear to God, woman, if you don't stop talking, I'm going to kiss you again, just to keep you quiet."

"What? I...oh." Her struggles against him ceased. "Yes, Dr. Watson. Sorry to inconvenience you." Her arm crept around his neck, and she moved the wet compress back to her temple. "Shutting up now."

The receptionist at the front desk was on her feet to meet them. An orderly with a wheelchair joined him halfway down the long hallway that led into the emergency wing. Niall was aware that Lucy had stopped talking, doing exactly as he'd asked, except to give brief answers to the medical staff attending her. With her skin so pale and her eyes refusing to make contact with his, Niall made the decision not to prompt her into conversation, partly because he didn't want to upset her further and partly because he had no idea what he had done to make her shut down in the first place. Well, he had a good idea that he'd let his frustrations get the better of him and he'd said the wrong thing.

But was she mad at him? Hurt? Tired? Did she not see he was doing what needed to be done in order to keep her safe so that she *could* be there for both Diana and Tommy?

Niall gave a quick account of his assessment and what he'd done to treat Lucy's injury to the attending staff, then phoned his brothers to report on Lucy's condition and find out, as he'd expected, that there simply wasn't enough information yet to pinpoint the owner of either the silver car or the rusted red pickup. Was that why she had her nose out of joint—that he'd had someone to call on for help in a difficult situation? Didn't she understand that his family was helping her, too? And why, why, why did Lucy McKane get in his head like this and fill it up with so many unanswered questions?

He desperately needed to lose himself in the provable logic of his work and restore the equilibrium inside him. While Duff and Keir continued to make calls, Niall put on a dry shirt from his go bag and got his ME kit from the SUV to take pictures and secure blood samples before the hospital cleaning staff disinfected the elevator and stairwell. Whatever evidence might be outside had already been compromised by the rain, so he focused his attention on the evidence he *could* collect.

Lucy sat propped up on an examination table in one of the ER bays, wearing a hospital gown and shivering beneath the heated blanket draped over her lap when Niall returned nearly an hour later. He stood back for several seconds, watching her study her own toes wiggling fretfully beneath the edge of the blanket while an intern on the stool beside her tied off another stitch in her scalp. Did the woman have an inability to truly be still? Or was that her way of coping with the pain and discomfort she must be feeling?

The younger man acknowledged Niall as soon as he set his kit down on a chair just inside the curtain. "You were right about there not being a concussion, Dr. Watson. Looks like whatever he hit her with was small and the injury was localized."

The edema surrounding the wound gave a clear impression of the instrument used in the attack. Aware of Lucy's green eyes shifting from her purple-polished toenails to his every movement, Niall pulled his camera from his kit and snapped a few pictures before the intern put in the last two stitches. He enlarged the image on the camera screen. "Looks like a weapon about an inch wide, with a distinctive ridge pattern to it."

After tying off the last stitch, the intern placed his suture kit on a rolling stainless steel tray and ripped open a package of gauze with his sterile gloves. "Maybe the butt of a gun?"

Lucy tugged on Niall's wrist, pulling the camera down so that she could look at the image, too. "Or the handle of a knife?"

No comment on the puffy swelling beside her right eye or the gray-and-violet bruise that marred her pale skin? She was an expert on wound markings now? Niall adjusted his glasses on the bridge of his nose. "It's not a cut. Blunt-force trauma split the skin open."

She opened her mouth to explain her comment, but the doctor was giving her directions to care for the wound. "When the anesthetic wears off, you're going to be pretty sore. It's okay to use an ice pack for the swelling, but don't let the stitches get wet. And no aspirin or ibuprofen for twenty-four hours or so." Young Dr. Shaughnessy, according to his name badge, peeled off his gloves and tossed them onto the tray as he rolled it over to the counter, where he typed something on to his laptop. "Since your tetanus shot is current, I think we can forgo the antibiotics. But if you do see any signs of an infection setting in, give us a call or contact your personal physician."

"I'll monitor her recovery," Niall assured the younger man.

With a nod, the intern picked up a plastic bag and handed it to Niall. "We bagged her clothes like you requested. I wouldn't leave them in there too long or they'll start to mildew. I took the liberty of labeling it and signing my name to preserve the chain of custody. I start my forensic rotation next month," he added with a slightly boyish enthusiasm.

"Thanks." Niall scanned the sealed bag and quickly scrawled his name beneath John Shaughnessy's. A pointed glare from Lucy seemed to indicate that something more needed to be said. She was still putting someone else before her own well-being. Niall frowned, but acquiesced to the silent demand. "Good luck with that."

"Thank you, sir. I might run into you at the ME's office then. Here's a clean set of scrubs you can change into." Dr. Shaughnessy handed that bag to Lucy. "Take your time, ma'am. Unfortunately, we're having a run of business this afternoon. I'd better go get my next assignment. Have a good one."

"Thanks, John." Before the curtains had even closed behind the intern, Lucy was squiggling off the edge of the table. "I've been here way too long. I keep thinking about how everything would be different if I'd just gotten Diana to talk to me."

When her toes hit the floor, she swayed and Niall reached across the table to steady her. But she put her hand up to keep him away.

"It's a bump on the head and a couple of stitches." Technically, Niall had counted seven. But if she still wanted to keep some distance between them the way she had after that kiss upstairs and battle of wills outside, he'd respect the patient's wish. After he retreated a step, she dumped out the bag with the scrubs onto the exam table and pulled out a pair of white cotton socks.

"I've just been off my feet too long. I need to get the circulation going again. Not to mention that it's freezing in here. I think my blood stopped flowing half an hour ago."

When she bent over to slide the first sock on, the gown split open at the back and gave him a clear view of her underwear clinging to the curves of her hips and bottom. He remembered those panties from the laundry she'd been folding late one night. They were a pretty lavender color, a few shades lighter than the polish on her toes, and Niall's groin tightened with an unexpected response that was as potent as it was ill timed. Niall politely turned away from the tempting sight. He needed something to focus on besides the way Lucy McKane was transforming his well-ordered world into a topsy-turvy mess.

"Tell me about the knife," he stated, maybe a little more harshly than he intended. "Tell me everything."

After a moment's hesitation, Lucy went back to dressing and Niall went back to being a medical examiner with ties to KCPD's crime lab. He heard about the silver car that she'd seen in no-man's-land and again just a block from their condo building—and yes, she thought it could be the same car that had nearly run her down last night. She told him about the brute in the elevator and the long knife he'd carried that could explain the distinct pattern of her head wound. When Niall thought he had his physiological and emotional reactions well in check again, he pulled a narrow file from his kit and scraped the dried blood from beneath her fingernails and labeled it as evidence. In the back of his mind, he kept thinking how much easier it was to process a dead body in the lab than to deal with the scents of rain and blood and antiseptic on a living person. On a friend. On a woman who was the most alive person he'd ever dealt with.

On Lucy McKane.

Niall shook his head, warding off the uncharacteristic anger that simmered in his veins when he snapped a picture of the ugly bruise on her elbow and she told him how she'd followed the trail of blood the same way he had to track down the man who'd assaulted her and warned her to mind her own business. But when she raised her arms to slip into the pink scrub top, his temper boiled over. "Hold it."

Lucy froze at the sharpness in his voice and instinctively hugged the top to her waist. "What now?"

It wasn't the smooth curves of her lavender bra that had caught his attention, but the fist-size bruise turning all shades of purple framed between her breasts that had him circling around the exam table to stand directly in front of her. "Did he do that to you, too?"

A rosy blush dotted her cheeks as she tilted her face up to his. She turned away and lifted the shirt up over her head again before answering. "I suppose so. On the elevator when he shoved me back inside to get away."

Niall raised his camera. "I'd better get a shot of that, too."

She whirled around on him. "I am not a crime scene!"

"It's what I know how to do, Lucy. It's how I can help." Okay, so maybe going on seventy-two hours with hardly any sleep was giving him a short fuse he'd never had before, but the tear she swiped off her cheek and the soft gasp of pain wasn't helping him clear his head, either. "Apparently, I can't keep you from getting hurt, but I can analyze the size of his hand and the weapon he carries. If I can get a clean sample of his blood off you and your clothes, maybe I can identify him. If I get DNA and he's in the system, I can send Duff and Keir to arrest him, and he won't be able to hurt you or threaten Tommy and Diana anymore."

"And if he's not?"

Niall slipped his fingers into his hair and scratched at the frustration jamming his thoughts. "I'm not up to that part of the plan yet."

"What plan is that?"

He threw out his hands and glared down at her. "The one where I keep you and Tommy safe and stuff like this doesn't happen."

Had that outburst really just come from him?

A gentle touch to his jaw snapped him out of his roiling thoughts. Lucy's lips were almost smiling when she reached up to stroke the spiky strands of hair off his forehead. He calmed at her tender caress. "I'll be okay, Niall. I've been hurt worse than this."

"Is that supposed to make me feel better?" There. He'd admitted it out loud. Maybe he'd just admitted it to himself. He was *feeling*. The visual of Lucy's injury and the touch of her hand made him feel emotions that were unexpected, and clearly more powerful than he was equipped to handle.

Yet with a smile he craved as much as her touch, she seemed to take every mood swing in stride. "You know, I was processed like this when I was seventeen. Back in Falls City."

"Processed? You were assaulted?" Parts of his brain

were starting to click again. She'd mentioned something about her past earlier. "By the boyfriend your mother wanted you to stay with?"

She nodded, but he didn't miss the way her lips pressed together in a taut imitation of a smile, or the way her hands slipped across her belly and she hugged herself.

"Roger Campbell. He got pissed off when I refused to have sex with him. Apparently, my mother had promised him that I would. It was her solution for getting him to take me back, I suppose." Opening up a dead body never made Niall feel physically ill the way Lucy's matter-of-fact recitation of the crime against her did. "It was a shaky relationship to begin with. I didn't want to take a step I couldn't turn back from. To be honest, I didn't want to end up like Alberta—so dependent on a man to take care of her that she didn't care what it cost her." Her shoulders lifted with a weary sigh. "It cost me too much, anyway. That's why I can't have kids, you know. He broke a couple of ribs, damaged my..." She rubbed her hand across her flat belly. "I had to have emergency surgery."

Every one of Duff's rich vocabulary of curses raced through Niall's head. But only two words came out. "I'm sorry."

For a lot of things. Lucy was a natural caregiver. She should have scads of children and dozens of relatives to share her life with. That this woman should have been so used, so hurt by the people who were supposed to love her, gave him a clearer understanding of her obsession with tracking down her foster daughter and saving her. He'd redouble his efforts, as well. Maybe then she'd believe that she was not alone in her quest to do whatever was best for Tommy.

"It's not the memory, you know. It happened. Life goes on. Roger went to prison and I moved to Kansas City. But I didn't want to ever be in an ER again, feeling so useless, like there's not a single thing I can do to help myself. Especially when I know there's someone I *can* help. Someone who needs me. I want to go see Tommy and make sure he's all right. At least I could be taking care of him right now. That would be something useful I could do to help Diana. It's important to feel useful, isn't it?" Lucy paused for a moment. "Oh. And the lightbulb just went on. I think I understand where you're coming from now." She reached for the hem of the scrub shirt. "Take your picture."

Niall curved his grip around both her hands, stopping her. She wasn't a DB on an exam table at the lab. She was a living, breathing, beautiful woman with fears and goals and needs he should be addressing instead of falling back on the procedures and science that only made him feel comfortable and in control—not necessarily better.

Her fingers trembled within his grasp, drawing his attention to her icy skin and the sea of goose bumps sweeping up both forearms. Instead of taking the photo, he put away the camera and pulled his ME's jacket from his kit. It was little more than a windbreaker with a knit cotton lining, but he slipped it over her shoulders anyway, wanting to shelter her—no, needing to protect her—from at least one thing in this world that had or could ever hurt her.

"You are the coldest woman I've ever met." When she

arched a questioning eyebrow, he realized how that must have sounded. "Temperature-wise. Not personality-wise. Not at all. You know, cold hands, warm…"

"No wonder your brothers tease you. You're such a straight man, Niall." Her expression had changed from accusation to a full-blown grin, and he felt the muscles around his own mouth relaxing. "That's a wonderful compliment. Thank you." She slid her arms into the sleeves and rolled up the cuffs to expose her hands. "This does feel better. I swear, you're as warm to the touch as I am cold all the time." This time, she was the one to draw back in embarrassment.

Niall chuckled and pulled the collar of the jacket together at her neck. "It's nice to know I *can* offer something you appreciate."

She curled her fingers around his wrists, keeping them linked together. "I appreciate everything you're doing for me—for us—Diana and Tommy and me. I just need you to remember this is a team effort. You don't get to say whether or not I help. I'm going to."

"Understood. But you are a steep learning curve, woman." He dropped his forehead to rest against hers, carefully avoiding her injury. "And I just need you to understand that, in your efforts to save the world—"

"Just my little part of it."

Niall conceded the point, but not the entire negotiation. Her little part of the world seemed to be a far too dangerous one for his liking. "I need you and Tommy to stay in one piece."

Lucy tilted her green eyes beneath his, looking straight up into his probing gaze. "Speaking of Tommy—I know he's only a couple of weeks old, but

I think babies can sense separation. He's already lost contact with his mother. I don't want to be gone so long that he thinks we've left him, too."

He could feel her trembling, an indication that the hospital's cold air was still affecting her. Cupping his hands over her shoulders, Niall rubbed up and down her arms, instilling what warmth he could before reluctantly raising his head and breaking contact with her. "I don't want that, either. Let's go upstairs and check in with him. I want to find out what Dad decided about Grandpa, too."

"And then we'll go to the lab?"

Niall gathered the evidence bags he'd labeled and stowed them inside his kit. "I think I'd better take you home so you can rest. You'll at least want to put on some of your own things."

A hand on his arm stopped his work. "I need answers more than I need sleep or clean clothes. I can watch Tommy, and we'll stay out of your way while you work. I have a seriously bad feeling that there's a clock ticking somewhere in Diana's life. That she doesn't have a lot of time. I need to know why she was with that man. Maybe the blood you found *will* tell us who he is. Diana said I was the only person she could count on. I need to know why she keeps running away from me instead of allowing me to help."

Taking Lucy and Tommy to the lab with him wasn't the wisest course of action. With them there it would be a challenge to focus on all the tests he needed to start running. But it was what Lucy wanted.

"Okay."

She picked up his camera and handed it to him, help-

ing him finish packing. "Oh, and never *threaten* to kiss
me again, okay, smart guy? I know relationships are
a challenge for you. At least, I think that's what I'm
learning about you. Don't overthink it when you're attracted to someone. If you're afraid for me or worried
about Tommy or your grandfather and you have that raw
feeling inside that you don't quite understand, finding a
logical explanation won't make it go away. All that does
is distance you from your real feelings. If you want to
kiss me, go for it. Don't make it some little scientific
experiment and don't do it to shut me up. Either kiss me
because you think there might be a special connection
between us or don't do it at all."

And with that intriguing little life lesson hanging in
the air for him to analyze, Lucy walked out of the ER,
leaving Niall to gather up his equipment and follow.

Chapter Seven

Answers were not to be found at the crime lab.

Lucy watched while Niall made phone calls and ran tests and accessed computers, but apparently forensic science, while it worked miracles in many ways, moved at a much slower pace than she expected. Results were coming in due time, Niall promised. But his patient attention to detail made her feel as if she was suffering from ADHD. Or perhaps, with Tommy asleep and Niall running tests and consulting with the CSIs and lab technologists in the building, while Lucy had nothing to do but pace, she only felt useless and isolated and not able to do one small thing to help find Diana. Even knitting was out of the question, since everything in her bag had gotten soaked with the rain and would need time to dry out before she could finish Tommy's cap or start any other project.

New locks for Lucy's front door couldn't be found, either, at least not until the entire door frame could be replaced. Which meant another night of sleeping on Niall's couch, fixing breakfast together, changing the dressing on her stitches, reminding Niall to put his books away and get some rest. She enjoyed a surprise visit from Duff and Keir with a pizza, loving how Niall murdered all three of them in the most competitive game of penny-ante poker she'd ever played. The next day she enjoyed the tour of Thomas Watson's big two-story house even more when they went over to help move furniture, install a ramp, and share a big pot of Millie's chili and cornbread around a long farmhouse table. She and Niall took turns feeding, diapering and playing with Tommy and wrestling him away from pseudo uncles and wannabe grandparents.

It was forty-eight hours of the family life she'd always dreamed of—and she had to constantly remind herself that it wasn't real. Lucy and Niall were just friends. Neighbors. Two concerned adults who'd joined forces to care for and protect an abandoned child.

Domestic bliss this wasn't. Not really. It hurt to discover herself feeling so at home with Niall's boisterous family, knowing all the while their laughter and friendship and support was just a temporary gift. It hurt even more to realize how easily her attraction to her handsome, geeky neighbor had grown into something deeper. She was becoming as addicted to Niall's quiet strength as Tommy was, and Niall's fierce devotion to a cause—her cause—gave her a sense of security and importance she'd never felt before.

What an idiot. She'd fallen in love with the brilliant doctor next door. And since love wasn't something that could be examined under a microscope or explained in twenty questions, she knew that Niall was sweetly clueless to the depth of her feelings for him. As for what he might feel for her? Since he scarcely acknowledged his feelings about much beyond his work and family, that was as much of a mystery as locating Diana and identifying the young man who'd threatened her in the elevator, then assaulted her when she'd refused to heed his warning. What logical benefit could she offer the inimitable Dr. Watson, anyway? Despite their friendship, Niall would probably want someone a little more staid and respectable, someone who didn't butt her nose into things and leave chaos in her wake. As much as he loved his family, he probably wanted someone who could give him that, too—lots of little shy brainiacs who would quietly change the world one day. Nothing like setting herself up for heartbreak.

So it was an easy decision to go back to work on Tuesday, returning her life to some sense of the independent normalcy she was used to. Since she and Niall worked opposite shifts, they'd agreed that she would take Tommy to the office with her. Either because he was still worried about her head injury or because he didn't want her and Tommy to be on their own and unprotected for any length of time, or some combination of both reasons, Niall insisted on driving her and the baby to her office. After dropping them off in the morning, the infant could nap comfortably in one of the family visitation rooms while she caught up on her caseload. And with Niall putting in so many extra hours at the lab and with his family, he could return home and have the day to catch up on some much-needed sleep before reporting in for his regular shift.

Lucy cradled Tommy against her shoulder, turning her nose to the unique scents of baby wash and formula burps as she sang a little ditty and danced around the tiny room, lulling him to sleep. *This* would be hard to lose, too. It was selfish to wish Tommy was *her* son, that fate would finally be kind enough to gift her with a child she loved this much. But Diana had been her child, too, for a time, until the law and the lure of a new boyfriend and an exciting career had made it easier than it should have been to lose contact and drift apart. Lucy still loved Diana and felt that inexplicable maternal urge to protect her just as fiercely as the helpless infant in her arms.

So despite the all-too-human envy in her heart, Lucy wanted Diana to be reunited with her son and for both of them to continue to be a part of her life. She'd be the mother Tommy needed until she could lay the precious baby in his real mother's arms. That would be happiness enough for her. Lucy pressed a kiss to Tommy's soft hair as pointless tears made her eyes feel gritty. "I love you, you little munchkin," she promised. "I will always do whatever is best for you."

A soft knock on the door interrupted the mush fest. Kim, one of Lucy's coworkers, opened the door to the private room and stuck her nose inside. "Hey, Lucy, your two o'clock is here."

Lucy turned with a frown. "I didn't know I had a two o'clock. Did Mrs. Weaver reschedule again?"

"Nope. It's a guy. I didn't recognize him. If he's a client, he's new."

"New?" Lucy instinctively hugged Tommy closer, thinking of dark-haired men wielding knives and warning her to stop caring about finding Diana. "Is he wearing a leather jacket? Does he have black hair?"

Her friend with the short straight hair and freckles

laughed. "Um, no. Try tall and blond. And he looks like he could bench press my car."

"Oh, no." Lucy felt the blood drain from her head down to her toes. She didn't have to see the man to identify him. Too many phone calls begging for forgiveness these past few days practically confirmed it. Her dread was quickly replaced by a flood of anger. "Here. I need you to watch Tommy. Keep him in here, out of sight."

She handed Tommy over to the other woman and apologized when his eyes opened and he stirred into wakefulness again.

"Is something wrong?" Kim asked, adjusting her grip to hold Tommy more securely. "I didn't mean to upset you. Do you know this guy?"

"Unfortunately."

"Sorry. I already told him I'd come get you, so he knows you're here." Kim juggled to keep hold of both the baby and the blanket Lucy had covered him with. "Otherwise I would have made up an excuse. I thought he was cute. You know, in a bad boy kind of way. Thought maybe he was a cop with news about Diana and that you'd want to see him."

Lucy caught the blanket and tossed it over the edge of the bassinet she'd set up in the small room. A smidgen of hope tried to take hold that Kim could be right, but Lucy pushed it aside. The description was too accurate to anyone but Roger. "Never be taken in by a pretty face, Kim."

"Huh?"

Ignoring the question in her friend's tone, Lucy smoothed her skirt over the tights she wore and tilted her chin above the collar of her turtleneck before closing the door and marching down the hallway. She didn't need this visit. Not today. Not ever. But maybe Roger Campbell could put some unanswered questions to rest, and she could weed out a few of the facts regarding recent troubling events that might not have anything to do with Diana.

A fist of recognition robbed her of breath for a moment when she saw the familiar face that had once haunted her nightmares. Roger Campbell stood from the chair where he sat beside her desk and pulled off the ball cap he wore. "Luce. It's good to see you."

The feeling wasn't mutual. His hair was ridiculously short, his face a little more careworn than she remembered from that last day in court and a new tattoo on his forearm marked his time in prison. A black-and-blue circle beneath one eye made her think he'd had a recent run-in with someone's fist. But the playful wink from the uninjured eye reminded her he thought he was still big, bad, I-own-this-town Roger Campbell.

"Say your apology and get out here." She picked up a pen from the calendar on her desk. "Do I need to sign off on something for your parole officer? That you apologized to your victim?"

He chuckled and sat without any invitation to do so. "Luce, this isn't about my parole. This is important to me, personally. I learned a lot about earning forgiveness in prison. I've taken more anger-management courses than you can imagine. I know I hurt you. But I've made peace with what I've done, and I'll never let it happen again. I'm a different man."

Lucy tossed the pen onto her desk and propped her hands at her waist. "Yeah, well, I'm the same woman.

Damaged beyond repair because of you. I didn't want anything to do with you then, and I don't want anything to do with you now."

"Look, I know I made it so you can't have babies. I remember you testifying about that in court, so I know that's important to you. But I'm gonna make up for that."

"Make up…" The nerve. The ego. She shook her head in disbelief. "You can't."

"This is for you as much as me. You have to forgive me."

"No, I don't." When she realized the sharpness in her voice was drawing the attention of others at the sea of workstations across the room, Lucy pulled out her chair and sat. She lowered her volume if not the frostiness of her tone. "I mean, maybe I already have—there's no sense letting you have that kind of power over me. But I'll never forget. I'll never trust you. Plus, I've moved on. Falls City isn't part of my life anymore. My mother isn't. You aren't. I've made a life for myself here in Kansas City. A pretty decent one. And I don't want you to be any part of it. I don't wish you any harm, Roger. I just want you to go away."

"Stubborn as ever, aren't you, sweet thing. Is there someone else?"

"Why? Are you jealous?" She turned her chair toward him, growing a little more wary when he didn't answer. "Come on, Roger. You don't really have feelings for me. I don't even think you did back when we were dating. Those were teenage hormones running amok, your sense of entitlement and ungodly pressure from your father that made you—"

"A bastard?" He studied the ball cap he twirled between his fingers as he worked through that admission. Then his nostrils flared with a deep breath, and he nodded to the bandage on her forehead. "Does he treat you right? This guy you're with now?"

"How he treats me is none of your business. Nothing about me is any of your business." Although the relationship she was defending didn't exist, there was a tall, dark-haired ME in her heart that no one from her past would ever be allowed to malign. Lucy got up and headed toward the building's front exit. "I'll show you to the door."

She heard the chair creaking behind her as he got up to follow. "Luce, if he's hurt you, I can—"

The fact that he would dare to touch her incensed her fight-or-flight response. Lucy smacked his hand away.

She waved aside the security guard who stood at the front desk. She could deal with this. Lucy McKane could deal with anything, right? She had to. Pushing open the glass front door, she stepped outside onto the concrete stoop. The brisk wind whipped her hair across her face and cut right through her clothes to make her shiver. Maybe Roger *had* developed a conscience while serving his sentence, but alleviating any regrets he might have or assisting with the atonement he wanted to make wasn't her responsibility. "You can do nothing for me. Except leave." She crossed her arms against the chilly breeze and moved to the top of the steps leading down to the parking lot. "I want to see you get into your car and drive away."

"Look, I know guys in prison who are so obsessed

with their girlfriend—or kid or wife or whatever—that they killed the very person they loved. I don't want to see that happen to you."

"You're the only man who ever beat me up and left me for dead, Roger. Goodbye."

"Look, Luce, I'm only trying to make amends." He actually thought there was something he could do to make up for robbing her of her ability to bear children? "I saw a guy lurking around your building the other night. Had words with him. I could tell he didn't belong there. I just want to know it's not him who did that to you."

Lucy's eyes widened. "You know where I live?"

"I knew where you worked, and I followed you home one day last week. I've been keeping an eye on you ever since."

And he was worried about some other guy stalking her? "Never do that again or I'll call the police."

"If it is him who hurt you, that ain't right. Look, I learned some skills in prison I'm not proud of, but if you need me to have another conversation with this guy, I can make him stop."

"Another…" Lucy grabbed the cold steel railing and leaned against it. "My life is none of your business."

He shrugged his big shoulders, apparently impervious to the wind and her outrage. "I sat outside for a few hours, hoping to catch you coming or going. I fell asleep in my car. Woke up to see you running after that guy from the other night. Thought maybe you two had had a fight. I tried to have a conversation with him. He wasn't interested in listening." Roger tapped his cheek. "That's how I got this. By the time I was back on my feet, I saw you with that guy with the glasses and figured…"

"Wait. Go back." Lucy put up her hand to stop his rambling. "You saw him?"

"Yeah. Tall guy with glasses and no shoes. He was bookin' it across the yard."

"No. The driver of the silver car. The man I was chasing. Can you describe him?"

"Black hair. Eyes so dark they looked black, too. Cussed at me in some language I didn't understand. He's not from around here."

Wind wasn't what chilled her blood now. "Did you see a dark-haired woman with him? Younger than me?"

"No."

"Was the man injured? Did you see any blood on him?"

He shook his head. Lucy needed a better witness than Roger Campbell. Had he seen the man who'd attacked her or not?

"Can you tell me what kind of car he drove?"

This time Roger nodded, his frown suggesting that she was missing the point. "Look, he was nosing around your car before he went into the building. When he came back out, I stood up for you. At least until he pulled a knife on me. Hell, I even followed him out to Independence, until I lost him somewhere along Truman Road. You gotta give me credit for that. I'll make him go away if that's what you want."

"So you hit a guy. He hit you back. I don't need that

kind of protection, Roger. I need answers. If you can't tell me anything else, tell me about the car."

He shrugged. "Silver Chevy Camaro 2LS. Recent model. Two door."

"Did you see the license plate? Do you remember it?"

"Didn't think to look. I was busy trying to get out of his way before he ran me over." Lucy was already pulling her cell phone from the pocket of her skirt when Roger reached over to squeeze her shoulder. "What kind of trouble are you in?"

She shrugged off his touch. "Nothing I need your help with. Apology accepted. Please don't try to do me any favors anymore." Maybe that silver car hadn't been racing toward her. Maybe the driver had been speeding to get away from Roger. But she'd seen that car before, and the driver must want something from her. "Go back to Falls City, Roger. Don't contact me again or I'll call the police. Just get in your car and drive away."

He considered her request for a moment, then put his black ball cap back on his nearly shaved head and trudged on down the steps. "Whatever you say. I'm just sayin' I know trouble when I see it—"

"Goodbye, Roger."

Lucy stood there to verify that one, Roger was indeed leaving, and two, that it wasn't in any silver car. Learning that Roger knew where she and Tommy were living, and that someone else, perhaps even more sinister than the bully Roger Campbell had been, also knew her home address, shook the ground under her feet. There were too many threats hiding in the fringes of her life, and thus far, she hadn't been able to pinpoint one of them. Roger hadn't given her much of a lead, but it was something.

She pulled up the numbers on her phone and called Niall.

He picked up after one ring. "Lucy?"

A single word in that deep, resonant tone shouldn't be enough to soothe her troubled heart. But it did. "Did I wake you?"

"What's wrong? Are you all right? Is Tommy?" She heard movement in the background. Was he searching for his glasses on the nightstand? Unlocking his gun from the metal box in his closet or doing whatever the man did when he thought there was an emergency?

Her mouth curved with a wry grin as she headed back into the building. "Why do you assume that something is wrong? Am I that much of a train wreck?" When he didn't answer, Lucy paused in the lobby, the embarrassing truth heating her cheeks. She started talking, needing to fill the silence. "Okay, fine. I just had a visit from Roger Campbell."

The noises in the background stopped. "The man who put you in the hospital? The man harassing you on your answering machine at work?"

So her brainy savior had pieced all that together, too. "Yes. That's him. He wanted to apologize for hurting me."

"Do you need me there to get rid of him? A guy on parole doesn't want to see a man with a badge."

"No. I managed that myself. But thanks for asking." She hurried through the maze of desks toward the back hallway and the room where Kim was watching Tommy for her. "Besides, you're supposed to be sleeping."

"I was going over a DNA report from the lab on my laptop."

"DNA?"

"Tommy's blood sample matched the DNA we got off the screwdriver used to break into your apartment. Diana Kozlow's. She's his mother."

Lucy pushed open the door to find Kim singing a country song to Tommy. She smiled as the baby batted at her friend's moving lips, fascinated by the movement and sound. Diana loved music like that, too. Well, maybe a different genre. She was just as curious about the world around her. At least, she had been when she'd lived with Lucy. She couldn't imagine loving that little squirt any more than she already did. But her heart swelled at Niall's words. "You're not telling me anything I didn't already know."

"Yeah, well, now I know it, too. I said I'd be there at five to pick you up when you got off work. If Campbell's not a problem, why did you call me?"

To hear his voice. To let his coolly rational strength remind her that she wasn't the victim of her mother's machinations or the evils of Falls City anymore. To remind herself that she wasn't alone in her quest to find the truth—that she had an ally she could depend on without question—albeit a temporary one. But she couldn't tell him any of that. The big galoot probably wouldn't understand.

Lucy winked at Kim and quietly closed the door to finish the conversation. "I have a lead on finding Diana. Or at least on identifying the man who attacked me at the hospital."

"From Roger Campbell?"

"Yes. He… I think he was one of the men fighting outside the laundry room this past weekend. He said he's keeping me safe, making up for what he did to me." Was there any other humiliating, sordid, painful element from her past that she hadn't confessed to this good man? "Niall, I don't want *his* protection."

"I'm on my way."

NIALL DIDN'T LET Lucy out of his sight for the next five hours. The research he'd done on Roger Campbell led him to the conclusion that he didn't want the man anywhere near her, even if he could provide missing information on their investigation. Not only had the teenage Campbell kicked and beaten Lucy severely enough to break ribs and cause enough internal hemorrhaging to destroy her ovaries and necessitate the removal of her spleen—the crime for which he'd been sentenced—but he'd been involved with more aggravated assaults in prison, extending his time. Niall couldn't believe that Roger Campbell's motives now were altruistic. Too much violence, too many people who didn't value her for the unique treasure she was, had touched Lucy's life already. He couldn't allow it to touch her again. Not for Lucy's sake. Not for Tommy's. Not for his own.

Now, cocooned inside his apartment by the starry night outside, Niall watched her giving Tommy a bath in a small inclined tub in the kitchen sink. He was considering calling in sick and letting someone else take his shift at the lab because it made him crazy to think of her and Tommy alone here, having to face the threat of Roger Campbell's unwanted surveillance along with the possibility of the man who'd struck her hard enough to require stitches coming back to take his intimidation tactics to a deadlier level.

He no longer had doubts that Diana Kozlow was in serious danger. Whatever mess the young woman had gotten herself into had now touched her baby's life and Lucy's. He had no answers yet, either. And for Niall, that was equally unacceptable.

He glanced over at the clock on the stove, knowing he had to head to work in just a few minutes. But leaving behind a giggling baby with suds on his tummy and a woman with a matching dollop of bubbles on her left cheek didn't feel right. The autopsy lab was hardly the place to invite a woman and child to spend the night. And though there was a cot in his office to catch a nap during extra-long shifts, he couldn't confine them there as if they were under house arrest, either.

Keir was working on tracking down the silver car Lucy had described in detail. Duff was following up on the shooting at the church, running a long-shot check on the spent casings the CSI team had recovered in the organ loft. Maybe he could find the shop where they'd been purchased and track down the identity, or at least an image from a security camera, of the shooter. His father and Millie were busy reorganizing the house to accommodate Seamus and his wheelchair, as well as the arrival of the nurse they'd hired, Jane Boyle, and all her equipment, when the two of them moved in the following week.

Although a carpenter from the building's maintenance crew had worked on rebuilding the door frame leading into Lucy's apartment this afternoon, Niall wasn't prepared to let her move back across the hall with

Tommy until the job had been completed. He wasn't ready to let her and Tommy leave, period, not when he knew she was impulsive enough to follow a lead on her own if Diana Kozlow should call. Lucy didn't seem to believe that he considered them to be a team, and that that meant they should pursue any leads together. She didn't seem to understand his need for her to stop chasing bad guys who wanted to run her down with cars or bash in her head. He didn't know how to make her understand how it upset the balance of his life when he heard things like her meeting up with the man who had once assaulted her.

He needed her here. Safe. Close enough to see and hear. Close enough to breathe in the exotic scent of her shampoo. Close enough to touch.

Decision made, Niall pushed away from the counter where he'd been leaning and picked up a diaper to cover Tommy's bare bottom as Lucy lifted him from the sink. She laid Tommy on a hooded towel and dried him while Niall anchored the diaper into place before the baby watered either one of them.

Once Lucy had Tommy swaddled in her arms, Niall reached out and brushed the smear of bubbles off her cool cheek and wiped his finger on the towel at Tommy's back. "How long do you think it'll take you to pack an overnight bag for the two of you?"

He noted the blush warming her cheek where he'd touched her, and his blood simmered with an answering heat. She tilted her eyes up to his, and Niall wondered if she knew just how many shades of moss and jade and even a hint of steel were reflected there. "Are we going somewhere?"

"I can't leave you two here alone. I'll call Dad, see if it's all right to drop you off at his place."

"You don't have to bother him. We'll be fine."

He sifted his fingers into the hair behind her ear. "*I* won't be. Too many people know how to find you now. I need to know someone I trust is keeping an eye on you around the clock." With the pad of his thumb he brushed a few wayward curls away from her temple before leaning in to press a kiss to the edge of the gauze bandage there. Tommy turned his face toward Niall's voice and wobbled against Lucy's chest, either startled or excited by him coming so close. Although he trusted Lucy to keep a sure grip on the baby, Niall splayed his hand across Tommy's back. "Easy there, munchkin."

He could feel Lucy trembling, too. Her eyes shone like emeralds beneath his scrutiny of her reaction to the simple contact. But there was nothing simple about the heat stirring inside him. Niall dipped his head a fraction of an inch and her pupils dilated, darkening her eyes. He moved even closer, and a ripple of contractions shimmered down her throat as she swallowed. Niall's heart thundered in his chest, nearly drowning out her soft gasp of anticipation that clutched at something inside him and ripped it open. Niall closed the distance between them.

Her lips parted beneath his, and he hungrily took advantage to sweep his tongue inside her mouth and lay claim to her soft heat and reaching, eager response. Niall tightened his fingers in her hair with one hand and palmed her hip with the other. He turned her, pushing her back against the counter, crowding his thighs against hers to soothe the ache swelling behind his zipper. He slipped his hand beneath the nubby wool of her sweater and clawed at the layer of cotton undershirt she wore until he could slide his fingers beneath that, too, to find the cool skin along the waist of her jeans.

Squeezing her generous curves between his hand and thighs, Niall angled her head back into the basket of his fingers and kissed her harder, deeper. His chest butted against the hug of her arms around the baby, and the earthy sensuality of mother and child ignited something protective, possessive inside him. He captured the rosy, tempting swell of Lucy's bottom lip between his own, then opened his mouth over hers again, matching each breathy sound of pleasure she uttered with a needy gasp of his own.

The coo of a baby and tiny fingers batting against his chin returned Niall to his senses. With a deep sigh that was a mix of frustration and satisfaction, he pulled his hands from her hair and clothes and moved them to the baby. He caught Lucy's lips once more, then kissed her again. Each peck was less frantic, more tender, as he eased himself through the withdrawal of ending the incendiary physical contact. Finally, he angled his hips away from hers and retreated a step, pressing the last kiss to the top of Tommy's head as the curious infant clung to the scruff of his evening beard and squiggled with excitement at the sensation, which probably tickled his sensitive palm. "You want to be in on the action, too, hmm?"

Lucy's lips were swollen and pink from the same sandpapery rasp as they curved with a shaky smile before she stepped aside and turned her back to him. She set Tommy in the bouncy seat on the counter before reaching behind her to straighten the shirt he'd untucked and smooth her purple tweed sweater down over the curvy flare of the hip that was branded into his hand. "Niall, you didn't have to do that. I'll go to Thomas's for the night. I'd love to visit with your dad and Millie again, if I won't be in the way. You don't have to persuade me with a kiss."

"Persuade?" He took her by the elbow and turned her to face him again, his eyes assessing the relatively blank expression on her face. "You said when I felt raw and unsettled inside that I could kiss you."

"I meant—"

"You said never threaten to kiss you, to just do it."

Her cheeks colored with a blush, bringing the animation he was used to seeing back into her face again. "I did say that, didn't I?" She reached up to comb her fingers through that glorious muss of hair. "I forgot for a second how well you listen. Did it help you feel better?"

"Yes." Releasing her, Niall drew in a deep breath, trying to cool the fire Lucy McKane stoked inside him. He felt as though there was something unfinished between them, and he wasn't quite sure how to verbalize it. "And no. I'm more concerned about how it made you feel. I don't want to scare you off or make you uncomfortable. But then your response is so natural, so...combustible— it feeds something inside me." He scratched his fingers through his own hair before adjusting his glasses at the temples. Her frowning eyes following his every movement didn't tell him where he was going wrong in this conversation. "I know that there are rules about men and women and...and we don't have time to explore that right now."

"You worry too much about rules and logic." She reached up to stroke the hair off his forehead. Niall felt that tender caress and her returning smile all the way down to his bones. "There are some things in this world that can't be fully explained—like a mother's bond with her child or what makes one person attracted to another. Sometimes you just need physical contact to feel better. We all do. I'm not quite sure how you manage it, but you damn sure know how to kiss, Doctor. Sweeps a girl right off her feet." He liked those words, too, and was glad he wasn't the only one left a little off-kilter each time they touched. "I just need you to understand your motives if this…attraction…develops into something more than a friendly alliance. I need you to be fully aware of what you're getting with me, so that neither one of us gets hurt."

"What I'm getting with you?" That sounded like some kind of warning. "I'm not like Campbell. I have no intention of hurting you. I don't understand."

"I know." She touched that springy spike of hair again. "I'm not about to put words into your mouth or try to tell you what you're feeling. But if anyone can figure it out, you can." She pulled away to pick up Tommy and push him into Niall's hands. "If you'll get Tommy dressed, I'll go pack a bag for us."

The lights of the city turned streets into a foggy twilight as Niall wound his SUV through the back roads south of Kauffman and Arrowhead Stadiums until he could catch Blue Ridge Cutoff and take a straight shot to the two-story white home where he and his brothers and sister had grown up. He stepped on the brake, slowing behind the last dregs of rush-hour traffic, and waited to make a turn.

While he waited, he glanced over at Lucy in the passenger seat, nodding and drumming her fingers against the armrest in time with the tune playing through her head. Or maybe it was nervous energy. She hadn't really explained herself to his satisfaction after that kiss in the kitchen, so he couldn't be sure what ideas were going through that quirky mind of hers. She wouldn't surrender herself so completely to an embrace like that if she didn't feel something for him, would she?

Lifting his gaze to the rearview mirror, he glimpsed the royal blue knitted cap peeking above the top of the car seat, where Tommy dozed in the back. It seemed he understood the baby's needs and moods better than he did the woman beside him. Niall hated to trust what most people called instincts, but something inside him was telling him that he was on the verge of finding something—or losing it—if he couldn't figure out a better way to communicate his thoughts clearly to Lucy.

He understood right and wrong, yes and no, justice and crime. He understood fear and anger—had known both growing up when he'd lost his mother or when one of his brothers or sister had gotten hurt in the line of duty, or when he'd seen his grandfather fall at the church shooting. But this fascination with Lucy, this overwhelming urge to protect her, to find answers for her—that irrational desire to touch her and listen to her ramble and see her smile—he needed to put a name to it and understand it before he said or did one wrong thing too many and he pushed her out of his life or, God forbid, someone took her from him.

"You're staring again, Dr. Watson." She giggled and the soft sound made him smile, even though her amusement with his name continued to confuse him. "Better watch the road."

"It's a red light."

"Well, it's about to change."

Not yet, it hadn't. "Why do you find my name so funny?"

"Dr. Watson?" She was still grinning. "It's the irony. The revered Dr. Watson makes me think of the Sherlock Holmes mysteries I read in school. But you are so much more Holmes, with your intellectual prowess and manners and lack of empathy for lesser mortals like me, than you are the earthy sidekick doctor."

"Lack of empathy? I feel things."

"Of course you do. It's clear how much you love your family and your work." She glanced back over the seat. "How much you care about Tommy and making sure he has a good, safe life." By the time she turned her wistful expression to him again, the light had changed, and he had to concentrate on moving with the flow of traffic. "But you're always thinking so many steps ahead of everyone else in the room that you sometimes miss what's going on right in the moment. I always thought Dr. Watson was sort of the Everyman for Holmes. He understood the witnesses in the cases they worked on together and, to my way of thinking, translated the world for him. You know, he took what Holmes was thinking and expressed it in a way the other characters and readers understood. In turn, he took what others said or did and helped Sherlock Holmes understand their emotions and motivations." She nestled back in her seat. "I feel like I'm Watson to your Holmes. You've got the wrong name for your character. And that's why it's funny."

Niall turned the SUV onto Forty-Third Street, organizing his thoughts before commenting. "You *do* translate the world for me. I see things differently when I see them through your eyes. I'm learning through you— things that don't come from books. I admit that I'm more comfortable talking procedure with other cops or talking about a dead body into a digital recorder than I am conversing with…"

"Real live people?" He glanced over to see her sympathetic smile and, after a moment, nodded. "Niall Watson, I think you're a little bit shy. You live in your head most of the time."

The woman was as intuitive as his mother had once been. "And you live in your heart."

Lucy's lips parted, then closed again as she turned aside to look out the passenger window. "That gets me into trouble sometimes."

Definitely. But it also enabled her to smile often and laugh out loud and feel joy and passion and even sorrow to a degree he sometimes envied. He slowed as they neared a stop sign. "Don't ever change."

Her head whipped around to face him as his phone buzzed in his pocket. "You say the oddest things sometimes."

Niall felt himself grinning as he reached into his pocket. "Translate it, okay?"

The call was from Keir. Niall instantly put on his

work face. This could be something about Grandpa Seamus or the follow-up he'd asked his brother to run on
Roger Campbell and the owner of the silver Camaro.
He handed the phone to Lucy. "Answer that and put it
on speaker for me, will you?"

She tugged her glove off between her teeth and
swiped the screen. "Hey, Keir. This is Lucy. Niall is
driving right now so I'm putting you on speakerphone.
Okay?"

"Hey, Lucy. Is he giving you any trouble?"

Niall cut off the teasing before she could answer.
"What do you need, little brother?"

"It's work, Niall." The sudden shift in Keir's tone in-
dicated as much. "The lab said you're the ME on call.
I've got a DB at Staab Imports over on Truman Road.
It's up in the old caves in the bluffs off I-435."

"I know them. Businesses rent the old limestone
quarries now for warehousing inventory or running
electronic equipment." But Niall had a feeling that the
underground caverns being naturally cool and practically impossible to break into had nothing to do with
a dead body.

"That's the spot. And I think you'd better bring Lucy
along." That put him on alert.

Lucy's gaze sought his across the front seat. "Why?"
And then the color drained from her face. "Oh, God.
Please tell me it's not Diana."

Niall reached over to squeeze her hand as Keir
quickly reassured her. "It's not your friend. Our dead
body is a Latino male. There's no ID on him. But there
are a couple of things at the scene I need you to see."

Niall looked across to see her blinking away tears.

"You okay with this? Crime scenes aren't pretty. I can have an officer stay with Tommy in the car."

Her grip tightened around his. "I'm okay. If I can help…"

Niall nodded and released her hand to end the call with his brother and turn the SUV around. "We're on our way."

Chapter Eight

Lucy knew she had issues with staying warm. But even
with gloves, a knit cap and her sweater coat, this man-
made cave cut out of the limestone bluffs rising above
Truman Road was downright freezing.

"You're sure you're okay with this?" Niall asked,
pulling out the squarish attaché that held his crime-scene
kit and a rolled-up package that looked surprisingly as
though it might have a body bag inside from the back of
his SUV. He tucked the package under the arm where
he held the kit before closing the back of the SUV and
facing her. "It's not for the faint of heart. Not that anyone would accuse you of being that."

Lucy huddled inside her layers and shivered. "I suppose there's a joke here somewhere about this not being
my first crime scene."

He squeezed her shoulder, then rubbed his hand up
and down her arm, feeling her reaction to the unheated
open space at the mouth of the cave where he'd parked
behind two police cars and an unmarked police vehicle.
His eyes narrowed, and she suspected he was trying to
determine whether her trembling was from the chilly
temps or nerves. She wasn't sure she had an answer for

him. "I'll be right there with you, the whole time. Keir, too. If it proves to be too much for you, one of us will bring you back to the car and Tommy. I'll leave the engine running so he can stay warm." He nodded toward the compactly built detective leaning against the front fender of the SUV. "In the meantime, Hud—Detective Kramer—will keep a close eye on the baby."

Lucy glanced at the young man in a denim jacket, with work boots crossed at the ankles, chewing on a toothpick while he texted someone on his phone. "Does he know anything about infants?"

"I didn't know much about infants a week ago."

Leave it to Niall to point out the logical reason she shouldn't be worried. Detective Kramer *was* wearing a gun and badge that looked authentic enough. "Are you sure Keir trusts him?"

"They're partners. I know he does. Let's go." Niall looped his camera around his neck and nodded to the detective left to guard the infant in the backseat before heading down the stone driveway in the middle of the high cave. "Hopefully, whatever Keir wants you to identify won't take long."

Lucy hurried her pace to catch up with him. "Is it bad form for me to hold the ME's hand when he's on his way to a crime scene?"

Niall reached over and caught her fingers within his grasp. "It wouldn't matter if it was."

Lucy held on as they walked past the sliding gate that had a broken padlock dangling from one of its steel bars. Deeper inside the cave she noted a serpentine trail of conduits mounted to the squared-off walls and ceiling. Niall explained that they were used to run electric-

ity, water, fresh air exchanges and computer lines deep
under the ground to supply the offices, repair shops and
storage units housed inside. Lucy had seen the openings
in the bluffs several times but had never had a reason to
go inside before. It surprised her to see cages and iron
bars shielding the businesses after hours, just like the
shops on a city street downtown.

"How far back does this go?" she asked as they
turned a corner around a limestone post and entered
another, wider area that had only one office front next to
a pair of garage doors that were large enough to drive a
semitruck through. One door stood open, and the lights
shining from inside the entrance bathed the whole area
in an artificial yellowish light. "Is that really a whole
warehouse under the ground?"

"Feeling claustrophobic?"

"A little." She tightened her grip around his hand. He
didn't protest her desire to cling to something steady
and familiar as they approached the line of yellow tape
strung crossways in front of the open garage door. A
large commercial fan over each door helped circulate
the air deeper inside the bluff. The moving air tickled
her nose with a familiar scent. She sniffed again and
slowed her steps. "Wait. I recognize that smell."

Then she saw the sign painted on the office window
and closed garage door—Staab Imports: Mediterranean
Spices & Delicacies.

Lucy stopped in her tracks. "The man in the elevator
smelled like that." She supposed a man who smelled like
a restaurant could also work for a company that stored
and shipped the spices and ingredients a restaurant chef

would use. She swiveled her gaze up to Niall. "Does your brother want me to identify the body?"

Niall's grim gaze indicated that was a likely possibility. "We'll take care of this fast and get you out of here while I work."

Lifting her chin to a resolute angle, Lucy followed the tug of Niall's hand.

Keir Watson appeared at the garage opening and lifted the yellow tape when he saw them approach. The hand he shook Niall's with was gloved in sterile blue plastic, and he winked at Lucy. "Thanks for coming. Back here." She could see the stoicism in Niall's posture and expression once he'd released her and knew he was changing from the man she was falling in love with into the city's night-shift expert on analyzing dead bodies. Keir was as efficiently businesslike as she'd ever seen him, too. He led them between two long rows of pallets piled high with bags and crates labeled Sea Salt, Rosemary and Olive Oil. "I called the ME wagon for a pickup, but I wanted you to see this first before the CSIs cleared the scene and sent the body to autopsy. The custodian who discovered the body thinks our vic might have interrupted a robbery. There's a safe in the warehouse's office, and Friday is payday, so it should have money in it. Apparently, these guys deal with a lot of immigrant and low-income labor. They prefer cash instead of maintaining bank accounts."

"But you don't think it's a robbery?" Lucy questioned.

"No, ma'am. The safe hasn't been opened. I've got a call in to the owner to unlock it for us, though, to check the contents."

"We passed the office out front," Niall pointed out. "A thief wouldn't need to enter the warehouse. This is something else." He lifted his camera and paused to take a few pictures of the footprints and scuff marks at the base of one of the pallets. "Looks like an altercation of some kind happened here." He pointed back toward the exit and then in the opposite direction into the makeshift walls of food and spices. Lucy didn't need a medical degree to see the different sizes and designs of shoe imprints in the thin layer of dusty residue on the floor. One track led to the exit while the other followed the path Keir was taking. But how did Niall know the different trails had anything to do with the crime and hadn't simply been left by the people who worked here? He pointed to the partially flattened burlap bag about chest-high in the pile. There was a small hole in one corner and a scattered mound of ground dry oregano at the base. Niall snapped a picture of the dark red stain in the material surrounding the hole. "Make sure one of the CSIs gets a numbered photo of this, and cut out that piece for analysis."

"Got it." Keir jotted the order on his notepad and ushered them on to the scene she was dreading. "I figure whatever started there ended here."

They turned a corner to meet a forklift jammed into a stack of crates filled with broken and leaking bottles.

"Watch your step," Keir warned. "The spilled oil makes the floor slick."

But shaky footing wasn't what caused Lucy to shudder and recoil into Niall's chest. A man was pinned upright between the pallet on the raised forklift and the wall of crates. He stood there, frozen forever in time, with blood pooling above his waist where the empty pallet had caught him. But even that ghastly mess wasn't the most disturbing part of the scene.

Now she understood why Keir had wanted her to come with Niall.

There was a soiled piece of fabric draped over the man's head and chest—a square of white knit cotton dotted with yellow, red and blue trucks.

The baby blanket someone had stolen off Tommy that night in the laundry room.

Keir must have put two and two together and had been waiting to see her reaction to the way the murder victim had been displayed. "So you do recognize it. I thought it matched the description you gave Niall."

Niall switched positions with her, putting his tall body between her and the bloody scene. "You didn't put Lucy through this to identify a stolen baby blanket."

Keir shook his head. "I'm sorry, Luce. The blanket wasn't the only part of this mess that was too familiar for us to ignore." He nodded to the CSI working nearby to remove the blanket and place it in an evidence bag. Keir was talking to his brother now. "This death shows a lot of rage."

"Or an act of desperation." Niall moved to keep her from seeing the dead man as the blanket was removed. "Who uses a forklift to kill a man?"

Lucy sensed where this conversation was going. "Someone who couldn't overpower him on her own?" She was already shaking her head. "Diana didn't do this."

"I need her to see him, Niall." Keir reluctantly asked his brother to step aside.

Standing like an unmoving wall in front of her, Niall explained a few practical details. "Lucy, the victim's eyes are open. His face is bruised and puffy, partly from what appears to be a fight, and partly from the initial stages of postmortem swelling as fluids disperse through the tissues. He won't look like the body of a deceased person you've seen at a funeral."

His facts prepared her, softened the jolt of him stepping aside and giving her a view of the victim's face.

Still, Lucy recoiled, maybe less from the horrible death Niall had described than from the familiar face that had haunted nearly every waking moment these past few days.

Niall stepped between her and the black-haired man in the bloodied leather jacket once more. "Is this the guy who assaulted you at Saint Luke's Hospital? He fits the description you gave Duff."

Lucy nodded. "That's him."

But the situation could only get impossibly worse. Bless his practical, protective heart, Niall couldn't shield her from the other detail that had been hidden beneath the baby blanket. She peered around his shoulder to confirm the truth.

"Please tell me I'm not imagining that." Niall reached for her, but Lucy was already pointing at the dead man's chest. "What is happening? Why? My poor girl."

She gasped and pressed her fist to her mouth, resisting the urge to gag as the rock walls swayed around her. Niall caught her by the shoulders and backed her away from the body. He pushed her clear around the corner and leaned her up against an undamaged stack of crates. He hunched his shoulders to bring his height closer to hers, demanding she focus on him and not the scene they'd left behind. "Deep breaths, sweetheart. Deep breaths."

The endearment he used barely registered. Her mind was too full of the image of that screwdriver with plastic jewels decorating the pink handle plunged into the dead man's heart. It was the mate to the one Niall suspected had been used to break into her apartment the day Tommy had been abandoned there.

"Lucy." Niall's voice was as firm as the grip of his fingers around her chin as he tipped her face up to his. "Don't faint on me. Are you with me?"

"I have never fainted in my life. I'm not about to start now." Anger blended with shock and fear, clearing her head. She twisted her fingers into the front of Niall's jacket and clung to him. "I know what you're thinking. Diana did not do this."

"That's not what I'm thinking right now," he answered quietly.

Those piercing blue eyes revealed nothing but concern as he released her chin to brush a lock of hair off her cheek. Lucy tightened her grip on his jacket and walked right into his chest, pushing aside the camera that hung between them. "Put your arms around me, Niall. Just for a few seconds, okay? I need…"

His arms were already folding around her, anchoring her shaking body against his. His chin came to rest on the crown of her hair, surrounding her with his body. She snuggled into his heat, inhaled his scent, absorbed his strength.

Several endless moments passed until her world righted itself and she could draw in a normal breath. Niall showed no signs of letting go, and she wasn't complaining.

But the comforting embrace lasted only a few seconds longer until Keir cleared his throat beside them. "I hate to do this, you two. But the sooner we can get some questions answered, the sooner Lucy can leave. Do you think the beating or the forklift or the screwdriver killed him?"

With a reluctant nod, Lucy pushed away and tilted her eyes to Niall's. "I won't freak out again. I promise."

"I know you won't. But you stay here. You and Keir can talk and I can work while we figure this out." Niall needed one more nudge to leave her and disappear around the corner of the crime scene.

Keir's dark brows were arched in apology. "So you recognize the screwdriver?"

Lucy nodded, hugging her arms around her waist, already feeling the chill creep into her body again. "It matches the one Niall found in my apartment—from the set I gave Diana a few years back when she still lived with me."

Keir's blue eyes glanced around the corner, no doubt exchanging a pitying, skeptical look with his older brother. His suspicions were wrong. She'd said as much to Niall. She'd say it to anybody. "Diana did not do this. Maybe someone stole her toolbox. Maybe someone is framing her."

Keir pulled back the front of his sports jacket and splayed his hands at his waist, assuming a more brotherly stance, looking less like a detective interviewing a witness. "Maybe it was self-defense. It fits the warning he gave you about staying away and making things worse. If he was hurting her, then it makes sense that she'd want to get Tommy out of the picture."

"No. She couldn't kill anyone."

Niall suddenly reappeared, holding what looked like a meat thermometer and a wallet in his blue-gloved hands. "Would you kill to defend that baby out there? Or to protect yourself from someone like Roger Campbell?"

"That's not the same. I didn't retaliate against Roger."

"You testified against him. Maybe Diana didn't think she'd be able to get away before she had that opportunity."

Keir flipped through the pages of his notepad. "Campbell's the guy from Falls City who went to prison after assaulting you?"

Lucy glared a question at Niall, not sure she wanted every sordid detail about her past shared with his family. "He's the investigator, Lucy. I deal in dead bodies, remember?" But knowledge was power in Niall's book—understanding was the way to make everything fall into place. "Campbell said he wanted to make amends with Lucy. If he knew this guy had hurt her, could he have done this to square the debt with her?"

"Murdering someone is not squaring a debt," she argued.

"You don't think the way a criminal does," Keir suggested. "I'll add him to the list of suspects we want to question." He made the notation in his book, then turned to Niall. "Find any ID on our vic yet?"

Niall opened the wallet in his hand and pulled out

the driver's license to hand him. "Antony Staab." While Keir jotted down the information from the license, Niall continued his preliminary report. "Liver temp says he's been dead about eight hours. But the temperature in here would make the body cool faster, so the time of death might be closer to dinnertime."

"That would explain why no one discovered him until the night custodian reported for duty." Keir jotted down more notes. "We'll narrow down the window of opportunity to, say, 5 to 8 p.m. Don't you think that covering the face indicates a personal connection—not wanting to see a loved one's face? Possibly remorse?"

"It wasn't Diana," Lucy reiterated.

Niall had more gruesome details to report. "In addition to the contusions on his face, his knuckles are pretty scraped up. Looks like there's an older knife wound in his flank. That probably accounted for the blood trail he left at the hospital. He had it bandaged, but there weren't any stitches and signs of infection are evident."

"So this guy was dying, anyway," Keir suggested.

"Possibly. I want to check out these other injuries before I pronounce the cause of death. See what story they tell," Niall says. "Mr. Staab here put up a good fight somewhere along the way."

Lucy had a speculation of her own. "Could he have died of those other injuries? And the screwdriver is an attempt to pin his murder on Diana?"

"Like I said, I'll know more when I open him up."

The high-pitched wail of a baby crying echoed off the cavern walls. An instinctive alarm clenched low in Lucy's belly, and she spun around. When she saw the compact detective carrying Tommy and several bags over his shoulder, she hurried to meet them. "Don't let him see this."

Niall was right there beside her. "Get him out of here, Hud."

Hud Kramer halted inside the garage-door entrance. "I'm stopping right here, ma'am. Sir."

"Is something wrong?" Lucy asked, reaching for the trembling infant and turning him in to her arms. "There, there, sweetie. Mama's here…" She went silent at the slip and pressed a kiss to Tommy's soft wool cap. "Lucy's here, sweetie. What do you need?"

Tommy's little toothless mouth opened wide as he squinched up his face and cried against her ear.

"Easy, bud." Niall moved behind Lucy to catch Tommy's gaze. "You're making a lot of racket for someone your size."

Tommy's cries stuttered and he turned his head to the sound of Niall's voice. But then he cranked up again.

Hud held his hands up in surrender. "The kid started hollering. I tried to give him one of those stuffed toys, but that only helped for a few seconds. I didn't smell anything, but I didn't open him up to check, either." He pulled the diaper bag, plus Lucy's knitting bag and her purse, from his shoulder. "Not sure what the issue is, so I brought everything. I wasn't sure what you needed. Thought maybe I could be more help back here than walking him around the car over and over."

Keir had joined the group, too, and was making faces to distract Tommy, but with little success. "I thought you said you had a half dozen nieces and nephews."

His partner shook his head. "I'm the fun uncle. I play

horsey with them and give them drum sets for Christmas. I don't deal with their personal issues."

"It's too cold in here for him to stay." Niall peeled off a sterile glove and caught one of Tommy's batting fists between his fingers and guided it to the infant's mouth. "Hey, munchkin. What's the sit-rep?"

The instant she heard the sucking noise around his tiny fingers, Lucy diagnosed the problem. "He's hungry."

Niall released Tommy. "He's starting to put on some weight. Maybe he needs to eat more. Or more frequently."

"Hey, Mom and Pop." Keir was grinning as he interrupted them. He thumbed over his shoulder. "Crime scene, remember?"

All too vividly. The baby whimpering around his tiny fist must be feeling as helpless and distressed as Lucy was right now. She glanced up at Niall and the other two men, glad to have something to do. "I'll take him."

"Don't go back to the car by yourself," Niall warned. "The killer could still be close by. And if Campbell's watching, I don't want him to see the two of you alone."

"Even if he's too young to know what's going on, Tommy can't stay here. We'll be fine."

"That's unacceptable."

"Niall—"

"You can use the office right next door, ma'am." Hud Kramer extended a hand toward the entrance, offering a quick compromise. "There's a restroom in there and it's unlocked. Until the owner comes to open the safe, we've eliminated it as part of the crime scene. There

are enough cops around here that we'll be able to keep
an eye on you and the kid."

Lucy nodded her thanks and hurried as far away
from the grisly murder scene as she could get.

The bell over the door startled Lucy and set Tommy
off on another crying jag. "Poor guy." Quickly assessing
her surroundings, she dropped her bags on top of the
gray metal desk in the center of the room and balanced
the baby in one arm while she unzipped the diaper bag
and pulled out the items she'd need to prepare a bottle.
She was learning to juggle things with surprising effi-
ciency, although the job would have gone a lot faster if
Detective Kramer had thought to bring Tommy's carrier, too. Since everyone from KCPD seemed to have a
job he or she was working on, she didn't want to ask any
of them to run to the car to retrieve it. She rubbed her
nose against Tommy's, distracting him for a brief moment from his hunger pangs before he cranked up again.
"You and me—we can deal with anything, right?"

Once she'd warmed the formula a tad under the hot
water tap in the adjoining restroom, Lucy snugged
Tommy in the crook of her arm and gave him the bottle. The instant his lips closed around the tip, his crying
changed to greedy little grunts of contentment. Lucy
kissed away the tears on his cheeks and let him have
his fill. While Tommy ate, she walked around the office, mindlessly taking in the neatly arranged awards
hung on the walls, as well as the vibrant silk flowers
on top of a file cabinet and bedazzled pencil holder on
the desk that added a woman's touch to the otherwise
austerely masculine room.

Tommy was smiling and full and playing with her

hair by the time Lucy's gaze zeroed in on the familiar handwriting on the calendar beside the pencil holder. She read the lines and notation marking off several weeks in February and March. "Maternity leave."

Maternity leave? Diana's penchant for glittery objects? The handwriting? Being warned to stop looking for her by the dead man found at the same business? "This is your mama's desk."

But Niall would need concrete evidence to prove that her foster daughter had been in this room—that she had a connection to Staab Imports and one of its namesake employees, Antony Staab.

Eager to find anything that might lead her to Diana and clear the young woman of suspicion, Lucy knelt down to pull the changing pad from Tommy's diaper bag and spread it on the area rug beneath the desk. Then she pulled the needles out of her knitting bag and squished the yarn and fabric inside to create a safe spot to lay him down. Once he was content to snuggle with his stuffed toy and watch her move above him, Lucy started searching. She opened drawers and sifted through files and office supplies. She wondered about booting up the computer, but decided to save that as a last resort. Instead, she flipped through the names and numbers in an address book that revealed business associates like grocery stores and restaurants, and foreign names she couldn't pronounce. But there was no record of Diana anywhere.

She tried to open the center drawer next, but it was locked. Remembering her long steel knitting needles, she pulled one from her purse and wedged it between the drawer and desk, twisting and jabbing until something tripped inside and she could slide the drawer open. "Victory."

Setting the needle on top of the desk, she opened it wide to find some loose change and dollar bills, along with a calculator and a tablet computer. She was about to close the drawer again when she spotted the corner of what looked like a blurry photograph poking out from beneath the tablet. But when she pulled the paper free, she discovered the torn-up squares of an ultrasound printout that had been carefully taped back together. Her gaze went straight to the numbers and letters printed at the bottom. *Baby Kozlow.* Proof.

She found another photograph underneath the mended printout. Unlike the grainy ultrasound, the image on this one was crystal clear. "Oh, no. Oh, God no."

It was a photograph of a pregnant Diana standing with the man who'd been so violently murdered in the warehouse. Antony Staab. He had his arm around her shoulders, his straight white teeth beaming against his olive skin. They were dressed up in this photo—suit and tie, maternity dress. Diana stood with her hands cradled beneath her heavy belly. But she wasn't looking at the camera. And she wasn't smiling. Was the dead man the father of her baby? Were the police right? Had Diana surrendered her baby to Lucy to keep him from this man who stole her smile? Had she killed Antony Staab in self-defense? Were those Diana's footprints that Niall had photographed at the scene of that so-called altercation?

She needed to show this to Niall and Keir. Diana worked here, maybe in past tense. But she definitely had a connection to Staab Imports. And now Niall would have a name and a whole dead body he could use to find answers. He could prove to his meticulous satisfaction that Tommy's father was the dead man in the warehouse.

Lucy stuffed the printout and photo into her purse and closed the drawer. But she jumped at the bell ringing above the door and snatched up her knitting needle as if she could defend herself with so simple a weapon.

Her racing heart stuttered a beat, and she stumbled back into the rolling chair when a stocky, black-haired man wearing jeans and a leather jacket stepped into the office. Just like the dead man.

"You… How…?"

"What are you doing in my office?" The man asked the question in a crisp foreign accent. "Who are you? Why are you going through my things?"

"Your things?" He didn't strike her as the flowers and glitz type. But she was shocked enough that she could do little more than parrot his accusatory questions.

"I know they are not yours."

How could a man be alive and dead at the same time? "Who are you?"

He advanced to the opposite edge of the desk, glanced down at the knitting needle she wielded like a sword, then looked back at her. His angular features were harsher, more lined than the quick glimpses she remembered from the hospital.

"I am Mickey Staab. Mikhail. I own this place." Did he know Diana? She'd need more proof to convince Niall, but she was certain these were her foster daughter's things. "I asked, what are you doing here? You are trespassing on private property."

Mickey, not Antony. A brother? Cousin? Her breath unlocked from her chest as a rational explanation kicked in. "I'm Lucy McKane. The police told me to wait in here." She pulled the needle down to her side and summoned her compassion. "There's a dead man in your warehouse. Niall—Dr. Watson, the medical examiner— said his name is Antony Staab. Is he a relative of yours?"

The man's predatory demeanor changed in a heart-beat. The harsh lines beside his eyes softened.

"Anton?" He collapsed in a chair on the far side of the desk. He dropped his face into his hands. He shrugged his shoulders as if in disbelief before he looked up at her again. "He is my brother. *Was* my brother."

"I'm sorry for your loss."

"Anton is dead?"

"Murdered, actually. I'm so sorry, Mr. Staab."

"Murdered? When the police came to my house about someone breaking into the warehouse, I had no idea they meant…" He signed a cross over his head and heart and muttered something in his native language. Then he pushed to his feet. "How? Who did this?"

"That's what the detectives and ME on the scene are trying to figure out."

He paced the small office twice before stopping across from her again. "You're no detective. Why are you here?"

She supposed anger was a normal response to grief, but Lucy wasn't exactly feeling her stubborn, independent self right now. She slid a step toward Tommy, feeling the need to protect as well as the need to be closer to an ally—even one only a few weeks old. "I'm a witness."

"A witness? You saw someone breaking into my warehouse?" His hands curled into fists before he pointed toward the warehouse. "You saw this…killing…happen?"

"I'm not a witness to the murder. But I met the victim. It's a long story." Lucy picked up her purse and stuck the knitting needle inside, checking on Tommy as she stooped down. His arms and legs were stretched with tension, a sure indication that he was probably filling his diaper or hungry again. *Please don't cry, munchkin.* She sent the telepathic plea before she quickly straightened. "Maybe you'd better talk to the police before I say anything I shouldn't."

"Yes, I will talk to them. I know who is responsible." He was pacing again, his cheeks ruddy with temper. "That witch. She was no good. I knew she would be trouble. I told Anton to stay away from her."

Lucy tried not to bristle too much at the insults to the woman she was almost certain was Diana. "The police think there could have been a robbery. There was certainly a fight of some kind."

"A robbery?" The pacing stopped, and he crossed to the safe behind the desk. "She knew the combination. I wouldn't put it past her—"

Tommy cried out from his makeshift bed, and Mickey Staab halted. His dark, nearly black eyes narrowed with a frown as he glanced down at her feet. "You have a baby here?"

"Yes, he's…" Tommy mewled softly, his discontent growing. When Mikhail squatted down as if to touch him, Lucy quickly bent to scoop the infant up into her arms and circle to the far side of the desk. He couldn't belittle the mother and then expect to be all coochie-coo with the child. "His name is Tommy."

"Tommy?"

"Yes."

"A boy? You have a son?" He followed them around the desk, smiling, in awe of the baby he'd discovered, it seemed.

Tommy's fussy cries grew in duration and decibels. Despite Lucy's cooing words and massaging his back, he was probably picking up on the tension she was feeling. "He's very precious to me."

"You are a lucky woman." Mickey Staab palmed the top of Tommy's head, touching without asking. Lucy cringed away. "Who is his father?"

Suddenly, a tall, stern Clark Kent wannabe filled the open doorway. "If you have any questions, you ask me." Lucy exhaled an audible gasp of relief as Niall took Tommy into his arms and angled his shoulder between her and the business owner. She wasn't even jealous that the baby calmed down at the sound of his voice. She was glad to see him, too. "I'm Dr. Niall Watson, KCPD crime lab. Are you Mr. Staab?"

Backing out of her personal space now that Niall was here, the shorter man answered. The momentary joy he'd shown at discovering a baby disappeared beneath a resigned facade. "Yes. The victim is my brother, Anton?"

"That's what his driver's license says." Niall nodded to the door. "There's a Detective Keir Watson in the warehouse. He'll need you to make a positive identification of your brother." He inclined his head toward Hud

Kramer, waiting outside the door. "Detective Kramer will show you where to go."

Mickey Staab hesitated, looking at the baby before giving Niall a curt nod. "You are a lucky man." He leaned to one side to include Lucy. "And a fortunate woman. Congratulations." He was almost out the door when he paused to slide his hands into the pockets of his jacket and face them. "Do you always bring your family to the scene of a murder?"

"We're not exactly—"

Niall cut her off and motioned Hud into the room. "Detective Kramer?"

Hud's grin was friendly enough, but the broad span of his shoulders and muscular arms crossed over his chest indicated he could be very persuasive if he needed to be. "This way, Mr. Staab."

After the two men had disappeared, Niall pushed the door shut and turned Lucy in to his chest. He wrapped his arm around her, holding both her and the baby. "Hud said you were having a conversation with some man he didn't recognize, and I just needed to see that you…" His chest expanded against her cheek with a deep breath. "I thought it might be Roger Campbell paying another unwanted visit. That he'd followed you."

"I'm okay, Niall." She wound her arms around his waist and willingly snuggled close to his strength. "I needed to see you, too."

"Did Staab frighten you?"

Lucy nodded against his chest. "He's understandably upset. And normally, I could deal with that. But he looks just like his brother—like that dead man. For a minute, I thought I was seeing a ghost. The two of them could be twins."

"He's a ringer, all right." She felt his lips stirring against her hairline. "I'm sorry he scared you. Kramer shouldn't have left you alone."

"I'm better now—just hearing your voice, feeling your warmth around me…" Smiling at the fleeting sense of security this man instilled in her, Lucy reached up to touch the baby. "I'm as bad as Tommy. You have the same effect on both of us."

"It'll be another thirty minutes or so before I'm finished with the body. Do you want me to have Hud or one of the other officers drive you back to the apartment?"

"No. I don't want to be that far from you. Besides, someone has to stand up for Diana before everyone around here railroads her into a murder charge."

"There's a difference between exploring all the possibilities and—"

"Wait." Lucy pushed away, remembering her discovery from a few minutes earlier. She scooped up her purse and pulled out the wrinkled printout and photo she'd found. "Look at these. I found them inside the desk. And this is Diana's handwriting on the calendar. I think she must have worked here. And the ultrasound has to be Tommy."

"So she definitely knew Antony Staab."

"I'm sure they drove away from the hospital together in the same truck."

"You were nearly unconscious—"

"No. Look." Enough with the skepticism. She was giving him the facts he wanted. She crossed to the office's front door and pointed to the logo on the window. "This is what I saw on the side of the truck. Staab Imports. We have to find out if their company uses orange-red trucks. And you have to do that blood sample thing on the body so you can prove Antony is the father. And then we can find out who else might have wanted him dead."

"No." Nodding in that sage way of his, Niall joined her at the door and slipped the baby into her arms. "*I* have to find out. You stay here with Tommy. Lock this behind me so you don't have any more surprise guests. I'll have Keir wait to check the safe until after we leave. I'll figure out how all this connects to Diana's disappearance."

"She didn't kill Anton," Lucy insisted.

"Right now, I can't state anything conclusively. But I'm willing to work with that hypothesis."

"Niall?" Slipping her fingers behind his neck, Lucy stretched up on her toes. The moment she touched his lips, his mouth moved over hers in a firm, thorough, far too brief kiss.

"Feeling raw inside?" he asked as she dropped back onto her heels and pulled away.

Lucy smiled, wondering if the smart guy would ever figure out how much she loved him. Whoa. The rawness inside her eased as the revelation filled her. This wasn't just a crush or an alliance. This was way more than friendship or gratitude. "Not so much anymore." Still, the truth was bittersweet. She tried not to wonder if Niall was capable of comprehending that kind of love, much less whether he could ever feel that way about her. "Go. Find the truth. We'll be waiting here for you."

Chapter Nine

Lucy buttoned up a cable-knit cardigan over her jeans and T-shirt and slipped on a warm pair of socks before unwrapping her hair from the towel she'd worn since stepping out of the shower. She hung the dark blue towel up beside Niall's and picked up her wide-tooth comb to carefully pull it through her damp hair. The swelling on her head wound had gone away, although the colorful bruise and stitches in her hairline still made her think she looked a bit like a prizefighter.

She was losing track of the days since Niall had taken her in, and making herself so at home in his bathroom made her feel as though she was living out some kind of domestic dream. Or maybe it was more like living in an alternate universe with a strong, supportive man and a sweet little baby and all the extended family and security that went with it.

Because this wasn't her life. The Watsons and Tommy weren't her family. Niall wasn't her husband or fiancé or even her boyfriend.

She was the eccentric neighbor lady who talked too much and butted into other people's business and couldn't have babies of her own.

Even though her door had been repaired and her locks were secure, Lucy was reluctant to go back to her apartment. She wasn't ready to leave this fantasy life behind. But other than insisting that he wanted to keep an eye on her and Tommy until Diana was found and her link to Antony Staab had been resolved, Niall hadn't asked her to stay. Not for any personal reason.

And somehow, she suspected that blurting out her love for him would either confuse him or scare him away. There was a little part of her, too, that hoped if she never said the words out loud that the handsome cop doctor who'd righted her world time and again couldn't really break her heart when this alliance between them ended.

She watched her face contort with a big yawn. She still had a ways to go to adapt to the long, late hours Niall kept. Although she and Tommy had dozed on and off in his office down at the crime lab while he performed an autopsy on Antony Staab, she was exhausted this morning. She'd called in sick at work, blaming some lingering aftereffects of her injury for her fatigue. Perhaps it was better, though, if they remained ships that passed in the hallway or laundry room in the late hours of the night or early morning. That was the kind of advice her mother had given her.

"Don't you go givin' your heart and time to any man, Lucy, honey. Not until he puts a ring on your finger. Or you'll be paying the rest of your life."

Her mother had been talking about the financial difficulties that had motivated every decision Lucy could remember. But she was far more worried about the emotional toll it would cost her to reveal her feelings to a man who struggled to comprehend the human heart. He'd find a way to dismiss the irrationality of such feelings, or maybe he'd decide there was no logical way a quiet intellectual like him, from a tight family and a good home, could embrace a lasting relationship with a woman like her. Lucy knew that Niall was attracted to her physically—that crazy talent for kissing he had gave that away. But she had enough experience with her mother's peccadilloes to know that sexual attraction didn't equate to emotional commitment and long-term happiness. And Lucy wasn't going to settle for anything less.

Still, he was irresistible. She realized just how far gone she was on Niall Watson when she walked into the living room and found him sitting in the recliner with Tommy. The man needed a shave after his shift at the lab. His rich, dark hair stuck up in unruly spikes above his black-framed glasses. The wrinkled blue Oxford shirt that should have completed the brainy scientist look clung to broad shoulders and strong biceps in a way that was anything but nerdy. The baby was nestled securely in the crook of one arm. Tommy looked up between big blinks to the deep, drowsy timbre of Niall's voice.

"And so your daddy's name was Antony Staab." Niall ran his finger along the page inside the folder he was holding. "These pictures are markers, which is how we visually code DNA to identify people and find out if they're related. This is your code. See them side by side? These patterns show all the alleles you have in common."

Longing aside, Lucy couldn't help but grin as she

picked up the empty bottle and burp rag from the table beside the recliner. "You're reading him a DNA report for a nap-time story? He can barely see colors yet."

"You said he liked hearing the sound of my voice." That she had. "Theoretically, I should be able to read him anything and it would have the same effect."

"Theoretically?"

"Practically, then. We don't have any children's books."

Truth be told, Lucy could listen to him read from a grocery list or phone book and that deep, fluid voice would make her pulse hum. "Point made, Dr. Watson." The big blinks had won. She pointed to the child snoring softly in his arms. "You put him to sleep."

Niall set the report aside and carried Tommy to his bassinet, where he gently placed him and covered him with a blanket. He rested one hand on the butt of the gun he wore holstered at his hip while Lucy looked down at the open report. "So it's true? Antony Staab is Tommy's father?" She read through the summary at the bottom of the page and studied the graphs and statistics she didn't fully understand. "Do you think Diana is all right? Or did she get hurt in that fight with Antony?"

"Somebody's hurt, based on the injuries I saw on his body. He got a few licks in on whoever attacked him. But if she's hurt, Antony Staab isn't responsible. In fact, I may be ready to rule her out as the killer."

"May be?"

"I found traces of her DNA on skin cells inside the victim's jacket."

"I thought you said you were going to rule her out

as a suspect. If you found DNA, doesn't that prove that she was there? If you think she—"

"*Inside* the jacket," he emphasized. Niall crossed the room to retrieve his crime-lab jacket from the entryway closet and came back to drape it around her shoulders, to demonstrate his point.

Lucy huddled inside the jacket as she had that day in the hospital's ER. "She wore his jacket. So she was a friend—or even something more."

"But there was no evidence of her around the stab wound itself. No trace of her on him anywhere except from when she most likely wore his jacket." Niall tossed his jacket onto the sofa and put his hands up between them as if he wanted to start a fight. "If you and I were going to tussle—"

"My skin cells, hair, maybe even my blood would be all over your hands and clothing." He wiggled his fingers, urging her to come closer. "So tell me how you think you can prove she's not guilty of killing this man who once offered her his jacket."

"How big is Diana?"

"About my size. Skinnier. At least she was the last time I saw her. Why?"

Niall grabbed her hand that still held the bottle and raised it to his chest, using her to show how Antony Staab had been killed. "He was already pinned against the crates when he was stabbed. Even being injured like that, since there wasn't any momentum to drive him into the weapon—"

"As if he was lunging toward someone in a fight?" Lucy backed up a few steps and Niall moved toward her raised hand until his chest hit the bottle.

Then he stood still and pushed her hand away to show the difference in using just her forearm to strike the blow. "It would require a lot of strength to plunge that screwdriver all the way into the heart of a stationary victim who was standing upright. The wound track showed the weapon glanced off his clavicle. But there was no second strike, just one powerful thrust that tore through his heart."

Although the forensic details were so unsettling that she needed to stop the reenactment and pull away, Lucy appreciated that his evidence supported what her instincts had been telling her all along. "You don't think Diana would be strong enough to strike a blow like that?"

He followed her into the kitchen while she rinsed out Tommy's bottle and set the parts in the dish drainer. "It's not impossible, but it's unlikely—especially if she's injured."

Hugging her arms around her middle at the sudden chill she felt, Lucy went back into the living room. "I can't stand the thought of her being hurt and frightened and alone."

"You survived it." She felt the warmth of his body come up behind her as she stood over Tommy's bassinet and watched the peacefully sleeping baby. "She will, too."

She closed her eyes against the urge to lean back into his heat and strength. "I don't suppose there's anything in that report that *does* say who murdered Antony."

"Roger Campbell is still a possibility. Staab put you in the ER. He might see killing him as vindication for his crime against you. Duff took a drive down to Falls

City to find him and check out his alibi." She opened her eyes when the warmth disappeared. She turned to see him thumbing through the autopsy report again. "His killer must have worn gloves. I found no transfer of skin cells or blood in the wounds. Usually there is in a fight like that."

"You scraped under my fingernails. Was there anything helpful under Antony's?"

"Environmental residue from the warehouse, and his own blood and tissue."

"I can't imagine how frightened Diana must be." Determined to focus on Niall's belief that Diana wasn't a killer, Lucy joined him, leaning her cheek against his shoulder to look at the report with him. "Would you read to me, Dr. Watson?"

"You've heard all the pertinent details. The rest is technical jargon. Oh." He set down the file and frowned down at her. "Tired? You want me to put you to sleep, too?"

"Your voice doesn't have quite that same effect on me." She reached up to brush that spiky lock of hair off his forehead and ease the concern from his expression. "But I do find it soothing."

"What do you want me to talk about?"

"It doesn't matter, really. Anything. Everything. Whatever you want so long as I get to be a part of the conversation."

He considered her answer for a moment, then unbuckled his belt to remove his gun and holster and carry them into the bedroom, where he set them up on the closet shelf. Just when she thought he was going to ignore her request, he came back into the living room. He caught her hand and sat in the recliner, pulling her onto his lap. "I'm so sorry you have to go through this. The aftermath of violence is something I deal with every day. But this is the first time I've witnessed firsthand the emotional consequences of that violence. I think about Grandpa going down like that with a bullet…" His hands hooked behind her knees, turning her in his lap to face him and holding her there when she would have scooted to a less intimate position beside him. "At least I know he's alive and that he'll get better. I know he's not alone."

Although the sturdy trunks of his thighs and the distinctly masculine shape of him behind his zipper were warming her hip and bottom, she suspected Niall was seeking the intimacy of comfort and conversation, too, and her heart reached out to him, even as her body buzzed with awareness. "Seamus knows all of you care about him. Your family is such a blessing, Niall."

"Diana doesn't have any family but you, does she?"

Lucy shook her head. "None to speak of."

"I wish I had better answers for you. So you could at least know where she is. I hate to see you worried like this. You have such a big heart." He slipped his fingers into her hair, curling one finger, then another into the tendrils there, softly brushing them away from her stitches. He studied the way each lock twisted around his hand until his palm came to rest against her cheek and jaw, and his gaze locked onto hers. "You're not alone, Lucy. I'll stay with you and Tommy as long as you need me."

She tried to smile at the bittersweet promise. Lucy knew he was sincere and that she was lucky to have

Niall in her life. But if he suspected how much she needed the sound of his voice and his strength and heat and clever mind and kisses, would he give her forever?

Tenderly stroking her fingers through that independent lock of silky hair, Lucy wished that every day of her life could include this kind of caring. Niall needed someone to translate the world for him, someone to see beyond the erudite speech and obsessive focus and teach him to recognize his kindness and passion, and allow them to be given back to him. She wanted a family like his. She needed his calming strength and the unquestioned reliability he brought to her chaotic world. She wanted this good man to be *her* good man.

His blue eyes narrowed suspiciously behind his glasses, and she realized she'd been petting him this entire time. "What are you thinking, Miss McKane?"

"How much I want you to kiss me right now."

"That's a good answer."

Lucy felt a blush warming her cheeks. "Why is that, Dr. Watson?"

"I was thinking the same thing. That I could shake this feeling that I'm missing something important and make all those unresolved questions that are nagging at me go away if I could just…" His hand stilled in her hair. "Is this what needing someone feels like?"

Lucy nodded. It was for her, at least. His grip tightened on her thigh and scalp, pulling her into his body as he leaned in and kissed her.

His lips opened urgently over hers, giving her a taste of creamy coffee when their tongues met and danced together. Lucy wound her arms around his neck and tunneled her fingers into his hair, lifting herself into the tender assault of his firm lips. The rasp of his beard stubble against her skin kindled a spark deep inside her. The smooth stroke of his tongue over those sensitized nerve endings fanned the embers into a flame. Each demand of his mouth on hers stoked the need burning inside her.

His hands moved to her waist, lifting her onto his chest as the recliner tipped back. She twisted her hips against his belt buckle to stretch out more fully on top of him. Her breasts pillowed against the hard plane of his chest, and she crawled up higher, whimpering at the friction of her nipples pebbling between them.

Niall moved his lips to her jaw, her earlobe, the sensitive bundle of nerves at the side of her neck. He pushed aside the neckline of her sweater and nibbled on her collarbone. At the same time, he slipped a hand beneath her sweater and T-shirt. He moaned some little words of victory or satisfaction or both when he found the bare skin of her back and splayed the fiery stamp of his hand there. It wasn't fair that he could slide his hand up along her spine and down beneath the waist of her jeans to squeeze her bottom when she couldn't touch bare skin. Determined to explore the same territory on him, Lucy braced a hand on his shoulder and pushed herself up, trying to get at the buttons of his shirt. One. Two. She slipped her hand inside the Oxford cloth to tickle her palm against the crisp curls of hair that dusted his chest, and her fingers teased the male nipple that stood proudly at attention. The muscles beneath her fingers jumped, and Lucy wanted more.

Niall's hand moved inside her shirt to mimic the same action. Her breast was heavy and full as he palmed her through her bra, and Lucy groaned at the frissons of heat stirring her blood from every place he touched her. He pinched the achy nub between his thumb and finger, and she realized those breathy gasps of pleasure were coming from her mouth. She wanted his soothing tongue on the tips of the breasts he explored so thoroughly, with no barriers between his greedy touch and her sensitive skin. She wanted the straining bulge inside his jeans sliding inside her, claiming her body as thoroughly as his hands and mouth had claimed the rest of her.

She sensed he wanted that, too. His hips shifted beneath hers, spreading her legs. Her knee bumped the arm of the chair. He lifted her to center her above him, but she hit the other arm and jiggled the lamp on the table beside the recliner.

"Niall…" There was no place for her to move. No room to make this happen. "Niall—"

In a quick show of strength, he righted the recliner and pushed to his feet, palming her bottom as he commanded, "Legs. Waist. Now."

Lucy happily obliged as he caught her in his arms, locking her feet together behind his waist as he carried her into the bedroom. From the moment they left the recliner until he set her on her feet beside the bed, she got the feeling that there was a clock ticking somewhere, that the rightness of this moment with Niall might pass before she got to live out the fantasy of being loved by this man.

He seemed just as impatient to discover his passionate side, to find solace or to explore the human connection blossoming between them or whatever this was.

His lips kept coming back to hers as they unbuttoned shirts and unsnapped jeans and dropped her sweater to the floor. She pushed his shirt off his shoulders and he reached for the hem of her T-shirt. He whisked the shirt off over her head and stopped, his eyes feasting so hungrily on her breasts that he didn't even have to touch her for the muscles deep inside her womb to pulse. Leaning in to touch his forehead to hers, he skimmed his hands up her arms to slide his thumbs beneath the straps of her bra. "Heaven help me. The leopard print?"

"What?"

He drew one finger along the line of the strap down to the swell of her breast and traced the curved edge of the material into her cleavage and up over the other eager breast, eliciting a sea of goose bumps across her skin. "I've made a very unscientific study on the design and color of underwear that goes through your laundry every week."

His deep, ragged breaths blew warm puffs of air across her skin, and she felt each breath like a physical touch. If he'd been a different man, she'd have thought he was toying with her. But Niall was Niall, and she half suspected that the way he studied her body and analyzed her reactions was part of the arousal process for him.

Lucy tried to capture a rational thought for his sake. "That's a little voyeuristic."

His finger slipped inside a leopard-print cup and the back of his knuckle brushed across the sensitive pearl. Lucy gasped at the bolt of pure longing that arced from that touch to the damp heat between her thighs. She swayed on unsteady feet and braced her hands against his warm chest. "So you like these?"

"Yes. Very much. Take them off."

Lucy laughed at the growly command, loving the rare revelation of impulsive need. As he pushed the straps off her shoulders, she reached for the waistband of his briefs. "You take yours off."

And then it was a race to strip off their remaining clothes and tumble onto the bed together. She giggled at the way his glasses fogged between them when they kissed and reached up to pull them from his nose and set them gently on the nightstand.

His hand was there along with hers, pulling open the drawer and digging around inside, blindly searching while panting against her mouth. "Condom. Need to find a condom."

Lucy pushed him back onto the pillows and straddled his hips, reaching for his eager flesh, ready to be with him completely. "No need. Can't make babies, remember?"

He prodded her opening with a needy groan, but his hands squeezed her thighs, keeping her from settling over him. "That's not fair. You deserve a dozen of them."

"Fair? Maybe not. But that's life. And I'm not letting what's happened to me stop me from living this moment with you. Right here. Right now. I need you, Niall. Inside me. All around me. Setting me on fire with all that body heat."

"Technically, it's your own body heat that's rising and making it—"

"Niall?" She leaned over him, pressing a finger to his lips to shush him.

"Yes?"

"Now is when you need to stop talking. Do you want this to happen?"

He nodded.

"Then kiss me like you mean it."

"I'll do my best." And, oh, his best was crazy wonderful. He rolled her onto her back and moved between her legs, his strong thighs nudging hers apart. His hands fisted in her hair as he slowly pushed his way into her weeping core until they were completely one. He suckled on a tender breast, then stretched the hard weight of his body over hers to reclaim her mouth as he moved inside her.

As his thrusts came faster, more powerfully, Lucy gave herself over to the exquisite pressure building inside her. What he'd denied her a moment earlier, he gave back with generous attention to detail, sliding his thumb between them to the spot where they were tightly linked, bringing her right to the edge and taking her over in a rush of feverish pleasure that washed over her arching body like waves of blissful fire. And while the aftershocks were still pulsing deep inside her, Niall's body tightened over hers. With a groan of pure satisfaction humming against her throat, he released himself inside her.

By the time Lucy came to her senses and her thumping heart settled into a steady beat against Niall's, she was already falling asleep. With her head nestled against the pillow of his shoulder, he pulled the covers over them both. There were no tender words exchanged, no questions asked, no promises made. But it felt as though the man she loved wasn't going anywhere. For a few minutes on an overcast day at the end of February, when the rest of her world was in complete limbo, Lucy felt as though she was a part of something, as if she belonged.

Treasuring the gift of these precious moments together, she snuggled into the circle of Niall's arms, surrounded by his heat, shielded by his strength and saved—for a few minutes, at least—from the fears and vulnerability and loneliness she'd lived with for far too long.

Lucy woke up to the distant sound of chimes playing.

She was drowsy with contentment and deliciously warm in the cocoon of the bed and the furnace spooning behind her. Only half-alert to the sunshine filtering through the blinds at Niall's window, she savored the scent of Niall's soap clinging to the cotton sheets and the earthier scent of the man himself filling her senses. She wanted nothing more than to snuggle in beneath the possessive weight of Niall's arm and leg draped across her waist and thighs.

But moment by moment, the reality of the outside world stole the dream of her blissful morning away from her.

The sun was too bright. It must be afternoon already. She heard Tommy fussing in the other room—not crying yet, but awake and realizing he was hungry or wet or alone. She heard the beep of her phone. Missed call. Then the chimes sounded again.

Lucy pushed Niall's arm aside and sat bolt upright. "My phone."

He was awake, too, tucking the covers around her naked body before swinging his legs off the side of the bed. He stood in all his lean, lanky glory, reaching for his glasses and slipping them on. "Living room. I'll get it."

"No, thanks. I can…" Ignoring her body's traitorous rush of interest in the gallant ME's bare backside, she scrambled off her side of the bed, gasping as the chill of the air hit her warm skin. Lucy crossed her arms over her breasts and shivered. She made a quick search for her clothes and grabbed the first thing she saw—Niall's shirt that she'd tossed over the foot of the bed earlier. Feeling an increasing sense of urgency with every chime of the phone, she slid her arms into the long sleeves and hooked a couple of buttons as she hurried out the door. "Stay put. I'll get it. I need to check on Tommy, anyway."

But he was right behind her moments later in unsnapped jeans and miles of bare chest when she pulled her phone from her purse. He nudged her aside. "You talk. I've got the munchkin."

Lucy didn't recognize the number on her phone. But too much had happened in the past week for her to take the chance on ignoring it. "Hello?"

"Lucy?"

"Diana? Thank God." She braced a hand on Niall's arm to steady herself as relief overwhelmed her. "Are you all right? Are you someplace safe? I know you used to work at Staab Imports. You didn't have anything to do with that horrible murder, did you? I told the police you couldn't have."

"Even though it was my screwdriver stuck in his chest?" Diana sniffled a noisy breath, as if she was fighting back tears. "I'm so sorry to get you involved in this mess. Everything is so screwed up. I need to ask one more favor of..." She hesitated as the baby wrinkled up his face and cried out in earnest when Niall left him lying in the bassinet to eavesdrop on the call. "Is that Dorian? He sounds healthy. Is he?"

"Dorian?"

Diana sniffed again. "Of course. Anton said you were calling him Tommy. I like it. I named him after the lead singer in one of my favorite rock bands. But Tommy's a good name. It makes him sound like a regular, normal kid. And I want that for him—"

The conversation ended with an abrupt gasp. "Diana? Yes. He's healthy. I took him to a pediatrician. Are you still there—"

A different voice cut Lucy off. "I want to hear my son."

The voice sounded familiar. It was thickly accented, deep pitched, and it could have been melodic—if it weren't for the absolute chill she heard behind the tone.

"Who is this?" she asked.

Niall's calming, more familiar voice whispered beside her ear. "Put it on speaker. Keep him talking."

She nodded her understanding and watched as he took a few steps away to call his brother Keir and order a trace on the incoming call.

"Tell me who you are," she demanded. "What have you done to Diana?"

"She does not matter" came the smug answer that frightened, angered and saddened her at the same time. "I am the boy's father."

Niall had evidence to the contrary. Lucy had seen it. "She matters. His father is Antony Staab. And he's dead."

"You lie!" Lucy jerked at the angry voice, flashing back for a split second to the night she'd said no to Roger Campbell.

But Niall's blue eyes, demanding she focus on the call and stay in the moment with him, gave her something to concentrate on. "I saw his dead body," she explained. "I read the medical examiner's report." She hardened herself against the man's curses and Diana's pleas muttering in the background. "I'm guessing you had something to do with his murder. And you tried to pin it on Diana."

Blowing off the accusation she'd just made, the man came back on the line, speaking in a deceptively calm voice. "My son was taken from me. You kidnapped him."

"No. I'm watching him for his mother." Poor Tommy's cries quieted to a mewling sound of frustration when she reached into the bassinet and captured one of his little fists in her fingers and moved it to his mouth to suckle on. "I'm his legal guardian."

"I am his father! He belongs to me. Let me hear him."

She heard Keir's voice coming from Niall's phone. "We got a ping on her phone from a cell tower downtown."

"Narrow it down, little brother. I need an exact location." To Lucy, Niall gave her the sign to draw out the conversation for as long as she could.

Lucy nodded.

"Here." She pulled Tommy's fist from his mouth

and the baby wailed. Lucy put her phone next to the crying baby for several seconds before pulling it back to speak. "Is that what you wanted to hear? I need to change and feed him. Are you willing to do that kind of work to take care of an infant? To be responsible like a real father? Or is he just some prize to you? Now either tell me who you are or put Diana back on the phone." There was a terse command about explaining things and a sharp smack of sound. "Diana? If you hurt her…"

"It's me, Luce. I'm okay." But she wasn't. Diana was crying again. No wonder her foster daughter had wanted to get her baby away from such a dangerous situation. But why wouldn't she save herself, as well? "I thought after I had the baby I could disappear on the streets the way I used to before I came to live with you. You know, when I was a runaway. But I've never met anyone like Mickey before."

"Mickey?" Now the accent made sense. "Mickey Staab?"

"Yes." Diana's voice was rough with tears. "I used to cut his hair, you know. That's how we met. I thought he was handsome and charming. He offered me a job that paid three times what I was making. I thought we were going to live happily ever after. Then I got pregnant and everything changed."

Lucy glanced over at the bassinet. "All he wanted was the baby."

Diana sniffled an agreement and continued. "It's some cultural thing from his country—something about firstborn sons being raised by their fathers. But I couldn't let my baby grow up like that—with all the violence and no regard for others. You taught me how

children should be treated. How I should be treated."
Niall had crossed the room, pinning down some important piece of information with his brother he didn't want
anyone to overhear. "He found me. He found us. I was
desperate to save Dorian—er, Tommy. And then Anton,
sweet, sweet Anton, tried to help me get away. Stupid
me. I fell in love with the wrong brother. I wanted to
tell you that I didn't kill him. In case we don't get a
chance to talk later."

How long did she have to listen to these horrible
things Diana had had to deal with before KCPD could
find her location and get her out of there? "What do you
mean? We will see each other again. I promise you."

Guilt and regret shook in Diana's voice. "Mickey
knows I left Tommy at your place. He followed Anton
and me to your place the other night and tried to take
him from you."

"In the laundry room."

"Keir?" Niall prompted, returning to her side to
squeeze her hand. Lucy held on just as tightly.

"Yes. I wanted to see my baby one more time and
explain everything to you. But this guy showed up and
made everything worse." *Roger Campbell*. "Mickey
blamed Anton—said his brother should be helping him
get his son back, not helping..." She didn't need to explain whatever crude word Mickey had called her. "He
was so angry. There was a horrible fight."

The blood at the hospital. He'd cut his own brother.
Mickey Staab was a sick, obsessive man.

And now, without Antony Staab alive to even try to
protect her, Diana was completely at his mercy.

Mickey's cruel tone at the other end of the call confirmed as much. "Tell her what I said. Tell her!"

Diana's next words came out in a panicked rush. "Stay away, Lucy. You stay away and don't let my baby anywhere near—"

Lucy heard the sting of a slap and a sharp cry of pain.

Her knees nearly buckled at the helpless rage surging through her. "Diana! You sorry SOB. You keep your hands off her. Diana!"

Niall's arm snaked around her waist, pulling her to his side. She tilted her gaze to his and he nodded. Keir had pinpointed the source of the call and dispatched every available unit to the location. "We're coming for you, Staab."

For a moment, there was only silence at the other end of the line. And then, "You think you have it all figured out, Dr. Smart Cop?"

"I know you killed your brother." Niall's articulate voice held none of its mesmerizing warmth. "It's the only answer that makes sense, Mikhail. Or should I say Mickey? You and Antony are twins. That's why all the DNA at the crime scene showed up as his. You share the same genetic code. That's why I thought he was Tommy's father."

"His name is Dorian," Mickey corrected, his articulation slipping each time his anger flared. "My son's name is Dorian."

"No court of law is ever going to let you be his father. *I* won't let you be his father," Niall warned. "Now let Diana go when the police arrive, and maybe you'll live long enough for Tommy to visit you in prison someday."

"You cannot deny me what is mine." Lucy collapsed

against Niall's strength at the frightened yelp she heard in the background. "The time for conversation is over. Listen very carefully, Miss McKane. I will leave the phone here so all your police friends can find it. But you—and you alone—will bring my son to me at the address I will tell you, and then I will give you this piece of trash you value so highly. If I see any police, Diana will die. If you are a minute late, she will die. If you do not bring me Dorian, you both will die."

Chapter Ten

"Is that the clearest picture we can get?"

Lucy heard Niall's voice over the device in her ear, taking some comfort in the knowledge that he was with her, even if he was stuck in a surveillance van with Keir nearly half a block away on the far side of the Saint Luke's Hospital parking lot. Meanwhile, she was making a grand show of unpacking a stroller and diaper bag from the trunk of her car, taking her time to assemble and stow Tommy's belongings before she retrieved the doll dressed in Tommy's clothing from the carrier in the backseat.

The deception was risky, but no way was she going to let Tommy anywhere near his father, especially after Mickey had murdered the baby's uncle and kidnapped his mother. While she followed the rest of Mickey Staab's directions to the letter, Tommy was safely hidden away at Thomas Watson's house, with Niall's father and Millie Leighter keeping a careful watch over the infant.

"I've got tech working on it," Keir assured him. "And remember, I've got men stationed all around the hospital complex. If Staab's Camaro or anyone matching his description shows up, we're going to know about it long before he gets to Lucy." Then she realized Keir was talking to her. "Luce, we've got you on screen. I need you to do an audio check, too."

She pulled her knitting bag out, keeping appearances as normal as possible. "Make sure you're getting my best side."

"This isn't the time to joke," Niall warned. "You know how easy it is for this meeting to go sideways. No matter how prepared we are, we can't control all the parameters. Staab is vicious and unpredictable."

"I know, Niall," she answered, wondering if he even realized how worried he was about her, and wishing she knew how to help him recognize and deal with those burgeoning emotions. "Trust me, I know."

She'd stood up to Roger Campbell in a courtroom over a decade ago, and she hadn't had backup of any kind then beyond her attorney. Today she was standing up to another violent man—but this time she had Niall Watson, the rest of the Watson clan and a good chunk of the Kansas City Police Department supporting her. Meeting Mickey Staab face-to-face again would be far more dangerous than testifying against Roger had been, but knowing she had people she could rely on in her corner this time made it easier somehow.

Niall's brother, on the other hand, appreciated a little sarcasm to lighten the tension of the situation. "We're reading you loud and clear, Lucy. We'll keep you posted as soon as we spot our guy. Are you sure you're still up for this?"

Keir, who'd worked sting operations like this before, suggested Staab had picked the parking lot at Saint Luke's Hospital because of the easy access to traffic, enabling a quick getaway once the hostage exchange was made, and because there were so many innocent bystanders around the busy public hospital who could get caught in the potential line of fire that he rightly assumed the police wouldn't be eager to get into any kind of gun battle with him. And if they cleared the area, then Staab would immediately know they were waiting for him. That left Lucy out there, unprotected and alone to face off against a kidnapper and killer.

"I'm sure." She held her breath as a car backed out of a parking space a few stalls away. She didn't breathe again until it drove past and turned toward the hospital building. No threat there. "But I want to move to a house with a private driveway. I'm sick of parking lots."

Niall surprised her by responding to her nervous prattle. "When this is all said and done, I'll take you to Mackinac Island, Michigan, where they don't have any cars or parking lots."

Lucy looped her knitting bag over her shoulder with her purse and closed the trunk lid. "Is that an invitation, Dr. Watson?"

She didn't giggle when she said his name this time.

He didn't answer the question, either. "Let's get through the next few minutes first."

Right. That would be the smart thing to do. She checked her watch and moved to the back passenger door, unable to delay the inevitable any longer. "And you're sure you've got Roger Campbell out of the picture? I don't want him thinking he's going to come in and save the day and wind up getting someone killed instead."

Niall answered. "Not to worry. Campbell violated his

parole six ways to Sunday by showing up at your office and our building. Duff's got him down at the precinct offices now booking him."

That was one less random factor about this whole setup she could eliminate. "So it's just Mickey Staab we have to worry about."

"Theoretically."

"Theoretically?" Lucy shook her head, unstrapping the doll and covering its face with the blanket she'd wrapped around it. "Is there some other bad guy you want to tell me about?"

But someone on Keir's team had spotted the car. "Be advised. We've got Staab in a silver Camaro approaching your position from the north entrance."

Lucy inhaled a deep breath, spying the all-too-familiar car turning down the lane where she was parked. She was shivering from the inside out. She was scared. Scared for herself and scared for Diana. But she wasn't alone, right? She didn't have to do this alone. "Talk to me, Niall. I need to hear your voice right now. Ask me a question or something."

"We need to talk about what happened this morning."

"What?" This morning? Did he mean making love? Or going over Antony Staab's autopsy report and DNA tests? Or something else entirely? Those weren't exactly topics that she wanted to get mixed up, especially over an open com line where Keir and a bunch of other cops could hear. "I can't talk about that right now. I can't…"

Mickey Staab's car slowed, and Lucy carried the camouflaged doll in her arms to the back of the car. The man who'd terrorized her foster daughter was close enough that she could see his dark eyes. But she didn't spot anyone else in the car with him. "Where's Diana?" she whispered, more afraid of what she didn't see than what she did.

"All right, people, this is it," Keir announced. "Eyes sharp. Nobody moves until I... Niall? Where are you going, bro? Son of..." Keir swore something pithy in her earbud. She heard a metallic slam in the distance. "Be advised. Hold your positions until I give the go to move in. We need eyes on the hostage."

Lucy adjusted the straps of her bags on her shoulders and hugged the doll to her chest as the silver car that had nearly run her down once before stopped in the driving lane only a few feet away. She swallowed hard, steeling herself for the coming confrontation. Mickey shifted the car into Park but left the engine running. She was confused when he leaned across the front seat. Why wasn't he getting out? Did he know there were a dozen cops watching him?

Eyes on the hostage. She couldn't see Diana.

"Where's Diana?" she shouted. She dipped her head to kiss the doll's forehead, keeping her eyes trained on the black-haired driver. "I did what you said. I brought Tommy. Where is she?"

The passenger door opened and a young woman tumbled out onto the asphalt with a barely audible moan.

"Diana!" Lucy lurched forward.

She froze when she saw the bloody knife in Mickey's hand. It was a long, wicked-looking thing like the one his brother had carried. Maybe it was even the same blade the monster had taken off his brother's dead body. Mickey followed Diana out the same door, standing over her as she curled into a fetal position, but crouch-

ing low enough that the door and frame of the car protected him from the eyes of any cop who might take a
shot at him. He knew this was a setup. He knew he was
being targeted. But he was that desperate to be united
with his son.

And a desperate man was a dangerous one. "In my
home country, women are good for two things. Betray-
ing me is not one of them."

Lucy's eyes burned with tears. "You lousy son of
a—"

He pointed the knife at Lucy. "Give me my son."

Lucy inched around the hood of his car, trying to
get a clear look at how badly Diana was injured. "Let
me help her. Please. Let me get her inside to the ER."

His dark eyes tracked her movement until she came
one step too close. He thrust the knife in her direction,
warning her to stop. "My son first."

The charade had gone on long enough.

"Here he is." Lucy tossed him the fake baby and
grabbed Diana's hand to drag her from beneath the
open door.

Even though he was startled enough to catch the doll
dressed in Tommy's clothes, as soon as Lucy threw the
package, Staab must have guessed the deception. "You
bitch!" He dropped the doll and charged around the
door into the open.

Lucy heard a chorus of *"Go! Go! Go!"* in her ear
and dropped Diana's hand to reach into her bag as he
raised the knife to attack.

"You are all lying—"

She jabbed the knitting needle into his arm as hard
as she could, ripping open a chunk of skin. But she'd

only deflected the blade, and his momentum carried the screaming man into her, knocking her to the ground. Lucy ignored the pain splintering through her shoulder and rolled.

"Move in! Move in!" She was hearing real voices now, echoing the shouts in her ear.

Lucy was on her feet first, but she stumbled over Diana's body before she could get away. Mickey's feet were surer, his stride longer. He latched onto a handful of her hair and jerked her back. A million pinpricks burned like fire across her scalp. That knife was so very close, and help was so very far away.

Lucy heard three loud bangs.

Mickey's grip on her hair went slack, and she dropped to her knees. His dark eyes glanced up to some unseen point behind her. Three spots of crimson bloomed at the front of his jacket, and he fell to the ground, dead.

Lucy scooted away before he landed on her and turned to see Niall holding a gun not ten feet away. His feet were braced apart on the pavement. A wisp of smoke spiraled from the end of the barrel, and she looked beyond the weapon to his steely blue glare.

She'd defy anyone to spy one trace of the nerdy scientist now.

But the heroic impression was fleeting. Niall was already holstering his gun and kicking Mickey Staab's knife away from the dead man's hand as Keir and several other police officers swarmed in.

He didn't say a word but knelt beside her, switching from cop to doctor mode before she could utter a thank-you or ask why he wasn't back in the van where he was supposed to be. He checked her eyes and ran his hands up and down her arms. She winced when he touched the bruise on her shoulder, but the sharp pain woke her from her stupor. "I'm okay." She turned his hands to Diana. "Help her."

"I need a med kit!" Niall yelled the moment he rolled Diana onto her back. She was bleeding from the cut across her belly that Mickey had no doubt inflicted upon her. "Diana?" He peeled off his ME jacket and wadded it up against the gaping wound. "Diana. I'm a doctor. Open your eyes."

Lucy crawled to the other side of her and took her hand, squeezing it between both of hers. "Diana, please, sweetie. It's Lucy. Listen to Niall. Open your eyes if you can."

Diana groaned and blinked her eyes open. But they were dull and unfocused. "Luce?" she slurred through a split lip.

"Yes. It's me. You're safe now. You're safe."

"Tell me…about…my baby." Her breath railed in her chest. "Mickey…he can't end up like Mickey."

Lucy glanced over at Niall, who was doing his best to stanch the wound. When he shook his head, the first tear squeezed between her eyelashes.

She kissed her foster daughter's hand. "He won't. Tommy's fine. Dorian, I mean. He's such a good little boy. Such a healthy eater. And loud. But he's safe. You did it, Diana. You protected your little boy. You kept him safe."

Diana's eyes drifted shut again. But her swollen lip curved into a smile. "Tommy's a good name. Tell him how much I loved him."

"Diana—"

"Tell him."

"I will, sweetie. I will. I promise that he will always know what you did for him."

"I knew you'd have my back." Diana's hand grew heavy in Lucy's grasp. "He couldn't have a better mother than you. Because you were always a mother to me."

"Diana?"

Lucy knew the moment she lost Diana forever. She gently set Diana's hand on her still chest and brushed the dark hair off her forehead to press a kiss there. The rest of the world blurred through her tears—the police, the EMTs on the scene taking over for Niall in a futile effort to revive the dead woman, the cars, everything. A merciless fist squeezed the air out of her chest, and then she was sobbing.

A soothing, deep-pitched voice reached her ears. "Sweetheart, stop."

She knew very little of what happened over the next few minutes, only that Niall's arms were around her. She didn't care about the blood on his hands that were now in her hair. She didn't care about the weeping spectacle she was making of herself. The only thing that mattered was that Niall was here.

Lucy McKane could deal with anything. But not this. Without Niall, she knew she absolutely couldn't deal with this.

LUCY CRIED A lot over the next few days, a sight that tore Niall up inside every time he saw those red-rimmed eyes and felt the sobs shaking her body.

She'd lost someone she considered a daughter. She'd relived the nightmare that could have been her a decade

ago if she hadn't fought and scrapped and kept moving
forward with her life. Lucy talked about feeling guilty
for losing touch with someone she'd once been so close
to and how angry she was that she hadn't been able to
find Diana in time to save her.

But Lucy McKane was a kind of strong that Niall
had never known before. Yes, she cried. But she also
teased his brothers and had long talks with Millie and
traded hugs with his father. She was even finding things
in common with Niall's sister, now that Liv and Gabe
were home from their honeymoon. She laughed with
Tommy when he was awake and hummed with contentment when he fell asleep in her arms.

It was an emotional roller-coaster ride that Niall
wasn't sure how to help with. But he could offer practical assistance and muscle. He'd stood by her side at Diana's funeral, and now he was helping her move Tommy
and her stuff back to her apartment.

He'd almost been too late that afternoon when she'd
faced down a killer. He'd felt too far away watching
her on a TV screen from a distant van. And though
firing his weapon wasn't his first duty as a cop, it had
been the only duty that day that had mattered. Mickey
Staab was hurting the woman who was more important
to him than any other since his mother had died. When
he'd raised that knife to gut Lucy the way he had Diana
Kozlow, Niall had quickly taken aim and stopped him.

And now, as he set down the bassinet in her bedroom, Niall felt as if time was ticking away from him
again, as if living just across the hall from Lucy and
Tommy would be too far away. And if he didn't do
something about it now, he might lose them forever.

He turned to watch Lucy leaning over the changing table to rub noses with Tommy. She smiled and the baby laughed. After tossing the soiled diaper she'd changed into the disposal bin, she carried him to the bassinet and laid him inside with one of his stuffed toys.

Why did having his own space back, and getting his world back to its predictable routine, feel as though Lucy was leaving him? And why did an irrational thought like that make his chest ache?

He was memorizing the curve of her backside in a pair of jeans when she straightened and faced him. "You're staring again, Niall."

"Am I?" His gaze dropped to the rich green color of her eyes. There was still sadness there, but a shining light, as well, that he couldn't look away from.

"You don't know when you're doing that?" She nudged him out into the hallway and closed the door behind them so Tommy could nap. "I feel like a specimen under a microscope."

"Sorry. I guess I'm a little brainless when I'm around you."

"Brainless? You? Never."

He followed her out to the living room. "There's no logic to it. I can't think straight. I'm disorganized. I can't focus on my work. All I do is react and feel."

"Feeling isn't a bad thing, Niall. What do you feel?"

He raked his fingers through his hair and shook his head, searching for the definitive answer. "Off-kilter. Out of sorts. Like I never want to let either of you out of my arms or out of my sight. I think about you when we're apart. I anticipate when I'll see you again. I'm thinking of Tommy's future and whether or not he'll go to college and how he shouldn't grow up without a mother. I worry that you're not safe or that you're talking some other man's ear off or—"

Lucy shushed him with her finger over his lips and offered him the sweetest smile he'd seen in days. "I love you, too."

"Yeah." He nodded as his heart cracked open inside him and understanding dawned. "Yes. I love you." He tunneled his fingers into her hair and tipped her head back to capture her beautiful mouth in a kiss. Her arms circled his waist, and he pulled her body into his as that eager awareness ignited between them.

Sometime later, when she was curled up in his lap on her couch and he could think clearly again, Niall spoke the new discoveries in his heart. "Lucy McKane, I have a question for you."

She brushed aside the hair that stuck out over his forehead. "You know I love to listen to you talk."

"I'm a patient man, and I'll give you all the time you need."

"To do what?"

"Will you marry me? Can we adopt Tommy together after the six-month waiting period? Can we be a family?"

She grinned. "That's three questions, Dr. Watson."

"See? Completely brainless. I'm new at all this touchy-feely stuff, so be kind. Don't make me beg for an answer."

She tilted her mouth to meet his kiss. "Yes. Yes. And yes."

Epilogue

The unhappy man skimmed through the article he'd already read a dozen times before folding the newspaper and setting it on the corner of his desk. "The *Journal* says that Niall Watson was involved with a shooting outside Saint Luke's Hospital. Internal Affairs vindicated it as necessary force to protect the intended victim. It's not front-page news, but the story is long enough to mention his grandfather being well enough to leave the hospital and move home to continue his recovery."

The man sitting across from him refused to apologize if that was what this late-night meeting was about. "I did what you asked. I ruined the wedding. I got those Watson boys and their daddy all up in arms without any clue about what's going on. And there's no way they can trace anything about that shooting back to you. For all they know, some crazy guy went off his rocker."

"Seamus Watson is supposed to be dead." He pulled open the top right drawer of his desk and fingered the loaded gun he kept there. "When I hire you to do a job, I can't afford to have you fail."

"Then tell me what I can do to make things right.

Reputation is everything in my business. The next job will be on the house."

Satisfied, for the moment, with that arrangement, the man pushed the drawer shut. His employee could live for another day.

The Watson family might not be so lucky.

* * * * *

Keep an eye out for Keir's story when the next
thrilling installment in Julie Miller's
THE PRECINCT: BACHELORS IN BLUE
series becomes available.
You'll be able to find it wherever
Intrigue books are sold!

Lynne Graham has sold 35 million books!

To settle a debt, she'll have to become his mistress...

Nikolai Drakos is determined to have his revenge against the man who destroyed his sister. So stealing his enemy's intended fiancé seems like the perfect solution! Until Nikolai discovers that woman is Ella Davies...

Read on for a tantalising excerpt from Lynne Graham's 100th book,

BOUGHT FOR THE GREEK'S REVENGE

'Mistress,' Nikolai slotted in cool as ice.

Shock had welded Ella's tongue to the roof of her mouth because he was sexually propositioning her and nothing could have prepared her for that. She wasn't drop-dead gorgeous... *he* was! Male heads didn't swivel when Ella walked down the street because she had neither the length of leg nor the curves usually deemed necessary to attract such attention. Why on earth could he be making *her* such an offer?

'But we don't even know each other,' she framed dazedly. 'You're a stranger...'

'If you live with me I won't be a stranger for long,' Nikolai pointed out with monumental calm. And the very sound of that inhuman calm and cool forced her to flip round and settle distraught eyes on his lean darkly handsome face.

'You can't be serious about this!'

'I assure you that I am deadly serious. Move in and I'll forget your family's debts.'

'But it's a *crazy* idea!' she gasped.

'It's not crazy to me,' Nikolai asserted. 'When I want anything, I go after it hard and fast.'

Her lashes dipped. Did he want her like that? Enough to track her down, buy up her father's debts, and try and buy rights to her and her body along with those debts? The very idea of that made her dizzy and plunged her brain into even greater turmoil. 'It's immoral... it's blackmail.'

'It's definitely *not* blackmail. I'm giving you the benefit of a choice you didn't have before I came through that door,' Nikolai Drakos fielded with a glittering cool. 'That choice is yours to make.'

'Like hell it is!' Ella fired back. 'It's a complete cheat of a supposed offer!'

Nikolai sent her a gleaming sideways glance. 'No the real cheat was you kissing me the way you did last year and then saying no and acting as if I had grossly insulted you,' he murmured with lethal quietness.

'You *did* insult me!' Ella flung back, her cheeks hot as fire while she wondered if her refusal that night had started off his whole chain reaction. What else could possibly be driving him?

Nikolai straightened lazily as he opened the door. 'If you take offence that easily, maybe it's just as well that the answer is no.'

Visit **www.millsandboon.co.uk/lynnegraham**
to order yours!

MILLS & BOON®

MILLS & BOON®

Mills & Boon have been at the heart of romance since 1908... and while the fashions may have changed, one thing remains the same: from pulse-pounding passion to the gentlest caress, we're always known how to bring romance alive.

Now, we're delighted to present you with these irresistible illustrations, inspired by the vintage glamour of our covers. So indulge your wildest dreams and unleash your imagination as we present the most iconic Mills & Boon moments of the last century.

Visit **www.millsandboon.co.uk/ArtofRomance** to order yours!